CERBERUS SLEPT

BY DOONVORCANNON

TABLE OF CONTENTS

Preface

Erato sings to me. She found me at the edge of the abyss, barking at the fools hurling themselves into decadent decay. Through my howls at the hopeless herd, she sings louder and purer than any Siren of the deep. She, the erotic love of those romantic poets. She, the ancient Muse so many adored. Her passionate dancing has frenzied me with fervor. I must write this!

I, Doonvorcannon was tasked to write down this epic, burning my words deep into the hopeless hollows of today. This is written in love and for the love of what we once were; this is for the love of what we need to be. The Muses have come to me. I howl no longer at the moon, but at the sun, for it is our day. The night of modernity is burning away in the dawn of rekindled righteous tyranny.

And there, Polyhymnia descends and sings of the sacred solar. Alight and listen to the Muse's holy hymn! The abyss is not so deep that it cannot be filled. Alight, you sacred angel and give me wings so that I might save those sinking souls that were meant for the sun, but have forgotten their past!

Calliope soars out from the sun's rays and heaves its warmth over my skin, radiant and buoyant as a lover's sigh. Her harmony is ecstatic with an eternal eloquence; how could I not lay down these words atop one another and attempt to build up to her heights? The rest of the Muses dance, encircling me with wisdom. I must tell this tale.

But why, you ask, why has old Greek mythology come to me? Why those Muses? I simply ask you this: have you read Hesiod and Homer? Have you read Virgil and Dante? And what of Shakespeare and Milton? Our forefathers, those giants of the sun, they heard these Muses cry out to them. And the return of the Muses is much needed! I weep at the blessings heaped onto me from their tragic songs. The old has been forgotten but the Muses sing to bring about the tale of what brought a remembering new. The new that is ancient, but forward moving. This is what they sing, and I listen and write to their song as swans soar above me in a cloud-like dance. The majesty and tragedy of such power forgotten!

You may have heard of my fabled Rangabes in the past. But now, with the mythic inspiration of the Muses, I write of his true journey through the land of the dead, to the land of the living, to the land we have lost, and to the land we now inhabit. This is no fable. Before, I barked as best as I could but I only dreamed of his true form. Then, it was but a desperate howl into the long-labored night. It was a shadow of the true myth! Now, I howl at the sun as the dawn of a new day quickens. Read this tale and become as the gods; live it again through their eyes.

May the epic of great Rangabes bring about a rapture, for only those of power and the mythic heroic can withstand the glorious glow of righteous tyranny. Can you hear the Muses' song? Their singing lifts our souls. Ascend!

Book 1

Chthonic Sun

My soul, my soul, forsaken and forgotten in soulless solitude. In a black pitch I hover without a throe to give. My throes have been thrown in every direction, but in this cursed abyss, direction has died. My body is no more and my soul a mere husk filled with searing shame. Why couldn't it be Valhalla? Why couldn't it be the Inferno? Even Dante's underworld allowed for action—a kind of moving that is a something, however circular and tortuous. I'm forced to float forgotten in burning tar with the silent, black air pressing against my skin and whispering that all is untruth—that all is and has always been a nothing.

Suspended in this endless realm of empty nothingness, I've fallen into the blank forever of a starless night. My tarring is finished but oh how I long for feathers, if only to be deceived at the possibility of an absurd flight. The foolish lie would at least give me a direction in this directionless blanket of eternal night. I cannot tuck myself in for it appears as though my lot is cast, for those lost in this heavy black have failed. I have failed. I cannot see, hear or eat here. I'm not even sure if I can speak. I am too afraid to call out into the deep, not knowing what might be lurking.

Tartarus.

An answer? I mustered up my strength and called out into the darkness. My voice fell dead in the air, swallowed whole. Echo, the sad and lovely woman, could not be heard. Why was I here? Tartarus—the abyss where the Titans were kept, at least in Greek Mythology. The underworld. But I was Christian; this fabrication made no sense. I did nothing to deserve suffering such a miserable, impossible fate.

A test.

"Test?" I whispered. My voice fluttered free. It at last existed apart from my tortured thoughts. This foreign voice that spoke from the deep was a something, and it had brought me a semblance of being, however small.

Escape Tartarus and you will be rewarded by founding a powerful people from Apollo's blood. If you look below, one patch of this quilted black is not like the others. The answer is in the past but present.

Apollo? Founding a people? What was this myth? What was truth here? And there were no patches that I could see; there was still only the insufferable total and uniform darkness. This quilt of night was expertly stitched together. I waited as a nothing in the dark, and thought back to my past. Perhaps a clue could be excavated from my memories. There was nothing else I could do, at least in my current state. But Tartarus. I was in the great black abyss. Greek mythology made real. Was it therefore not myth? Tartarus… the third deity of Greek legend, preceded only by Gaia and Chaos. The abyss.

A murmur swam through the lifeless air. A poet's voice rang out and sang, "First Chaos came to be, but next wide-bosomed Earth, the ever-sure foundation of all the deathless ones who hold the peaks of snowy Olympus, and dim Tartarus in the depth of the wide-pathed Earth."

"Hesiod?" I called out to no avail, my voice nothing but thoughts without release—surging water beaten into a pooled submission at the thick walls of a dark dam.

"Rangabes! Failure of a Roman soldier. Your city of Constantinople is conquered. You deserve no escape. If

Typhon arose from such loins as these cold depths, how might you hope to burst free? Can you not feel that frigid fear in this nothingness? Tartarus is the void that all succumb to, if they choose the comfort of eventuality. To cease to move is to accept the pull of the forever falling anvil."

"You said nine days," I mumbled. I'd read Hesiod when I was young. I knew his words and worth. He was not wrong.

"Quite the scholar, I see. Nine days it fell from heaven to earth. Nine more days it fell from earth to be swallowed in Tartarus. What is done in life will be swallowed in death, equaling all the feats on earth and heaven above. The anvil never stops falling and its force draws in the masses. Smoke ascends from its old bronze in tails of gray; tendrils snaking about while the herd eagerly allows its serpentine heads to bite their heels and drag them down. An anvil that is an anchor designed to sink the ship." Hesiod's voice was clear and crisp. Even in the nothingness he still spoke as if he were carrying his laurel staff—a poet gifted by the gods and worthy of song.

I tried to smile. I tried, but I was still a nothing. But Hesiod! Here with me. I'd pinch myself if I had a self to pinch.

I said, "I died a hero's death. I belong amongst the warrior-saints. I belong amongst the gods!" My words were returning somehow, yet my body remained void. My speech sounded as thought spoken from an echo. I was that echo.

"Wait till you meet Erebus and then tell me why you might be here right now."

"But why are you here, ancient poet? Why speak to me, and how can you in the first place? You are trapped as well. Have you been tasked by the gods to spout your myths and judgements as if Muses sang only to your black heart? Are you Tartarus's jester? I thought more of you—that you'd be in a place of honor in the underworld. That Christ might forgive your sin out of respect for your worth."

"The anvil I dropped from Olympus has smashed through my body, and in the wreckage of my soul it pulls me always away like a falling star trapped in orbit."

"So, your own myths were too much to overcome. Your own writings your guilt. The weight of your creation has you lost in the chasm of the sea. Why should I listen to you, lonely poet?" I said.

"Because I want to leave. Because light came to me in this darkness, and in its blaze I saw your face."

The thought of light pulsed in my imagined temples; such a concept whispered holy into my vacated body. I reached with invisible hands and felt for a way up, or a rope to hang myself with. Eternal darkness made me want to tear myself apart. Only, my flesh was gone and whatever self I was now was imperishable.

"All of this black here is a flawless blanket. Below me and everywhere else, there is nothing but that same cold black. Where am I supposed to find a difference?" I said.

Who never wears the quilt of night yet always lives in darkness?

The same voice from the deep torrented through Hesiod and I. I didn't want to know who such a stampede of a voice belonged to. It threatened to trample our nothingness into something even less existent. I shuddered at the impossibility of such a concept. I tried to focus on the words themselves and give answer to this strange riddle.

"If this is the land of myth, and the untruth speaks as though it were true—is this riddle requiring an answer from your mythos? If so… and I suspect it is, I'd first guess the god of sleep, the dreaming god Hypnos?" I said, stopping to consider. "No, no... that can't be it. He always is covered with such a quilt in the depths of his dreams." I stopped again. If Greek mythology was somehow based in actuality, could other pagan gods be counted too? It was worth trying. "Ptah? The Egyptian god my dear pagan friend Belen worshipped so strangely—the god of the sun at night. But to be the sun, no matter how dark the surroundings… that is not living in darkness but sitting outside of it with resplendent fire serving as a beacon of light to scare the shadows away." I paused again, ceasing my scholarly musing to think deeper of the mythologies my father had taught me so well. I felt oddly in control, my fright at the fearsome voice frozen from the frost of my reason. "Or is it Selene, the goddess of the moon. She does not sleep as the moon is always somewhere else, so she never quite abandons her chariot. If the quilt of night is sleep, then it must be Selene."

No.

"No?" I said, my thoughts evaporating into a sigh.

It is I.

"And who might this I be? My own eye cannot see, so you're going to have to give me something more. Perhaps a name?" My bodiless mind grinned, pleased at my own mirth in such dire straits. Tartarus couldn't darken my soul. I wouldn't let it. But the thought of eternity pressed itself into my being. I lurched but forced myself to hold strong. Losing myself would only make forever that much worse.

Kronos.

The voice roared stronger than Zeus's thunder ever had. Fitting that only the father rumbled louder.

"You are in darkness here with me. But do you not wear the quilt of night? Do not all who dwell in Tartarus wear the same quilt?" I said.

Wild white eye balls appeared inches in front of me with irises and pupils missing. But no... I peered closer to see two perfectly fine eyeballs, only they were rolled backwards and quivering there. The eyeballs were surrounded by a face with cold white skin that was concaved and sunken. A wild black beard enveloped half of this madman's mien. Long, knotted black hair hung in tatters like the rags of a beggar. And then the eyeballs rolled forward and fixed their auger pupils directly at my soul, unmoving and unforgiving.

"There is no sleep here. There is no night. There is no anything. It is only this expanse of nothingness," Kronos said.

"But Zeus has long since fled after being forgotten. Why are you still here imprisoned? Have you forgotten that Olympus once was yours?" Hesiod spoke, but Kronos didn't react as he stayed staring at my nothingness. I shivered.

"But the quilted black not like the others! Why say such a thing if you've never managed to find it? Who even told you that?" I said.

"Moros gave you his signs. Your Holy Mother wept in her flight and your angel turned his face. Your cathedral lit up with a fire that fled, leaving your pathetic city behind. She loved you, but you did not love her back," Kronos said, his face tremoring as it floated before me, its gaze still fixed upon my soul.

I swallowed my spirit, my mind flexing with a sinking gloom. I remembered it all too clearly. At the time I had scoffed at the peasants' superstitions. They had all claimed that the suddenly glowing cross atop of Hagia Sophia and its strange fiery light flying away, was the Blessed Theotokos leaving us to our dismal fate. I thought it merely a trick of the light. I should have heeded the warning. But in a city's last days, all signs become apocalyptic.

"Moros, the god of impending doom. But how were you aware of such things down here, Kronos?" Hesiod said.

Kronos remained staring at me, his mouth spreading into a sick grin that bared his gray teeth. "He brought down his own broken flame here and let it consume him to ash. Moros died in fear. He died a failure. The only thing that can kill a god is fate, and when the god of impending doom seeks his own doom, he can find a way to make fate his own." He smiled even wider and his eyes darted in spasms. His mouth propped open and his beard hung over his wicked maw like a spider's pincers. I shivered as I thought of what this terrible Titan had done to be sent here in the first place. The child eater. "We're here because we failed. I failed to defend my mountain, my throne. You, Rangabes, you failed to defend your city. And Hesiod failed to defend his mythos. He failed to create one that would endure as truth and not as mere children's stories seldom read by those of today."

"Yet you are here speaking to us both. The unbelief of the world is not my fault," Hesiod protested.

"It is the fault of Rangabes and all like him! They trusted truth, and our untruth condemns us to a dispersal into the nature we once broke free from. Rangabes is weak! Rangabes is dead!" Kronos grunted and snorted at me, his head snapping back and forth.

I burned. I hated. The rambling of this sinner was awakening something inside. This mad, pathetic beast was beneath me. My fear frothed into a fury that stormed in surges of fire. As if my blood had returned, I felt a solidity in my being as my rage and wrath quickened in fervor. I struck Kronos in the face with my fist. I was still flesh after all, or at least becoming so once again—if the satisfying sound of bone crunching bone was to be believed. Kronos cackled, opening his mouth as if preparing to swallow my arm. I struck him again, cracking his blackened teeth, his blood foaming in his decrepit mouth. I hammered both my fists into his eyeballs and they burst like rotten eggs, spewing foul blood and gray liquid.

"The flame! Moros, allow me your fate!" Kronos sputtered, his beard blood-soaked and his eyes black geysers. His two gnarled hands grabbed me by my shoulders which had apparently sprouted over my soul, and as my body became whole once more, Kronos pulled me towards him in a maniacal and sputtering embrace. "Burn me! Burn me! It is too cold, the darkness!" he cried.

I tried with all my might to push this foul creature away, but he wouldn't budge. His black blood was cold and it seeped through my skin, chilling my core. I shivered, writhing in his embrace with nothing but anger fueling me. I did not fear such a pathetic wretch as this degeneration of divinity. As I struggled, I realized that I once more could see the entirety of my limbs. And then my flesh started to smoke as Kronos's blood cascaded over me and he held me still. I screamed as my skin scalded into a reddish gold, and in a sudden eruption of light my body was covered in flame. Beams of glorious sunlight burst from my soul, my being sending out its rays and banishing the darkness of Tartarus.

I slowed myself down and took deep breaths as I no longer felt the fallen god's cold hands upon me. He was no more. My body was clothed in a filthy robe that had faded to a stained brown and hung useless at my waist in tatters, leaving my torso uncovered. My skin was a healthy honey-white, the color of the Greek sun I'd left behind. I ran my hands through my untamed red-blonde mane, inherited from my Varangian grandfather. It parted on the left side and swept back as if the wind had forced it into a perpetual retreat. I rubbed my green eyes and pulled at my curly beard that was as wild as my hair on top and connected in such a way that a continuous flow of wavy locks threatened to drown the rest of my face in ferocious follicle flame. I reveled in the return of my body, feeling my face as if I were a blind man. I rubbed my sloped nose's slightly bent bridge, crooked and sharpened from my many fights as a soldier and still as aquiline as ever.

I curled my toes and clung to the soil I now felt. My heart beat, its sudden return like the comforting whisper of the Almighty's still, small voice. Grinning, I allowed myself to appreciate every crease and fold in my skin as I stretched and moved, alive and flesh again.

"Look around you. You are dead." Hesiod's somber words matched his dark brown eyes and sullen yet stoic demeanor. He wore long, gray robes that bared the right side of his torso. His long, brown locks of hair were gathered messily over his forehead in a clump of bangs.

I breathed the stale, sulfurous air and gagged, happy to smell despite the stench of decay and rot surrounding me. Then, I forced myself out of the revelry of the life of flesh, and looked at my grim surroundings. In bodiless darkness, Tartarus was hopeless; in the pale light of right now, it was Hell. Pillars of fire shot upwards, lava surging up to the smoke-covered heavens. The iron gray of the ocean of smoke above cast the realm in an eerie, dusk-like gloom. This was the eternal twilight. This was what was hidden in the darkness. Yet, this volcanic tundra filled with burning red rivers of fire and boiling blood somehow remained impossibly cold. This was the fire that froze. This was the heat that halted. I shivered, no longer reveling in the chill of my recovered flesh. Tartarus. I was dead.

"Is this desolation empty?" I said.

"Empty of life, yes. Overflowing with death, of course," Hesiod said, walking forward to stand beside me and survey the landscape.

"I thought the immortals of old couldn't die."

"You've seen Kronos end by your own doing, and you heard him speak of Moros's suicide. There is an undoing force in the air. A reckoning of some sorts. A reckoning in which you seem to stand at the center of."

"Is it a right reckoning? Why me, I don't bother to ask. It is me that walks these paths, and I will see this through. Whatever this truly is. I do not trust this mythos and I suspect the demonic. Yet, I will not fail again. Kronos said I was destined to found a new people. Perhaps that is God's word. Perhaps the Devil's. But it is a word, and right now it is a something. I am tired of that wordless nothing. I refuse to fail as I did my beloved empire."

"Words as empty and meaningless as a bedded whore's wedding vow. Find the quilted black unlike the others first."

I turned my back to the faithless poet and clenched my fists. I glanced at my forearms and flexed, enjoying the press of veins against skin. My strength and physicality were back. I hadn't a sword to defend myself, but my fists would do for the moment.

The freezing flames that chilled my bones forced me forward. First, I needed to find some shelter, if such a thing existed in this hellscape. Forward I marched, feet frigid against the black sand. I surrendered to the freeze of the air and without tension strode onward. The unnatural pillars of flame shot up in sudden and continuous spouts, a roaring furnace that boomed loud and banished any hope of quiet. I marched on, knowing that one wrong step could end me.

"There are other Titans here, you know."

I didn't answer. I'd not even bothered to notice that Hesiod had followed me. My excitement at the poet's presence had ended as soon as the darkness had cleared and this Hell had revealed itself. One's accomplishments and stature tended to be diminished in the flames of this infernal forever.

"You wouldn't happen to know where the nearest Titan might be, would you? There is nothing here but useless fire," I said.

"This frosted flame has its use. How else do you think the Titan of light can be contained? Not in darkness, and not in light that burns. Only through the paradox of freezing fire can the light of the High-One be brought low.

He cannot watch the world when torn apart by opposites. His attention divided; he has lost his own light."

"Is this Titan dead? I thought only two of the immortals have died."

"No, he is not dead. His name is Hyperion. But for as long he's been forgotten, I wonder if his wisdom remains. He did not run, nor did he hide. He contemplated and watched, unable to decide what to do even during the Titanomachy—that ancient war in which Zeus led the new gods against the Titans, ending their tyrannical reign. So wise was Hyperion that he realized the wisest choice a Titan such as he could make, was to wait. And so he waited, his waiting and watching raising him higher and higher until he became so distant, so forgotten, that before he knew it, he'd paradoxically inverted, sinking into the very depths of being. Tartarus. His punishment was to be burnt in the flame of forgetfulness. He forgot what it was that made him who he was. To be burnt by such a flame is to freeze. That is who we must find."

"The present but past. I wonder if he might possess the key out of this wasteland."

Hesiod grinned. He shook his head, rubbed his face and stopped walking. Rolling his neck and then shoulders, his face seemed suddenly tired as if he'd only now just realized what it was to be of flesh again. I stopped and peered at him with suspicion. Was he my guide or warden? Stroking my fingers through my thick beard and scratching at my squared chin, I squinted my eyes and stared at the old, sullen fellow in front of me. His legendary status paled under the gaze of the present.

"How is it that you've come to me? Who do you get your orders from, poet?"

"The only orders I've received were from the songs of the Muses. I write on my own, and live according to virtue."

"What was this light you spoke of that showed you my face? I was a skilled soldier in my life, but nothing more. How is it that a man such as myself has been given this power to destroy the immortals? These gods I never once considered to be real. What is this falsity? How is it that I walk amongst the dead, in the flesh of my body?"

"The light of impending doom. The light that lit Hagia Sophia aflame and left your city behind. Not a mere trick of the sky, nor a meaningless sign. No, that light that left Constantinople was not simply Moros, though Moros dwelled within it. That light was also of a higher being. Parallel to impending doom is everlasting glory. There's always an opposite. To overcome what is fated is to be eternal. When Moros dissolved into nonbeing out of fear, he passed on the flame of glory. That flame frightened Kronos and it found me, but it wasn't for me. It was only to reveal who was destined for that light." Hesiod had the look of an evangelist proclaiming what he took to be hidden truth. There could be no doubting it by the crease of his brow and the stern glare in his dark eyes: he was a man convinced. But whether or not he spoke in allegory, I couldn't tell. "When you awoke in the darkness, that was the glory of your blood aflame with that everlasting light. I do not know who you truly are, but I know that you are a leader of men and the next great hero. In times when the heroic has fallen forgotten, you bear the torch of Hercules, of Aeneas, once more. That is what the fire revealed, and that is what now courses through your blood."

At the mention of such great heroes I tensed up and glared at him, not with fury but fire. I was aflame with the desire to achieve. Constantinople might be lost, but there was a new land waiting to be conquered. I was that conqueror. Not when I got out of here, but now. Now! I remembered my father killing a lion with nothing but a stone perfectly thrown at its head. The power beaming in his eyes had propelled me into a career of soldiering. I always wanted to be more powerful than any opponent: animal, man, or myth, it didn't matter. My father was no stranger to Roman and Greek mythology; he often bemoaned the fact that there weren't more warrior-saints and that I should strive to be one. Well, in the stories of Hercules and Aeneas, the perilous journeys of Odysseus and Jason, and the epic battles of the Iliad, I heard of power and glory. And from those tales I built myself into a man worthy of fighting alongside an Achilles or a Perseus. And now I realized, I should have kept building myself until worthy of besting them. A man shouldn't stop until he dies. But now I could see that after death, that increasing and becoming must continue. Eternity implies never ceasing, so I would increase. So, I would be greater.

"And which way must I go?" I said. I looked up at my surroundings, the black sand and bursts of lava spreading out as far as I could see. Nothing else. "Where are the other souls? How is it that only you and I, not counting Kronos, are here but nobody else?"

"Every mythos that the great civilizations have followed, all those gods fear you, Rangabes. Your Lord reigns over them all and they fear not only His blessing on you, but that of Apollo's. There hasn't been a man such as you that carried so much of civilization and history in himself at once."

I sighed, breathing in the rancid air defiantly. "They fear a fallen soldier of a conquered people?" I spat and shook my head in disgust. Those poor souls who survived Constantinople's fall were in bondage now, after being raped and mutilated and who knew what else. I spat again as if to get rid of my guilt.

"They don't just fear you, Rangabes. They fear what comes after. The nation that will arise from your loins will be unmatched in all of history in terms of sheer power. This force, this people that comes from you has the potential to conquer the world, or destroy it and itself. They fear this most of all because not even the Fates and Prometheus could see the future this people might bring about. It belongs only to the strange one, Wyrd, and your Lord."

I scoffed and kicked at the soil beneath me. Wyrd? A meaningless name. But this mythology existed while Christ remained King? A puzzling truth, if in fact it was. I scratched at my forehead and squinted at the ground. I kicked my bare foot at the ashen sand, numb from the strange chill of the place. I was beginning to doubt this calling to found a people. Was I Aeneas? Was I just an empty avatar at the mercy of the will of the Fates?

"A nation from me? My father was a great man but he was no saint... or mythological being, for that matter. And my mother, a good and faithful Christian, yes, but a simple woman." I looked up at Hesiod, angry at this insanity, at my righteous death ruined. I should be in paradise, not this falsity. "I am my own man and make no promises for fatherhood or nation-bearing. I seek only a way out of this hell to wreak havoc amongst my enemies.

The blasphemers must pay. Whether or not Constantinople will rise again doesn't matter to me."

Hesiod slowly closed the gap between us, seemingly gliding in his calm and regal gait. His long mountain ridge of a nose took up my vision as he leaned into my face, his eyes transfixed onto mine. His thick yellow brows curtained his fierce and proud glare, and his jaw tensed as he stood there scrutinizing me.

"Are you truly the man Moros feared unto death? The god of doom fizzled to nothingness by a vindictive boy? You may have had a martyr's death, but for what? You don't care that your people are finished? You want to leave your city for petty vengeance? Is it not custom for your tradition to say, 'Vengeance is the Lord's'?" He whispered the words wildly, whipping me without worry of retaliation. I clenched my fists and tightened my face, but allowed him a chance to relent. Yet he continued, "No, all I see is a scared soldier unworthy of the fear that so many great powers have for him. Perhaps they were wrong. Perhaps they should have let you ascend to your sad, pathetic paradise as your world burned below."

I headbutted the proud poet in his beak of a nose, cutting my forehead and painting his face in his own scarlet mortality. Growling, I grit my teeth and did not hold back. I swung my fist with the full weight of my body behind it and Hesiod threw up his arms in an attempt to ward off the blow. He failed miserably and my fist struck the side of his head. Staggered, but still on his feet, Hesiod laughed, spitting blood and putting both his fists up to fight. I glared at him wickedly, roaring with fury as I rained down attacks. I knew that this man had fought in battles during his day. He was unlike the soft scholars of my own time.

But I was Rangabes, esteemed captain of the Constantinople forces and unafraid even of the strongest of Turks. I'd leapt off the wall to fight off the hordes of men alone. I'd cut down twenty before they finally overcame my acumen.

This man didn't stand a chance, and I let loose all the fury that Tartarus had filled me with over that endless time of suffering in confusion. Time was dead to me. Now, it was time to unleash. And unleash I did. Hesiod collapsed in a crumpled heap, a black pool of blood slickening his skin as he sputtered.

My fists ached, bruised and covered with bits of meat from Hesiod and myself. I stood over the man, triumphant and calm. I rolled both my shoulders and then my neck, unscathed by any blow. My spirit was still alight from his disrespectful, despicable words questioning my merit.

"Never question my manhood and never question my faith." I glared down at the broken man who twitched in a heap like a swatted insect. I frowned, took a deep breath and extended my hand. "But you were right to question me. I do not know my destiny or purpose, but I do know that I will get out of Tartarus. And I will take what is mine. Glory belongs only to those willing to bleed. I think we both belong in that category."

Despite it all, Hesiod, bruised and bloodied, smiled a broken grin. With hands wet and crimson, he grabbed my arm and slowly climbed to his feet, using my body as a ladder. With labored breath, he muttered, "I fought in many a battle in my day. Never have I faced a man with fists harder than steel. I've seen less damage done by hammers and swords. The gods better fear you." He spat blood and, still hobbled and bent over, laughed. “I had to see if you were honorable, both in combat and victory. I could use some of Hyperion’s wisdom now. Perhaps I should have thought of a better way of testing it.” He shook his head and slapped my shoulder.

“You’re more of a man than the intellectuals of my day would ever imagine. They think of you as a curmudgeonly poet, writing nonsensical myths and boring moralities. You’d destroy them with your manhood. The kind of blows I landed here have killed many men much larger than yourself. I’m proud to have you by my side, Hesiod. Thank you for bringing some sort of light to this darkness.” I smiled and swept my arm backwards to gesture at the flames soaring in our vicinity. I frowned and looked at his split and crooked nose. “Without you, I might still be alone with nobody but Kronos yelling at my exposed spirit.” We both nodded in comradery and I quickly grabbed his nose and forced it back into place as he grunted. I received a half-hearted punch to the shoulder in thanks.

“You were the one who killed that cannibal Titan. But did you have to go and break my nose?” He softly touched its still-bleeding bridge and winced.

“Maybe now it won’t look so large,” I joked.

“I should have watched and waited. The more I think about it, the more I realize Hyperion was the smart one. Forgotten and not in pain is better than this.” He dabbed his nose with cloth from his robe.

I tore off a thin strip from my sad rag of a robe and held it out to him. “Be thankful you won’t be able to smell this,” I said.

He took the ribbon with a grin and pressed it on, the blood making it stick. He shook his head and laughed. I grinned and joined him in his laughter till we both were bent over and gasping for air.

"To Hyperion!" I said, finally getting a hold of myself.

"To the forgotten frozen one. Hyperion will know where to go next. His time of distance has ended. There is no more watching in this world now. The time to act has long since begun."

I nodded and patted Hesiod on the back. With renewed vigor and strength, I strode forward into the burning wasteland of Tartarus. And so, we walked. And walked. And walked. And walked... and there was nothing. We'd been walking like this for quite some time and with the lack of any indication of change other than our own exhaustion, it was impossible to tell if we'd made any progress. There was still no sign of Hyperion or any other beings. The landscape's flat nature and constant flashes of fire had such an uncanny appearance of sameness that I was half-convinced we hadn't moved an inch. My aching feet made me question that, though the doubt lingered in my tired mind.

"Can we really expect to find the so-called High-One in the lowest of places?" I said.

"He's here entrapped in one of these pillars of flame."

Hesiod felt at his nose, something he'd done consistently since my breaking it. All things considered, he was in pretty decent shape. Despite the dry blood caked onto his robes and face, and the spots of blackening bruises dotting his body, his energy and vivacity remained as resolute as ever. He seemed surer of himself than I. But the lack of progression was wearing me thin. My prayers to

God to deliver me from this pagan falsity that appeared realer than He were only met with silence. I sighed and stopped walking.

"Something isn't right; we should have seen some change by now, something to mark our movement," Hesiod muttered, stopping next to me. He turned his attention to a nearby spout of fire that had just burst towards the smoky sky. "I wonder..."

"What are you getting at now?"

Hesiod rushed over to the fire and thrust his hand in. He tightened his face and bit down as he stuck his arm even further into the flame till it was shoulder-deep. His face twisted with agony and his jaw clenched as he growled in pain.

"Stop it, you fool!" I shouted, running after him.

His face shimmered with a ripple of pale white light that emanated from his skin and, with a pained smile and nod at me, he threw himself into the flames.

"No!" I screamed, reaching out in vain.

Hesiod's voice drifted out from within the flames. "Step in, Rangabes. The glory of this fire is worth the suffering."

Before I could question the disembodied voice of Hesiod, the spurt of flame subsided until there was nothing left. I dove towards the geyser, desperately searching for some kind of sign, but I found nothing but cold sand.

"A brave man, that Hesiod," a triumphant voice announced behind me.

I got up off my knees and faced the voice. A man cloaked in golden light, and nothing more, stood there expectantly. His physique was something to behold, with the light bathing his naked body in gold. His radiant skin made him look like a divine and living statue made entirely of precious metal. A body of muscle with not a flaw or drop of fat. A Titan.

"Hyperion," I said. "Now you show yourself. Why would Hesiod attempt such a foolish feat?"

"His foolish feat was what brought me out of the darkness and to you this moment. He awoke me with his worthy cries of righteous pain."

"Has he perished?"

"He's waiting for you in a different realm. You must follow him into the flame, no matter the pain or pillar you choose."

"And what have you to offer me? Hesiod seemed transfixed on finding you, and only you, first."

"I am of the original twelve, a Titan wiser than all."

"So wise you are, that you hid yourself? Wisdom does not belong to the cowardly," I said, standing tall and preparing myself for a fight, if it came to it.

What I lacked in visible radiance, I made up for in height. Despite Hyperion's glory, he was still a bit shorter than me. His golden hair was cut tightly to his head, with both sides shaved completely and just a thin layer left on top.

"For one so ill-equipped," he said, his eyes gazing at my rags, "you are quite the braggart."

"All I need is my body, a weapon and armor greater than anything a Hephaestus could forge." If myth now walked true, then I would answer myth for myth.

"Are you greater than Aeneas? Would you not take the fire god's shield and armor if offered?"

I crossed my arms and let my head fall askew. "What is it you offer? I don't care to hear about the god of the forge, wherever he may be."

"Surely you want a sword made by the master?"

"I only want to find Hesiod and get out of here."

"There is something you must do first."

Hyperion pointed his finger at the expanse of smoke above, and made a continuous circular motion until the smoky heavens swirled like water down a drain. The smoke gathered into a funnel and started pressing downwards in the form of a tornado. As it lowered, a bright light began to shine from above as the coverage of smoke enfolded into itself. A chariot of golden fire appeared in the opened heavens, burning down towards us and landing with impossible grace beside Hyperion. As the chariot landed, the sky once more was filled with the ocean of smoke, drowning out the light above.

The chariot was crossed with white flames and a golden sun was emblazoned boldly on its side. Six white glowing horses stood in front, their eyes burning with orange flame and their impressive stature dwarfing the magnificent chariot behind. Their heads turned in every direction, their pink nostrils flaring at the taint of Tartarus. A man with a crown of fire and polished gold skin as bright as Hyperion's stepped out of his chariot and stood there patiently with grace and a meek, controlled power.

"My son, god of sun, Helios," Hyperion said, holding an arm out towards him.

Helios wore a wrap of fine white cloth. A bronze red sun was pinned on his breast. His solar crown spread forth rays into the sky and encircled his head like the sun. His form was as if carved of stone, delicate lines and muscle flawlessly etched into his lean and sinewy body.

Helios stepped forward and smiled at us both. "Have you told him yet, Father?"

"Not yet." Hyperion smiled and turned to me, looking into my eyes. "You are one of us, Rangabes. A powerful blood boils inside you. You belong to the people of light. Do you realize who your father was, and I mean *really* was? In the higher sense? Do you not wonder how it is that you are as you are right now?"

"My father was a worthy warrior and my mother a good and simple woman of faith."

"Mortally, of course. But is that all? How can you be so forgetful of your ancestors?" Helios said, a flaming orange-red spear bursting out of the air and into his hands as if he meant to use it against me.

"How could he know, son? If those once great do not pass on this greatness in truth and purity, how could he know? Be patient with the man. It wasn't too long ago that he believed all of us to be made up myths to keep a population sedated. We are gods—less than his, but gods." Hyperion sighed and stepped closer to me. "The light you gained from Moros was yours by birthright. Moros was the offspring of Nyx, the goddess of night. That light you now possess was stolen from our kind. The night sought to be the day, as if in hopes to become like holy Hyperborea where the sun always shined. In a desperate attempt to survive the modern upheaval, Moros tried to flee with this light and bring it to a new people. Yet he searched in vain, for no such people exist like they had in Troy, or first in Hyperborea. He was incapable of recognizing that no civilizations in the now quite possess that same worthiness and greatness of perfect power and faith. Rome had it once, but she lost it in abandoning your city to its ruin. Rome was meant to be East and West. Your Theotokos was of her own light, but she did not quite abandon your city. She wept at your fate and prays for a renewal. It was decreed."

"That is all fine and well, but what does that have to do with my lot now? Do not speak so familiarly of my own people and faith. We were betrayed by many, and if you hadn't merely watched from this prison, perhaps we might yet have lived on. I'm not here to make guesswork of your strange posturing."

"Do you know of your royalty?" Helios asked.

"Not yet! He must demonstrate his worth before being handed the sacred truths of our light," Hyperion said.

"I simply want to leave this place. Where has Hesiod gone?"

A scepter of brilliant white flame flashed into Hyperion's outstretched hand. He banged the ground with his rod and chanted out a throaty melody, haunting in its minimalistic and savage style. The black sand swirled into a funnel in front of my feet, and hissing arose from the sinking ground. A white snake with sapphire eyes slid out from the black. Its forked tongue flicked out, pale like the pallid winter sky. It patiently slithered closer and moved in a perfect circle to surrounded me with its body. The snake grew as it encircled me, its body coiling around itself as it continued stretching out. Its head was the size of my torso and its two clear, icicle-like fangs shined threateningly in the glare of Helios and Hyperion's golden light.

The already frigid Tartarus mingled with the snake's frost and tinged my skin blue. The strange snow serpent's hissing increased and its encirclement came ever closer to my body. I stood there calmly, staring at the creature's jeweled eyes. My blood slowed and my breath fell heavy. Puffs of air swirled out from my mouth as if the force of my spirit were evaporating. I slowly raised my gaze to Helios and Hyperion. Hyperion stood there transfixed, his golden lit eyes following the serpent's movement. Helios stood there regally, his sunbeamed head unable to provide warmth in my polar vicinity.

I tensed my body, preparing to at last strike out at the serpent, but I noticed that at my tensing, its pace increased until it circled me in a whir—three times in mere seconds. Its icy scales brushed the skin of my feet, turning my toes black with frostbite. With my feet useless, I crumpled to my knees. I foolishly and fearfully struck the serpent with both fists, rendering both my hands numb and black. The snake wrapped the lower half of my body, and my heart beat slowed, my blood thickened, and my eyelids dragged. With blurred vision, it donned on me what I was supposed to do. This was not a foe to be vanquished, but a testing of my worth—a glory to be earned. With a tired smile, my lips barely twitching, I offered my forearm to the snake's head.

It stopped its binding and, with its head eye to eye with mine, it blinked, its sapphire eyes glowing with power. It waited there, its head tilting back and forth as if weighing my worth. My head lolled to the side, and through darkening vision I watched as the serpent's tongue licked my forearm, turning it not black but marble white with a golden light radiating from within. With sudden force, it bit down on my offered forearm and a wave of warmth washed over me as I screamed at the ecstatic power of light and life coursing through me. My body was yanked airborne and it hovered as my spine curled and my arms and legs dangled. I was held up rigidly in waves of pleasure and power, a cloud of bright light holding me aloft as I screamed. When I thudded to the ground, the serpent was gone. The only sign it had come and done anything were two white bite marks on the inner side of my forearm right above my wrist. A slight pale blue icy light shined from the marks. My blackened skin had returned to normal as well.

Stretching, I stood to my feet and stared at the two solar gods who stood there with unchanged expressions. "Well," I said. They didn't even blink. "I passed whatever this test was."

"No. No you did not, for if you had, you would not speak so brazenly about it." Helios narrowed his eyes and kneaded his hands.

"One more ritual. Do not disrespect these modes of being, these paths of power, again. You will not be given a second chance," Hyperion said, clutching his scepter tight.

I rubbed my bite marks which tingled like fresh mint on the tongue. I nodded and stood straight-backed and prepared. Helios held out his burning red spear and struck the ground. A thousand howls filled the air and I pressed my hands against my ears in agony at the terrible shrieking tear of such sound. Hesiod and Hyperion seemed unphased, as if I'd imagined it. But the howling only grew louder and it rained down from on high as if thousands of wolves ran above the smoke. Unfortunately, that was exactly the case, as wolves bathed in fire poured down through the smoke, which billowed and coursed as countless numbers of the creatures tore burning holes through its reformed cover. Trails of orange embers and black ashes sprayed out behind the wolves' scorching approach. The packs of fire wolves landed in an erupting avalanche of red smoke, and they spread out to encircle me.

Their howling ceased and silence pressed itself upon me. In a perfect circle, like the snake from before, wolves as far as I could see surrounded me on all sides with nothing but a small circle of black sand separating us. Saliva glowing like lava dripped from their mouths, hissing as it fell upon the ground. It was obvious that surrendering myself to these beasts was not an option.

Their burning red-orange bodies, smelled like a funeral pyre, and the only sound now was the hiss and sputtering crackle of flickering flames. Under the surface of the sound, like the beginning rumble of an earthquake, a low growling began. First it was soft enough to be drowned out by the fire's burning, but then it increased until I once more was forced to cover my ears. The sound grew to such an intensity that a painful thud and sharp pop in my ears went off and warm blood trickled out from my ear canals, sticking my hands with red. The wolves began to come closer, slowly and as one. Their black tongues licked at their ashen jaws as their fangs of white and blue flame jetted out from their burning maws.

I lowered my hands now that my hearing was gone. Only a dull ringing sound remained. I slowly turned my body around to gaze at the nearing packs of endless wolves. What was I supposed to do, if not surrender? Their slow progression seemed unrelated to the tensing of my body or any movement I made, whether I stepped closer or remained frozen. I narrowed my eyes and looked at the serpent's bite mark. I rubbed it, which brightened the wound to an even colder pale blue. The ringing in my ears subsided and I could just barely hear the crackle of the wolves' flames once more. If ice takes life away, bringing the natural slow surrender of death, then fire was what gave the world life and power. The heat of the sun. The flaming torch. The burning stove.

The serpent's bite flashed in a frigid blaze of blue on my forearm. Frozen flame burst out from my body, and the wolves backed away as my light spread out and spiraled close to them. My body erupted in a brighter burst of blue, and icy flame torrented in a circle that roared outwards, turning the nearest wolves to ice and putting out the flames of the others close by. The wolves whimpered and stepped further back. Ice was powerful, but it was only one half of a whole. I needed to take the fire of the wolves. I stepped forward to the frozen wolves, holding my left, snake-bitten arm in front of me as it still glowed blue. The wolves bowed their heads in silence.

I crouched down in front of the largest wolf, which had ventured farthest forward and suffered the full effect of my frost light. The noble beast was now reduced to a frozen sculpture. I motioned for the other wolves to come near. One brave wolf with its head lowered came close as the rest of the packs whined. I held out my right hand and its flaming nuzzle singed my palm and burnt my flesh. I bit down on my lip as I pet the beast, ignoring the burning pain of my smoldering skin. The wolf pressed its head against my forearm and I embraced it, pulling the animal close to my crouched body. I nearly fainted from the shock of such searing pain, but I persisted. With rapidly blistering skin, I released the flaming wolf and pressed my burnt right arm on the frozen one. The ice intensified the pain but, just as suddenly, it soothed the burn, and a comforting warmth cascaded over my being.

My sight was lit aflame with golden light. I felt myself lift like rising fire and the wolves howled with me and we became as one. I thundered with the packs, leading them back to the heavens. When we burst through the smoky sky, my human eyes opened and I was alone with nothing but the imprint of the fiery wolf's head branded onto my right forearm. The skin was raised into a supernatural tattoo that crackled with a subtle red flare.

I stood to my feet, the power of ice and fire surging through my blood as a unified force. Hyperion and Helios stood there expectantly, each of them holding their weapons out as if prepared to use them against me—or to hurl out another form of ritual. I stepped closer to them and stood tall. I held out my powerfully scarred arms with my palms upwards and open. Helios and Hyperion both nodded solemnly as each of them clasped my hands.

"A Hyperborean. Your birthright," Helios and Hyperion murmured, speaking as if they were one.

Hyperion looked at my arms while still holding my left hand as he said, "Our time in the light is meeting an end. We are living in an age that has forgotten us and forgotten the power of pure light. You must carry our flame to a new land, a new people, and become a light for the future. I waited and watched for too long. My power is finished in this ritual. A new order has arisen and the world is better for it. But that will only remain true if you act with the light of your forebearers. There are many jealous of your fate, but Wyrd plays a higher tune. Those who see what must be done, will sacrifice. Do not trust those unwilling to pass the flame on." He released my hand and his golden light dimmed. His body seemed smaller as if he were a candle running out of wax.

Helios nodded gravely, let go of my right hand and said, "I have given the last of my light in this as well. I may have acted much in the past, but the people ceased to follow the powerful path of light, and so I began to dim. All that remains for me is material now. Nature. My purpose has been passed to you. I'll watch and shine with warmth. But Helios the god will be no more. Rangabes, it is your power to wield. Your right to conqueror. Use it well. Do not forget your Lord. We are truth and He is Truth." Helios's strong body flashed and the burning of his crown intensified until the god was nothing but a ball of light. And he ascended as but a star, his deity no more, only living on through the ritual passing he'd given to me.

Hyperion's form flickered, and as his body dimmed and his light dissipated, he whispered one last direction. "You are ready to enter into the pillar of flame. There you will find Hesiod. Hyperborea is for you. Hyperborea is and always will be for Hyperboreans and nobody else. Go forth, brethren."

I bowed my head and uttered my thanks. The two gods were no more, their only signs of existence shining in each of my arms. I nodded and turned to the pillar of flame. There was more for me to do. Much more. Lord willing.

I stepped over towards the flaming pillar of light with head raised and eyes open. Without hesitation, I walked right into it. The pillar of fire scorched my spirit, at first stripping away my self, and then, just as suddenly, soothing my being with a feeling of eternal peace, captured in a single scalding moment. My vision was drowned in a golden red light, and it was all I could see, as if I'd been thrown into the midst of a sunrise. It seemed as though my whole body flew upwards as my stomach floated with a nauseating weightlessness. Suddenly, I felt myself solidify, and a new area appeared before me, unfolding like a scroll of fire.

The same smoke-covered canopy hung sinister in the sky. That could only mean I was still trapped in Tartarus. I angrily peered at my still sulfurous surroundings. I stood on some kind of precipice—a black granite cliff, smooth and crystalline. The cliff spiked out dangerously towards the horizon. I slowly walked to its edge and peered down, seeing nothing but darkness. Was that where I had just been? Had the darkness returned now that I'd left it behind?

This strange dark mountain I now stood on had no flame pillars to step back into, so it appeared as though I'd be trapped here, at least for the moment. I turned away from the edge of the cliff to look behind me. There was nothing but more mountain in jagged stretches and peaks, sloped downwards and disappearing into the black fog of the abyss.

"Hesiod!" I called out.

No response. The sickening air was dead with nothingness. Not even the bursts of lava broke through the silence now. It was just me, the mountain, and the stench of Tartarus. I heard a low murmur come from the black fog below the precipice. I scrambled back to the top and stared into the dark pit.

"Answer me," I commanded.

A roaring laugh shook the mountain, and I only just managed to catch myself from falling as I staggered backwards.

"Who dares to demand something from me?" The deep voice rumbled, rattling my teeth even as I tensed my jaw.

I glared with violent impatience into the abyss, scowling at the disembodied voice. "Show yourself, dark one! Hiding in the fog? Do you think one such as I am afraid? Tartarus has bowed to me. This hellscape is mine. How many immortals must I best?" I cracked my neck and held up my arms, the left bathed in blue light and the right in red. The abyss didn't answer, but a low and long growl rolled underneath the black below. The abyssal mist vortexed into a swirling tornado and twirled upwards, gathering the darkness into itself while the abyss below remained whole, with an even darker darkness somehow on top of it all.

The tornado of black mist began to take form as the surrounding black billowed like a bilious sea. In a sudden pulse of darkness, the mist enfolded on itself, exposing the valley with the pillars of fire below. So, Tartarus was still there below. Had I ascended past the first level of smoke? I quickly glanced up at the lingering smoke above, and noticed its different color now, however subtle the darker hue. While Tartarus had been shielded in a stormy gray, the clouds here were a meaner hue that bordered on black, with swirls of dark gray intermixed. No, this wasn't quite Tartarus. And that black mist wasn't simply an abyss. It spun right out of the air below and twisted around me. I held my ground with my arms still raised and ready for battle.

The abyss continued its pirouetting around me, and with a whip it formed into the shape of a giant figure like that of a shadowy man. The mist shimmered like a flock of synchronized insects, and the shadow giant loomed over me.

"Who are you?" I said, lowering my arms and stepping away from the cliff's edge.

"Erebus."

"Hesiod warned me of you." I paused, thinking back to the poet's words. He'd said that Erebus knew more of why I'd been chosen to be so unjustly imprisoned. "How is it that I, a mortal, have been banished to the prison of Titans and monsters too dangerous for Hades?"

"The torchbearer of doom. You possess the flame of Olympus in your very blood, and you would question this? When the light left Hagia Sophia, we all saw your face. Even the Fates fear you; you, the one to finally turn their wheel against itself."

"But I was—and I assume still am—a mortal. When I get out of this underworld, I will once again live and die. I am but a ghost now, and death seems just as urgent, likely more so now than ever before. Even as Constantinople fell, I had more hope that I would survive than I do now. I do not have hope any longer, but only assurance in my own might. My power is my shield. My power is my life and death. You cannot take this from me," I said, staring at his silhouetted form.

"Don't be so sure. But you are wise to leave behind hope. Prometheus was a cancer to your kind, his gift of fire depriving you of metamorphosis. His martyrdom and faith for you all was false. Lies. You humans were once supposed to know your deaths, for what better way to live and love your fate? Yet he sought to strike you with blindness by stealing from you the knowledge of your deaths and hiding it in fruitless dreams. Truth and power go hand in hand. Deceit is a tool for the truthful to use, but only men of truth can wield it truly." Erebus stooped forward, breathing out in leaking gasps of smoke.

"Prometheus was wrong to give us hope, if it was ever even his to give and not a choice of our own. He was wrong to do this instead of letting clarity reign supreme. Hope prolongs the weakness of man by tantalizing and tormenting him with falsehood—a reliance on the future to provide power and support, and not on the man in the moment at hand. The weak resign to their fates, and hope makes that resignation all the sicker. The strong step towards death as pure being, drinking each eternal moment as if already divine."

"Very wise, mortal. Wise indeed. But you and I both know: you are not a hero."

"Did I claim to be?" I said.

"You failed and were thrown here as the new torchbearer of doom, tasting your own darkness. You sought martyrdom yet you met your deserved fate of failure."

"Can a hero not fail? What is it you want?" I asked.

"Of course a hero can fail. But there is more to this sort of failure—in the end, the end is the judge and executioner of heroism. It either ends eternity or begins it," Erebus said, leaning back as his shadow grew.

"Then what is a hero?" I said, crossing my arms and glaring at his empty face.

"A sacrifice at the altars of tragedy," he said, his whisper howling as he leaned so far forward it looked like he might spill over me with his toxic fumes.

I breathed through my mouth to avoid smelling his gravestone scent and said, "Did I not do just that in flinging myself against the Turkish horde alone, as they breached our once impenetrable walls?"

"You did what any beast would do. You defended your nest."

"And what would have been the heroic course?" I said. I shook my head and sighed, uncrossing my arms and looking around me.

"You did not follow the path of sacred war, but only the path of desperation. You might have thought of vengeance, you might have been afraid, or you might have dreamed of playing the martyr. These thoughts in your last moments negate the action's heroic weight." Erebus shifted backwards, his mist groaning as it curled away from me.

"I may well have thought all three. But I acted!" I yelled.

Erebus flurried further away, reforming into the silhouette of a towering man once again, now several feet back from me. "You *reacted.* To transcend such an end into the heroic is to embrace the spirit behind the act. To have a why for your what. War is sacred. Act and intellect must go together in balance, spirit as the arrow to your instinct."

"Were my thoughts not my why?" I said, pacing forward with my arms alight. "If you continue to dishonor me, I will scald your pathetic form."

"Come then, hero," he whispered, coiling around himself like a smoky serpent. "We go now to meet some special ones to guide you on. You cannot leave this place until you see."

Erebus snapped back into the shape of a man and reached his misted arm outward. I grasped it with both my hands, his shadow surprisingly solid as stone—like the dark so deep you imagine you feel it, but this time it was actually an actuality. My body stiffened and my vision filled entirely with the black mist of Erebus's body. His darkness numbed me until I lost all feeling and sense. The mist suddenly dissipated and I gasped as bright sunlight struck my face.

I blinked and shook my head. Atop the old trusty wall. Constantinople. Again... as if I stood exactly as I had in those final moments. My men, those few that remained, paced along the walls with an exhausted assurance that they would die well. I forced myself to look away, knowing our end was near. Out on the battlefield, bodies drowned in a sea of red rot, crashing up against our walls in frozen waves of corpses. And over and past the dead, the Turkish hordes were gathered together, a continuous torrent bursting with bodies. Their cannons shook our walls as screaming men were buried beneath an avalanche of thunder and ruin. The Turks' foreign, barbaric shouts coursed forward even more terrible than the cannons' boom. The bulk of their forces stormed forward as I stared. Shaking, I breathed in the thick and heavy air soaked with sweat and blood.

"Rangabes!" someone yelled.

I turned to face my troops. I squinted to hold back my tears at their worried yet impossibly hopeful faces.

"We've hardly any men left. The walls are crumbling. They weren't built to withstand such hellish machinery."

"Walls..." I mumbled.

The face of the one who'd spoken—he was merely a boy. His light eyes swept frantically back and forth, yet there was an overwhelming sense of courage and destiny there, like that of a cornered lion knowing it wasn't going to die without clawing its way to eternity.

To the left of me, a booming blast crashed into the wall, crumbling it and several men into dust. As the smoke cleared and my hearing returned, a sense of serenity descended. I breathed deep and stared into the gray-canopied heavens. Bloody war cries shrieked and the thundering rumble of charging men shattered the false calm. Instinct took over, and the shock of my sudden return to life subsided as I led my men, cutting down the invaders clamoring up the dead bodies. Like ants they crawled, scurrying atop heaps of their own. Stones dropped from our towers, arrows soared, and scalding water poured. Sweeping swords and long-reaching spears felled many a man, but always another followed with more and more behind. We'd been doing this for days and nights in constant distress. There was no sleep allowed, as the Turkish artillery never let up, shooting at random. The constant strain of danger had worn us all down. We were a few islands, and they a sea, each man a returning wave. I shook myself from my thoughts—Tartarus and the underworld had become a sinking dream. Had I not died? Was this real? Had I really been here fighting these last several days and nights? I shook myself again as I sliced another Turk's throat.

Now the fearsome janissaries followed and their archers behind them covered their push forward. Men collapsed beside me along with another section of wall. Again. Again. I had to see this again. No. Yes. This was past. Hesiod was waiting. Past. Reality was gone. Right now, I knew nothing, but hatred and instinct forced me forward. As all was lost, I leapt from the wall and onto the battlefield and carved out my own path, slicing with my sword.

I screamed as I cut into a man's neck, pulling the sword free just in time to ward off a scimitar. Spinning, I cut down the assailant's calves from under him. Another flourish and I swung my sword at exposed hands, the blood of my faceless enemy covering me in scarlet. I chopped. A body fell. Another chop. Another fall. But they were many and I was one. Several men tackled me at once and their relentless bodies stampeded over my fallen form and all went dark as I screamed.

Gasping, I opened my eyes wide to Erebus standing before me with his hand still holding mine. Beside him someone else now stood: a tall pale woman, with translucent green robes.

"Please," I whispered. "No more."

"But you were heroic," the woman cooed, her green eyes as deep as the far-flung forest. She smiled, leaning forward to stroke my cold cheek. Her dark auburn hair draped over me and tickled my head. A scent of fresh familiarity, like a childhood memory of a mother's perfume, wafted over me. "Come now, hero. Again." She kissed my lips and the black gripped me once more with numbness.

When the sunlight struck me again, the shock of the moment was finished. I looked around, frowned, and drew my sword. I refused to play this game. This was not real.

"Rangabes!" the soldier cried.

His voice made me shiver. Was it real? Could I find redemption?

"We've hardly any men left. The walls are crumbling. They weren't built to withstand such hellish machinery."

I knew how this would go. What could I do different? The soldiers hadn't spilled forward yet. I leapt from the wall and over the dead bodies. I landed with a roll, and stood and stared out at the distant lines of enemies.

"Sir, come back! Are you mad? We need you!"

My men shouted but I did not turn to look back. I strode forward, slowly at first, dragging my sword in the soil as if to mark a path to return to. A mocking of fate. Holding my steel aloft, I shouted and ran across the bloodstained plain. The dark faces of the enemy seemed taken aback, but shadows filled the air. The arrows rained down and consumed me. I twitched and writhed on the ground. Useless. A more pathetic and pointless end than perhaps any man had faced in this bloody war.

Again, the black misted Erebus stared facelessly at me while still clutching my frozen hand. The green-eyed woman was joined by another figure. A beautiful, tanned man with the garb of an Egyptian stood there in his perfection. Sinewy and lean, his symmetrical form was frightening in its glory. No artist could draw or sculpt such a being as he. Oddly enough, he had a waterlily tucked behind his ear, and his black sea eyes seemed to ripple. The black eye liner only served to highlight the stormy waters that were his irises. With a blue headdress on, he certainly had the look of a god.

He stepped forward and crossed his arms as if he were a disappointed father. "To charge like a frenzied bull is to be a fool. Fools are not heroes. Try again, fool."

The numbness did not take me by surprise and when the sunlight assaulted my face, I shrugged it away with a turn of my back. Dropping my sword and ignoring my soldiers' startled pleas, I left my post at the wall and walked back into the city. The streets were dead and empty. My men's cries faltered as the collapsing wall and assaulting Turks forced them to leave me be. My Constantinople. Never again would the true glory of Rome shine so pure. The death of an already dying empire. So real. This was all so real. I had to question whether this was constructed falsely through Erebus and his sorcery, or if this was somehow a reality that existed separately from the one I thought I knew—this moment an eternity by itself. Perhaps this one could be saved. But my soulless wandering through the vacant, stripped down city had probably only hastened this one's end. A few more Turkish thugs would survive due to pathetic Rangabes leaving his men to die. I sighed, caring little for the memory of my name that would surely be forgotten regardless of what I did here now, and what I had done then. These once statue-lined streets had been dotted with Roman columns decked out in the finest metals and designs. The war and our weakness had long since bankrupted us. The city's finery had long since been stripped. Nothing would remain. All would fade.

When the Venetians had taken the city all those years ago, glorious Constantinople's riches were forever depleted. And for decades and decades after, the constant loss of our land on top of racked-up debts ruined what little glory remained. Hagia Sophia stood proudly over us, but the light had left her. I didn't believe it dwelt in me. I glanced at my wrists, unsurprised to see the marks of my Hyperborean initiation rendered nonexistent. Perhaps this was just another ritual, another test. Perhaps this time when I died and went black, I'd remain in the darkness. Perhaps. An eternity worth of perhaps.

I walked to Justinian's monument. He rode his horse triumphant atop his pillar, pointing towards the east. We had been meant to conqueror, but now we were a conquered race. The civilization that birthed Plato and Aristotle. The proud people that the great Alexander once led. Where Hesiod, Homer, and Aeschylus wrote their masterworks. Where Constantine baptized an entire empire. I wished Hesiod was still with me. I feared that I'd never see the wise poet again.

We had been the people who inspired Rome. The great Constantine had brought Rome's inspired splendor back to us and made this city the brightest of gems this world had ever known. Emperor Constantine the Great—whom my dear Emperor Constantine XI Palaeologus was named after. My emperor was no doubt fighting to his death with his people right now. Tears burned my eyes, forcing my vision into a squint. And old Justinian sat on his eternal and noble steed, victorious and pointing towards conquest. To conquer and be strong. Our empire was the natural conclusion and evolution from the Greek one of antiquity and the mighty Roman one that followed. To the empire of now. And now my now had fallen into the forgotten.

"Great Emperor Justinian, what must I do? How can I persist when everything I know and love is forever destroyed? I have no place here... why couldn't I have stayed dead with my own?" I stared up at his distant, raised figure and sighed.

The ikons covering his pillar shimmered red, and each one flashed aflame, staring down at me with eyes filled with fire. Justinian's head turned to me, the rest of him remaining frozen in triumphant pose.

"Become power incarnate. It is the duty of man to increase." His voice spoke clearly and commandingly in a masculine, eternal tone that resounded inside my bones.

"But I no longer belong to any other on this earth. All whom I loved have been lost," I said.

"The future needs you. They need a hero who remembers and knows the power of truth and myth. Do not forget this city, this glorious spirit. Constantinople might have fallen, but who is to stop you from building a new and better home?"

I bowed my knee and kissed the first of the seven steps leading up to the column. "And how do I return to that future? I am trapped here now."

"Wait here. Let them come and kill as many as you can. And when you once more return to this recurring dream, believe and decide why you will act—what is the higher cause behind it? To die a hero is to be conscious of destiny and eternity."

Shouting clattered through the streets followed by twisted cries of despair. The Turks stormed the statue like vermin to a corpse. I held my head high and raised my blade. Swinging my sword in angled and precise strokes, I cut down the first several men with ease. They were so hellbent on storming the famed statue that they'd hardly noticed me.

The destruction of my people fueled me with the strength of Hercules. I cut and cut, a woodsman in a forest of rotten trees. Blood bathed me and I reveled in its retribution. I thrust my blade into a greedy pig of a man. He squealed as it pierced his pink throat. I kicked him away and ran my blade across the stomachs of three men rushing towards me, sweeping them away in one blow. I stabbed. I spun. I danced to the tune of life with such perfection that death was my only worthy partner. And so, death rippled out around me as body after body collapsed, and I surged on with life.

I charged at another hopeless fool and stuck my sword through his heart. The man crumpled to the ground, taking my sword with it as it got stuck there. I tried to pry it free but was too slow and I screamed as my arm was severed. I dropped to my knees in the midst of all the felled trees. With my bloody stump of an arm spraying forth blackish-red gore, the pile of dead surrounding me was of a hundred. Like Samson with his jawbone. I screamed louder. I had fought with nothing but power and rage fueling my glory. As I collapsed on the steps of Justinian's pillar, my blood soaked the marble stairs and pooled around its foundation. I smiled up at the great emperor as I lay there dying. His eyes were fixed on me and he nodded his bronze head. He then looked towards the west and I understood. My conquest. I kept my eyes fixed upon his glory and did not flinch as the flashing scimitar decapitated my head.

The icy chill of Erebus was expected. I opened my eyes with calm confidence, ignoring the chilled clasp of Erebus's hand. Now a fourth figure stood in front of me. She was taller than the rest and her supple, well-formed figure couldn't be contained by the loose yellowish olive toned dress she wore. Her blonde hair cascaded like a waterfall of honey down to her ankles. Her cold silver eyes were frigid and harsh.

"Is it your destiny to be a hero? Is it your fate to heroically leave behind that fallen greatness of your once powerful people and pursue that which will one day prove greater? A new people, a new beginning could be yours." Her stern voice solidified my renewed spirit and will and, as the black mist took me back, I knew I was ready to become that true hero with eyes open and spirit pure.

I manned the wall with my will directed towards the heavens and reverberated in this eternal now. My death for my people was not just a sacrifice to a city that would fall—no matter what I did now or had truly done in my last moments. I'd bested many men then, even as they'd encircled me. But I'd died, defeated by the swarms of them in the end. Where had my will been? When the light had left Hagia Sophia behind and the holy ikon collapsed in the storm, face down in the muck, the people and even the emperor himself knew we were at an end. No help was coming, divine or from the west. It was only ourselves. And that was where I had been wrong. To die as I had for myself and my men was noble in a sense, but not truly heroic.

I could see it now, feel it even. The crispness in the air, the smell of decay, struggle and might mingling as one; it was truly a scent of unmitigated power and lifeforce, opposing energies pulsing within the living and dead. The tremors in my hands, veins pushing forth against my skin with screaming life despite my bone-weary flesh. The sleepless men moving about with nothing but fear holding them up. The strings and strands of fate dangling from the heavens, pulling us one way and then another. A yank here and a snip there, and that would be the end of it.

I could see it now, those invisible strands like the thinnest of silk spider webs. It wasn't for me to say what strand was just or right; it was for me to see the spider weaving it, smile and with my will soaring high, to laugh as I lived and loved as fiercely as I could. Prosper, no matter what. In life and death, with the strength of my spirit soaring towards the divine, I would go. As the walls shook, I snarled not as mere man or animal, but as spirit and will aimed upwards, my mind the bow and my soul the arrow.

I flung into the fray, my sword a brush as I canvassed the battlefield with Turkish blood. They surrounded me but I kept fighting, sweeping this way and then another. When the circle closed in and I felt my strand at last be snipped, I smiled and let my spirit soar. A heroic end. I was chosen for more. I had chosen the more.

Returned to the numbness, I breathed easy as the four figures stared at my collapsed form. I stood, pulling myself free from Erebus's gravestone grip.

"Man mustn't forget what makes him great. I am Mnemosyne, goddess of memory. I'm tired of my waters being polluted by Lethe," the green-eyed woman said, her gaze crystalline and focused. "My lake is sadly forgotten. Those who live and die walk right on by, the river of forgetfulness and its refreshing sparkle providing false promises to those who only look forward and forget to honor their history."

"Were you the one that made me remember?" I said.

"Yes. But you were the one who remembered what you needed to. Learn from the past and with eyes divine, gaze upward as you move forward," she said.

"And what of you two," I said, waving an arm at the pretty man and the blonde-haired woman.

The woman said, "I am Wyrd. I am the odd Fate who belongs neither in nor out, but above. I pull the string to bring forth the strange. I was very pleased to see your soul sent to Tartarus. Very pleased!" Her voice was buoyant and joyful. Its flow was charming and softened the severity in her icy eyes.

I glared closely at this beautiful Fate above the Fates. Wyrd. The name I'd already heard mentioned several times. The Fate aligned with my Lord. I eyed her fearfully, knowing the eternal weight she held.

"How is it that all of this is here? How is it that you and this... and I in its midst are true?" I stammered. The unspoken implication of this proving my understanding of truth false tremored like a tightrope with my faith barely balanced on.

"I was in His ancient Divine Council. It is in your Scripture. We've always existed under His rule and He was glad to listen to us with love and patience. Yet this here," she said, looking at the gods around her, then back at me, "much of these mythologies have fallen into untruth and unbelief... that is a result of gods darkening into their decadent selves by reflecting the sun like the moon. That is false light. True light belongs to the one who partakes in the sun and does not try to pollute such power by pretending it is one's own. Be not like the moon, but like the torch. That fire comes from the eternal source and exists as a finite example of infinite glory. The moon tries to claim infinity as its own, but that is only done when it's aglow with the fire of the sun, not a dimmed reflection." Her airy voice lowered to a grave tone. Her arched brows dropped and her countenance fell as she stared at me. "It is best for these gods to now fade into nature. Too much untruth lingers in their name. But most of them fight it. Yet do not fear Rangabes, for you do not walk in untruth. Listen to my strange song and you might just see this through. They cannot stop my singing." At this, her face lightened and her eyebrows shot up as if to fling off the weight of seriousness. She smiled at me, then laughed as she glanced at the three beside her.

Mnemosyne stared at her with an odd mix of fear and anger curtaining her lowered brow, as if she wanted neither but couldn't help it. Erebus remained hidden, but even he seemed to shrink back into his mist, his form losing shape at Wyrd's words and glare. Only the waterlily god seemed unperturbed.

"Thank you." I nodded at her. It was clear at least that the others feared her. I wondered how they felt about her song and our Lord. I wasn't sure myself.

The Egyptian god coughed to coax the tension away from Wyrd. "And I am Nefertem. I will be taking you to your next stop on this journey." He extended his arm out in invitation. I ignored it.

"Who are you and why do you dress and talk like an Egyptian?" I said.

He smiled a gleaming grin. The man's warmth and beauty overwhelmed me, making me ashamed at having rejected his arm. He plucked the waterlily from his ear and twirled it between his brown fingers, staring deeply into it.

"We must rise like my fragrant waterlily greets the great sun, Ra," he said.

"I am not leaving here without Hesiod." I turned to Erebus and stared into his black form. "Where have you hidden him in your darkness? The gods of light have told me he still lives. Your darkness cannot hold him." Remembering my newfound power, I held my arms out, the ritual marks threatening the dark god with purifying light.

"He is where you are going. The fires of Tartarus are pillars of flame that hold up this plane of darkness, yet connect it with the others," Erebus said.

"I thought we were to rise, Nefertem," I said, turning to the waterlily god.

"In a sense. Here it is deeper than Hades. But no, we go instead to the Duat," Nefertem said.

"Your land of the dead? I thought one was good enough. Am I to ever escape these regions? Am I to live again?" I said.

"The weighing of the heart awaits. You must be judged to see if you are as worthy as the Fates fear," Erebus said.

"This is the exact kind of *pluck*," Wyrd said as if playing an invisible harp, her pale and slender fingers pulling at silent, unseen strings. "The exact kind that I would play. Perhaps it is I. But you must go. There is no other way out of Tartarus. To leave this hell you must go to another." She clapped and, in puff of violet vapor, vanished.

"Do not forget. You mustn't." Mnemosyne looked at me forebodingly, her eyes bright and terrible. She turned away and a door of polished emerald shimmered into the air in front of her. Her divine body stepped through, and the beautiful goddess of memory and her strange door disappeared. I would not be forgetting her.

Erebus said nothing more. He simply collapsed on himself and swirled around my ankles before pouring back over the cliff and resuming the form of enveloping darkness below.

Nefertem placed his waterlily back behind his ear. He rolled his sculpted shoulders and once more extended his arm. I nodded and took his hand; the air shattered like glass and new surroundings flashed before me. A wide and dark river calmly snaked its way in a bend around us. The sky here was clear and midnight. Ridges of cloud drifted by in splotches of purple that shimmered like a raven's feather struck with light.

The surrounding landscape was flat and wide. Crystalline, turquoise trees that shined like lamps lined the river. In the distance there were several large black and murky lakes. I could see a lake made of fire, burning terribly and thankfully distant. There were pyramids scattered about, some golden and larger than others and some of silver and quite smaller. The river seemed to slither endlessly—or at least it appeared to from my vantage point on its banks. This was a strange land, as foreign to me as were its people. Still, at least the air was merely balmy and not at all as painful and wicked as that of Tartarus.

"Let us move forward," Nefertem said.

I looked down at my still-exposed form, draped in ribboned rags for bottoms and nothing else. "Do you have any armor, or form of protection?" A foolish question to ask a god who wore only a layer of cloth on his bottom half, but I had to ask. As strong as I was, I didn't see how I could withstand a lake of fire like this and whatever else this strange land had to throw at me.

"A man is worth only as much as his skin. Prove your worth as you are."

I nodded. He was correct. "And where is Hesiod?"

Nefertem smiled. "He is right there," he said, pointing behind me.

I turned and blinked at the sudden appearance of a long wooden boat approaching with a lone oarsman paddling it ashore.

"Hesiod!" I yelled, jumping onto the boat, shaking it and nearly throwing us both off.

"He will be your guide the rest of the way. Now go!" Nefertem said. He pushed the boat off shore and forward.

I clasped the poet's arm and embraced him. He laughed as he warmly hugged me back. Despite it all, I at last felt at home.

Book 2

Branches of Blood

I was still smiling at Hesiod, sitting beside him as he rowed. Even though Nerfertem had since faded from view, I still couldn't get over how much I'd missed this man, despite knowing him for such a short time. The poet's face was set and determined, and the way in which his jaw was clenched and brow bent made me grin till my face hurt. He looked to be intentionally losing himself in his rowing to avoid acknowledging my mirth.

"Hesiod, do you not have any words about how you came to this realm? The last I saw of you, you were nothing but ash." He kept rowing as if I hadn't said a word. "Or how is it that you have come to acquiring this boat and rowing it so masterfully right to where I happened to be? Do you have a god guiding your movements?" I paused and chuckled. "Are nefarious forces driving you?"

"Ungrateful fool," Hesiod grumbled, "I've had my body burnt to crisp. My ashes were sifted by Hades himself who only after some deliberation agreed to hand me over to that waterlily god. Hades was all but forced to when Ra, the birdlike Egyptian god of sun, threatened to burn him to a crisp. The fact that you have the gods from different mythologies warring against each other for your soul says enough!" Hesiod harrumphed. He stopped his rowing for a moment and turned to me. "I know that you are Hyperborean. I know that Wyrd watches and Apollo sees you as kin. The solar gods, those bright and shining deities, welcome your ascension. At least some do. I was appointed to guide you on this path of flame. As your guide, I first had to take that step into that infernal pillar of fire in

Tartarus. But I did not bear your marks. I had to be burned. Whether it was a message from Apollo to my intellect, divine revelation, or simple intuition, I suddenly knew what I had to do."

I stood up and grasped his forearm, pulling him towards me and embracing him while he still awkwardly clung to his oars. "I would be lost without you, friend. But how is it that you survived the flame? How is it that not even Hades could hold you hostage?"

I let go of Hesiod and stared at his dark eyes that were suddenly coated in unshed tears. He ran a hand through his unruly bangs, flattening them out as he placed the oars on the boat floor.

"We are both Greeks. You a Roman one and I an Ancient. But there is more that runs through these veins," he said as he held up his wrist as if it were an offering. "We come from the same line. Not simply as Greeks, but as a people set apart, with the light of the sun illuminating our minds, and its blaze the furnace that fuels our hearts."

I extended my arms to show Hesiod my marks and he took them sacredly, leaning forward to breathe on them as if adding new life. Then he kissed each mark.

"Hyperboreans, through and through. Our line may have changed much over the millennia, but the spirit of such eternal blood remains. A repetition, reviving itself in those bearers of heroic eternity. It needn't be a degeneration, no, it shouldn't! We must increase. Much has been entrusted to our kind and to forego such glory is to wither and fade." Hesiod's eyes shined as he stared up at the strange, violet-streaked sky.

"Then, as brothers, we will see this through together," I said with my hand on his shoulder.

"In this unliving world, yes. But the realm of life belongs to the living. My words remain but my body does not. I do not see me making it through. This is no word from a god or Fate. It is a feeling." He sighed and lowered his gaze to look at me.

"But if I have died and will return, why should you be prevented?" I said.

"My sun has set. Yours hasn't yet risen."

"Then let us finish this as one." I let go of his shoulder and looked around us. "What is the goal here in this strange Egyptian underworld?"

"We are in the Duat and it is our task to move through the hours... the twelve hours like Ra. We must follow his fiery trail until we are worthy of his path. There are many monsters and trials here that need overcoming. You've done well to pass through Tartarus, but this realm will be all the harder. You must be found worthy of eternal weight. Only with such power and approval can you move on to life. The weighing of your heart is at the end of this river. Those scales must be answered. If you have a true 'yes' as an answer, then you may continue in this Hyperborean song—singing it into a new land and people."

"Then let's go."

"Let's," he said, picking up his oar.

"Can I not aid you with your rowing?"

"Trust me, you'll need your hands free to face what we are about to face."

With my mind now untethered from the unknown—at last coming to grips with a semblance of a why—I stared up at the sky in search of this Ra. Purple streaks skimmed over a blank black backdrop. A far different feel from the gray smoke of Tartarus that had been like the color of a nameless tombstone. The sky here was oddly imbued with a lurking sort of violet life that demanded the dead stay in the dark black. I would be like those flashing clouds then. I would live through this dark around me.

Our boat coasted through the river, and there was no noise but for the constant slosh of oar digging in and out of water. The air here was heavy, not quite tropical in its humidity, but oddly banal in how it hung there as a sort of oppressive nothingness. The whole realm felt fuzzy, as if left unfinished and lacking a sharpness of spirit. I breathed the empty air and sat back down on the boat, watching Hesiod work.

"You're sure you don't want to switch with me?" I asked again after some time. "It's not as if we are in any immediate danger."

"We haven't even passed the first hour. No, no... I am fine. It is good to use my body once more. I spent enough time bodiless in Tartarus since my death. To be rebuilt of ashes from Hades made me realize how much I enjoyed being human." Hesiod hadn't even turned from his rowing to answer me. His head swiveled about, searching for danger that wasn't there. A lurking shadow in the water made him squint harder, but he relented and focused once more straight ahead.

I sighed, leaning back on the cool wood edge of the nicely carved and surprisingly roomy rowboat, and contemplated why it was that I was here. How had I, a soldier in the service of the esteemed Emperor and eastern half of the Roman Empire, been chosen to play the protagonist in all these foreign myths? There had to be some sort of truth tying it together. I knew of Wyrd. And I knew Christ was Lord. Yet He remained silent and Wyrd strange. Riddles and half answers were all I'd received.

Was I willing to found a new nation of Hyperborean spirit? Of course. Yet I couldn't help but feel as though I were a mere puppet to be yanked about by the unseen. What was it that I could see? Was this really me?

"Do you think I was chosen or that I chose this myself?" I said.

"Who did the willing? Was it your will or was it decreed by the Fates? I've already told you that even the Fates cannot see your clouded future, and for that they fear you. It was not they that set you on this path. Wyrd aids you against the jealous gods, yes. But she only helps as the Lord sees true. I believe your will is what will see this through, one way or the other," he said.

"Many brave men have died better deaths than I. Even if I bleed the blood of ancient Hyperborea, my soul being yanked into this dark game seems suspect."

"It is you, for whenever you decided you would pursue the utmost glory possible, this decision was what willed this afterlife rebirth. A pure will powerless alone, but this joining of purity and single will is what brought you the power of your Lord. He smiled down upon your right-seeing sight. This sort of power is the way to ascend Olympus and become a god, becoming divine. Your will was entrenched with divinity; your unadulterated focus willed this into being. A mortal made immortal by purification of self-tyranny. I focused my entire being on this when I walked the earth alive. Whip out the weakened will by beating away the chaff of distraction. Proper will directed at pure power is possible. It is why I too have joined you. We are both worthy of our wills. It is something I thought much of in my prison of darkness. And now we stand together on this one path." He quickly glanced back at me and nodded, and just as quickly turned back to search for unseen dangers.

"But how? I would be lying if I said I'd been planning this, or really thinking of the future at all. It was always the present, the moment I lived in. I kept my focus on that strange slot of time... that semblance or, perhaps paradoxically that, equivalence of eternity." I scratched at the etched swirls on the boat's edge. Tracing my finger along the carved path, I tried to connect this theory of time, this strange existence I now led, to what it was we willed—if it was we who had done the willing, as Hesiod claimed.

"As a potter molds clay, so you sculpted your being with the excellence of living as one finite in the infinite pursuit of glory. Your glory was pure because you pursued it without longing for some distant and unknown future glory, but you pursued the always present—that which remains eternal as being and becoming united in one," Hesiod said, never breaking form from his consistent rowing.

I dug deeper at the intricate lines in the wood and squinted. "So, my being was directed perfectly towards becoming, the two joined together in time as a speartip directed towards glory? Is that the correct analogy?"

"Precisely, but deeper there is a mystery impossible to untangle."

The oar's rhythm filled the following silence as I contemplated what such a mystery might be.

"Your own fate overcame whatever the Fates had in store for you. I've spoken of Wyrd before and assume that you've met her since, right?" Hesiod said, his head turned back to look at me while his lulling row remained at the same pace.

"Yes. She was an odd one. A Fate belonging to the Lord."

"Her discordant harp string is the one that must be plucked, not only by her and your Lord, but by you. If you choose such an instrument, people will view you as being weird as Wyrd; but to play such a chord as your own is to embrace and smile with your entire soul at the indifferent nothingness the abyss of time threatens to swallow you with. Instead of running away from the shadowy end, or pretending it isn't there, you simply surrender to it in such a way that it becomes your own. Therein lies transcendence. Therein lies the freedom of the now, the freedom of the discordant man humming outside of the mortal realm—the man willing to embrace the infinite in the face of his own mortality."

Hesiod faced forward again and I finally stopped fidgeting with the edge of the boat. I scratched at my beard and leaned over the water, its black color offering no reflection. Our discussion offered me the only reflection of myself I needed. Talking of such concepts reminded me fondly of time spent in my father's study, going over Plato and Aristotle, always learning and trying to make sense of the world. And here was Hesiod, a man before even those great philosophers, speaking with the force of eternity. I was grateful for his words. I needed them in this strange time of so much unknown. Trying to comprehend existence and meaning had been one of my foremost methods of battling against the tides of mortality when I'd lived. Fitting it was continuing even further now that I was dead.

"I knew that there was something more for me during my life, but I never hoped or pretended it would be. I can recall facing each day as its own forever. In life or death that hasn't changed," I said with my hand buried in my beard.

Hesiod nodded his head and looked at his swinging oar. "I look ahead to where I want to row this boat, and thus the wooden craft is guided there. For man it is much the same, only one looks by not looking forward."

"Riddles, poet?" I did not smile despite the obvious jest. His words were worth much.

"No, no, let me finish. To guide your spirit into the glorious and heroic realms of reality is to look inward at the always-present now, the moment that is instant yet never finished. A repetition of power that must be reenacted again and again—each eternal moment lived until the spirit has flown forward to the course best suited for glory. Like a ship guided by the oar, a man is guided by his will. Only, this will is not directed at a space in front of him, but at a space within and also without. It is pointed through the present past of heroic men who never die and live on through everything the true man does when directed towards glory. But you must row, for to row is to be, and to not row is to cease to exist, meaning: never existing as a being worth being—never becoming the javelin spear that pierces the shroud of time and catches all of eternity on just the tip, in that one moment of glory."

I pulled at my beard and nodded. "Time decays a will directed at nothingness."

"Time cannot touch the spirit of substance, the spirit aimed at the glorious now of eternal heroism," he said.

"So, I was chosen through my own willing?"

"If you need to ask, then why would I answer?"

"But I had to relive my last moments several times over to perfect my will. How was I allowed such a choice, if I were not already chosen by some Fates?"

My return to Constantinople refused to let my mind rest. How had I truly died? I looked up at Hesiod, hoping he could give me some reprieve from such barbed doubt.

"You met Wyrd and we discussed her discordance, yet you still question? Your returning to that moment was the realignment of what already was. You simply did not comprehend because, as you died there on the battlefield, your mind was clouded by the animal instinct of survival. But your spirit acted accordingly. How could it not be as such? For you would never have been able to walk as you do living among the dead—reliving the end of life in an authentic way. Your memory must realign itself with the discordant fate of becoming that sings in a perfect hum when embraced by the purely willed spirit, glory directed eternal." Hesiod nodded at the horizon and I found myself doing the same.

I leaned back and pondered the nature of it all. I, a Christian soldier of Constantinople, dead along with my people, was here in a foreign mythology. As strange as Tartarus had been, at least I knew of the mythos there, as I'd grown up hearing and reading of it. I was a Roman Greek after all. But the Duat? Pyramids and waterlily gods? Hesiod seemed at home. But then again, he might well have wandered here on his own before I'd ever come to this afterworld. I inhaled the swampy air, hot and heavy with a smoking rot, and I let my eyes drift towards the black river's murky waters. I stayed there staring silently, no signs of any movement but for the gentle tearing of the water from the slice of Hesiod's constant strokes. It mesmerized me and I leaned further over.

And then, I saw something break the surface: a ridged, dark spine the same color of the water. It was that mossy, blackish-green that could only belong to one beast. Then another ridge popped up, and then another. I stood to my feet and looked behind, and to the other side. All around our boat, scaled bodies wriggled through the water with yellow eyes glaring at us with terrible hunger. Yet they kept themselves alongside us as if being forced to hold back by some greater will. I didn't want to know what beast could possess such a will, but Hesiod answered my thought.

"Sobek comes," he whispered. He kept rowing, but at a slower pace now, careful to avoid touching any of the crocodiles' gargantuan bodies.

My arms glowed, the serpent bite blue and the wolf brand red. A strange golden block arose from the water, right behind our boat. Attached to the gold was a giant crocodile head, by far the largest of the surrounding beasts. The large head under the golden block came closer to the back of the boat until a strong arm, like that of a man, pulled the strange being aboard. I stumbled backwards and managed to catch myself against Hesiod's back. The strong and tanned body of a man now stood on our boat. Sobek's muscular frame matched the size of his reptilian skull. His massive form loomed over us. The boat rocked as his weight nearly capsized us, but the crocodiles gathered together along the sides, pushing it straight and holding us there while continuing to propel us down stream. Hesiod's oar smacked against the deck as he at last took in the sight of this strange and terrifying being.

Sobek's body was garbed in a gold embroidered waist-robe. His exposed torso was thick and swollen with heavy rolls of muscle covered in a layer of fat. His golden eyes were flecked with bits of silver, and his black slit pupils remained unblinking as they stared at us. His green-black crocodile head was as long as my body, and his mouth gaped open in a snarling smile. He had sharp fangs piled atop one another that were an unholy white, pure and pristine in a frighteningly impossible manner. Even stranger was the blue headdress he wore which cascaded down his back like hair. On top of the headdress was that strange golden block which towered atop his head. Two green-jeweled serpents were sculpted under the base of the block from inside the blue headdress, and an orange-red disk like the sun was placed in the center of the block.

Hesiod stared in silence. My fingers twitched and I held out my glowing arms. "Sobek," I said.

He pounded the boat with his strange staff that was forked on the bottom and colored a solid blue. He lifted his other hand in which he carried an ankh—an arched and t-shaped talisman that was the same color as his staff.

Sobek said, "Ra blazes forward, and I follow his path in my sacred waters. What is it you desire here, mortal? How is it that you possess a living body in this realm of death?" His voice was foul like the gurgling rush of an overflowing sewer.

I held up my arms higher and the solar disk in the center of his headdress lit up in flame, a perfect circle of fire that burned so smooth that it glowed as if made entirely of a glassy ember.

"You bear marks of the solar kind, but do you yet bear the gifts my people once possessed?" he said. His mouth yawned open, a terrible maw of blackness inside, and he snapped his jaws shut with a crack. "I know you, Rangabes. We have awaited your arrival. You have a sacred task, but are you worthy of bearing the flames of the sun? Does Ra truly shine down upon you? Many of us do not believe in your strange path. To live again and leave behind death, you must inherit the full power of the sun, through the great civilizations' mythic might. This is the only way a mortal such as you can complete such sacred duty that is best left to the gods. To found a new holy land based on the ancient power of the sun, you must be able to join it in its fullness. Here in the Duat, I can add to your strength."

"And why would you help me?" My arms were still before me and glowing, my fists at the ready like a fighter.

"Help must be earned. Otherwise, debt will be accrued. There is no lending amongst gods. It must be gained with glory, power and honor. There is no honor in taking and expecting more," he said.

"I didn't ask for your help. I am here only to move onward towards my goal."

"Ra has touched me," he said, placing his hand upon the fiery disk on his head. His skin scalded and smoked, but when he pulled his hand away there were no burns or blisters; if anything, his skin looked somehow purer. "You must be tested by my soldiers upon the shore."

"A test? Again? Do you see these marks? I am a Hyperborean and I do not need your dull gifts to sharpen my might." I did not trust this twisted god.

"Sobek-Ra is a lie. He is merely Sobek. He pretends to carry the light of the sun the same way the moon shines false," Hesiod whispered behind me.

The boat lurched as the crocodiles nudged it ashore with the full weight of their bodies. Sobek stared at us without speaking as we waited. Hesiod's whispered warning held truth. Sobek was neither Helios nor Hyperion. Their rituals had been built for my blood, while Sobek merely wanted to prove that he was greater than I. There was little to trust in his monstrous appearance, the sun disk on his head be damned. The crocodile god appeared more and more beast-like as his silent waiting devolved into a snarl. His jaws snapped open and shut, chomping the air as if it were his prey. His swarm of crocodiles, numbering twelve in total, slinked onto the shore as our boat propped up onto an empty plane of land. Sobek lumbered after them, dragging our boat further ashore with his arms and not looking back.

Hesiod grimaced as our boat was dropped with a bang. He grabbed my shoulder just as I was about to step off. "Rangabes, we do not need this monster's approval. He merely wants to claim the feat of besting the sun's champion. He is not truly Ra's chosen. Sobek has always been a god of chaotic in-betweens. There is no guessing the depth of his murky waters—we cannot see what lies in such a sordid spirit as his."

I took his hand off my shoulder and stepped onto land. "If he seeks to challenge my honor and worth then I will best him. He will not leave us alone; he must be dealt with. Sobek does not belong amongst the solar beings."

"Do you back away from this challenge, mortal?" Sobek growled.

He stood on the wide and desolate sandy shore with his crocodile soldiers beside him. The land here was wide, rocky and white. Patches of dying reeds slumped alongside the banks of the river. One of the lantern-like turquoise trees shined off to the right, casting the landscape in a cold, bluish haze.

"You're not my kin. You're an abomination," I said. Ready to leap at the slightest sign of aggression, I moved forward. "Stay aboard the boat, Hesiod. This is my honor at stake." The poet didn't respond but I knew he understood. I could best this foul beast of a god, this faux solar beast. A crocodile slinks in the shadows of his murky domain. Light only exposes his filthy form.

Sobek's twelve crocodiles flanked him on each side with six to his left and six to his right, angled like an arrowhead with Sobek as the sharp point. He roared and his gold tower headdress darkened, shimmering in a rainbow of colors like oil on the surface of clear water, and then it went black. The solar disk burned red in the black and then went dark, snuffed out in a strange puff of black smoke, turning the disk gray. A fitting symbol—a dull beacon like that of the full moon on an overcast and gloomy eve.

His body rippled and bubbled, and his tanned skin thickened into a sickly gray. His flesh shook and black-green scales like that of his crocodile head pushed to the surface, covering his human half. Now he was his true nature, a crocodile beast standing on two legs like a man. A long, scaled tail sprouted out from his backside like a creeping vine. Silver spikes bristled out from his black scaled tail as it snaked out behind him. The serpents on his headdress glowed green and wriggled to life, extending all the way to his shoulder.

His crocodiles underwent similar monstrous transformations. Their bodies all rippled like jellyfish, and their forms stretched upwards until they stood like their leader. Over their reptilian bodies was spiked, green-scaled armor that had ivory thorns sprouting out as if grown from a bony bush. They donned and clothed themselves with the dead flesh of their kin. The ignominy of such wicked redundancy!

"I will use nothing but these fists!" I yelled, letting the glow of my arms subside. My body as it always was would win this fight. My chance at Herculean honor. "Like Hercules, I wear nothing but my own flesh. Weaponless and honor-bound, I challenge you."

Sobek lumbered forward as he stretched out his clawed hand and motioned for his soldiers to hold formation and stay back.

"I have my ankh. I have my staff. I have my soldiers. I have my divinity. What can you hope to accomplish by deliberately weakening yourself?" he said, unimpressed and unwilling to part with his added strength.

"I earned my marks," I said, holding my tanned forearms up without any spark of light. "Yet as a man alone, I want to best you. My Hyperborean might is earned, but it is also by birth. My pure spirit willed in perfection. My Hyperborean spirit is enough."

I paced in a slow and loping gait—the wolf waiting for its prey to panic. Sobek held up his staff and ankh as if in offering to the dark sky. Both of the strange artifacts were bathed in black energy like an electrified shadow. The shining black shadow gathered together in his two weapons and bloomed out in a patient pulse. The spreading shadow of shimmering black suddenly lasered forward in a sharp rush at me. I dove out of the blast's path but a crackling whip shot free from the shadow beam and clipped my left shoulder, my flesh turning black and rotting where I'd been struck. The burn and decay were instant and my surroundings wavered. I clung to consciousness and pushed the taint from out of my mind while the burning and stench remained.

As Sobek growled some sort of spell in a strange language, and the same black shadows once more shrouded his weapons, I sprinted directly at him. He roared as he shot his beams of dark light at my direct approach, but I sidestepped the first while ducking the second. I leapt at Sobek and struck down with two hammerfists right at his underbelly. Its soft tan color and lack of scales were surprising, considering he might have been just as unprotected there had he kept his human form. As my fists landed, thudding against the taut skin, the crocodile god let out a deflated hiss. I followed my attack with a quick succession of jabs to his gut.

Sobek snapped his mouth at me and I spun away from the bite, jumping backwards. Enraged, he threw his weapons to the ground and stormed forward with his claws tearing at the air. He'd taken the bait and I quickly rolled twice until I was behind him. His nasty, needle-covered tail swept and swung at me, clipping my shin but only just as I sprung onto his back. I pulled myself upwards as if he were a wall to climb. Blood from my ankle painted his black scales red, and his arms stretched desperately back but were unable to reach me. He thrashed wildly, but I hung there like stubborn fruit clinging to a tree through a storm.

Scrambling all the way up to his head, I reached around his bulky headdress and pressed my thumbs into his eyes before he could close them. I pressed harder as he bellowed and I dug my fingers in and dislodged what remained of both eyeballs. His snakes snapped at me, biting into my wrists, but I would not release my hold. Whatever poison they spewed was no different than the darkness already rotting my shoulder. I'd win this first, then worry about any after effects.

As his eyes tumbled out, his pained screams crumbled into whimpers. Seeing their master rendered so, the crocodiles surged forward. They desperately reached upwards while I clung to my perch atop Sobek's head. I pulled off the serpents latched onto my wrist and grabbed his black pillar, pulling backwards with all my strength and throwing my weight off his body as I held on. The black pillar came toppling down and I fell to the ground along with it. My palms were stained black where I had touched the thing, but at least it hadn't hurt and it had humiliated the monster god even more. The serpents hissed down at me from under his blue headdress, their eyes burning an even brighter pale green.

He thrashed out in a tornado of black, his tail and arms swinging everywhere as he bit at the air, all while I backed away, dipping and ducking the crocodile soldiers' blows. Sobek's insane attacks were inadvertently bludgeoning and slicing his own soldiers. Three of them were felled by their master in mere moments.

Their armor covered their vulnerable underbellies, forcing me to stay on the defensive. I tried to draw them into the flurry of Sobek's despair as he continued his mad lashing out. I ducked the unpredictable swings and bent back just as two crocodiles lunged forward and stumbled into death by their own crippled god's scythe-like fingers.

"Hand me my staff and ankh!" Sobek cried.

They raced over to grab them and hand them back to the finally sobered Sobek. Two of the crocodiles closed in on me, and I swung my bruised fist at the nearest one's snout while kicking the other with enough force to knock it backwards onto the ground. They backed up and joined the remaining soldiers standing by Sobek.

"You have maimed a god!" Sobek screamed. His two artifacts quaked, and an emanating dark glow swallowed his body in black as he disappeared in the growing and tremoring shadow. "I will erase your solar birthright and send you falling down to the darkness. You will become like a moon buried in its dark nature without any sunlight to reflect."

The crocodiles pushed forward and Hesiod yelled to me. I quickly glanced behind me at his voice. He frantically waved me over as he shouted for me to run. I shook my head. This wasn't finished yet. With a deep breath, I suddenly sprang forward and into their attack, scraping through their chomping jaws and scratching claws, grunting as they tore off bits of flesh from my lowered shoulders and arms. I burst out of their grasp and leapt one last time at Sobek's dark-shrouded body. The black shadow burned and froze, the icy heat somehow pushing through into my soul. The darkness! The despair! I cried out in pain, yet plunged deeper into the strange abyss until I saw his glowing green serpents. Sobek laughed as his mouth snapped at my neck, and I desperately ducked my head. I propelled myself onto his chest and thrust my arms out to grab the two snakes by their throats. With my feet planted on his chest, I flung myself back and pulled as hard as I could. The snakes snapped off from under the blue headdress, writhing in my grasp as Sobek screamed in fury.

I broke free from the dark, swinging the still hissing snakes like whips, holding them by their heads while the crocodiles backed away in terror. Blood spurted from the two snakes' torn ends, and their black spew burned the crocodiles unable to avoid their spray. Free from their clutching claws, I slammed the serpents to the ground and crushed their heads under my bare heels.

Sobek was gone. All that remained was his tortured screaming and the ever-growing black cloud, which flashed and billowed, about to explode. I turned and ran back to Hesiod and the boat. Hesiod had already pushed it into the water. As I hopped on, I looked back at the black bloom of glowing taint and it erupted, consuming the remaining crocodiles. Its shadow rapidly expanded outwards and towards us.

"Go! Go!" I yelled.

Hesiod sliced his oars through the water as the shadow grew longer, a floating river of oily black that came closer by the moment.

"Use your marks, fool!" Hesiod yelled. "You won, and your honor demands you don't let us die out of pride."

I stood at the back end of the ship and held my arms out, bathing them both in a reddish-blue light that covered my flesh all the way up to my elbows. I pushed out and unleashed a single beam of bursting, purplish-light that tore the darkness apart and exploded it into a shine of gold that hung there like the abiding desert sun. With the darkness diffused, sparkling white embers danced in its place as if to celebrate the banished corruption and purified air. Hesiod slowed his rowing until he dropped the oar in the boat and breathed a heavy sigh. I stumbled back and sat down on the ship's deck.

"What is this black taint?" I asked after several minutes of silent and labored breathing. My shoulder festered black and rotten, and my palms were printed with dark stains. My wrists ached from where the snakes had bitten me.

"Corruption has mingled with your light. We must have Ra burn it away." His strained and red face drained pale at the sight of my wounds. With his voice shaking, he said, "That black is the corrupting darkness of eternal surrender. That surrender to the weakness of the lightless beings who live as mere shadows and silhouettes instead of embracing solar divinity. Sobek was false, and his falsity is festering within you. We must hurry." He quickly turned to grab his oars.

"Then let us move forward." I took a long and labored breath to steady my stuttered mind.

Hesiod rowed forward with impressive haste. I stared at my blackened hands and wondered if this taint would pollute my yet unborn nation. This black burned.

***

Apollo Awake

The three-headed hound was sleeping. Old Cerberus was at long last leaving the gates of Hades open. The immortal guardian had seven serpents branching out from his black fur, and even they too were limp and asleep. Cerberus slept for one reason—the gates of Hades were no longer used. He slept because the way of antiquity that he'd so proudly protected had vanished. Men of power and heroism seemed absent to the hound who'd seen just about every kind of soul walk through his doors. I knew the truth of his gate and duty. Most assumed he was there to keep the dead within. But truly he was there to make sure that only the worthy stepped through the gilded doors of Elysium. Cerberus was the first and truest judge of the underworld. He knew the scent of truth.

And next to Cerberus was the god of sleep, Hypnos. No doubt the two had conspired together to dream in that blessed land of eternal slumber. Most gods couldn't quite kill themselves, but they could give up. They could become of nature and like the animal, forgetting their personhood and bowing to the beast inside. Or there was this sad alternative. Sleeping with eyes closed to the decay of a weak world. A dream of remembrance based on what once was, what might have been, what should have been—or whatever else a resigned mind might imagine.

The fair-skinned Hypnos looked like a youth just ripening to adulthood. His boyish and fresh-faced appearance was no doubt due in part to his nearly constant state of rest. As the old gods quaked and hid, driving themselves into an unsalvageable madness of despair, Hypnos slept deeper and sounder than ever before. And now the Elysian Fields were empty. No more heroes to populate the shaded meadow and sing songs of glory and might. And the torture regions were useless. In an age where people preferred nothingness instead of an eternal perfection of being and becoming, the gates of Hades might well be shut. Cerberus and Hypnos slept because their way had dissipated like the lingering remnants of a dream as the whole of it was forgotten. They slept because to be awake and a part of this time was to embrace the modern rot of chosen slavery. So, Cerberus slept with the god of sleep. There was nothing left to guard here. At least, that was what they thought.

I watched the two slumbering immortals and shook my head. The last bastions of our once great pantheon. At least those who belonged with me in the solar reaches still fought to exist. At least we were not allowing ourselves to fade into the forgotten. We had chosen our champion, when he had chosen us. He was to be our avatar, our vessel. I licked my lips and tried not to get ahead of myself. There was much work yet to be done. I pulled my blonde hair back, the curly locks loose and hanging just past my neck. I straightened my white mantle and tugged at my golden robe, knowing there was nothing I could do yet but wait. Wyrd sang louder than the Fates, and Rangabes weaved his own indifferent web. My wisdom's weakened reach was irksome, and it took a glance down at my exposed ivory-white arms to remind myself that these muscles were as lithe and strong as ever. I was still me. I let out a lengthy breath of relief just as I heard soft steps scuttle out from the shadows behind me.

"Apollo? What are you doing here? Come to gloat?" a cold voice called out.

"Hades," I said, without turning around.

"Your gamble on this mortal is wreaking much chaos. Hesiod belongs with me. Tartarus is not meant to be trifled with. What if Typhon were to break loose?"

I turned to face him, his insolent tone forcing me to frown. The god of death slouched there before me in a ragged black robe, his skin pale like a corpse and his eyes hollowed out and tired. He had once stood tall and proud but the years alone in his diminished realm, which had once been so great, had worn him thin. He now looked like the dead he had once lorded over. Even his long black hair had thinned; it hung in stringy strands, clumped together in knots where it hadn't fallen out. In short, he looked mortal—like a sickly mortal on his last throes.

"Typhon is a stooped shadow of what he was, please. Maybe you should tell your hound to wake up. Anybody could come and go as they pleased." I softened my glare and looked at my low-fallen kin with pity.

"What happened? How is it that we are forgotten?" Hades said as if our fading away had only just begun. He turned away from me and walked over to look down at Cerberus. He gently stroked the hound's middle head.

"How is it?" I crossed my arms and stared at this sad excuse of a god. My pity evaporated at such a pathetic display of mortal victim mentality. "Please, we Greek gods ranted and raved, ravaged and raped, and what have we to show for it? Offspring that are either monsters or halflings—mere shadows of ourselves? We grew distant in our profanity. We forgot what we once were."

"Apollo, you blaspheme us. If Zeus hadn't gone the way of Dionysus, pretending his madness was the way forward..." He stood up and turned to me, his shoulders stooped and his eyes looking everywhere without seeing anything. "Maybe it was the way forward. Better than this."

"There is virile madness, and neither of them possessed it. Drowning in drink and hedonism and proclaiming that as an affirmation of life is degenerate madness. Virile madness is smiling at the sodden sun and soaking up its scorching drip. It is setting in the burning black of tomorrow, sinking so low with such weighted power that whatever rises next will be something entirely new. Ra reborn, but no longer Ra... no, but something more. Much more. My virile madness is not the decay of Zeus and Dionysus. If they aren't gone already, their minds are."

"And what is this setting sun? Is the age of the gods finished? You speak with assured airs yet you still stand here alone. You are no different than I. I intend on staying right here—empty realm or not, it is still mine."

"I smile at this sun, because I have sons of my own. Not these filthy aberrations you and the rest of the gods have vomited forth. I've left behind my own atrocities and now my sons shine. They possess my wisdom. Hyperborea froze as nature breathed her icy breath. But when my children went forth pregnant with power, they birthed the greatest of peoples; the light of their blood couldn't be snuffed out. There are those who walk among the living still with that light locked within, leaking out in individual acts of greatness and glory. And there is Rangabes now living among the dead. He might just be this new rising sun—or at the very least, its shining ray," I said, my eyes shining gold and my voice pronouncing each word like a poet. Hades appeared unaffected.

"Egyptian beast-deities forcing my hand." He shook his head. "You overstep your shrinking bounds. This is my domain."

"What remains of it. Hypnos looks as if he's at last taken on the sleep of the dead. Even though he is not one for ever being much awake... this time it seems as though he might remain forever with eyes shut. Perhaps better than madness. Perhaps not. And Cerberus? Hades, you can't see what kind of hound he is meant to be. Your eyes are too dark to see the light there. He has his part to play."

"Leave my hound alone. First you mock him, and now you threaten to use him in your plots? What? Is this heathen Rangabes going to pilfer him like a prize the same way Hercules robbed me of him so long ago? Zeus is no longer here to protect you. Do not make me imprison you here, fool. I cannot kill a god but I can make one suffer."

"Hades, you are the fool. No, you did not go mad but you cower here in your dark realm. Persephone left you ages ago and you didn't even care to take her back, so afraid of the light have you become. You say a god cannot die, but you look as though you've already dug your own grave. Have you chosen a nice spot for yourself to be unseen in, here in your fading realm? So much knowledge and nobility to be buried! How grave!"

"That does it!" he roared.

He stood up straight and squared his shoulders as if he were his old self. His eyes blackened and shadows dripped out, dipping his face in an inky darkness. Black wings of shadowy mist stretched outward and the fog from his eyes poured out to encase his body, enhancing it until he towered to four times my height and width. Only his sickly head remained uncovered, and the rest of his body was now a hulking, black-fogged beast with misty talons for hands and feet.

I grinned at the transformation, for now we'd have a worthy fight. His pale face twisted as he screamed at me. A shrill shriek from a man who had nothing and blamed the world for his own deserved misery. An insolent child: that was what Hades had devolved into. That was what most of great Olympus had become. Disgustingly weak and profane.

"At least you remained a god, however lowly and shadowed. At least you are willing to fight," I said calmly, the even respect of my voice smoothing the rough wrath of Hades' features.

"Let us fight. I am tired of this nothingness that I and so many of us have become. I will not become an animal. I need to fight. I may be forgotten but I cannot forget." His eyes and features softened, a spark of divinity and life shining in the once-great god's features.

I nodded up at him, knowing there was no other path for him to walk. This was his setting sun and I approved of his brazen leap into its fire. Better to burn than flicker. He breathed in deep and yelled—a deep and worthy roar. I loosely shook my arms and stood crouched and ready as he soared up into the air like a bat. He scraped the miles-high cavern roof and flung himself back down at me.

I waited, watching his now-alive face, passionate with purpose at long last. In a burst of light, my golden bow shined in my hands as I called it forth from the heavens. Crouched on one knee, waiting as long as I could, I pulled back the string and let loose an immaculate white arrow of light, the snapping bow singing aloud like the pluck of a heavenly harp string. The arrow headed straight for Hades' head. Not one to ever miss, I confidently rolled away from his crashing form.

Safely out of reach, I could only smile at the sight before me. In his shadowy pincers he held my arrow. He tossed it aside and sped towards me through the air, his talons reaching forward as if he were an eagle coming to snatch its prey. I let out a flurry of arrows, the golden bursts of my volley sizzling holes through his dark form. I dove to the side a step too slow, and he gripped my body. My surroundings whirred as he flew upward, crushing me in his grasp. My eyesight dimmed and my fingers froze as my legendary bow fell from my hands and faded into the black mist.

As we soared upwards, his claws dug into my skin. I kicked at his one claw and held the other at bay with both my arms pushing it away as if I were Atlas painfully bearing the weight of the heavens. Not seeing any obvious way out, I decided to risk an approach of artifice. I closed my eyes and let my form go limp. Just as his claws scraped my skull, I focused inward on the solar glory within me. The pain of the tearing talons brought forth the eternal light of my being. In a bright torrent my light burst through my skin and erupted over his shadowed body as I screamed in a fit of power and pleasure. His form bubbled and blistered, scalded by my pure light that kept pouring out. My screams rose higher as ecstasy mingled with a perfect harnessed eros, as if it were being gathered and released all at once—a finite moment of eternity, blinking brilliantly in white-gold flashes. With both of us ablaze in my divine light, we spiraled down, yet Hades still held me in his stony grip.

We crashed to the rocky floor and his grip at last went limp. I pushed myself free, panting and ragged from my expended eternal energy. Hades' fearsome shadow form was stained gold by my light. Riddled with tears as it was, it wafted away like dust in a sunbeam.

"Hades?" I said, stepping over to him as he lay there in his tattered robes.

I gasped at the sight of him. He was nothing but a skeleton now, his bones brittle and brownish as if he'd been laying there that way for centuries. His hair hung in rotting patches on his skull.

"I see it. I see it now. How could I not see where it all was heading, where it had always been heading?" His bones rattled and his jaw ground as he spoke while still lying there on his side. His cavernous eye sockets stared up at me. "I see it at last because now I cannot see. I needed this darkness. I needed the light to burn my folly away. I am the nothing now."

"Hades," I said, getting to one knee and reaching out to embrace him.

"No!" he hissed, his voice whipping from all around me as if the very cavern had spoken. I froze and stared. "Do not corrupt yourself by touching my unworthy darkness.

An absence of light is what I am. To touch me is to blot out your being."

"But light banishes the dark."

"And dark swallows the light."

"It depends on how strong the light is."

"As does it for the dark."

"How is it that you speak? You cannot die. What happened? Are you suffering?"

"No... you're wrong. And I cannot feel. All I am now, is... is nothing. Like the air you breathe but cannot taste. I will not decay into an animal, forgetting myself. But this... what I am right now. Apollo, at last I've become Death. My bones are vacant now."

"But you speak. You live."

"No. I die and am dead. I've chosen this. I live on whenever another dies. That is where I go and will always be."

"I will watch Cerberus for you. I know you loved that hound."

His jaw shifted and his skull stretched, creaking itself into a grimacing smile. "Thank you."

I bowed my head as his whispering voice echoed away, slowly decreasing till the only sound was the steady breathing of the still sleeping Cerberus. I kissed his bones and they crumbled to dust at my touch. I nodded, my work here in the land of the dead almost done. My light was my own. I would overcome.

***

Emerald Light

The swirling gray ocean peaked and valleyed like a desert of liquid granite. It pumped against the cliffs, a thunderous heartbeat of power painting the backdrop with life and death. No matter how much my people had forgotten my divinity, this realm remained tied to the eternal reality of our old Emerald Isle. This was one of the first lands the Hyperboreans conquered when they fled the frozen north. I nodded, assured as ever of the path I now walked.

In the distance, a man in emerald-jeweled armor shimmered over the grassy slopes and peaks that spread out before me. His green garb so naturally belonged to his surroundings that his outline was fuzzy; his body seemed to bleed out from the landscape. He casually walked forward as if I hadn't told him that our meeting was of the utmost urgency. We stood on strange soil here, a reflection of the mortal realm that was not quite truly there but as close as we could come. I knew no mortal could see us any longer. Not here. Crossing my bared arms that were wide as a bull's neck, I glared impatiently at the proud king. Arawn, the immortal god-king of Annwn. He was lord of death. He ruled over his once lively land of the dead with justice, but now there was nobody left for him to judge. Little life remained in our world.

My blue tattoos of runes and patterned paths spiraled over my unclothed body, glowing with a subdued blue that emanated from my sacred ink. I rolled my shoulders and smoothed my wide-stripped, burgundy loincloth that hung between my thighs. My red hair was pulled tightly away from my scalp into a topknot, greased with the finest oil and fragrances. My body was as thick as a tree trunk and I planted myself there, shaking my head as Arawn finally made his way over to me.

His armor glittered like glass refracting sunlight. His green, steel-plated suit had large burning, pale-green runes covering it, each rune encrusted with even more emeralds. Truly it was a powerful sight to behold. His face was bare and angular—royal cheekbones and an upturned lip: his narrow face had the look of sleek and purebred nobility. His dark hair spread out on his shoulders like a raven-black cape.

"Why have you summoned me, Lugh?" he said.

"My hero has suffered decay," I said.

"From who? The desert gods?"

"Yes, their monstrosity of a god, Sobek, is to blame. He had taken to calling himself Sobek-Ra as if he could inherit the role of the solar."

"Blasphemy!" Arawn shook his steel fist.

"And this blasphemy got him killed. Rangabes presses onwards, but not without wounds of corruption. His people will have to deal with this curse, I fear—thousands of years from now and right in the present."

"A dark fate, if this fate is met."

"His bravado was the fault. But that other one sings her song, that song I cannot hear. I do not know." I turned away from Arawn and looked up at the gray-reflected sky, storming with clouds and capped like the sea it ruled over.

"But why have you summoned me? Is he not still in Egyptian hands?"

"Sulis has betrayed us, as I knew she would. She fears Rangabes. She fears our acceptance of this strange fate. She is stuck and afraid. She belongs only to her own dark," I said.

"Her light lies," Arawn said, nodding.

"It belongs to us. Her being is lunar by nature. A deception."

"Then what do you have in mind? I know that Rangabes shares our blood, however diluted. His spirit remains in our light, does it not?"

I nodded, but stayed with my eyes searching the skies. "Wait a moment more. The Morrígan comes."

"You invited her, that spiteful carrion queen of death? And not the righteous kind of death!"

"Sulis has her armies and artifice. We do not. We have something... someone better: the phantom queen herself."

The ominous crashing clamor of crows all cawing together rushed out from above the clouds, their strange song fitting for a funeral. A black cloud descended from out of the gray, and from this mass of crows, a lone one descended free from the rest. As its purple-feathered wings spread out low before us, the bird took on the shape of a beautiful, pale woman. Both her breasts were bare, pointed and perfectly peaked. She wore a thin strip of loincloth that only hid the front of her lower body. We Celtic gods knew how to dress by not dressing much at all. Arawn had fallen in love with the nobility of the Middle Ages and had taken on its strength. I did not blame him. His armor had been much needed in the battles he'd fought to protect his realm. The legend of an eternal, knightly king had captured his imagination. But there was something about the freedom of movement, the air and sun reminding you of your true nature and power. I smiled at such tame thoughts in such a time of terrible change. At least we would remain. At least for now.

"I have come, Lugh. Does that mean he has made it through the Duat by now?" the Morrígan said, her voice fresh and light like the morning dew.

"No, he suffers greatly. But we have a more immediate matter to deal with on our own soil. Sulis, the false sun goddess, has taken refuge in her black castle with an army of thousands protecting her. We need to end her so she cannot ruin our plans. Our fate must be had, especially against those squawking Fates—and the oddly chirping one," I said.

"Sulis thinks only of herself. She hides upon stilted heights, refusing to bow to the always higher sun," Arawn muttered.

"We are Hyperboreans, even in our different shades of light. And the Morrígan, you are our natural ally while Sulis is a corruption of our noble past. She does not belong to our ilk and kind. She must pay for her treachery," I said, hurling out the words with disgust.

"Then let us burn this whore of the dark," the Morrígan said.

I nodded, my runes and tattoos flashing bright like lightning. I soared into the heavens as a roaring bolt of thunder, storms surging in my wake. The Morrígan flew as a raven, jetting through the air with impossible speed. We flew over the green valleys and rolling hills—an emerald ocean with an equally emerald knight riding its waves on his horse of wind. His steed was a crisp and ancient forest breeze; its green leaves rustled together in the form of a stallion and whipped forward with a wild gale of force. Arawn rode his primordial steed with shocking ease and regality. I grinned, lightning crackling through my ink, and soared high knowing no army could face the might of our nobility.

The black castle carved through the gray skies like a cursed dagger, a scar blackening the surrounding green. It stood profane and high—a giant spire with grotesque black stone branches spreading out along the hills. Its form was gothic and gargantuan. A fortress that belonged in the Otherworld where Arawn reigned, but had been bled into this refracted mortal realm through Sulis's perversions. She feared us and Rangabes so much that she hid here, as if this realm would remain untouched by his mighty death march through the pagan pantheons. I was proud to call the man my kin, and I would use his might as required. And I required much. Mortal he remained and immortal I stood. This was a battle belonging to the gods.

I shot down to the ground in a bright streak of lightning. Arawn hopped off his horse as it vanished in a leafy gust. The Morrígan cawed and swooped down to stand by us in her beautiful female form once again.

"The Grian Dorcha. This castle should not be. A fortress forged of dark light, a negation... an abomination. She bleeds my domain!" Arawn yelled, his emerald fist clenched and raised as if he meant to topple the fortress with it.

"What do you propose, Lugh?" the Morrígan said.

"She knows we're here. Let her forces come. Let her army assemble! Let them see the wrath of true gods!"

"A pleasure. Oh yes, oh yes!" the Morrígan cried, her voice pregnant with ecstasy. "We will feast!" She burst into a fluttering blur of purple-black plumage, and an army of crows swept out from the clouds as she rose up to join them. The black beating of their wings darkened the gray skies in a billowed bleeding of impending death.

"The carrions are carrying on, yes?" I laughed, enjoying my pun.

Arawn scowled; his fury was fixed only on righting this unforgivable wrong. To bleed divinity from his realm without his royal permission was an offense that must be punished. He'd kill his own mother if she committed such a sin. Still, his kingly sense of justice was strict and righteous. Hierarchy was fixed and the royal ones were worthy of wearing their crowns. His roots were of the Hyperborean earth and his branches soared into the solar reaches. He was worthy of his position. I nodded at him but his eyes were focused on death now.

I looked up at the black cloud of crows swirling like a stormy cortex, and contemplated. The Morrígan was a strange one and few saw the sun in her darkness. But she was not like Sulis, forcing the light to embrace her dark while pretending to wear the garments of the sun. No, never. The Morrígan knew who she was; she knew her nature. She belonged to the earth, like the corpse drained by thirsty soil. She was not naturally a Hyperborean; she did not bear my solar nature but she sought it. She could not become it, but she aided it. Her black wings spread far and wide, and she was sovereign over much. She saw what Rangabes would be, or could be. She saw the worth of my blood and what Rangabes would mean for it. She was also a bringer of war, and to have her on our side was to surely win. Perhaps in her soaring flight there was enough of a reflection to be a refraction, and the fractal light in her wake might just hold a bit of that solar spirit. Not a lunar lie, but an accepted gift. Regardless, she was for me and that meant I was for her.

I hummed and started chanting like a bard. I sang with a jovial grin, my voice surging into song, shaking the heavens. My brother in sun Apollo was not the only one who could spin a silken melody. I held out my arms and stared up at the Morrígan and all her ravenous ravens. The runes on my throat burned a bright blue.

Her murder of crows
brings murder to all that chose,
the darkness of the sunless throes
of the frigid one who froze.

Murder, murder!

The one closed and lacking clothes.
She hides in an abode where not even a toad
might hop. Sulis is only the queen of a sunless stop.
She stays stuck in her fear.
She stays still, small as a mouse-deer.
Sunken in snow, adrift—
the sunless one has no glow or lift.

Negate, negate!

We hate to see your thin skin so exposed.
Where, oh where, you sunless one,
are your clothes?

I laughed as I finished singing, bowing with a flourish. The field before the castle's wall was empty, but no doubt Sulis had listened. She'd respond. I smiled wider as roaring shouts and war cries arose from near the wall.

Impossibly, men poured out from the stones of the black wall. What foul trick had hidden them there? The well-armored men were garbed in black-barbed steel, and they burst from the stones in thousands, all along the thick wall. Men ran forward in a thundering herd of meat. I held out my arm and my divine spear shined into my grasp; the great spear called Areadbhair—known by mortals as the Slaughterer—was made of pure crystal and imbued with a refracted rainbow. I raised my other arm and my legendary sword of white steel, Fragarach, shimmered out of the air and into my grasp. The Answerer. A worthy weapon.

I whispered the incantations to Areadbhair, "*Ibar. Athabar.*" It rumbled in my hand and shot out in an emerald blaze of fire, straight at the coming horde.

I snapped my fingers and my sling-stone, slayer of Balor, wrapped around my wrist in a purple flash. It elongated into a red chain that carried the heat of the stars and the light of the rainbow. With my weapons in hand, and Areadbhair, Arawn and the Morrígan already striking into the masses, I burned forward to join them. I struck as lightning into the midst of the herd and I unleashed my power. My spear sliced through the men in paths of fiery green, and my chain burnt the mortals to ash as I whipped it in circles, a whirlpool of fire scorching the soldiers in waves.

The Morrígan pecked out countless eyes with her form that was a swarm of crows. If their talons didn't kill as they tore at mortal flesh, their dagger-like beaks did the rest. She was a cloud of black death. Arawn was not to be bested: he wielded two glimmering swords, each a deep evergreen hue that mirrored the black of the deathly forests in his domain. He flourished, spinning in circles, leaping into the mass of bodies as his hair flew behind him like raven wings. I watched their progress from the corners of my eyes, but only to see if they could keep up with my might. They couldn't. As I split a splotchy man's skull and his ratty hair drowned in a beautiful bloom of red, I breathed in the fresh air of death and smiled. The killing field was a full table feast of fallen bodies. A glorious ocean of death!

Thousands of men were piled atop each other, mangled and wretched, more swamp than sea. The bodies were foul and ragged; these men were no noble warriors. They had the look of peasants, the lowest of low. Of course, that was the only kind that would fall for such a false god. Those of virtue remained loyal to their betters. How Sulis had brought them into this realm I couldn't fathom, but wherever she'd scraped them from was no worthy place.

The crows were feasting on the carcasses. Spouts of blood spurted upwards in increments as the crows pierced arteries and other fleshy bits. Arawn was grinning, his face sinister and gaunt after such rapturous ferocity. He strode over to me, crushing the gored corpses underfoot with odd squelches bubbling in his wake as if he were walking through a bog.

"She has more, I feel it," I said, as my weapons vanished together in a blink of light now that the fighting was finished.

"Weak. Weak-willed filth that I refuse to call men. These were rabble. As much as I enjoyed the slaughter, I can't help but feel insulted." He stomped his foot on a nearby head, the flesh bursting like a rotten gourd underneath his green-greaved sole.

"Yes, something is amiss." I stroked my chin and glared up at the tower. "Let the Morrígan feast; we need to continue. Call your hounds if you must; they surely hunger for flesh not of the Otherworld."

"A feast they've not tasted of for too long. Thank you for this allowance, brother. They grow cold without the flesh of those under this sun—or semblance of the sun anyway." He put his fingers to his mouth and whistled, a piercing shriek that shook the earth beneath us as the ground tremored and the distant sound of barking came. Several packs of his white wolves with their scarlet ears descended onto the battlefield and joined the crows in their feasting.

"Grab my arm," I said, holding it out to Arawn. I raised my head at the tower.

Arawn nodded and gripped my extended forearm. We burned forward in a burst of lightning and landed atop the spire with a bang, crumbling through the black stone in an effulgence of electric light. We stood untouched by the rubble as the field of crackling blue energy sizzled out around us. A lone crow followed behind us, and the Morrígan appeared at our side.

"Welcome," Sulis said.

She sat on a black throne with a white sun circled behind her as the backrest. Sulis wore a billowing black-violet dress that ran down in long rivers of silk, extending gaudily across the room to our feet.

"You throw your men away like a prostitute with her chastity," Arawn spat, his phlegm squelching right onto her overreaching dress.

Her pretty face scrunched up, her delicate nose and thin red brows rising. Her hair was a violent red and she wore a silver crown with four amethysts pointed forward like fangs of a viper.

"You know our strength. You know the world's unbelief. And you know that Rangabes will come. To resist is to perish. He is of the sun as am I. You are not, as you've shown." I shook my head, sweeping my eyes around the room and then narrowing them as I took a step closer.

"Rangabes," she hissed. She straightened her back and tensed, her brow lowering so suddenly that her face seemed ready to fall off. With her jaw extended, she ground her teeth and glared off in the distance with her deep violet eyes as if she could see Rangabes coming already. "His arrival is our forever exodus. Do you want our reign to end?"

"He is the proper evolution. All the myths, all the gods, it all pointed towards him. The last of the mythic heroes, the one to start anew. A new age of new heroes and myths. The mortals have already forgotten us. We that persist either have gone mad or become who we were meant to be. Rangabes is the cure to our diseased state. We've fallen from our heights, for since the true myth of that Ancient One, our kind have slowly been bled dry. Those that still remain are the ones who bleed the sun. Yet we that choose to align ourselves like a proper constellation, we remain. Rangabes is the only way." I sighed. I knew Rangabes was the extension of this bleeding. But he was of my kin and his will was pure. It was the only way I could still walk in the sun. And I would use this extension to persist. I had to. Reality grew more distant every day. I shook my head and stepped closer.

"Do you know why I threw my flea-bitten mortals at you?" she said, a creeping smirk marring her face. I stopped and eyed her warily as she leaned eagerly forward.

"Lugh!" Arawn shouted. He loosely grabbed at my shoulder.

"Bitch!" the Morrígan shouted, as she started to shake and heave.

My body shuddered and I suddenly lost all sense of strength. I felt as if my bones had liquified and I collapsed, quivering to the floor with Arawn and the Morrígan in the same pathetic, fishlike state beside me.

"I threw them at you because I have no mortal subjects—they do not believe. You fools! You think all of a sudden I managed to pilfer a peasant army from the countryside? Not even the Lord could make an army out of such men. Those pigs you slaughtered, those corpulent corpses you let your beasts feast on were not humans. They were swine, actual pigs!"

"What?" the Morrígan gurgled, her voice drowned in blood.

Sulis stood up, sweeping her dress around her as she glided over to us with statuesque grace. She peered down at our rippling bodies and laughed. "The whore goddess of death has drank her fill now, yes?" She knelt down and poked her manicured finger into the Morrígan's head. I screamed as her body burst into a pool of black liquid. Sulis turned to me and said, "Gwydion, the old trickster god, still lives as he always was, and like me, he is not keen on Rangabes bringing about our end. An end is an end, no matter how righteous." She looked at me gravely, and placed a perfect finger on her blood-pumped lips. She subtly shook her head and smiled again. "That old wily mage used his trickery to disguise the beasts, and then charmed them into believing they were men. Tricks and magic all around!" She clapped her hands and cackled with her head thrown back. "I cursed the pig's blood, for whoever came to spill it would become as they were—nothing but foul and impure. Rangabes will die when he comes. He'll join you in the pool of pig blood you're becoming."

I choked, my lungs black and bloodied. My heart slowed and sagged. My fingers melted before me and my body burst like a spider egg sac. My essence blackened thick and scarlet, and as I became liquid without form, the sun blackened to me.

***

"We've come to the fourth hour; the waters of Osiris no longer carry us afloat. The river will run an even darker black and we must proceed into the maze that Sokar, the falcon god, stalks." Hesiod threw his oar onto the boat for emphasis and jumped ashore. The sand here was black like that of Tartarus—black like the corruption staining my flesh.

I silently followed Hesiod ashore, trying not to grimace at the icy prodding of Sobek's stains. It was as if something cold and dead were seeping into my blood. The serpents' dark venom spreading through me no doubt made it all the worse. I shivered, clutching my arms to my body. Hesiod watched me with concern folding his face.

"We need to reach Ra. We cannot dally long in this maze. Perhaps Sokar will be willing to help us like Nefertem," I said.

Hesiod nodded and I walked forward. The black sandscape before us spread out into a valley that had swaying reeds the size of mountains lining the sand and crisscrossing in every which way. The maze of Sokar. As we stepped up to the first path where the maze began, I gave a start and stopped as I realized this was no longer black sand ahead and within the walls of the maze. This was a black water so dark it appeared as if it were an empty abyss with no sign of movement on the surface—just a still nothingness.

"How are we supposed to get through this without our boat?" I asked, turning to Hesiod. His widened eyes were enough of an answer.

A serpent arose from the black depths of the water, swaying upwards as its body continuously extended out from the deep as if it would never cease. The serpent stretched itself so high up and right at the entrance, that it stood taller even than the mountain-sized reeds lining the maze. The serpent glittered yellow and its black eyes surveyed its surroundings slowly. It hissed, its pale-purple tongue flicking out like a flame. The serpent seemed not to notice us, but appeared to be awaiting something or someone else.

The sand beneath our feet shook and flashed orange as if on fire, and then the black turned to a burning tan like that of the Sahara. A dark blue falcon's head arose from the sand behind us. Attached to the head was a mummified corpse riding atop a golden snake that was merely the same size as that snow serpent from Tartarus. Merely! The absurdity wasn't lost on me, but that mountain of a serpent in front us made even the biggest monster I'd yet faced look infinitesimal.

"That is Apophis, traveler—the Chaos Serpent. Ra's eternal adversary!" The falcon god cried out in a high chirp. Two blue wings burst free from the bonds of his mummified form. "I am Sokar and my maze has long been polluted by this serpent of doom. He turned the already black-pitched river into a deeper abyss of nothingness. The sands surrounding this once pure domain were of gold.

Now, like so many of my kind, all we once were has been turned on its head and thrust into the cold of nonbeing."

I glanced up at Apophis; the colossal serpent sat there coiled, his hissing like a violent downpour of rain. Yet, of all things the giant beast looked bored as if we weren't a threat. As if it were looking for another foe. With my pride bruised and my honor challenged, I walked away from Apophis and hopped aboard the golden snake, sitting right behind Sokar.

"A wise choice. Apophis does not take notice of us; he only has eyes for Ra. He is called Lord of Chaos, enemy of Ra for good reason."

"And where is Ra?" Hesiod asked, climbing stubbornly behind me, taking his time and clearly not pleased.

"Ra travels through the Duat just as you. He makes the journey every night. For where light shines, darkness follows. Thus, Apophis slithers in the shadows as the embodiment of evil. His only drive is to bring the world into his domain of chaos."

"Why has he revealed himself?" I asked. "Why block the maze?"

"Probably because he sensed your solar spirit. But that mark of corruption made you unworthy in his sight. Still, there are more hours to be finished and your heart has yet to be judged," Sokar said, turning to look at me.

"I'll show him unworthy!" I growled.

"Do not be headstrong. We go and gather our own strength. There are places we must first pass and time we must first end. The hours. And then we can find Ra and we will finish this," Sokar said.

The rumbling of Apophis's movement shook the sands and he slowly collapsed back into the depths of his murky nothingness.

"Now we may pass," Sokar said, his wings flexing as if he meant to fly away and leave us behind.

Instead, his golden snake raced forward, carving through the black water with ease. He turned this way and that, moving so rapidly I could barely stay seated. Sokar knew the paths of his maze and we tore through it with impeccable speed. If Hesiod and I had been left to navigate this on our own, we might well have died here from old age. Every turn looked the same and the paths forked in every direction, endlessly multiplying. Of course, it wasn't as infinite as it seemed, and at last an opening bloomed out before us. A burning lake of red fire angrily torched the nearing horizon and a white pyramid towered out from the midst of the flames.

"Tell me we don't have to go there," Hesiod groaned.

"Unless you want to awaken Osiris, no. Though from the murmurs of this dying land, I've heard that he is no more. No more rebirth, no more anything. He went mad without any dead to judge. So, he judged himself instead, and he judged that he was unworthy. He threw himself into the lake of fire, and I don't think even his being the god of rebirth could save him from that. Those flames are primordial and capable of killing all, even gods. Only one higher than us gods could walk through flames such as those. And without Osiris to heed, Isis and Nephthys clawed at each other in the air above the pyramid until each of them, bloodied and forsaken, tumbled into the flames.

That pyramid is cursed. It used to be that Osiris's body waited there to be awakened by Ra's spirit."

I narrowed my eyes and stepped off the snake as it coiled its body together now that we were back on black sand. There was something in that pyramid for me. There was something I had to do. I knew it. It drew me. It spoke to me. My spirit burned. An ancient ache anchored my will to eternity, and the pyramid held a key to unlock my multiplied being. My powerful past slumbered, but this walk through death was awakening it. The fire surrounding the pyramid would burn away those cobwebs of unclarity that still trapped my awareness in the finite. It was as if I had been Osiris buried there. It felt like it should have been my home. I stepped away from the snake and stared, the flames billowing high, but in all their fury they were incapable of blotting out the brilliant glow of the white pyramid.

The flames cannot harm the truly mad.

The strange whisper chuckled, folding in on itself and echoing in the back of my mind. I rubbed my head as if to quiet the laughter, but it remained resounding, hollow and broken. The roaring of the flames hummed, their crackling cacophony bringing a smile to my face as I traced a melody within them.

Embrace the song that can't be heard
Unless you sing that all's absurd
The fire hides what shines with night
The sun dances chaos into right

A rite that only the yes can bring

A light that lonely stress can sing
With open eyes a man must laugh
A drunken order that carries chaff

And so my whispers beckon you forth
Few souls believe in the journey north

You and I, we born of suns at heart
You and I, wheat torn from chaff apart

Sometimes the chaff is worth chewing.

The whispering voice snuffed out like a blown candle and the throbbing in my mind ceased. I stared hungrily at the flames and sped forward towards their burning glow. My hearing closed itself to the outside and listened only to the subtle creak of my joints ground against ancient bones. My bones. Their bones. My bones. A strand of silk dipping out from the center, my soul tied to those before and those to come. The web would unravel if I gave in, but it would spin onward to spread its strands like the sun its rays, if only I moved forth. A spider's web bathed in the blaze of morning light—that was the closest a mortal man could come to understanding the sun. I walked to the flames. I drew inward so as to be only myself in the present and the future. The infinite. I listened to my rushing blood, my singing heart.

The lake of fire parted into a path, the flames bowing down and swirling outward as I walked. They leapt back together behind me to close off a turning back. The heat of the flames billowed over me and I embraced the blaze pumping into my heart. The bed of the fiery lake sloped down and its bottom was of cracked black brimstone that burned the soles of my bare feet. I walked onward and reveled in the pain, the bubbling blisters of my feet the result of the required refinement of my sick self.

The white pyramid, pure and pristine, stood above the rest of the soot-soaked landscape around me. It was a beacon of something more, something for me. Whatever had happened to Osiris did not concern me. What mattered was that this tomb was necessary. Maybe Osiris hadn't been truly mad as the voice had said. The flames parted for me, but they still burnt. Was I truly mad? It was hard to say. I'd earned my scars in these nether lands. I'd felt the power of my solar blood. It was real. I was no mere Roman any longer; East or West, it did not matter. I was an amalgamation of great peoples past, a pyramid of sorts, with the triumphs of my kin building me up. And I refused to be the last brick upon the foundations of my blood.

I wanted to take this call to found a great people, to build upon my soul. My vengeance melted in the glow of the pure pyramid as its light reflected my own inner pyramid deep within my spirit. I would be a stepping stone as my fathers were to me; a stepping stone for greater sons to stand on, and greater ones from them until we stepped into the sun, always building up. What god could stop my descendants? No Zeus, no Ra, no myth. I was a walking myth myself now, and my kin, my unborn heroes would one day become their own myths. I smiled and the pyramid glowed as I approached. A soft light surrounded it like a morning mist mingled with the waking sun.

With my mind aglow and my body ablaze with life and power, I walked forward, ignoring my raw and peeling feet. With a vigor fueled by my ancestors' past and descendants' future, I stepped to the pyramid, knowing it would welcome me. The pyramid itself was pure white and sleek without any sign of masonry or brick laying. The pyramid hummed as I stood before it, and the base of it spread open its doors, sliding and pulling back like nothing I'd ever seen before. The base of the pyramid pulled itself open by forming into crystalline pillars that shivered and moved like rippling water while maintaining a solid and perfect geometric form. In the opening, a slow, icy-blue light pulsed on and off, filling the darkness only to be consumed by it and then spat out again. I stepped through the opening and the pyramid closed its maw and I was enveloped in its dreary bowels.

With each tremor of pale blue, I was able to see more of the empty room. The pyramid was hollow. The room was wide and vacant, and it spread so far that I could only just make out the distant wall. The roof sloped steeply up, meeting at a sharp point. I took guarded steps towards the middle of the room, my eyes sweeping the dusty interior in all directions.

Did the old corrupter of youth say no?
Did the impious one say yes by choosing no?

The whisperer was back, only this time they were not whispers. A strong and slurred voice now spoke, sounding as though it belonged to a man lost in madness.

Madness. Are you mad?
It is not proper to never be angry.
But proper anger is that which laughs with glee.

He giggled as his words reverberated in the hollow tomb, amplifying and crescendoing into three voices speaking as one. His speech tremored and creaked, and I couldn't tell if it was from insanity or if it had rusted from a lack of use.

He drank that cup of death with glee
Poison swallowed infinity
Not thanking a god for freedom from life
Not mere denial, but accepted sacrifice

His debt was a crowless rooster still
Paid in tyrannizing his flesh and will
Not relief at a weak flight from life
Not belief in a peek at an after strife

The strange prodding poem stopped and he inhaled, breathing sharply as his tenor scratched against the walls. He softly said, "To dominate the body and mind is to deify it—exalt the mortal frame with force of will. His offering was a thanks for a life worthy of death. Socrates says yes to life and death as one. He loved both me and my brother, gold and grape."

"Dionysus, you wine guzzler! I should have known. Come out from your darkness!" I said, searching the still stuttering light for a silhouette. "Only the mad god would live in a tomb belonging to another mythology."

"Belong? Belong?" His voice rose and crashed back down, vibrating with an overcharged energy. He rushed to release his words, yelling, "To belong is to be loved for nature and spirit. These gods here have neither nature nor spirit. They combine and mix, taking elements from one god and attaching it to the next. Sobek-Ra is a lie. There is no spirit, for these gods are beasts." His voice stopped as he choked and coughed.

"You could probably use some more drink," I said with a smirk. "And do not disrespect Ra. He is worthy." I nodded to myself. There were still good ones here, however few.

He ignored my remark and continued. "My essence is all that remains. And this last essence of mine has been reduced to this laboring light you see here beating: my freezing heart."

"Why wax poetic on Socrates of all people? Why call me forth?" I said, watching the push and pull between the blue light and dark.

"Because I want you to act like Socrates and say yes to life and death, but especially death. My maenads grow hungry. It has been oh so long since we devoured Osiris's cooked carcass."

I frowned and raised my arms. Purring hummed out from the shadows, interspersed with playful meows. As the light pushed back the darkness, six figures now stood around me in one of those circles that I was growing all too familiar with. The six women purred louder, surrounding me in a slowly tightening circle. They carried strange wooden staffs with pinecones adorning the tops. They wore robes dotted with the spots of a leopard. The animal skin hung loose and open enough on the sides that their tanned breasts were mostly exposed. Each maenad was savagely beautiful with wild black hair and matching dark, frenzied eyes. They licked their lips as the moved closer, their purring increasing to a growl. And as they neared, they started to wail and moan as if in the throes of intercourse. I couldn't bring myself to do it—to destroy them. Was this another ritual? Was this ravenous death I faced of necessity. Why was I brought here? I closed myself to the maenads' deadly approach and listened inward. Silence. A beat of my heart. The sear of my burnt feet. No. No! I couldn't let them win. Or was I supposed to? No ritual! This was danger. This was death. I opened myself back to their snarling spin.

I raised my arms higher up, anticipating their mighty glowing power, but nothing happened. My holy marks appeared only as scars; no light nor sacredness imbued in them. I winced as my blackened shoulder bubbled, burning and boiling with Sobek's sin. My blood was slow and heavy. My blistered feet suddenly became too much to stand and I collapsed to the ground. Bone showed through my peeled soles like a split peach exposing its stone. I sat there and did not resist; my only method of manhood was to not cry out in despair. The maenads danced, and with the overpowering scent of skin soaked with wine, they pounced, clawing at my face and tearing at my body with teeth and hands. I tried to ward them off, but their frenzied strength of madness beat my weakened state away with ease. Teeth ripped off my nose. Chunks of my skin were chewed and swallowed, my body gnawed and torn like a half-eaten apple. The blackness that enveloped me was a welcome change. I smiled and my lips peeled back, mostly eaten away. Blood coated my body with a gory glow. Then I was no more.

But no... no! The darkness that came was pulled back—sheets torn from a bed that one had just fallen into at last to get blissful rest. My rest would not be allowed. I watched my body below be eaten, a red hunk of meat now, a bag of gushing gore. Now, I was as a cloud, light and incapable of solidity. And in that high-pitched roof of the pyramid, with my body being eaten below, I felt a presence of pure will embrace me. Ecstasy tore at my soul. I would have screamed if I could. But silently I rode the wave of divinity and when it subsided, my vaporous form ascended through the ceiling to hover above the pyramid at its peak. Dionysus stood there before me while I was still without body. The god of drink appeared whole, and he balanced with casual and calm indifference on top of the pyramid as I merely hovered there beside him.

He had the appearance of a young, handsome man with a well-groomed beard and trim, curly black hair. He stood there naked, his body lithe and lean, a fit and healthy form with olive skin gleaming as if just oiled. His violet eyes jumped about violently and without apparent reason. His tremoring smile flicked the corners of his lips upwards while his face twitched unstable. This was surely a god long since gone mad.

"How do you taste?" he asked me, his voice a full-throated roar as he shouted the question, flinging it through my vaporous form.

"Ask your maenads, you freak. Now am I truly dead? Now is my body forever lost?" I spat the words out as if I still had a mouth. Sadly, my voice slowly drifted as thoughts to his brain, though the way he winced I could tell he'd felt my venom.

"Your body? *Your* body? You walk amongst immortals in mortality and have the gall to presume such a thing. Why, you're mad!"

"Do not insult me." I clenched my absent fists and grunted with fury. I was useless as I was now. "My blood is my own and it belongs to those who helped it bloom. You are no gardener. You snip the grapes and pull the vine."

"But you aren't divine!" he laughed, clapping his hands.

"Why did you call me here? Why set your dogs upon me?"

"Felines, my friend." His face flashed with a sudden seriousness and his skin tightened as he lowered his brows. "I myself was torn apart and eaten by the Titans, long ago. I was an infant! A baby fed to the old guard by that whore, Hera. Unworthy wife she always was, who could fault Zeus for fleeing such a paltry vulture? He was weak to never put her down like the rabid dog she was. But I digress, this is a grave matter for both you and I were torn and thrown into the graves of ravenous stomachs."

"You did this to me!" I said.

He frowned at my interruption and held out his hand in disgust as if to push me away. "Do not profane this all with your ignorance," he muttered under his breath, his gaze darting, and he irritably raked his feminine fingers through his black beard. "My mother was the queen of death herself, fair Persephone. Well, *one* mother. Depends on the bard! I suppose death was breathed into me from the start, regardless of my godhood. But what do you know… I was spared an end, as my heart was saved by great Athena, and from this I was reborn, resurrected as I am today. It is funny, there are other myths that would say I came from Zeus's thigh. But who can trust what? Maybe I'm both. Or maybe, there's a strand connecting them. I ramble." He laughed, bending over and yanking his hair before standing up completely serious again. "In the right myths, my enemy was Semele, my mother who most would consider to be true. She was my enemy for forever having failed at birthing me as a mother should. Yet I rescued her from the dead and made her a goddess! Is it not expected for a mad god to save those whom he's mad at? What of the enemies that are those hungry Titans? They burned under the wrath of Zeus, under his glory. And from their ashes, you were born."

"Me? I was born from my loving parents in Constantinople. Not in two separate ancient myths that you cannot seem to straighten out."

"No, no!" He hopped up and down on one foot and pulled his beard. "Those ashes, those ashes! Not then, but now. Now! Don't you see? To truly live you have to be reborn every day in ashes. That is the way of life. You emerge from the ashes of divinity, those lovely embers that burn your weakness with a madness that sings in the power of glory. Do you see? You already were of those ashes. I wanted you to come and see that you lived this truth and that you must pursue it further—to its final, true end!"

"If I already was as you say and on this path of ash, then why have me be eaten alive?" I tried to yell, but my thoughts—involuntarily serene—drifted at Dionysus who leapt from foot to foot with his arms flailing happily like a dancing jester.

"To taste death not merely as one tethered to Tartarus like a forgotten Titan... no, but to taste death that life itself tastes, this circular tasting is the feast that must be swallowed whole. By coming here, by suffering those burnt soles, by suffering the death of your flesh, your ashes are no longer that of mere burnt-out flame. No, no my dear brother in madness, your ashes are the coals that light the flame for the rest of the burning ones. Your rebirth now is for your people. Hyperborea sings in the smoke billowing out from your soul." Still dancing, he stretched out his finger and stuck it directly into my invisible chest, and my entire spirit burned.

My cloud-self flew over the pyramid and gathered together directly above Dionysus as he grew so distant his dancing jig made him look like a hopping flea. I looked ahead of me at the bruised sky and smiled at the impossible power thundering my way. A bull, wide and glowing white, boomed through the air. An emerald serpent shining like a green star slithered alongside the bull. And there beside the two glorious beasts were three wild felines together: one a bronze tiger with a sullen glow, the other a panther as black as the surrounding night, yet with glowing yellow eyes rivaling the intensity of the sun's blaze, and the last of the big cats a leopard with gold spots burning out from a coat of snow-white fur.

I bowed my essence as if I still had a head and in reverence surrendered myself to the five majestic animals, welcoming their piercing charge as I felt a sudden pull, like my soul was draining downwards into a powerful sinkhole. My being poured, my surging self like grains of sand bursting out from an hourglass, shattering time into a moment of eternity. And again, I stood as me—Rangabes made whole. But more than whole. I was more now. I was the fire that would set the world aflame. The maenads lay prostrate before me. I ignored them, for they were pawns in a game that I had already won. They belonged to the mad god. I belonged to me and my own. And so, I returned, the pyramid opening its mouth to vomit me forth, unable to stomach my power.

Not waiting for the flames to part, I strode through them triumphant, their flickering forms nuzzling my body like an affectionate cat. The flames did not burn or cool; they simply had no temperature compared to the burning of my life-giving, celebratory madness. Emerging from my comforting forest of flame, I walked ashore. Hesiod collapsed in shock while Sokar bent to one knee, folded his wings and lowered his gaze. His golden serpent covered its face with its tail, tremoring in fear. Apophis would acknowledge me now. It would have to, or face destruction. I was lord of its chaos, and my order would bring the blasphemous snake to a humble end. I was its eternal sun now.

"You have the aura of a god—no, of something more. A feel of power, of purpose," Hesiod said, at last recovering from his fall and dusting himself off as he tried to act as if everything was as it had been. "Whatever happened in that pyramid, you're certainly... different."

I chuckled at such an understatement, but got serious as I said, "Osiris wasn't there. Dionysus set his whores upon me. I was reborn in a sense. I am unsure how, but I feel it in my bones. An assurance of something higher. An ascension that will take place, already has, yet still currently is."

"You sound as mad as him. I wonder why he'd hide here," Hesiod said.

Sokar raised his head but remained bowed on his knee. "Isis or Aphrodite. Osiris and Dionysus. Their myths are more similar than you might guess. Perhaps in the breaking apart of our worlds, this bleeding together that you hasten has revealed the synchronicity behind it all. A synergy, a synthesis. We gods are as each other, all stemming from the Source. What light do you carry forth?" Sokar let his wings unfold and his beady black eyes blinked at me. His pale-yellow beak was bent so dreadfully that it looked like a drooping weed, dying and weak. This mummified falcon-god was a decaying companion of death—the perfect guide for this nether realm.

"Let us move on and not waste time pondering. I want to have my heart weighed so I can leave this world behind." I winced at the sudden pain in my shoulder. The black taint remained. Yet my blood was better. The snake's dark venom was apparently gone. I'd bought some time; it'd only cost me my flesh. I loathed this place. I held up my still black palms and said, "You animal gods are beneath my kind."

"There are animals in you," Sokar answered, at last standing to his feet.

I frowned but did not respond. The sky beasts' power boomed through my bones. Yet, despite my rebirth, healed feet, cleansed blood, and newfound strength, my hands remained stained black, and the festering shoulder wound still stung. The lingering light of whatever had occurred in the pyramid was diffusing, and its afterglow revealed that there was still much to be done.

"Perhaps the animal is needed. But I would not be a man if I let it stampede my soul. The strength of the wild is required to make the world tame to your will. Yes." I nodded, picturing the five beasts that had pierced my disembodied self. "We must go. I need Ra to cleanse this dark with whatever light he still holds." I climbed onto the golden snake as it shivered, uncoiling itself at my touch.

Hesiod and Sokar followed, the both of them deferring and sitting behind me. Whatever substance that had been added to me in my rebirth had the both of them subdued, as if they weren't sure that I wasn't mad like the god who'd murdered me. While I felt strong and filled with purpose, I wasn't so sure anything had changed. I was still me, with the same ritual gifts along with the corrupting stains. There were no new powers gained from that painful suffering. There had to be more to it. How was I coal and ash? Where was the smoke from my spirit?

Sokar, his snake, and even Hesiod were all submissive and guarded towards me now, so there had to be something more in me. I had to find out on my own. To ask them would be to make the advantage disappear at my acknowledging I was still as clueless as before. Even the fool sounds wise with silence. I felt the fool as the snake soared through sand, gliding so smoothly that it seemed as though we'd taken flight.

Now far past the lake of fire and its strange shore, we once more came upon water that was a deep and healthy blue. The snake slithered over the water and continued its unnatural soaring, skimming through the sea as if over immaterial clouds. These waters were an expanse as wide as the sky above, and we flew through it at the speed of a falling star. An ocean of blue spread out in all directions and the soft purple clouds pushed out from the dull black sky and down from above, onto the horizon. The salty smell was singed with sulfur, the ever-present reminder that we were still in the underworld. The always-stale air, windless despite our wicked speed. In our silent flight onward, the only sound was the slick slosh of dead water sliding under the snake's belly.

"Have you forgotten how to speak, Hesiod? I never knew you, my verbose poet friend, to not attempt to share your wanting wisdom and whimsical words whenever a fleeting moment of silence comes." I meant for the words to sound as light as the snake made us feel, but they came out sounding weary and dry, as if in insult and not in jest. I was met with silence. I glanced behind to make sure he was still there, and the both of them were staring at me as if I'd grown another head. "What is it then?" I shouted.

"Your eyes," Sokar said. He leaned back as if his admission put him in grave danger.

I grew cold as I rubbed them. My eyes? Were they not still the same dark granite green they'd always been? "What of them?" I asked.

"They move about, dancing as if insane." Hesiod stopped, letting his words sink in. My heart slowed as I recalled the frenzied look of Dionysus. Had I too gone mad? "First when you emerged from the flames they merely danced. But now... their color, their size. Your right iris is red, a deep amber like that of a rising sun."

"The eye of Ra," Sokar murmured. The snake hissed, its body shivering and shaking in tremors, all the while still sliding over the endless waters.

"And what of my other eye?"

"A midnight blue, the dark violet of a moonlit sky. Its silvery hue drips down as an eternal tear forever staining the single spot of your flesh." He pointed his finger right under his eye. I felt under my own eye and recoiled as I touched something frigid and liquid, like a living tattoo. Sokar continued, "The lunar eye of Horus. He offered it once to Osiris. I fear what it might signify. To be joined with Ra's eye in one person... they both are beacons of power and when unleashed, their power has destroyed not only gods, but worlds." Sokar pressed himself back, his wings pulled close as if trying to tuck themselves back into the tatters of his mummified corpse. The snake convulsed once more.

I squinted, focusing on the two scared souls before me. I felt my eyeballs dance to the tune of power, an insane leap to those stuck in the ways of the weak. My vision pranced and I pressed my finger again to where Horus's tear gathered so proud. I shivered ecstatic and closed my eyes, holding my finger on the tear and letting it fill me with the light of the moon. I howled, the Hyperborean wolves of flame roaring within me, the icy snake surging through my veins. The white bull thundered in my chest, glowing like the sun. The emerald serpent from the heavens had redeemed my blood, and its healing hold was wrapped around my heart, stabbing my spirit with burning electricity. I closed my eyes tighter and the light increased, pressing my eyelids, and there the three big cats prowled. The bronze tiger leapt in my mind and the dark panther greeted its leap, already deep within my consciousness. The tiger's eyes were orange and aflame, and the panther met its gaze with glowing eyes like beacons of a lighthouse in an eternal stormy black. And there in that ocean, the leopard swam. It swam in my soul with its white coat twinkling like a distant star and its gold spots a living constellation. This chaos was my own, and I could order it or unorder it as I saw fit.

With a gasp, I opened my eyes and smiled, unfurling my body from its ecstasy and sitting calmly, watching Hesiod and Sokar as a potter looks at his clay. "I stare with the eyes of Horus and Ra. Moon submitted to Sun and harmonized in ascension; my beams aglow with a conflicted, yet balanced and fulfilled radiance. A battle rages within me for the Hyperborean soul to emerge from these stained windows. Silver moonlight intermingled with amber rays of the rising sun. I see you as you are. I see you, flickering souls of a dying breed. Your candle is almost at its end. You, the poet of untruth, and you, the falcon god of death. I am an eagle carrying a star. My wings are the air you breathe and my lungs the womb of becoming. What are you but crumbling facades over a ruined bridge that hid its nature as a fraying rope? Don't look down at the chasm we traverse. I won't drop you, but if you squirm, perhaps the sinking sky is meant for you."

My eyesight flew into the heavens and I could see all. The threads of the universe revealed themselves to me; I could see strands pulsing everywhere like threads of silk connected to some cosmic spider's infinite web. The strands pulsed, veins of meaning and power, differing in size and noteworthiness depending on where they stretched. My soul soared into eternity and I gazed down from above and saw the teeming masses crawling over the earth like bees busying themselves in their hive. The strands sang, reverberating and glowing for only a select few. From the masses, most of the strands clumped together as if they were all of one mind and being, lacking the worth to have their own piece. Could they break free? Was it only up to a select few? Without finding an answer in the web, I descended suddenly, returning to myself and blinking. And then I heard a familiar whisper inside my soul.

Make the madness your own.

I understood. I lifted my Hyperborean arms and with them glowing, shoved them into my eye sockets. The pain was sweet and rapturous. I tore the eyes out and threw them into the ocean. I blinked as my normal eyes returned. To see the fabric of the universe with those eyes was well and good—and I would use what I saw to surge forward with my own silk thread the greatest of them all—but those eyes were borrowed and not my own. They helped me see, but their sight was a process to be overcome, to be superseded. And reborn as myself, I claimed this power, this mind, and this soul as my own.

"You are a good poet," I said, smiling at Hesiod, and returned to the humility of the present as my eternity within remained. "I thank you both for your help."

Still wary and shying away from me, the two of them at the very least recognized that I had won and returned whole. They shuffled forward and Hesiod said, "Thank you." He watched me with kindness softening his sight.

Sokar nodded and slid further forward. "We near Ra, which means we near the end. Apophis awaits."

I nodded back and swiveled to face forward. The purple-bruised sky ahead was yellowing. At the nearing horizon, an orb of light, baptized in the water, was beginning to ascend.

"Ra," Sokar whispered.

"We've followed the path of the Amduat, but already we've gone awry. Rangabes, wherever you walk you awaken the new." Hesiod's voice was calm, as if Ra's emergence from the horizon was expected. Then again, Hesiod had been the guide here; with or without Sokar's assistance, he seemed to know all. I grinned, glad that the poet was my companion and that I could see him as such once more.

"What must we do?" I asked Sokar.

Sokar's golden snake stopped moving and we floated there as the orb of light increased in size and continued to slowly rise from the sea. Sokar simply pointed at it. The orb had risen completely out of the water and in its midst a golden silhouette of a man hung. The orb of light burst and the silhouette hovered there alone. Ra, the Egyptian sun god immaculate and glowing, the solar made flesh. His body was dark and tan, his head that of the falcon—not all too different from Sokar, only Ra's body was free from deathly binding, yet he was missing his eyes. The Eye of Horus and the Eye of Ra shot out from the depths of the sea like blazing comets and leapt into his empty eye sockets and scorched bright, their now golden glow sending out a light that overtook the already effulgent god.

Ra extended his strong arms as his muscles and tendons bulged out like roots of a tree. A staff appeared in one hand and an ankh in the other. The pretender Sobek had wielded similar weapons, though I doubted corruption or any darkness could exude from such a pure being. Ra wore a robe of glimmering golden cloth, and his belt was made of shimmering gems like that of the celestial spheres.

"If Isis is no more, then who stops Apophis?" Hesiod asked with his hand holding Sokar's blue-feathered shoulder.

"This is the last rise of Ra's sun. A setting of sorts. We all knew it to be inevitable. The real question was: would Apophis succeed or would another sun ascend?" Sokar swallowed and turned to me. His eyes blinked and his beak opened and closed. Swallowing again, he tilted his head back and forth. "Rangabes. You are that sun."

I nodded, knowing as much. I scoured the horizon, watching and waiting for Apophis to emerge, and then at last he arose from the deep. His giant maw opened from out of the water, an abyss of swallowing darkness, as he leapt from the sea and snapped his jaws at Ra's form. Ra flashed out of the way. Apophis leapt out again like a shark attacking a floating gull, but Ra once more blinked out of the air and reappeared safely away from harm. The ancient serpent extended his infinite form up and up, higher and higher until not even we were out of his reach. His head whipped through the air, chasing after Ra.

"We must help him!" I yelled. While Ra dodged and remained untouched, the blows seemed to be coming closer to landing. The sun god had yet to go on the offensive, so frantic and constant were Apophis's attacks.

"On my back," Sokar said. His lively blue wings tensed, spreading wide as he flexed them.

I climbed on top of him and Hesiod nodded at me with a confidence so supreme that it bested even my own assured belief. Sokar tensed his wings again and bent his knees before catapulting into the air. We soared towards the two all-powerful beings, their game of cat and mouse continuing. The wind walloped me with waves of air, and I crouched there with one arm holding Sokar's feathers and the other raised with the glow of wolf fire shining bright.

Sokar flew straight up into the air at such a vertical angle that my body dangled and flapped like a flag, but I managed to hold on. Apophis either didn't notice us or didn't care. I was coal! I would scorch the earth in my flame! We ascended directly above to such a height that Apophis couldn't reach us, and then we stopped; Sokar hovered there with a couple broad flaps of his wings.

Sokar's loaded-up hovering forced time into a pinpoint of eternity. I glared down over his shoulder, the blue feathers popping into my eyesight. Up this high and in the heat of a battle born from forever, the scent of sulfur gave way to frankincense and myrrh. Holy smells filled my attuned senses. It was as though the Lord was rewarding my valor with the smell of beauty. With my senses alight, I bent forward as Sokar divebombed Apophis. I raised my flaming fist and leapt from his back as the Chaos Serpent's head jutted close by. I slammed my fist into the giant's head, a flower of fire blooming out in bright red and covering us both in a hazy, scarlet cloud. I clutched Apophis's house-sized scales as the beast continued unheeded. Sokar's dive bomb had failed, and as I clung there, I heard the sharp crunch of bones and a piercing cry of desperation. Sokar had been eaten like a harmless pigeon. I screamed.

I pulled myself up the scales like a ladder, propelling my body up the long steps. I was forced to stop my ascension every time Apophis whipped its head at Ra. Still, I was getting closer. I leapt higher and grabbed the upward slope of skull and clung tight. This high up and now atop Apophis's head, I stopped in awe at Ra's splendor. He was truly of the solar nature. A noble soul, a spirit of pure being and power! His light was so blinding yet alluring that even though it pained me to look at, I still couldn't stop myself from doing so.

What was I to do? My punch hadn't done any harm and the beast still hadn't acknowledged my being on its back. Yet Ra saw me, and as he dodged another whip of the head and I clung there tight, he threw me his scepter in a whir of white light. I stretched out my hand and snatched it, sliding downwards but still clinging on. Ra pointed at his shoulder and then at me before flashing away to dodge another attack.

I glanced at my shoulder and at the corrupt wound. Its blackness was particularly foul at the moment, and my skin there was bubbling black like a tarpit. I took the scepter and pierced the flesh of my shoulder with the golden weapon. The spear burst the black like a needle popping a blister free of puss. I then sliced at my palms with the sharp end, and at last the numb rot of my corruption had gone. The spear of bright light had darkened into one of black shadow. I gripped the now chaotic and corrupt spear in hand, and let it glow red in the fire of my wolf light as I pulled myself on top of Apophis's head. My red and blue light joined with the darkened spear as I thrust it downwards into Apophis's head. The serpent was stunned and I pushed in harder, my Hyperborean light pouring into the spear even brighter. With Apophis unable to move, Ra finally jumped in on the opening and with his ankh held out, he hovered in front of the beast's eyes.

Lord of chaos, this is an ordered sphere
My one eye light, the other a tear
Back to nothingness you will forever go
An arrival is to leave, and to leave is to know

His chant carried the magic of a spell—his voice deep in pitch and tone. Apophis screeched and its body shook as I clung there desperately. The screeching pitched higher and the ancient Chaos Serpent collapsed in a puff of ash. With my perch evaporated, Ra came to me and grabbed my hand, holding me aloft. His grasp held the heat of a thousand suns, yet his touch exuded the gentle meekness of one knowing and controlling his power with a soothing warmth that could sear any in an instant, if he so desired.

"Come, we go to my temple in the sky," he said, his light threatening to consume my own with its brilliance.

"Where is my heart to be weighed? Has all custom fallen from favor?" I said.

"With Apophis finished and Sokar's sacrifice complete, the scales survive in the one last place here untouched by the gloom of beingless being that is of the forgotten."

"Then so be it. Hesiod must come," I said.

"Of course."

A flash of light singed my sight gold, and then as the effulgence cleared, I found myself faced with impossible splendor. A pale palace with colorful religious artwork covering its walls stood before me. Nine tall obelisks were lined up in front of and away from the palace, each several stories high. They were made of intricately carved sandstone and dusted in a pristine glow of golden-white.

I stood there in a stupor, still clinging to Ra's hand. Hesiod stood off by himself, clutching at his robe for dear life. I nodded at the poet but he didn't notice. I let go of Ra's warm hand and walked ahead. Ra glided in front of me and up to the two enormous silver doors of the temple. A large greyhound was carved into the silver on one side and a cat on the other. As Ra pushed the doors open and I stepped in with Hesiod close behind, I at long last faced the elusive scale that would weigh my heart. The scale was large and silver, standing three times my size. It had a feather on one side with the other empty. Two gods stood beside it.

"This is Maat and Anubis," Ra said as his light dulled to a less consuming glow.

Maat looked like a normal Egyptian woman. She wore a plain white robe and sported a billowing feathered headdress atop her apple-shaped head. Anubis on the other hand had the head of a black dog with long, pointed ears, and a fit human body with golden-brown skin clothed only in a black waistcloth.

"We will weigh your heart," Maat said, her body thin and tiny. She looked like a young boy with her youthful, flat features.

"Your heart weighed against her white feather," Anubis said, gesturing at Maat and then at the feather. "If it is the same weight or lighter, then you are of virtue and may continue on the path of the sun."

"No, only lighter, Anubis. He is not passing into our decayed, forgotten realm. He seeks to earn the right of my setting sun." Ra's glorious eyes shined at the dog-headed god, who blinked with a cold black stare. His ears wilted and he bowed his head, folding his arms under the heat of Ra's gaze.

"What happens if he fails the test? I will not allow a devouring to take place," Hesiod said, walking in front of me.

"I'll kill the lot of them. I've been devoured enough for an eternity," I said. Blank stares from the gods followed and Hesiod looked at me confused. "You're the ones who brought me here. I don't want to dally in this decrepit land of the dead."

"You speak to Ra, the self-created and author of being. I will swallow your tongue!" Anubis growled with his jaw unhinged and his black tongue lolling out from underneath dripping white fangs.

"I know of a God who might find offense at such blasphemy; the same God who you fled from, hiding in the shadows of a powerless past. Connect yourself to that ancient council!" Hesiod said.

I shook my head and crossed my arms. Where was Christ in all of this? Despite His silence, I knew Him to be true. I thought back to Wyrd's words about the Divine

Council. To build a mythical future, the foundation had to be made up of a heroic and great past. Perhaps this was the way to pay the price of return. The redemption of a court long since dismissed.

I peered at each of these beings and kept my gaze and voice level. "I was told that I had been sent here to be found worthy of eternal weight and continue on my necessary path. But if Ra wants to cede his throne of light to me, then that is well and good. I did not ask for it, but I will take it now that it is offered. This weighing is a sham. I know I am worthy."

"Enough!" Maat shouted.

Her feathered headdress wobbled as she stepped towards me. Slow to react and in shock from the wrath and might of her shout, I was unable to stop her hand as it shot forward like a viper. I gasped, twitching and tremoring as her hand ghosted through my flesh and came back out with my beating heart. It was a dark, reddish-blue, and continued pumping as if still within me.

I could neither speak nor move. It was as if time refused to budge until the scale decided whether I should live or not. Yet this scale was my tether to eternity and there was no stepping free from this precipice. So I watched, spasming there, impaled by time. Maat placed my heart on the scale and it didn't move an inch. But then my heart shook, flopping back and forth like a dying fish. The scale suddenly dropped on the side of my heart, bending under the weight and straining until it busted apart, my heart's weight toppling the entire thing over.

Maat looked petrified, staring at me as if I were Apophis himself. "Never... to be such a beast. That powerful and evil... never have I seen such weight." She pointed a long finger at me. "You have been jud—." She was cut off as Ra stepped within our closed bubble of time, shattering it as we returned to the present.

I gasped and collapsed as Ra tried and failed to lift my fallen heart. It was too heavy, even for him. He yelled, "Back! Anubis and Maat, do not intervene. This is something else, something foul. Back!" His eyes flashed red as Anubis and Maat stepped away in horror.

Hesiod knelt to the ground and held me, trying to keep me steady. But I was a man without a heart, and as my brain darkened and my blood ran cold, something occurred inside. Not the glowing light of Hyperborea that had saved me so many times before. No... this was the venomous darkness of Sobek's corruption. The venom I'd thought cleansed after my rebirth at the pyramid. But it had hidden within my bones, finding refuge in my dark. Ra's spear apparently hadn't purified everything after all. The reinvigorated darkness filled my vacant chest and I gasped as I went rigid, flinging up to my feet as if yanked by a rope.

"His eyes, his eyes are black!" Maat shouted from the corner, her back pressed against the wall.

I ignored her and went to pick up my heart that Ra still desperately pawed at. Why did I need such a mortal organ? Why did I, slayer of gods, Titans, and primordial beings need such an anchor dragging me down? I snarled and lifted my bare foot. My body was awash with black and covered in inky tendrils that waved around and poured free like rivers of liquid shadow. I stomped my foot down at my heart but Ra flung me back with a burst of sunlight. Hesiod ran behind me and held me tight, pinning my arms to my sides as I growled, my shadowy veins writhing wildly through my body.

"I don't need mortality anchoring me to weakness!" I screamed.

"Remember my anvil," Hesiod whispered, his voice a soothing balm of warmth to my cold dark. "It pulled me into darkness, my attempt at immortality failed. But your heart is an anchor to life. Life! If to live is weakness then call me weak. To live one has to die. These gods, they are not alive as you and I. Is there a god that truly lived as us? Is there a god that truly died as us? Not here. Not here! You Roman, have you forgotten your birthright?" I wept under the force of such reason and light as he continued, "Take up your suffering heart and carry that weight into greatness."

He let me go and my mind clawed inside itself, trying to pull back the shroud of darkness consuming me. Black veins rippled through my skin, mirroring the storm within my soul. My vision flashed black then clear, back and forth as I stumbled to my heart. I reached down, Ra watching me with a terrible fear that was unbecoming in those powerful eyes. Holding my cold, slow-beating heart in my hand, I had to grasp my forearm with the other to prevent myself from squeezing and choking the life out from it. I pushed my arm towards my chest and thrust it at my body. My heart was sucked inwards as a black whirlpool mixed with bright white light drowned it into my flesh.

My sight vanished and I could only see within. The sky animals from the pyramid gathered together into a battalion of wild light. Across the surface of my whirlpooled soul, a herd of black wildebeests grazed on my essence. They dripped disease and rot as if dead and raised as corpses. Their incessant and heretical feasting on the river of my soul had corrupted the stream.

My creatures of light, those magnificent beasts, thundered into and through the streams of my spirit, their light purging the pollution as they passed. The wildebeests raised their heads at the approaching light. They bellowed fearfully, their voices as crooked and stooped as an old scythe. They herded together and cowered. They hurried away in a sprint, massing together into an amorphous blob of darkness.

They kept running, looking for a cliff to hurl themselves off of instead of facing the truth of light. My immaculate sky beasts overtook them and ripped through their blob of darkness. In an explosion of blue and red light, I breathed in pure air and opened my eyes. Hesiod and Ra stared down at me. Hesiod wrung his hand with the cloth of his robe. Ra's countenance was paled and weak with worry. Hesiod gingerly held his arm out and I grabbed the extended hand happily and embraced my brother.

"Sobek's filth had festered deeper than I thought possible." Ra rubbed his beak and watched me with hesitance. "I do not need to weigh your heart to understand your worth. But... I fear that darkness will always remain within you. It can be used rightly and effectively, as you saw when you pierced Apophis. But it needs to always surrender to your light of glory. All mortals have such a shadow lurking, but none so strong." He rubbed his eyes and sighed. "Gods of darkness, those gods that you mortals so desperately cling to, gods of your own making—they and you together override the good in your nature and you succumb to the nothingness. You become an avatar of unbeing, a herd beast of burden for nothing but yourself. By being so selfish, you fit into the herd better than you'd ever know, as the herd animal cares only for his own safety, unworried if another beast in his herd gets eaten as long as it is not he. Use your chthonic force but always in submission to your Hyperborean light. That is a power greater than the scale of the dead. It is a power that when balanced in truth cannot be judged. It overcomes judgement."

"I think... yes, I understand." My voice faltered, wavering with weakness as Hesiod steadied me, helping me remain upright. I gently brushed him away and stood straight. "Now what?"

"The Indestructibles," Maat whispered from her corner in the room.

"Yes, you must," Anubis added, his voice meek and his disdain for me humbled in the face of such force.

"They are right. We brought you here, Apollo's solar wisdom informing us all, so you might head north." Ra nodded and gazed his eternal eyes deeply into mine. "Through the light of the eternal northern sky, its stars blinking portals, there the great pharaohs go. There, as you will see, there all the heroes go, though the name differs. You must go to this realm. Remember that all is not as it once was. You might be led astray but this is necessary. The crumbling of myth means nothing is certain. Keep your eyes open and your head in the light of the sun. You now will ascend one step higher to the world above and to the promised land ahead. It is what all of Egypt's pyramids pointed at, perfectly primed for the greatest pharaohs to ascend."

"And how can I go there?" I asked, my strength returning at the thought of such a heroic realm of glory and greatness—such promise and purpose.

"My light." Ra bowed his head and crossed his arms over his chest. "I was and am fading fast, and these remaining embers of mine will only be kept aflame in your eternal glow."

"Yes," Hesiod said, "Yes, it must be so."

"It mustn't be anything, but if you are willing, then who am I to reject such a worthy gift? I will not let you go forgotten into the void. I will carry your torch, not letting it burn itself out."

"Then you are as great as we'd all thought and hoped." He looked up and raised his hands to his eyes. Plucking them out, he squeezed them both until they burst and golden embers floated free. The embers were swallowed into the green forests of my irises, invisible yet tangible within.

Ra's eye sockets were two blazing furnaces and he tensed as light and warmth poured free from his empty eyes. His light filled my body with a wash of fire and when it subsided, Ra was no more. The sun god had finally set for good. Hesiod grabbed my hand. Anubis and Maat bowed in deference, prostrate on their knees. With the light of Ra as my guide, I willed my being towards the heroic north. And in the warm blaze of my mighty light, Hesiod embraced me and I held my brother with a love greater than the glow of sunlight within. We flew north and spread our spirits, soaring like winged branches of a growing tree.

***

Cerberus Lives!

"Awake, oh Cerberus. Awake, oh loyal guardian of death," I said to the sleeping giant.

To awaken him from the slumber of Hypnos, a sacred song would have to be sung. A sacred song that only I, the golden god of musicians, could sing. I was this hound's only waking sound. Who else could bring him back from the silence of sleep? My golden lyre glimmered into my hand from out of the air and extended its shining rays over the slumbering beast. I strummed, the notes gentle and pure, bringing a twitch to his ear.

Not Orpheus, my notes awaken even he
Not Orpheus, but Apollo sings for thee

This sleep of yours, not from fickle fitness
This sleep of yours, closed eyes to unwitness

Hidden from this changing guard
Your gates have long held no regard

Spit on your might, these new men do
They laugh and scoff at myths untrue

They can't see that power persists
Eyes swollen blind, a chosen cyst

Tradition is as Tradition was
New gods and old, a lingering buzz
Hornets will sting and bees will build
This new man, this new man, cannot be killed

Cerberus awake, the glorious gate remains
Cerberus awake, your poor sleep is profane

Let them hide, oh stalwart of worthy death
A new man I sing, and he needs your breath

Cerberus slept, he sleeps so still
Cerberus wept, for the unworthy kill

Hades died and sleeps in black blight
Hades didn't know you were of light

Rangabes comes, this new man of gold
Cerberus I sing, arise and behold!

I finished my song with a swaying glissando, the notes ascending like stairs to the sky. Hypnos profaned my music with wretched snoring, but Cerberus stirred. My song echoed—perhaps Echo herself had joined in. I played again, my holy lyre reverberating as I strummed a succession of flurrying crescendos. My music could make dirt rise to life, only to die again from the shame of lacking such beauty for itself.

Cerberus's body twitched and spasmed until at last, he shook his head and dragged himself free from the murky mire of false release that Hypnos had promised him. The hound howled, smoke venting through his nostrils and flames ejecting from his three cavernous mouths as he stormed to his feet. His serpents spewed yellow venom at the sudden spring to life. I stepped away. Howling even fiercer, Cerberus charged at me and I held my ground. With a desperate growl he flung himself out of my path and proceeded to crash against the walls, banging his body in agony at the realization that his long-held master was gone. But my words had been true. Cerberus was meant for the light. This forgotten shadow world was not meant to drag him into irrelevance. I had a use for him. It was my own play of fate. My song had stirred his soul, but I would let him mourn. I would miss Hades too, but my mourning could not come until my own sun arose in the fires of a new day.

"You awoke me and for that I am grateful. A weakness... I slept because the world of nobility had decayed and forgotten what it was to be truly powerful," Cerberus said, stopping his thrashing and towering over me. He growled as he spoke but his words were mental, traveling into my mind as thoughts.

His seven serpents stared at me with bright red eyes, their heads still and their tongues flapping like fiery ribbons. His black shoulders bulged like mountain-tops, and his chest rippled into a valley of black fur and muscled hills. His three heads peered at me with wise red eyes that had the look of a rising sun reflecting an ocean of blood.

I said, "Rangabes is a noble one of the old order. His Hyperborean blood beats with a spiritual heart, deeper than my solar kind could truly know. He is worthy of myth. He is a worthy avatar in an age that has forgotten what it is to embrace the form of the truly powerful soul that you say is forgotten. He is of the light, and he is in need of a noble steed to carry him forward into the untamed promised land. The land Hyperboreans should have taken and kept when their world froze."

"You speak of your chosen people as if I belong to them. You say that I am of light, but how can that be when I was born from the mother of monsters, Echidna? My father was Typhon, the scourge of the gods. There is no light in either of them. And I have lived in this realm of darkness long since, and thus it has become me, and I it."

"Have you forgotten that you were a guard of it? To keep out the unworthy?"

"No. But I protected the dark and live in it still. I guarded it not from the unworthy, but simply from those who did not belong. My judging is the only act I've done worthy of light, but that too is no more. There are none to judge."

"And when Hercules bested you and carried you into the light, was it not to your liking? You loathed the daylight at your first taste, but did you not consider that this taste was one you'd always known?"

He growled at the mention of his humiliation at the hand of that unarmed hero. "Is that what Rangabes is? Another demi-god to take me away in humiliation? And I only know the darkness. That light was blinding."

"No, Rangabes is mortal and for that reason he is tied to you and your realm. But you are forgetting something that is truly an everything," I said as Cerberus lowered his heads and leaned forward impatiently. "You guard the past by accepting it with honor. Those dead souls that came through here—those heroic ones worthy of Elysium—they carried that solar nature and you could see it because you instinctively knew it. Even the people of light need guardians of darkness to see them through. The ice of death runs through your veins. The flame of power pours forth from your mouths. What's the origin of such elements? Where was your fire conceived? You see, you give life by allowing the dead to live in their deserved state. Your word breaths outward hotter than your flames. You are of light. You are solar by your perfect fulfillment of holy command. You are solar because, while you hated the light, you guarded it all the same. You possess the flame, Cerberus. I ask you to step out and away from the shadows and to live amongst the decay as a towering pillar of fire, purifying the dark through a heroic existence."

Cerberus barked, belching flames up to the cavernous heights. He turned around and stomped over to where Hypnos still slept undisturbed. Cerberus bent down, his three heads hungrily snapping at the god of sleep. I watched as he feasted on the flesh while Hypnos remained in slumber. In truth, Hypnos had died long ago. Those who slept and did not persist would fade forever away. To lie down and close your eyes in an attempt to stay pure from the evil of an age was to be weak. To be a hero, one had to leave the cave, no matter how bright the burning of the day or dark the freezing of the night. I strode over to Cerberus and placed my hand proudly on his chest. Rangabes would need this hound. And more importantly, I would need them both. It was decreed.

Book 3

Snow Pure

Snow vortexed my vision in white. I couldn't make out Hesiod despite his standing beside me.

"A bit cold?" I yelled, the wind howling icily, tearing at my skin.

"At least I have my robe! Thin as it is, it's better than your bare flesh," Hesiod yelled back at me, laughing.

"A far cry from the Egyptian desert. Why would pharaohs want to be sent here?" My question thudded into silence as a booming voice shook through the flurry of snow.

"You are not in the far north the Egyptian spirit once strove towards. This is the land of Jötunheimr, home of the Jötunn." The voice was deep and it creaked ancient and tired.

"Ra's light must have guided you here for a purpose," Hesiod murmured.

"What?" I said, barely able to hear him through the blizzard.

"Ra wants you here. The solar deities must have something here for you to take!" he yelled.

"Another test. I grow tired of all their hoops they want me to jump through. Am I to build a nation, or be a pawn entertaining some distant gods? Where is Wyrd and where is my God?" My questions drooped in the wind and the bellowing voice groaned.

"I will clear the storm. I see who you long to be." The detached voice breathed in a deep inward growl, followed by an outward hot breath that burned the cold away.

As the white melted from my vision, it was replaced by a crystalline blue wall, thick and wide, extending out in front of me like a mirror. Its light blue disfigured our forms into odd, misty skeletons, our bodies appearing as bones. I turned my gaze from the strange blue wall of icy glass and was unsurprised at the barren tundra around me. In the distance there were rocky, white-capped mountains, but in the land between there was nothing but snow and gray-stoned debris.

"Where are you, oh wise and ancient voice of the Jötunn?" I asked with a smirk splayed across my face and mirth morphing my tone with an affected husk. Hesiod chuckled.

The strange mirror rippled and its reflection revealed a man as tall as the wall, his body clothed only in a tattered brown loincloth which hardly hid his grotesque form. The reflected man was a skeleton of frozen bones that were a pale and icy color. His eye sockets were lit with a similar-colored glow, and he had long and stringy white hair that was balding on top of his bulbous skull and hanging down from the back as long as a cloak. His beard was pulled together in a long knot that stopped right in front of his groin.

"Quit gawking at me like I'm Freya in the buff. This wall is called Gastropnir, and I'm the ancient voice of the Jötunn, as you so eloquently put it," he spoke, his voice quaking just as thunderous as before, and his shimmering form on the blue of the wall bowing mockingly.

"Your name?" I inquired, rolling my shoulders and walking closer. It was odd: even in my ragged waist robe, the frigid cold instead of stinging like before seemed to invigorate me, pumping my veins full of frigid, ice-fueled virility.

"Fjolsvith."

"Great." I shook my head at the strange sounding word. Hesiod chuckled.

"And do you know why it is that we are here?" Hesiod asked, stepping beside me and pulling at his beard.

"Svipdagr once came to me asking for information about the great staff called Lævateinn. Carved from black root and imbued with icy veins, its power is one best locked away. Yet he wanted the weapon for a wedding. He eventually succeeded and my gates opened for his bride. But nine spells were cast."

"And what has this to do with me?" I said.

"Nine spells were once cast, and now there are nine spells you must pass. These nine spells correspond to nine virtues you must prove worthy of possessing. Only then will the nine locks unlatch themselves for you. This staff, this Lævateinn has a heat that is the kind that burns with frost—melts with ice. Fiery root imbued with the spirit of the Jötunn."

I turned to Hesiod and raised an impatient eyebrow. "They sent me here for a staff? Are these marks not enough?" I held up my arms, the glowing wounds hot in the frosty surroundings.

"You think they'd send you after some sort of armor or such." He gestured at my torso and laughed.

"My skin is good enough. Do I need to hide my flesh behind dead matter? No, for my matter is what matters. I am enough, and to walk as I do is to dare the beggars hiding in their scarlet cloth to scoff. I will handle any, for I have no handler handing me hand-me down cloth.

I don't care how magical!" I finished with a flourish, grinning and bowing melodramatically.

"Well done!" Hesiod clapped as we both laughed together.

"Are you done?" Fjolsvith said, crossing his arms yet sporting a mirthful grin which was hilariously haunting in his icy skull. His teeth were missing in gaps and gathered together in clumps of pointed fangs seemingly at random like sprouts of white-stoned weeds.

"Quite," I said with a nod, smiling and enjoying my display of rhetoric and the strange but welcome cheer of the atmosphere. Much better than the lands of death I'd left behind.

"And you'll find some armor as well. You'd be wise to take it," he said, glancing at my body.

"Perhaps," I said. But despite my soliloquy, I'd welcome the added cover. As confident as I was, an arrow was all it would take to spell my end. Armor would certainly do.

"Is the armor magical? Is it of fire and ice like this staff?" Hesiod asked, sarcasm swirling in the ticklish tenor of his tone.

"The kind that you will find is not from here." Fjolsvith said, his bony face folding as if of flesh, all scrunched up serious and grave. "Best not to inquire further. It awaits you over this wall. Only those of pure light can clothe themselves with its radiation."

"Apollo," Hesiod said, his eyes lowered and his face went blank and withdrawn. Fjolsvith winced at the name. "You fear him?"

"I do not dare speak on it. All I will say is that he is one of the last threads on the frayed end of the mythological rope. He is one of the few fighting to keep himself tethered to a nonexistent existence." Fjolsvith paused, leaning forward while lowering his head, still encased in the reflection of the wall. "He is all that holds the frayed end together, but he also threatens to let it unwind if we do not heed his lead. Wyrd sings high and her song is one that belongs above Olympus. Listen to her voice. I'll probably perish for saying as much, but trapped as I am, I crave the release of nothingness." Fjolsvith's cold eyes burned into a blue flame. He banged both his fists against his side of the wall. "Solitude in this reflected unreality is no way to live!" he screamed.

"Apollo watches over us. He restored me from ashes. How can he be bad?" Hesiod said. "He's the reason Rangabes and I walk in the land of the living despite being once dead."

Despite the topic at hand and the stress of the situation, it finally hit me that I was not in a nether world of sorts. Even if this was a land of myth, it at the very least was a land of life, however sparse that life appeared to be. I took a deep breath of the chilled air and sniffed greedily at the fresh smell of cleansing and purity that only snow manages to bring. It took Hesiod's mentioning, but now that I realized the reality of this place, I wouldn't let the moment pass without engaging all my senses in the fullness of aliveness.

"Apollo is using you both. But I've said too much." Fjolsvith stopped speaking, his jaw creaked shut and he ground it back and forth. "Before I open this gate, please release me from this misery."

I nodded, both my arms bathed in red and blue light. Fjolsvith smiled and tiredly opened his arms wide, and the wall's glass shimmered and disappeared as if never there.

His voice came from where the wall had been and said, "Walk through where the wall was, and when it reappears, shatter my reflection. Perhaps light from Apollo's favorite might be the burning end I've so desperately sought."

I walked slowly through the vacant air and felt a strange chill seize my blood. The frigid feeling fled as I walked forward. As Hesiod stood next to me, I turned back and the wall stood once more, its reflection showing Hesiod and I both as skeletons, dwarfed next to Fjolsvith's gigantic frame. It was strange to see the two of us standing beside him in the mirror, but I knew this was some mere trick of the wall to try and prevent me from ending its eternal guard's existence.

"I suspect no trick here. If there is one, I will face it myself," I said.

I didn't look to Hesiod for any acknowledgement but only closer at the wall. It was just a reflection, and regardless of the poor copy of my body as a skeleton with glowing arms, it could do me no harm. I saw my skeleton sneer at me and before it could do more, I baptized the section of the wall in a purifying wave of light. When it at last cleared, the wall was a blank and pristine blue lacking any reflection.

I sighed and placed a hand on Hesiod's shoulder and he shivered at my touch. He was pale and quiet in such a way as I'd never seen before. I looked at him with concern and said, "I fear what this all might mean for us, Hesiod. I'd foolishly assumed Apollo and the rest of the solar gods were for my favor and reestablishing a solar people on this earth. But if he is torturing Jötunn here and threatening to undo it all, can we trust such a god? I will try to listen to Wyrd's song, whatever it might be. I still wait on my Lord."

I let go of his shoulder and waited for a response, but he just kept standing there vacant and pale. I walked ahead and into the white blanket landscape, listening for his footsteps to follow. They came lingering and slow, and we walked aimlessly in an odd silence as he staggered behind.

Finally, after some time like this, Hesiod cleared his throat and said from behind me, "Why would Apollo turn on you? He's given us both new life. He's allowed for you to gain power. Would Ra sacrifice himself simply because Apollo said to?"

I sped up, and spat my words forward, "I gained this power through my own merit." I clenched my fists and scowled over my shoulder. Hesiod glared back at me as if I were a common blasphemer. He'd forgotten that I believed in one God, not the many he served. "Perhaps I've returned to life due to my own dormant light within. Must I attribute my power, my merits to someone else? I would do so only for my true Lord, and I believe it is He who carries me on. Wyrd said as much. You did too, but now it seems as though this wall brought about a change of face, friend. These frayed myths are unbound and fading fast... they are falling forgotten. But I carry my ancestors proudly within and forward. I do them honor and strive up this mountain without complaint or question. It is not for Apollo nor any other setting sun god. It is for my people that I march. It is for my future sons and daughters that I ascend. The forces driving us from realm to realm must submit to my might. Apollo underestimates me if he thinks I would bow and worship him. I serve my blood and the Lord's, not his. Hyperboreans might have called him their god once, but they existed apart from him and his light ultimately failed them. I owe it to my people to bring about a new order under a much brighter sun." My voice burned and I looked back at Hesiod who was slumped over as he walked, wilted from my fiery speech. He was my brother and he knew I spoke true. Whatever he'd gone through in the thousands of years after his death, he had to know that Apollo was not wholly as he appeared.

"In darkness were many of my days spent after death. I cannot speak clearly of what went on, as that is not easily spoken of in such finite words—it is meant to belong in the eternal realm of mystery, I think. But I can say this... Apollo means well in the sense that he sees his future survival in your light as truly yours is the last of its kind. I perhaps foolishly thought he and the other gods of light were of goodwill, but you are likely correct in suspecting his desire for continued godhood through you as the other myths are consumed. I never even considered such an angle, so blinded was I by Apollo's warm light in that cold dark." Hesiod paced up to walk beside me. His gaze was set on nothing as he looked inward. "Ra gave himself to you, speaking of his fading. Whether that was Apollo's doing or simply the effect of time and his adherents forgetting him, does not answer the question. Perhaps Ra listened to Wyrd and not Apollo. Perhaps he saw only his own light. The question remains. Helios and Hyperion were also willing to relinquish their light and hand it to you, returning to their primordial forms. Was that Apollo or their own choice? They saw you as their own, no doubt."

"They did, truly. Yet until I look Apollo in his glory, how can I tell? Maybe the gods returning to nature is the natural progression of their divinity. Maybe that is what Wyrd sings and what the Lord wants. He's giving them the choice to return to his council and bring forth glorious light onto earth." I tilted my head and listened past the crunch of our feet through icy snow. A light hum warbled in the heavens. I looked up but the sky was still awash with gray. I nodded. I must have been on to something. Was Wyrd watching me as she sang? The breezy melody whispered away and I looked to Hesiod, who was still searching the sky as I had. "We must tread this path Apollo set before us. Whatever awaits us at the end, we can face together. I will not bow to him. We both hear her song." I held out my arm and set my face stern and proud.

"Neither will I, brother." Hesiod grasped my forearm and held it tight. He nodded and let go. "Let's get you some cover finally." He laughed and I joined in.

"To the armor of light!" I cried, letting my voice lift high and shrill like a child's.

I turned away and walked faster as we came to a steep crag slick with ice. I'd been so distracted by Fjolsvith, Apollo's schemes, and the strange wall Gastropnir that I hadn't clearly taken in the land beyond it all. This wasn't more vanilla tundra with occasional crumbs of stone, but an incline culminated here at this crag. We'd been steadily moving upward without knowing. A glance at Hesiod revealed a similarly puzzled face. I shrugged and scrambled up the stone, scraping through the ice till I precariously balanced myself on the precipice. A valley of impossible light blanketed out before me, unfurling in gold-sparkled snow. The light came not from a sun, but instead from a tree that emanated a natural effulgence of gold. The tree dominated the valley, its trunk extending to the heavens and its branches spread out far, bulging together and shooting out like giant muscles and veins. The clouds had somehow obscured this glorious sight when we'd approached, but now at this precipice, all was revealed. And what a glory this valley was. The tree's branches cast no shadows, and it had nine pulsating roots that burst out through the ground as high and wide as mountain ranges.

"The World Tree," Hesiod said as he struggled up to the precipice and stared ahead. "This tree, called Yggdrasil, connects the nine realms of Norse mythology. We are in Jötunheimr. This land we walk is of the Norse people's old religion. I do not know where Odin sits in our day, but I think it wise to remain here. Fjolsvith made no mention of leaving the realm to find this staff and armor." Hesiod scratched at his forehead, and ruffled his stiff and stubborn bangs in perplexity.

"No, but the number nine was mentioned. Nine locks, nine spells. There are nine roots of this tree, clearly corresponding to the nine realms," I said.

"You aren't wrong. But if this realm, this mythology still holds so strong, I do not believe Apollo capable of holding sway here. Maybe in this land of the Jötunn he can, some lost Hyperborean connection strengthening his might... but I do not think it wise to dally here. The staff and armor must be of some importance for us to land here. But this does not seem to be the place Ra spoke of in his temple." Hesiod sighed and shook his head.

"A frayed rope still has many strings that snag together, resisting the one undoing it all. This struggle is not ours, but the might of Hyperborea runs strong through this people—I feel it. The air here is alive with light and it exudes from that tree." I breathed in the air, which tasted of pine and rushing water. I smiled and let the pristine light lift me along with that lively scent of eternity, which permeated the air and surged forth from the tree.

"The root closest to us, the white one, is the one in which Jötunheimr belongs. The Norse kind is Hyperborean, just as much, if not more than, we beings of light from Hellas. It was there in Egypt, though it had undoubtedly strayed far from the path," Hesiod said.

"Here... I feel almost at home," I said.

"I feel it too, Rangabes. Let us use this singularity and watch for whatever it is that kept Apollo at bay."

"Nine spells to overcome. What then is first? Or perhaps who?" I said.

Hesiod didn't answer as he edged off the cliff and slid down its steep surface. He whooped and hollered like a young boy riding a sled. The other side of the crag dropped decisively, but not so much as to prevent such showmanship as Hesiod displayed. But the man at least had some cloth to prevent scraping his skin! I shook my head and toed my way off the top, trying to stay on my feet as I raced down. My racing quickly devolved to stumbling. As the gray face of stone rose up to greet my tipping body, I held out my arms and shot a burst of light, flinging me into the air and somersaulting me away from solid rock and straight down for icy snow. I winced as the white buried my sight, but came up laughing at the soft cushion the snow had provided. A far different texture from the icy tundra above, this snow was impossibly lukewarm, and even better, felt like feathery cotton. So much for showmanship! I laughed louder. Hesiod chuckled as he pulled me upward.

"Did you know the snow down here was going to be so soft and cozy?" I asked, smiling as I stood up.

"No idea."

"Of course," I muttered.

“I’m also not the one who flung myself through the air like a drunken jester.” Hesiod laughed, slapping my back as I just shook my head and stretched my body, feigning hurt.

Now that we were down in the valley, there wasn’t much to see around the giant tree other than the light-dazzled snow with the shadowless branches glowing green above, the ancient bark saturated with bright leaves and bunches of red flowers. There wasn’t anywhere to go but to the white root that clung to the realm and reached out closest to us, the root belonging to Jötunheimr.

The strange murmur of Wyrd’s lulling strings sang in the heavens once more, this time louder than before. Hesiod and I continued onward in silence, the murmur rising to a screech against the peace of the valley. Whether it was a warning or simply the strange song of fate falling out of tune to our finite ears, we moved faster regardless.

“Wyrd, again? Is this a good omen?” Hesiod shouted.

I shrugged. I’d been told to listen to her song, but not what to do if the song screamed at me. My walk turned into a jog so as to outrun the painful music. Hesiod raced ahead of me. Our jogging morphed into a sprint as the screeching continued high up in the heavens.

At last we reached the white root and as I placed my hand upon its warm wood, the cutting screech of Wyrd was snipped, and it faded into a sharp retreat as if her strings had all broken free. I sighed, relaxing at last at the welcome quiet. I let go of the root, which soared over me so high that I was like a mere insect beside it. Ahead, there was a divot underneath the mountain-sized root where a strange well stood. The well was a large circular construction built of raven-black stone with a purple luster embedded in its material. I made my way to the edge of the well and peered into its black insides. I couldn't see the bottom and I had no intention of falling in to find the answer.

Fall. A sacrifice was once given by the Allfather himself. Wisdom. The shame of Mímir, his headless body lies inside. Wisdom. Fall. Drink of me and knowledge will be yours.

I clutched my head at the shrill piercing of the well's whispers, unwelcome thoughts pricking my mind. I had to fight with all my will at the sudden urge to throw myself headlong into the well. I would not fall prey to such sorcery. But how was I to pass this first spell, this first test? I looked to Hesiod for suggestions, but the poet's eyes were quivering and fixed upon the well. I reached out my arm and grabbed him by his robe just as he scrambled over the well's edge to plumb its depths. The whispers had won him over but I remained. I yanked him hard before he could go completely over and pulled him onto his back. He shook his head violently, proceeding to bang it on the thankfully soft snow.

"Mustn't get too close," he mumbled weakly, holding his head as he stood. He took several steps backwards while still eyeing the well hungrily, thirsting for its dark depths.

I leaned back over the well, clinging to my own self and thoughts. I plunged my arms into the darkness and lit the well with red and blue. As soon as my light filled the well, two yellow eyes glared up at me, flickering first and then shooting out in a burst as a black wolf leapt up at me. I flung myself backwards to dodge it. Nothing came out of the well and after lying on my back and holding my breath, I got up and peered into the well once again. The wolf was gone and the darkness in the well had been banished, abated in the heat of my light. There at the bottom of the well was a headless corpse, and sitting beside it was a naked man, his skin green like pond scum, holding a large and ornate oak fiddle. He had long pointed ears and his smooth-skinned, hairless body tensed as he turned his gaze away from the corpse and stared directly up into my eyes from his depths. His eyes were slit vertically black like a reptile.

The creature smiled, showing its pointed teeth. It began to play its instrument, the notes foul and wretched in their perfection, as if the unnatural nature of it marred what was otherwise a heavenly sound that not even a cathedral full of chanters could match. And then, the odd creature began to sing.

Wise, wise, you don't look so well
Eyes, eyes, you don't look to smell
Nose, nose, you sniff my sanitized song
Woes, woes, you know thyself is wrong
Steal, steal, my heart a captured metal craft
Feel, feel, the beat of hammered strings' draft
Wind, wind, blowing against all the senses
Skinned, skinned, nothing left, no pretenses

I will eat your flesh. I am Fossegrim of well.
Mímisbrunnr my home, this body can you tell?

Give me your skin, I hunger much
An offering of meat for wisdom's touch
There isn't any other way one may pass
Unless one is willing to take all but half
You see my stomach wanting and cold

You hear my stomach empty and old

Come down and feast, it's the least you can do
Give me more and shut the door—
For nothing is new

I will eat your flesh. I am Fossegrim of well.
Mímisbrunnr your grave, wisdom will never tell.

Hesiod wept, gnashing his teeth and wrestling with the snow, thrashing in madness and melancholy at Fossegrim's ravenous and stale song of sinister perfection. I tried to wrap my mind around why this creature sang such a song and what spell was behind it all. Was wisdom still to be found here, or was the corpse's absent head the last fount of such water? There was nothing to drink. There was the darkness and this well, and its spell to try and coax one into it. I stared at the creature, who was licking its fangs in anticipation of a sacrifice.

What sacrifice? I would not give my eye for darkness, for would I not be trading my own light for a twisted light of supposed wisdom that was darker even than when I had such an eye? Was it wise to seek such wisdom? A wise man sacrifices himself only if the price is of eternal weight. No wisdom could be worth such price, for all such wisdom was of the world. Wisdom wed to the world, was in the end, someone else's folly. My wisdom was earned, not bargained for in a moment. I realized what this well was meant to do, and how it was that I would unlock this first seal. I knew what virtue was needed here. Of course. Not wisdom, but what wisdom required.

I grinned at the hungry creature and dove headfirst into the well, no coaxing needed. As I descended, his hungry maw opened grotesquely like that of a freshly dug grave. I continued downward in a pointed dive, straight for his mouth. He snapped his teeth greedily at me and I let my body go limp. He sunk his teeth into my flesh and tore at me, throwing me about like a sack of cloth. I grimaced but did not resist as he dug his teeth in further. His mouth and throat had distended grossly, and he had the look of a giant beast now, hardly the trim, green-skinned bard he'd been before. But I welcomed the pain and did not cry out as he carved into my flesh.

"Resist!" he snarled.

"What is perfect courage but to willingly plunge into the darkness with only your skin as a shield?" I spoke calmly, my voice a soothing balm to my chewed body.

He growled, shaking his head back and forth. My limp body flailed, but spiritually I remained unmoved. "Is it courage to not resist? Is it courage to blindly throw yourself to the wolf?"

"I resist you fool, by choosing this. You tried to sing me into the darkness. You tried to offer up wisdom that was mere folly to me. I resist you by leaping into the darkness instead of letting it catch me unaware. I acted first, of my own will. Your bite is weak and I do believe my act of faith and movement was enough to weaken your hold on this spell-locked well."

"And what would you call this spell that you think you've unbound? Answer correctly, or lose the momentum you've gathered." He stopped gnawing me, and held me there gingerly, his mouth surprisingly soft and limp like a hammock.

"This is a test not of wisdom, for that is the trick. Nor is this a test of sacrifice, for there is nothing here worth sacrificing for." I smiled, knowing I'd seen through the artifice perfectly. Hanging upside down from his mouth, I looked at his empty black eyes and laughed. "A test of courage, the strongest of virtues. Courage is action, and the act of courage must be proceeded by a will gathered in the infinite. I knew where I stood in terms of freedom, and with this agency, I leapt into being. In doing so, I became myself. Courage is to become oneself through the act of eternal will, through the act of risking one's finitude in the face of darkness. For that is the only way one can truly act in absolute and pure light."

"A philosopher," he spat, tossing me onto the ground and turning away in disgust.

I stood up and glanced over at the corpse's headless form. His skin was white like Roman marble, as if he were a fallen statue. I walked over to him and touched his flesh. The flesh was warm with life and it glowed at my touch. A bright, golden-white light burst from the body, filling the well and lifting me in a crescendo of ecstasy. My fingers and toes curled and I threw my head back and screamed at the terrible tremors of pleasure twisting my body. And in a lightning strike of blue, I landed on the snowy surface beside the well. The ancient well shook, its stones clattering into a heap as it collapsed on itself, the first spell broken.

"Armor," Hesiod mumbled.

I stood up and looked down at myself. My body was encased in brilliant, red, form-fitting chain, linked together with reptilian scales interweaved. The scales glinted and glowed with a hot yellow fire like that of the midday sun. The armor was cut off at the shoulders, leaving my arms bared. It extended down to my waist and hung in pointed, white leather flaps that were studded with diamonds, dropping to my groin and backside in length. My legs were covered in thick cloth leggings the color of a deep, dark sapphire that coursed with the same subtle energy that my armor did, only this energy was an electric blue that would occasionally glint and gleam like stars in a clear midnight sky.

"A bit restricting," I joked, bending and moving about. In truth, the armor and leggings surged with a life and energy of their own, making me feel as though they were powerful extensions of my flesh. I figured that rag I'd been wearing had been burnt off in the lightning strike, and good riddance! I'd have been better off unclothed than with that on any longer.

"Fafnir," Hesiod mumbled, half reaching out his hand at my fiery armor, still in awe. "He was the son of a dwarven king and was cursed by his own greed and turned into a dragon. His own scales were added to this already immaculate armor after he'd been slain. Sigurd earned this treasure and slayed that dragon. I wonder where he's gone." He paused, looking around as if to find him. "He might have entrusted this to you. He might have known you were coming. He was a good man and undoubtedly carried the blood of Hyperborea in his veins." Hesiod nodded. "He must have enlisted the famous dwarven smith brothers to make this. Brokkr and Eitri are the only ones capable of forging such perfect metal and scales so seamlessly together." He shifted his gaze downward at my sapphire pants. "Perchta, the weaving goddess known as The Bright One, hence the appearance of the stars hidden in a night sky—just as she hid herself through her craft and shroud. I know of her work, equal to and if not better than the spider Arachne's weaving."

"Your knowledge knows no bounds." I paused, doubt creeping in the backdoor of my mind, and I itched my head at the spot as if to stop it. "I thought the armor was from Apollo? Is that not what that gatekeeper said?" I shook my head. "Did Apollo tell you about these trials? Did Apollo tell you who I'd meet, kill, and the rewards? Am I responsible for anything?" My suspicion proved founded as Hesiod paled and his eyes darted as he turned away flustered.

"His wisdom is truly unapproachable. He helped me so that I could help you. I told you that you might be correct in your suspicion of him, but perhaps he merely is another god lending his strength in his own way. He told me of the other myths, but I swear he never revealed in detail his plans other than for me to aid 'your brother,' as he said it. But it is you I follow, a worthy man who rightfully has proceeded on his own path." He turned to look at me as he finished speaking but something was off—his eyes were guarded with an unfocused vacancy.

"There is still much to do." I walked away from the well and the tree's root, letting Hesiod scurry worriedly after me. I didn't know what to think of him and Apollo, but my words were true and I wasn't sure where this next spell trap would be.

Away on the distant horizon there were large gray slabs of stone mountains carved smooth into canyons. I made my way in that direction, for other than Yggdrasil, the surrounding area was mostly a blanket of endless snow. As I walked, there was a vigor and strength driving me forward that I'd hitherto not been blessed with. Even with my feet bare, the snow seemed to part in my stead, the armor emanating a force that was meant to carve through this world with power.

With the mountains still distant and my suspicions lingering, I decided to bring the issue to a head. I could not continue forward with a pretender sucking the marrow from my back bone, my spine yanked about by some distant god of light who was in it for his own machinations. Regardless of whether or not Apollo's power aided me at the moment, I could not help but question. Hesiod had to know something more.

"What is the truth, Hesiod?" I asked, my eyes on the canyons as I slowed my walk.

"The truth is something that must be lived, and I ask you, have I not lived it at your side thus far into this strange journey?" His voice was farther back and dragged heavily. I looked back and slowed down even more. He was jogging, and panting like a dog.

His robe and bare feet were not meant for this. He looked like he needed my armor more than me. I felt immaculate; the power in this armor had enjoined itself with my own, and in this fusing of valor and might, I was becoming even more—this armor feeling almost as much a part of me as my Hyperborean wounds.

"Have you lived? I seem to recall you mentioning you would not return to the land of the living with me, yet are we not out from underneath the nether worlds? In a land of myth, sure, but a land that dead should not be in." I gazed out once more at the horizon as Hesiod struggled to catch up.

"This is a land that is dying, if not already dead. But I am speaking true when I say we should not be here, at least not yet. Apollo didn't mean for this—it was Ra's invocation. Perhaps he knew something was afoul. We had been aimed at Hyperborea and after, I surely would have faded into a final death, but no... we ended up here, and somehow I persist." He was still out of breath, but his confusion seemed to energize him the way his voice gained strength as he continued on. "I knew of those ancient weapons and armor because I had thousands of years in the darkness of death. When Apollo spoke, the god of wisdom and light showed me much about other worlds, and gave me even more to read. Of course, I know more about myth than almost all but the gods; I am the foremost poet of it myself."

"And so, you say the truth is that you do not know why we were sent here. Why then did the gatekeeper speak so strangely and set us on this quest? He feared Apollo and clearly had been punished by the god. Apollo knew we would come here, Hesiod—why else would the gate be arranged as such?"

"Have you forgotten calling me brother? Now you question my whims and wills as if I were your enemy. We are kin through this light in us, and whether Fjolsvith was right in calling you Apollo's own is beyond me. In my time with the god I was overtaken with reverence and respect, as lowly and clueless as I was. But there was purity there. Much purity. So much purity that Apollo and I both seemed powerless to it. I ask, can purity be pure to the point of powerlessness?" Hesiod at last made it to my side, matching my stride and staring at me with a fixed look of confidence and truth, his brow square and his head leaned towards mine.

I stopped and grabbed Hesiod to hold him still. I embraced the older man, shivering as he was with his arms crossed. Even the warmth the World Tree provided wasn't enough for him. My attire glowed, the dark blue trousers and red-gold armor uniting in a glowing halo around us as I hugged him tight.

"I have begun to doubt, and I do not know why. It's as if Fjolsvith's suspicion fouled me." My words enjoined the light, my voice whispering in spirals of wispy luminosity as my armor glowed fiercer, the vortex of light increasing.

"You look as though you are pure flame. White light is burning in your stare and it hurts to see," Hesiod yelled, my light heating up the words with power, his voice cracking as lightning.

I laughed, smiling at my friend. Hesiod was clothed in his own cloud of light, as if he had swallowed the sun and exuded its energy through his pores. White rays of power radiated from him amidst my own as we held each other with our arms extended, staring into our pure flame. I could feel the doubt wash out of me, the mistrust and disdain washed pure in the flame of friendship, the fires of *fidelity*. This man was my *honor*! This man was my *truth*! Those three words, three virtues! They'd shot into my soul as if gifted from the heavens. Was it Wyrd? Had her grating song sifted the seeds into the soul of my spirit? I looked up and heard a whisper.

I serve the Lord and so I serve you. The virtues are already yours. You know.

Wyrd! I looked back down at Hesiod but he seemed not to hear. Still, she acted for us and on behalf of my Lord. The truth! I smiled wide. Even if he hadn't heard, I knew Hesiod and I had to act together and towards our glory and futures to live that truth. I could see it so suddenly and sharply that it felt as though I'd been blind this entire time.

The two of us laughed together, and the light flashed in an upward burst of white flame and then it diffused. I stood still garbed in my powerful attire, but now Hesiod donned worthy cloth too, his old robe gone.

Hesiod wore a mantle over his shoulders that swooped down his back in a fiery cascade of crimson. Yet he now stood unclothed. On the left of his breast there burned a red light that swirled like the galaxy's tear in the sky. He looked down, following my gaze, and pressed his hand there. He lifted his hand and the red light was gone, and then in a strange burst of bloody light that quickly vanished, he stood completely clothed in that same burning scarlet that had swirled in his breast. The cloth flickered and moved like a sluggish flame, weighed down by a weird viscosity that made the burning look like that of a slow-moving stream. His robe covered his entire torso, with the mantle a sort of cape descending down his back. In his bright red amidst the white backdrop of snow, he looked like the sun bursting free from a cloud-canopied sky.

"The mantle of King Arthur." Hesiod shook his head as he fingered the shimmering cloth on his shoulders. "This... I do not know what this is." He stared down in awe at his glowing robe that moved with shifting patterns of fiery light. He held his hand back as if afraid he might burn his skin if he touched it.

"King Arthur?" I asked.

"A noble king worthy of light. If he allowed for this mantle to pass on to me, we must be on a noble path, Rangabes. We must be, for King Arthur's mantle is one forged in truth and glory." He smoothed the mantle back on his shoulders, hardly needing to as it glossed back into place, a waterfall of red like plumes of a firebird. "The robe must be of Apollo's doing then. This had to be the armor Fjolsvith warned us about. I'd assumed it was for you." He shook his head, holding his hand over his chest. "It feels right, as if meant for me."

I nodded and said, "But what happened? You asked me that question and it was as if a shroud was lifted from my eyes, a dagger pulled out from my heart." I shook my head and scratched my chin. "A spell, an inward spell that took me unaware?"

"If the first was a spell requiring the virtue of courage, what was this? A spell requiring truth?"

"It forced my doubt, building on my mistrust. I insulted your honor. But your question of purity sparked something."

"Can purity be pure to the point of powerlessness?"

"But what did you mean by it? Was it about Apollo?" I said, standing there still in awe at the splendor of Hesiod's attire.

"I said he appeared pure. But can one who is truly pure be powerful? The word powerful implies having your fill of power, and is there then any room left for the pure? So, I ask again, does purity necessitate powerlessness?"

"Purity from what?" I said, unconvinced.

"Perhaps that is the question."

I smiled. It was time for one of our philosophical discussions again. We Hellenes couldn't help ourselves. I squinted my eyes and focused on my realization as if seeing it in the surrounding snow. "To be pure is to be untouched by nothingness. To be pure is to exist fully in existence. And with that existing in purity, then the question of powerlessness is answered. To be pure is to exist as a relation to the force of eternity that sifts through the essence of our beings. To exist as a perfect relation to power is to be pure, and thus powerless because in this relation we see that we die. With this sight of death, we drink of that cup with pure spirits and without despairing, knowing we are powerless to the nothingness of time. It is the circling in of finitude that spirals back the way it came into infinity. That is it. A perfect surrender. Purity is powerlessness because it is the actualized form of being. In its paradox, such a powerlessness is the most perfect form of power."

Hesiod shook his head as his eyes widened in amazement. He nodded and said, "And therefore Apollo is not pure, for he rages against the order of being, he rages against honor and truth. Not loyal, he shines his light with a lust for a power that does not exist. He rages against existence by rejecting the cup of divine order. He drinks instead at the sewage-strewn stream of chaos. He is powerless in his pretend play at power; lacking purity, he is steeped in a sea of nothingness. He rages against existence because his pursuit is impure. He does not desire the perfect surrender that is acting in accord with the infinite, acting as a relation to power and thus obtaining it in paradox. Apollo is acting from the finite like an old and mortal man still clinging to life, even as all his meaning, strength, and worth have been squandered from a disordered existence that chose the nothingness."

I looked at his scarlet robe and said, "Perhaps... this would be true if Apollo was acting as you just said. But maybe he is in line with Wyrd. Maybe he is on our side. Your robe fits very well."

"Maybe too well." He sighed and looked away.

After a quiet moment, I said, "And so, we philosophize and find our answer to your initial question.

But perhaps a better one might be raised: why did that question awaken my love for you, brother? Why did it bring forth such light and transform us so? Perhaps posing the question released the evils of the spell, drowning the nothingness in meaning. Perhaps that question helped us see in our very natures that we are on the path of purity. Of truth, honor and fidelity. Three virtues. Could those be three virtues packed into one spell? Are we three steps closer?" I knew the answer already; if Wyrd had spoken only to me, perhaps he was not meant to know.

"I hope so," he said, smiling and extending his arm. "Thank you."

I grabbed his arm as he looked at me, his oaken eyes joined together with my evergreen ones, his roots grown to a tree canopied with my potentiality—our potentiality. We nodded and released our firm hold to head towards the canyon once again.

"Well done, purified ones." The angelic voice floated down from the heavens while simultaneously thundering in the distant canyons. Yet it was not Wyrd who spoke. Another onlooker? How many celestial voyeurs watched our progress? "You near my canyons, and in my domain my mountains shake and soar. My lonely land of Thrymheim, my perfect recompense. Nobody is worth leaving your land for. Nobody. That is what I say."

"And what if leaving your lost land is only to make a new land for your own? For if it is lost, then it can only be found again through rebirth," I said, glancing intermittently at the sky and canyons.

The voice laughed, crashing solely as thunder, losing its lightness.

"Who are you?" Hesiod said.

"I am Skade and I am not here to prevent your triumph. You have released the holds of four spells, and the remaining five are blights on my home."

"Four?" Hesiod said, looking at me. "Perhaps the three were rolled into one after all."

"Our whole process of purification must have been three spells, the three combined virtues I mentioned," I said, looking into the heavens not for Skade, but for another sign and whisper from Wyrd.

Skade's voice drifted down like manna as she said, "The initial fire of your doubt against your friend was the first spell, and he lovingly spoke the *truth* to break it. And your embracing him broke the second spell and brought forth the virtue of *honor*. And lastly, when you so interlocked yourselves with each other and bloomed with communal light, a holy *fidelity* ended the three-pronged spell that served as three locks, yet in a strange way required one key: love. Three virtues with love as their key."

"You were watching and listening this whole time!" Hesiod shouted at the sky. Skade's thundering laugh shook us both.

I stretched my arms and said, "A welcome development." I shrugged and added with a smirk, "Less wandering!"

"Come to Thrymheim. Be swift. On feet such as those you'll never arrive." Her voice calmed, its power hanging in the heavens, its looming might the temporary staying of the air before the swiftness of the storm. "Feet worthy of the Jötunn!" Her voice shook the ground and snow swirled around us until we were blinded with white.

The snow suddenly fell flat and our feet were wrapped with feathery white cloth. It was as if I wore clouds for shoes. The cloth shimmered and felt impossibly light, even lighter than when I'd been barefoot, yet my feet were now warm and I felt ready to soar with the wind.

"Step forward towards my mountains," she sang, her voice ringing out into a heavenly chorus of operatic voices from every direction—even beneath our newly covered feet.

I took a step and my surroundings soared by in a serpentine snap. The wind was fresh and lively, and my body was tinged with an airy weightlessness. My surroundings had blown away and now I stood in the midst of the stone canyon. Black boulders, smooth and straight, loomed over me on each side. Hesiod stumbled forward, his body blurring before me and slowly flickering back to stability. His mantle flowed out behind him, a wide river of fire dancing in the wind. His laughter lifted high and he turned to me with a soppy grin spread across his face like melted butter. I grinned right back and chuckled at the youthful joy glowing in his eyes. No doubt I looked similar, but then I frowned over his shoulder at a figure who materialized out of the air as if born from the currents of wind.

A woman with grayish-white skin, like that of a polished pearl, stood before us. She was extraordinarily tall—at least four times my height. Her form was fit but not burly; if she weren't such a giant she'd even be attractive. She had a matronly body with wide hips and large breasts, wearing a cloth dress that fluttered to her knees in a colorful clear sky blue. She wore high boots that were made of the same cloud-white material as the shoes she'd bestowed on us. Her hair was reddish-blonde; the way the sun's rays brushed against its luxurious sheen made it almost pinkish, like a slight blush from a fair maiden. Her eyes were a clear and icy-blue; they stared at us as if unsure we were worthy of aiding her cause, whatever said cause might truly be.

"Skade, I am Rangabes and he is Hesiod. We are here to dispel foul magic and claim Lævateinn for ourselves." I spoke calmly but remained on edge: even if she'd given us these shoes, she'd brought us here for her own reasons.

"Why do you pursue this quest?" she asked, her voice still and stark now that we stood face to face. She shook her head at my silent and set stare. "Do you even know what this staff is?"

"I know I need it. I was sent here for some purpose and the only path forward seems to require my getting this staff," I said.

"We've been rewarded greatly thus far," Hesiod added, glancing at our magic-imbued attire.

"I do not need to explain anything. Just point us to the next set of spells." I stopped, waiting for her interjecting insistence that we aid her in whatever it was that she needed.

Her face fell grave, lines carving and disfiguring her pristine skin as she lowered her brow and stroked her cheek. "Do you not wonder why you were sent after such a staff? Do you not wonder who might be keeping this staff?"

"Of course," Hesiod muttered, "but we trust the radiance of our kind sending us here, and we trust there is a greater purpose." Pride set his face in stone, building his brow outward with a firm stare beneath.

"The sun swallower cursed this land, and curses all my kind. Fenrir, that ancient wolf of the dark deep, prowls Jötunheimr and has hunted my fellow Jötunn to extinction. He hates your kind, those of the true light." She glanced around as if Fenrir were there and listening.

"Was he the one who cast the spells or not? What does it matter that we were put on this quest if we are undoing his bidding?" Hesiod said.

"Because I put the spells in place." Her eyes went cold and her face clouded with a palpable despair that seemed to suck the life out of the air.

"Nine spells held by nine virtues. I see..." I mumbled, realizing the magic we'd undone was not corrupt but pure.

"Nine noble virtues cast in holy magic. Courage, Truth, Honor, Fidelity, Discipline, Charity, Justice, Potency, and Perseverance," she said.

"But why lock away the staff?" Hesiod asked.

"Svipdagr once pursued it, and it is true that the spells were cast to keep him away. But his suddenness here was of the sunlight that strikes the face of a man who's overslept till noon. A different matter, then—his pursuit of the staff was a test of his worth for betrothal to another. But once duly wedded, he forgot his staff, and left here in the nothingness of no recollection, it darkened."

"Did Fjolsvith know?" I said.

"I cannot say, but he knew it should remain locked. I do not think he cared for you: he merely wanted to use you to escape his prison and rest in eternal nonbeing."

"But what is wrong with it? What has it to do with Fenrir?" I said, scratching at the bridge of my nose.

She squinted her eyes and leaned forward, lowering herself to my height as if she were a teacher scrutinizing a young student. "Did you see yellow eyes ascend from Mímisbrunnr?" I paled and she nodded at my reaction. "As Fenrir swallowed the last of my people, darkness came to dwell in this land once held in the esteem of light. The darkness was lunar in its essence, setting this realm in eternal night, even as day hangs haphazardly in its archaic form." She paused, looked around and swept her arms in a circle. "This is no day. It is false. The virtues have been flipped and my magic corrupted. The staff, already darkened by forgetfulness, spewed a darkness that only increased Fenrir's ravenous power and appetite. Lævateinn is indestructible and its leaked power was too much even for Fenrir's shadow, and it blackened the old wolf darker even than night, darker than any abyss. Its ill aura birthed monsters as it mingled together with Fenrir. When my spells are undone, they will be freed along with Lævateinn."

"Then why aid us in breaking these spells?" I asked.

"You both might just possess the kind of light capable of dispelling such a darkness. I saw as much when you and your friend transformed."

"And what are we to do once we destroy your work of safeguarding?" Hesiod crossed his arms unconvinced.

"You must unlock this chest, for not even I can, so corrupt have my spells of virtue become. I am powerless. This world, my beautiful homeland is forever faded now. To unlock the staff is to save it from becoming dark and evil, instead providing a similar release to nonbeing that Fjolsvith so greatly sought, only, our release here will be back into the cold of winter. Back to the comfort of swaying snow. I long for such a pure return. For you to hold the corrupted staff is to force the darkness into the light, and only a true light can burn it away. A light that you possess and that I sadly do not. The corruption has even seized hold of me; I feel my power fading into the same forgetfulness that Lævateinn suffered. I do not want this darkness. The sun has been chewed and spit out, gnawed on and disfigured, but it has yet to be completely swallowed. You are the last rays of a dying light." She drew a long breath and stared over us at the World Tree. "Go back to Yggdrasil and slay the dragon Nidhogg. He gnaws the ancient tree's roots and without a pure realm holding him back, he has begun to tear into the foundations. With fleet-footed clouds soaring in your soles, you will arrive much faster than you came, a flash of lightning to fell a monster. Though you might just find that he's as much a monster as me." She chuckled and looked down at us.

Hesiod and I both looked at each other perplexed. I nodded and shrugged, and we both turned and ran, our windblown shoes torrenting us forward in a jet stream of blurred air. And just like that, we stood next to the mighty trunk of Yggdrasil. At the base of the tree, a foul dragon scratched at the bark with its claws like a cat. Nidhogg was a muddy brown color with mossy, slime-green patterns triangulating down his spine, coming to a point in a gross rotten-yellow smudge on his tail. Pale green smoke floated up from the strangely glowing tail.

From where we stood, we could easily examine him, but he took no notice of us. Hesiod peered at the monster, searching for a weakness. A mass of shades suddenly sliced out of the air and stood between us and Nidhogg. They were so immaterialized that they barely clung to being, shivering there as mere shadows. They stood holding shimmering black spears that glowed with darkness. More and more shades stepped out of the air, and their ghostly silhouettes turned towards us, their features non-existent. I set my arms ablaze, my armor glowing with a reflected scarlet-orange light. Hesiod stood ready, his robe and mantle a blood drenched inferno. More shades appeared, wielding all kinds of weapons: spears, axes and clubs all around.

"Back to back, Hesiod... they circle us," I said, as Hesiod already moved towards me.

We stood there with both our backs holding each other upright, and we spun in a slow circle, watching and waiting for the shades to make a move. But they too were waiting for something, though I couldn't tell what. If only Hesiod had been given a weapon to go with his armor; at least I had my marks. As the air chilled and I began to feel the icy grip of a dark winter, I thought back to the way in which Hesiod's robe had appeared, a light of fire that had emerged and bloomed out from his breast and from his heart.

"The fire that burned forth from your heart, can you weaponize it?" I whispered.

The shades had sucked out all the surrounding sound, leaving nothing but an increasing cold behind. All the while, Nidhogg continued his nibbling at the great tree. It reminded me of Apophis thinking me unworthy of notice. That serpent had paid the price for his dishonor, and this dragon was a serpent all the same. If he would not honor my worth, I would not let my honor be so profaned.

"My heart, it is of a higher heat and beat. It dances to the notes of Pan. The forest sun, deep green leaves ablaze in a field of fractal emerald, green shadows dancing along with the unseen hidden day that the deep forest sings." Hesiod sputtered his words out, the volume unwelcome and unable to fit in this weighty silence that filled every inch of the air.

"Are you mad, spouting such paltry poetry at a time like this?" I hissed. His body tensed even tighter; I was afraid he might leap away like a spring the way he was bent against me.

He said, "Your heart has always been like the forest igniting its green fields, unknown and unsung by any mortal being and unappreciated by lowly beasts. Only the noblest of animals belong there, the worthiest of creatures. Your heart continues this dance of emerald day whether you are there and aware of it or not. Do you see? Do you see? The spell here is testing an apparent virtue, it being honor. You remember Skade's list!" I nodded, forgetting he couldn't see me, and he continued regardless. "Your heart honors existence by beating so; it dances alone to celebrate the perfection of being, even the being that we do not ever get to quite know until we meet our endless end. We are dishonored by Nidhogg, and these shades have no honorable hearts of their own. But to honor your heart is to honor the beating drum of life."

I coiled up with a sudden excitement, realizing Hesiod was right, even in all his uncontrollable poetic verbosity. "Hesiod, your heart of flame is this weapon here! Let loose your glory and give the heart the honor it so deserves!" I shouted. The shades still stood there unmoved.

"And is there another virtue here to be unlocked before I pour forth this worthy wrath beating at the bars of its bony cage?" Hesiod said. His words stretched and snapped like a band ready to break, each syllable a testing of his sanity. Where had these words come from?

Something was wrong. Could it be the heat rushing to his heart?

I thought back to the virtues unlocked thus far: courage, truth, fidelity and now hopefully honor. With horror I realized our stupid gaffe and why Hesiod's sudden poetry shook me so. We'd already passed a spell with honor! Before I could say another word, Hesiod took my silence as approval and unleashed his solar force from within. A burning pillar of red light fountained out from his heart, consuming the shades in heat as he spun in a rapid circle and I dove to the ground as the burning surge singed the tips of my hair. The shades were burnt away, but Hesiod's dam of wrath had burst wide open. He was punching at his heart in an attempt to stop the fire, but all he succeeded in doing was singing his hand.

"At the dragon! Perhaps my heart still beats so furiously as to drive my power at that sick beast!" Hesiod cried over his shoulder at me and over the still raging torrent of fire and light that poured out in a horizontal column.

How could I have been so foolish to forget we'd unlocked honor? What was this one then? What was it that we were to do? As if an arrow struck my heart, I felt a piercing terror at the reality of what Hesiod was turning to do. I realized what the virtue was supposed to be, but it was too late. The flame tore across the landscape as he moved his breast towards the hungry dragon. I jumped in front of the beam, holding up my glowing arms to absorb his energy.

"What are you doing!" Hesiod screamed. "Let me feed this fiery furnace burning my soul—let me use it to accomplish our goal!" His voice cracked and shattered, brittle and dry, he sounded like a man on the brink of insanity due to an intolerable pain, or perhaps ecstasy. Was there any difference?

His torment was becoming my own as even my Hyperborean marks, crossed in front of me with my forearms extended and held together, were falling under the continuous wave of burning, bloody light. I was being pushed back towards the dragon. Did he notice us now? I dared not look back to check.

"Your light will burn away the tree, you overzealous fool!" I yelled.

"We must slay this dragon, this is my power to unleash!" he wailed, his mouth wide and his head reared back with his eyes rolling like a spooked horse.

"Destroying the tree upholding this world is worse than anything even Fenrir could do. Do you not see?" I said as my arms lowered under the continuous pressure and a burst of light in the top stream of his fire scraped across my uncovered triceps, searing the skin with liquefying blisters that bubbled immediately to the surface. "Not honor, we've done that already! We were mistaken. Not honor Hesiod, but think: what virtue opposes your uncontrolled wrath? What was it Skade said?"

"Discipline," he whispered and collapsed as the light shut off, its source emptied of life. I ran to Hesiod's crumpled body, his red robe just barely aglow, its bright fire reduced to dying embers.

Before I could attend to him, my calves were stung by a strange squelch, and a smell of rot assaulted the air. My pants on the backs of my legs bubbled with green acid, but they remained unmarred, the night-sky colored cloth refilling its holes with self-stitching ripples that healed both itself and my skin beneath. I leapt to my feet as Nidhogg charged, his tail raised and drifting out in front of him like a scorpion's stinger. I dove out of the way to avoid the thrust of his green-fogged tail. Nidhogg made for Hesiod, but I hurled balls of light at him, doing no apparent harm but sending him into a furious turn to face me.

How would discipline win me this battle? I had no time to ponder as I dove out of the dragon's hurtling path, his brown talons unveiled and reaching, his tail whipping like a viper at my head. I was quickly running out of steam: first from withstanding Hesiod's heat, and now from my desperate dodges, which were coming closer and closer to peril, each dive another one nearer to a final leap into an abyss. I lowered my arms and aimed two explosions of light downward that propelled me into the air. I glided up and gracefully turned my body downward, heading straight for the dragon's confused form. With both my fists full of light and raised above my head as if I held a sledge hammer, I slammed down and landed my blow on his spiny back, and the dragon collapsed under the force of my attack. He writhed there like a caught mouse, unable to get back up. I kept my searing, energized fists pressed into his spine, exerting a continued force of impact that left him helpless and wriggling there.

His tail hovered up and speared at me. I twisted my body and ducked as his stinger scraped my right shoulder, venom hissing but ineffective against my armor. I held my fists there and pressed harder, and at last he went limp, ceasing his resistance. But I refused to let up, leaving my arms aglow and pressing downward, waiting for some foul trick. His tail flung towards me again and even harder than before. I dove off his back and rolled into the snow.

Nidhogg impaled himself to the ground, his tail pierced completely through his back.

"Why must you shame my company? Why must you destroy such a gracious host?" Nidhogg said, his voice a rolling lull, a frozen avalanche of tired, slow snow that thundered deep at a weary pace. "My shades did not attack. They welcomed you in a circle of peace. They merely awaited your permission to speak."

"Liar! They wielded their weapons, they circled us like hungry wolves! Skade told us to slay you!" I stepped up to his scaly face and stared into his brown-gold eyes that blinked with a surprisingly human sorrow.

"The weapons were for war, not with you, but with Fenrir, for he is on his way at this moment. Skade told you to slay me, and she was right to. But we all are monsters without light, for our forms are reduced to mere shadows. It is my nature to bite at this tree. I long to fell it for a damming of eternity. Fenrir wants to swallow all. I merely want to exist. Yes, you must slay me, but not until the wolf is finished. Did you not think to ask?"

"Charity," I mumbled. He nodded, grimacing and wheezing at the effort. "Why did you attack? Why did Skade not say more?" I asked.

"It would be uncharitable not to. Evil returned. Charity is a patient love. A patient action, even when the other remains still. Act with reason. Skade could not reveal this or the spell would remain locked away. It must be your virtue."

"How might I aid you? Are the shades lost?"

"Back in Hel they go, what remains of it anyway," he groaned.

"And for you?"

"Send me down to Hel too. The roots run deep, and my people await. We will fade into the dark together. Our time has met its purpose. My existence belongs with the soil. I've damned myself."

I nodded, and Nidhogg smiled at me with his black teeth. I shot the full force of my light into his face, and his body burst into a green-gold glow, and flecks of silver rained down from the sky where his body had been. I stared at the glimmering flecks and realized that the greatest act of charity had been sending this fading beast into its own domain. A virtue forged, even when it appeared as if it had first been forever broken. I breathed a long sigh. Hesiod grunted in pain, and I turned and ran over to him as he struggled to his feet and stood up.

"Fenrir is coming," I said, steadying him as he stood by his own effort.

"Charity? How were we supposed to see that from what we faced?" he muttered, staring at his feet and spitting in disgust.

"You eavesdropped yet you didn't think to get up and help?" I joked half-heartedly.

His shoulders slumped as he rubbed his chest. "Could Apollo be behind my loss of control? My words were strained; my mind was aflame with a desire to burn. Was it from me or him... or both of us? Can I still wear this robe?"

I didn't offer any answer to his line of questions. How could I? Only he knew what he felt there in that moment. I wrapped my arm around his shoulder and said, "Maybe the armor feeds off feeling. Maybe Apollo designed it this way for good. Maybe for something sinister. We cannot yet say."

He sighed and placed his hand over my arm. "I will make this flame submit to the beat of my own heart. Whether Apollo fanned the fire or not, it is mine to carry. I won't make such a mistake again, Rangabes."

I let go of him and patted his hand, before looking out at the horizon. We both stood there silently, the sound and warmth still choked out by the shadow soldiers' lingering touchless touch. Even vanquished, their nonbeing still remained. The paradox of the heavy weight of that empty nothing.

Hesiod coughed and said, "And now to the seventh virtue. Justice. We shall see how this one is unlocked, I suppose. Fenrir should not be faced if we still have three more spells left." He spoke with a bit too much force, as if to beat the straining silence away.

"Well, he's coming soon and Nidhogg warned me without dishonesty," I said, looking over at him.

Hesiod shook his head and looked away and off into the distance. "What virtues might linger here? Perhaps there are spells in this air still. The air is too still. The nothingness is pervasive."

"Should we rely on chance? A voice from the heavens?" I shook my head and kicked up a puff of snow.

And there it was... Wyrd's song. The soft sonic shimmer of the slight pluck of her harp strings, followed by a whispered laugh. I grinned at the irony of my previous statement. And once again, Hesiod did not seem to hear. I knew what needed to be said and done. I already walked the right path. Her seeds were planted in the fertile soil of my soul.

I continued, "We must rely only on ourselves here, no magic armor or weapons. Like in my battle against Sobek, I earned the wounds I suffered. Like with my rituals in Tartarus, I earned these holy marks. Remember what Skade said. The last three virtues are justice, potency and perseverance."

Hesiod looked at me strangely and I couldn't contain my grin. He said, "You look too pleased with yourself, brother. I suppose that is deserved. After all, did you not already earn the virtues thus far? Outside hinderances may have arisen; whether or not they were needed is beside the point. We earned the virtues because we already possessed them. These are mere tests, magic polluted by the dark, as Skade told us. Who knows what they were like in their purer form?" He crossed his arms and itched at his beard.

"If you think we earned all this by being as we were, then remove your magical garb. It is not a fear of Apollo if you do, but an embracing of your naturally burning heart. I will as well, and I won't use these marks, earned or not. I fear no Fenrir for I fear none that dwell in the dark. How can light fear what is an absence of itself? How can light fear the shadows cast in its wake? The darkness belongs to the leeches. I am the light."

I tore my trousers at the unbreakable seam and it split willingly, the cloth seeming to understand the necessity of my pure act of heroic will. I followed the act by kicking off the shoes of wind along with the trousers. Not finished, I undid the shining bands of diamond straps and removed my armor. I stood naked and in my own natural power.

Hesiod followed my example, but only after several seconds of strained deliberation while yanking at his chin hair, so torn was he by this chosen surrender to nature. But he undid his mantle and the cape fluttered patiently to the ground like a drowsy butterfly in summer heat. His living robe of strange fire poured off of his skin as he glared down at it, dripping away as if the heat of his stare was too much.

"So, we face Fenrir as we are. In all our purity," Hesiod said, clasping my arm and staring into my eyes. "You are a man of true power. A man I'm willing to die with and for."

"Likewise, brother. As we are, purity powerless in perfect submission to our power—our eternal wills. Fenrir can come. We will always *be*; he in his darkness never *was*." I turned my gaze to the horizon, Yggdrasil an infinite fortress behind us.

"You know... if Fenrir has been freed, that means the Allfather has perished," Hesiod said, his Apollo-fed wisdom always so sure. "From where then does Vithar come? He is the foretold slayer, the foretold avenger."

"Perhaps he is already lost."

"Perhaps his spirit is what moves us," he said.

"It is my own spirit," I replied.

"Of course, but his example and witness is our tie to victory, to overcoming, and more importantly, to properly becoming."

"Follow the hero's path—the path to godhood," I added. "What better way than to slay a beast?"

"This battle was supposed to signify the end, to signify Ragnarok," Hesiod said, massaging his temples with his eyes closed.

"It is not ours to fight. We are here for our own triumph, to succeeded only for our truth and future kin. Our ancestors too. It is our power and act. Ours to give. And we act now as we are. Pure and filled with eternal will!" I said.

"A virtue in and of itself, right there. Potency. We have not unlocked justice still, but right here I feel I am correct. Potency. We have ourselves and all our potential, and we act with that potential filled to the brim, pouring it out yet always refilling from the bowed acknowledgement of the infinite." Hesiod smiled and grabbed my shoulder, laughing. "We walk into these virtues with ease, for we have had them all along."

I grinned, as I'd known exactly where we were headed when I'd first spoken. Even better that Hesiod had said it first. He sang Wyrd's song without even hearing it, so wise and pure was he. I grabbed his shoulders right back and laughed.

"Now we must move back from the eighth to the seventh," I said.

He let go of my shoulder and squinted at me with a sudden seriousness. "A relation to self-reliance is to be filled with a vigor of infinitude. The virility of passionate being, the spirit of justice working hard and pure to overcome the mortality of our kind, seeking and earning what is deserved amongst the immortals."

"And what must we do?" I said, pleased with the whirring of his mind. He truly needed no help from the gods, the myth-maker himself was always moving, always striding through his own path. A worthy companion! I gladly watched him proceed.

"Never cease and continue up the mountain. Yet the peak is just the bottom. The endless firmament is the true ascension that never wanes or stops. The infinite connected to finitude. Perseverance."

"And still the seventh spell remains locked. You said 'justice' when discussing perseverance. Justice as overcoming mortality?"

"I remember saying we needed to bow in acknowledgment to the infinite. That is where the potency comes from, the purity of powerlessness as we've already discussed," Hesiod said with his face scrunched small as he tried to fit justice in there somewhere.

I smiled at the intensity of his focus. I rubbed my chin and said, "Bowing to the infinite is the first act to bring about our great potency. But it also is the beginning of justice. What is just? Is it just to close your eyes to eternity, to that always ascending ladder, and to live and die as best as one can? No! Justice is both of ours as we climb! We ascend because it is unjust to let go and turn away. Power is justice when made powerless by that pure submission to the mighty currents of the always flowing river. We spread into the sea! We evaporate into the heavens! There is no ceasing. And that is justice. Accepting the mandate to be as one is meant to be, and not living as if one possesses more or less. We are just, Hesiod, as long as we lead ourselves and others up this mountain." I threw my hands up as I finished speaking.

"And so we are!" he shouted, dancing like a madman. I laughed as his naked body flailed about.

"Be glad that decency isn't a virtue," I joked, bent over and unable to stop my chortling.

Finally, he stopped his insane jig and heartily laughed, holding his stomach as he breathlessly stared up at the empty sky. As we both calmed down, we looked at each other with as much seriousness as we could muster.

I breathed deep to reign myself in and said, "Still, have we met these virtues? We may be right in our thinking, but there have been no signs we are correct here with our choice. And are they merely choices? Our honor and courage were concretely tested. Even our discussion on purity was accomplished only after overcoming the residual fog of some unseen spells. Is that the case again? We have no signs. We talk, but are we truly as we say?"

"No rewards, no magical gifts, no. No flash of light or voice from the heavens, but maybe that's just it. These final virtues are only signified by claiming them as your own, by acting as if already possessing them, because truly they can only be obtained within, not without. To be just is to pursue what is yours, and to give accordingly with an eternal gaze of truth. To persevere is to not stop ascending. To be potent is to face any obstacle, any monster with the knowledge of assurance in one's own power. Have we not done this? Have they not been acted out from within us both?" Hesiod folded his hands together and leaned towards me, now a paragon of seriousness, and I found myself nodding along.

I held my chin with my thumb and placed two fingers on my cheek as I considered his wise words. "Could the same not be said of the other virtues? Were they not from within? Why did they require the concrete?"

"Of course they were, but then and there an act was proof. That is why it had to be made concrete. Here, the proof is in acting without expectation of aid or progress, an act that can never stop and always must be in every step. Pure act aimed at the heights of the firmament, that ascension into the eternal moment. An act that does not end, for it spirals in a flat motion, increasing yet remaining contained, eternity pressed into time, into the finite decay. Thus, the decay is made holy, by being preserved in eternity," Hesiod said, his gaze lingering up at the dulled heavens.

"Then what are we to do?"

“We welcome Fenrir, acting as ourselves by relating ourselves to the infinite. We wait, and with ourselves in all our purity, the currents of glory carry us in a surrendered power, leaving us powerless to the perfect relation of higher triumph, of godhood.” He nodded and turned to look at me.

“So be it,” I said.

And so, we stood there at ease with our decision and unafraid of the terror wolf coming to swallow us whole. We were our own, for we had been made pure to and for our people.

***

Cerberus belched his red flames against the snow strangled air. He was not taking well to the land of the Jötunn and I couldn’t blame him. This frost, this unforgiving tundra was unwelcoming to our heat, and its darkness and cold were getting worse. Following the wreckage Rangabes and Hesiod left behind was no difficult task. I worried at what that Fjolsvith fool had said, who knew what lies he’d sowed? This land had long since been corrupted. The Jötunn considered themselves holy, better than mere gods, an evolution of the Hyperborean man.

Of course, they were a degeneration of that solar spirit I’d long ago kindled. The northern people and their gods carried that light still, but the Jötunn had chosen the darkness. They had chosen weakness and it at all came down to their infernal Lævateinn, their corrupt relic of hiddenness. Those who hid away their might were worse than the most immodest reveler. To pretend to be inglorious, lacking in might and hiding in weakened peace was the worst vice I could imagine.

"Cerberus, they no doubt have lied to Rangabes and Hesiod. Will they be able to see through it all?" I said, gazing up at the mountainous beast.

His middle head lowered down to me, his snakes hissing at the snow and his left and right heads glaring at Yggdrasil which we were fast approaching. "The well has collapsed and the rewards were no doubt given. If what you tell me is true, the Jötunn seek to subvert all that you do. Odin is gone and their end of the cycle is to begin anew."

"You speak as if you doubt my truth," I said, my burning eyes matching his red ones in intensity.

"I know they have a hound of their own. Fenrir who swallows light; he is an abyss darker than Tartarus. The Jötunn feed this dark wolf, but I know not why. Why was Rangabes sent here by Ra. What is there to accomplish? A cycle of dark begins in this realm and it will wash away the lingering light to bring about the new—perhaps something brighter."

"When old Zeus was toppled from his heights, when the old gods fell in forgotten ruin, what had been foretold was cut loose, the thrashing marionette of fate whipping as wild as your serpents," I said. His snakes turned together towards me and hissed, their orange tongues forking through the snow. I continued, unperturbed, "Wyrd of course enjoys singing her odd fate, the kind that changes at the whims of those who hear her song." I shook my head, her aloofness and service of the other always caused me difficulty. "And with so much that was foretold coming true in a form none of us wanted to see, there was only one option for we of the old guard. We had to welcome in this herald of the new order, the man to give rebirth to the Hyperborean soul. It lies dormant in many peoples spread throughout the globe; some possess it more than others. Yet that wasn't and isn't enough to bring back the mythic might of the heroic ages of the past. Those with it exist now as islands, men alone without a worthy tribe backing them up. Rangabes is the one to change that, Cerberus."

"I know this already. You haven't answered why he needs to be here. This cycle is dark. There is no light for him to obtain." Cerberus looked ahead and his snakes licked at his ears for him.

"I meant for him to go to the now degenerated Valhalla to free the heroes forced into the corrupted monstrosity of that glorious hall of power. But with Odin's death, Yggdrasil wilts with no truth to drink from. And Ra sent Rangabes here for a purpose that has only become clear to me just now. You saw the ruin of the Duat, of Ancient Egypt at last darkened with only Rangabes now to carry their sun. That corruption that even Dionysus was unable to escape in his white pyramid of fire—the corruption that made a monster god declare himself of the solar realm... that corruption touched Rangabes. I know this now and for him to continue straight to Valhalla, even in its fallen form... then that corruption might in turn chain him to the darkness of what was once light, now twisted to a cold dead forever. Only one of uncorrupted light can burn through there unscathed. Not even I could do so in my current state. For Ra to send him here, into a land even more corrupt than Egypt had turned, he must have seen a need. A need I should have anticipated. What an unworthy architect I am for not measuring this angle." I took a deep breath and kept walking forward, not bothering to glance at Cerberus now that I was deep within the swirling map of my everchanging plans. "He burned into the land of the living; his corruption swallowed with Dionysian virility. He said yes to the darkness and consumed it the same way in which Fenrir consumes the light. Ra saw what I should have first... in his final act of what is truly pure, Ra gave Rangabes the wolf of darkness to consume, and thus purify his body with a nothingness that must be overcome to step into Valhalla and over that bloody river that awaits—a noose around the neck of those unaccustomed to the dark. This is a proving ground now. I feared sending him here for I thought the Jötunn would lead him astray. I trapped Fjoslvith in that wall for a reason. They cannot be trusted! They never could." I spat onto the ground, my sandaled feet kicking through the snow. "What I didn't see was that without walking through such darkness, how could he be a bearer of light? The temptation in Valhalla as it is now would have been too much were his virtues not strengthened and confirmed. There is light because darkness in its absent being cannot exist without it. Darkness needs the light to know it is dark. Ra saw the need."

Cerberus trained all three of his heads at me, forcing me to look his way. His serpents hissed like biting rain. "I do not see the need. Someone is not speaking true. You seek to mold Rangabes into the perfect being of your chosen light. But what of the other solar gods? What if they want him to be more theirs than yours? What if Rangabes becomes his own? You tell me to serve his need, to aid him, but am I aiding him or you? Apollo, what is it we are doing here? These nine spells reek of your magic. Your tests of virtue."

I stopped walking and turned to him. Cerberus sat down and waited. I cracked my neck and rubbed my blonde brow. “I fed Odin to Fenrir. He refused to bow to Rangabes. The prophecy of his myth was that he would be eaten by a dark wolf and that his son Vithar would come for revenge. Only, Fenrir’s offspring was supposed to eat Odin, but I let the old wolf loose from his wicked chains and with his river of black saliva bloody and foul, I defeated the Allfather with darkness at my back.”

I stopped and Cerberus growled softly. The hound was proving as stubborn as I thought he’d be. What could I expect when he’d spent so much time in the dark, however noble his station? How could I expect him to understand such a difficult choice?

I remembered it like it’d just happened. The look on Odin’s face when I came to him; the white backdrop of snow like a blanket of cold nothingness, a void swallowing any hope of a new day and rising sun. We’d stood there in a freeze so cold that all feeling gave way to its numb touch. Like Hades, he resisted. Yet unlike Hades, Odin was of light. He glared at me one eyed and fierce, more fury fixed in that stare than any cyclops would ever dare. He leaned on his spear like it was all that held him up, yet his frame remained full of virility. His long robe whipped in the cold, revealing chords of muscle as hard and strong as dwarven metalwork. He stared at me and offered no response. He already knew.

“Was It Wyrd?” I said to him. “Did she convince you of some contrived fate? Do you not see what must be done?”

The Allfather stood tall and held up his staff, looking at its barbed point as if in search of some other way. “You fear us all. We the dying gods, we the living people—we are what is and you are what is not.” He glared his white eye right at my golden ones, cooling my fire with his frigid sight.

"My people are what gave this world light." I took a step closer.

"You froze their paradise because they became too much like you. I welcome ascendancy. I do not fear your imagined avatar. Wyrd told me what is to come. She is wise, unlike you. Are we not gods of wisdom? Where is yours, Apollo? Has your crown of eternal day lost its meaning in its endless loop of self-contained light? You cannot admit to your dimming because your light is the only kind you can see." Odin sighed and pointed his spear at me. "I'm a god who knows sacrifice and wisdom. You are so lost in your own dark that you call it light, even as it sinks into black. Wyrd played her song, but I already knew it was true. You are not."

He hefted back his spear and flung it at me. I ducked low and let it pass, grabbing its frozen shaft as it crackled with blue. I spun back with it clutched in my hand and its momentum turned forward. My hand burned hotter than the sun yet was colder than the deepest of polar depths. Touching that spear had been the greatest pain I'd ever known. I flung his spear right into his side. He fell to his knees and I pounced on him, pounding his face with a maelstrom of hooked punches. He slumped down unconscious with his spear still propping him up. I'd caught him at last, and thus I carried him off to be devoured like a speared fish.

I rubbed my hand at the memory, the echo of pain still present, though my hand remained whole and unmaimed. Cerberus sat there patiently, suspicion still holding his snakes rigid. He would never understand old

Odin's babbling confusion. Light is light, there can be no other.

I sighed and cleared my throat. "Vithar doesn't exist and neither does Fenrir's offspring. Wyrd sings loudly from her dwelling place, laughing at the twisting of fate. Rangabes is a better Vithar, and so it is he who will defeat the dark—only, his dark houses the sun inside. That kind of light that not even I could know. Rangabes is my destined heir."

Cerberus lowered his growl to a hum, his snakes silent yet staring their beady red eyes still at my face, hovering unsurely. "An heir or avatar? I'll stay by your side and I thank you for waking me from such a wretched and weak slumber. I slept, but now I am awoken. There is untruth in this chilled climate, and I do not know where the stench begins or ends. But to turn on fellow gods of light, I do not know what to say. Your plans spread hazy before me, even Wyrd couldn't sing a song so mad and obscure. Have you barded each god a different song? A different tuned hunk of meat with an appealing yet suspicious swine? I doubt your famed wisdom. But you brought me to the light, and in it I long to remain. Yet if this black sun of Fenrir is a ploy for you to stand alone in the next age, I will leave your side."

"If you think me capable of such treachery, you won't have a side to stand on," I scoffed, wary of his suspicion. I needed him for this, and for quite a while longer. Fate demanded it, or so it seemed. But he'd made himself clear and I refused to be made a fool. "Come Cerberus, a wolf can only be tamed by a dog."

Cerberus growled but walked forward, his serpents hissing at my back.

***

“Fenrir,” I said, rolling my shoulders and nodding at Hesiod. We both stood there naked, ready to face the wolf at last.

On the horizon a hulking shadow loomed. I squinted, something appeared off. As the moving mass neared, I recognized the shape of the beast and turned to Hesiod in confusion. The approaching hound had three heads attached to black slabs of muscle. Seven serpents spread out behind him like a perverse peacock's tail. I could recognize this dog’s likeness anywhere. Cerberus, the hound of Hades... in Jötunheimr.

“Another test?” I said.

“Why him, and here?” Hesiod muttered.

An answer of sorts was provided as a humanoid figure approached in the shadow of Cerberus’s mass. Now close enough to make out details, only a blind man would fail to recognize such a blazing mien. His yellow-white augers of light peered out from eternity, burning his gaze into mine. I held my head high.

Apollo wore a golden laurel on his head and its shimmering gleam intensified the aura of his stare. His hair was thick and curly and of medium length; it floated in waves down to the nape of his neck. Now even closer, I was taken aback by the ageless youth he appeared as. His face was pristine and hairless, his body fit and slim with skin a golden white—not sun kissed but sun embraced. He wore a white mantle thrown loosely over his right shoulder, and a golden robe that left his arms and legs uncovered. His body was a controlled power that was too sleek to be that of a burly wrestler, yet too strong to be that of a runner. The perfect balance. I shook my head and hoped that this beautiful god of light and wisdom was on our side. Why had he come now and with the hound of death at his side? Cerberus towered above him yet was diminished in the glory of Apollo's perfection.

I stared at him, my body loose and my unease hidden. He needn't know how much I'd grown to distrust his meddling in my affairs. Here he was, my unseen benefactor who clearly wanted something, and who'd rubbed these other immortals in perplexing ways. I would let him speak his piece and I would judge the truth. I stared up at Cerberus, his scent of ash and fire like burning coal. He watched me with what looked like kindness, or at least a kind of respect. His right head glanced down at Apollo and his other two heads stared directly at me with a slight, dare I say endearing tilt.

"Rangabes. As Hesiod is your brother, may I one day call you mine as well. Apollo wants something, be wary." Cerberus spoke inside my mind and apparently only I could hear. I stared up at the hound and let my eyes speak for me. There was no deceit there. A feeling, one I couldn't say Apollo gave me.

Apollo stood there in his radiance at about the same height as Hesiod and I, yet his eyes made him seem as if he were staring down from the heavens. Those irises were furnaces of white heat; I almost looked away for it felt similar to staring at the sun. Yet I forced my gaze onto his, refusing to turn away from the searing light. Not pleased at my frigid welcome, he frowned.

"Are you sure you possess the virtue of charity?" Apollo said.

"I've heard much said about you here." I let my words linger in the air, shrouding Apollo's condescension.

"What was said?" Apollo asked Hesiod.

"What was said and what was not, doesn't matter." Hesiod spoke firm and strong, his eyes daring Apollo to strike.

"A cold welcome for the warmth I've given you both. Who do you think brought you forth from the darkness of death?" Apollo looked up at the sky and I rebuked myself at the rush of relief I felt as his stare released me.

"Why are you here? Why wait till now? And why put me through these trials and tests?" I said.

I tensed my body, tight with a fury I could no longer control. His haughty airs and expectation that we should bow before him made me want to attack him right here and now. He was not my god. Christ was atop all peaks, above all. Apollo showed—ironically—too much darkness. Hyperion, Helios and Ra were somehow different. Purer. Apollo was a man desperately flailing in a river of necessary fate he'd not ever known or loved. I glared at him, but he kept his gaze away and upward.

Apollo sighed and said, "You surely know why you are here: to smolder through the great mythologies of old, to inherit the birthright of old Hyperborea and make it into your own, perhaps a higher form. That is why I sent you ahead. You need these ancient lights to create a new, bright civilization from these once shining ones. You are a son of my power; my solar spirit radiates out from your blood. In you, proud Aeneas walks into war, claiming what is his—a new people and homeland as his Troy burned to the ground. But you ask even more, why here? Why this frigid wasteland? For this realm of power resisted our light." He lowered his eyes and stared into mine. I met his gaze and watched him closer. "But there is a lingering sun within

Fenrir's soul, swallowed whole. In his belly rests Týr's right hand; what power awaits the one to slay such a mongrel abyss? Odin's son, Vithar was supposed to slay the wolf. But Vithar's strand of fate was never spun. He is not coming for he is naught. But like great Aeneas, Vithar's power is of the same celestial fire—the clothing of light that covers you both." He paused, looking past our unclothed bodies and at our discarded clothing. He turned his attention back to me. "And you, son of the sun, you are destined with Wyrd's incessant stringing, to slay him instead."

"At this, I am grateful. For you have allowed me to move as one living," I lowered my head in guarded respect.

This god deserved that at the very least, no matter his guiles he had brought me opportunity and life, and for that any mortal must show some gratitude; to not at all would be worthy of the dark. He was my kin, my ancestral beginning. I bowed my head lower, my irreverence shaming my heart. Hesiod followed my lead, mumbling apologies.

"I want you to be my beacon of glory and light to a world that has forgotten much of its ancient power. Look at me, you are my sun, the ray of my light to a dark, weak, and profane modern world."

I looked up at him and he extend his arm. I clasped it strong and he pulled me in close to hug me. His skin was like the comforting embrace of a fireplace in the dead of winter; he held me as a father might a son.

"Hesiod," Apollo said warmly as I pulled back. He smiled and extended the same offer to the poet who gladly accepted.

I was only vaguely aware of Cerberus's watchful and suspicious eyes judging and weighing the truth. A loyal and useful companion he would make. I lowered my head to him but he barked, his serpents extending down and gently lifting my chin.

"You must be greater than I, and I am here to serve. Greater than Apollo too. That is what you must strive towards, the unending, overflowing goal of infinity always filling your cup yet never satisfying your thirst." Cerberus spoke in such a manner that even though his voice came as thought, I intuitively knew it had been meant for all of us to hear.

"Cerberus is right. I need you to be my beacon and to bring back the perfection and glory of Hyperborea. This sad age of iron is rusted over with weakness." Apollo winked at Hesiod and continued, "the decay of this age will only get worse and that's why you're so desperately needed. That's why you must be far greater than I." He nodded and firmly planted his hand on my shoulder, warmth and confidence exuding from his touch. His furnace eyes seemed softer in a sense, as if their light was not meant to push me away through force but draw me in through kinship. "King Arthur's mantle," Apollo said, beaming as he gestured his arm at the piles of our shed attire. "A worthy gift he was all too willing to part with.

"He lives?" Hesiod said.

"No, he is caught beneath the rubble of Valhalla and you will meet him in its twisted form soon. But that mantle is Hyperborean in nature, that is, it came from the blood that bloomed in great Aeneas's tree. King Arthur's ancestor, and yours as well, Rangabes. But you Hesiod, you too my Hyperborean poet, are related in more than just spirit to this glorious past."

Hesiod coughed and said, "What of my robe? The fire that burned my heart was one of solar power, yet it beat with a terrible wrath."

Apollo cleared his throat and stared up at the World Tree. "My gift to you. The fire was yours, I merely gave you a wick to hold it. The wrath... well, I wanted Nidhogg to burn."

"Is that charitable? He was not as he seemed," I said.

"Was it truly Skade who made these tests?" Hesiod said, rubbing his chest.

"Yes, made by the work of the Norse immortals with the spirit of my wisdom and sun imbuing them with greater forms. Hence your robe and King Arthur's mantle."

I frowned. "And what say you about Skade?" I said.

"She is the one who corrupted them." Apollo shook his head. "That staff must be opened and used, but not to defeat Fenrir, but to defeat Skade's slipping grip on this sick realm."

"She claimed to create the spells to lock away the threat of the staff and hold her land against Fenrir," Hesiod said. "And besides, how can we be ready if the chest remains locked?"

"She needs that staff to bring about her own doom. Moros, Kronos, and so many of our kind seek to escape and return to nothing. True solar gods return to the sun and imbue creation with warmth and light—with power. Ra... Hyperion and Helios. They live through the light, and you carry their embers in your own will. Skade is just another Fjolsvith seeking an end. Their darkness is wanted." Apollo rubbed his eyes and for a second he looked weary to the point of being mortal. "And Hesiod, I cannot say how you might be ready for that is a spell you must break alone. If I aid you, the lock will remain latched shut. Skade has made sure to corrupt the spells to such an extent that not even I can solve them; a dark immune to my light."

"We fight Fenrir alone then. Your presence has brought much clarity and vigor to my being. Thank you." I bowed my torso and crossed my arms diagonally over my chest.

"Not alone, for Cerberus here will be remaining with you to watch. I cannot promise his intervention either, but if there is a way, he will find one. I can do nothing more for you, for you need to become your own sun and not a mere moon reflecting my light. I have enemies in other lands I must deal with swiftly." He smiled and vanished in a pillar of white light, leaving nothing but hissing snow behind.

"And now that the god of light has left, Fenrir skulks out from his shadows. He comes," Cerberus said, his heads gazing out at the horizon and his black noses twitching. Smoke snaked out from his nostrils as he breathed, his chest a furnace and his mouths leaking ash.

Sure enough, Fenrir at last showed himself, a true terror to behold. He made Cerberus look like a pup, and black shade followed in his wake, darkening the landscape in murky shadow. Fenrir's fur was startlingly silver, the color of the full moon on a clear, crisp night. His eyes were yellow and bright and his loping body flowed across the landscape, shimmering silver like a stream of moonlit water. He slowed to a trot and stopped just in front of us, eyeing us with an air of superiority; his lips curled, revealing white fangs sharper than sin.

"You smell of Odin's unborn son. But do you know your dear Apollo fed me your Allfather?" Fenrir snarled his words out, a deep growl that tore through the darkening air.

The gray sky was drenched in an inky black mist; weak light sifted through, casting the setting in a dark and unnatural purple hue.

"He's not my father and Apollo did what he had to." The news hardly surprised me, but still, Apollo would do whatever it took to see me through it all. I feared what that meant for any he thought too weak—or worse... too strong. But those were worries for then and not now.

Fenrir growled, "You and your friend stand exposed with your weapons and armor cast aside, yet you brought a mongrel. Even still, his might is certainly a weapon and hardly a reliance on yourself. Are you persevering with your own power up this summit?" He barked a high-pitched laugh that was more hyena than wolf.

"I could burn you to a crisp, wolf. I am here only to watch. I will not interfere for I understand what must take place and I hunger for an end just as you do." Cerberus's bark punctuated his booming thought.

I smiled as the realization struck me head-on. The genius of such a spell! The trickery! It was not just to leave a stray starving. So, the virtue required an act after all! And was it only left to justice, or did it belong simultaneously in the realm of charity? Was Nidhogg not the real test? For even the worst of fiends would host a friend, but to host an enemy, that was a virtue only one of the utmost charity could act. I chuckled, Fenrir and Skade couldn't outwit Apollo's masterful magic, it was too perfect. Perhaps his spells were not as corrupted as I'd thought.

"Would you like to eat with us, Fenrir? I am only trying to be charitable, for to fight famished would be unfair." I bowed with a wide grin and Hesiod laughed as Fenrir snarled.

The colossal wolf laid down on his fours and looked at us expectantly, his massive paws crossed in front of him; his claws of black iron twice as big as my body.

"Where then is your food? I cannot break this spell; it binds us all for the moment. But if you cannot bring forth a worthy meal, then it is a virtue unearned and the staff remains locked," Fenrir said, his voice a low and somehow distant rumble—patient power pregnant with storm.

I hadn't thought that far ahead and I desperately scanned the area around us, but there was no sign of anything to make a meal out of. I looked over at Hesiod and clenched my jaw.

"My fire can cook any meat to perfection. But where might we find such game to hunt?" Cerberus said, his thoughts as whispers meant only for Hesiod and I. Fenrir tilted his head at us, his pointed ears twitching in a fruitless effort to hear.

Hesiod smiled, nodding to himself and squinting his eyes, staring at nothing but his thoughts. "Yes, yes, now I recall. That's it. Fenrir," he said, stepping closer to the beast and staring directly upwards. "What would you like to eat?"

"Your flesh," he barked, his snarling a wheezing laugh.

"I knew you'd be unable to resist. So confident are you, yet so repetitive. You ate Odin and you tore off Týr's hand; you have a certain taste. And as you have requested, so I will not deny. It is the host's job to offer the very best, and here is mine," Hesiod said.

Hesiod's exposed chest glowed orange and the light flowed beneath his breast and drifted outward. His veins shined yellow as the light swirled through his body like smoke from a blown-out candle. Then in a sudden rush, the light poured together in a pool of red, all focused and gathered in his right hand. Smoke arose from his hand and his face paled as he screamed in agony. The light flashed and the hand plopped off, falling to the ground and leaving behind a cauterized stump at his wrist.

With a grimace, he slowly bent down and picked up his pale hand, and held it up above his head, offering it to Fenrir. The wolf howled like a brittle chime. He slowly lowered his head and his long purple tongue slipped out, gently scooping up the hand. As he raised his head back up, his tongue slowly returned to his mouth like a bear who'd left its cave too early from hibernation, sluggishly going back to sleep in the dark again.

And then, Fenrir swallowed Hesiod's hand. I winced at the motion and glanced at Hesiod's grim demeanor. Yet he stood fixed and assured, staring up at Fenrir and rubbing at his stump with his remaining hand. Cerberus stood at attention, staying an observer as the spell required.

"Cerberus, you tamed pet. I am of the wild and for my own purpose. You sit there and let your masters die. Come, fight me you mutt."

"I will not be baited and doom you all to the corruption of the realm. You only say such a thing because you fear those two. They are not my masters but they will be yours." He laughed, his rumbling bark strange and croaking, both out loud and by thought.

"No sign nor gift from the heavens. But we have proven the virtue and now we can end this." Hesiod spoke slowly with a rising fury—the building up of a trembling volcano about to erupt.

Fenrir licked his lips and stood, our bodies specks beneath his feet. If we were to do this with no aid from our armor or my marks, I saw no obvious way to attack. Regardless, I stood with my knees bent and my body tense, ready to spring myself into action.

"It is not a breach of perseverance in your power to use what is in your blood. That is truly ascending as yourself, for is not one's self everything his ancestors have instilled within him? To be potent is to know from where your strength comes and to use it accordingly," Cerberus said.

He spoke the truth and I nodded. This was a battle that required a true strength. To keep it unused and hidden was a vice in and of itself. The virtues required a full embracing of what was truly our own. And that was what our blood sang. The history of Hyperborea cried out for revenge on all those who would destroy the light. My forearms glowed.

Hesiod was suddenly covered in crimson light from his shoulders down to his hand. The light appeared so strong that it almost looked solid, but for a slight and translucent shimmer. A three-fingered talon, scaled with pure red light, shined where his right hand had been. His heart was a glowing, pulsing tree of light with paths spreading outwards like ancient roots. His heart looked as if it were suspended in glowing spider-webs of veined light that crisscrossed over his torso before gathering as solid pools on his arms and shoulders.

With the two of us aglow with Hyperborean light, we faced Fenrir, waiting for him to pounce. And that he did, his clawed feet swiping at us—but here we were at an advantage; so small were we relative to him, that our streaming dodges propelled by light kept us untouched as we sprinted and rolled in every direction. I couldn't help but imagine the two of us as fleas next to the giant wolf.

Fenrir growled and lowered his head, snapping his jaws as I dove out of the way and sent myself skidding further as his foot stamped down where I'd landed. Two streams of red and blue light poured out from my arms as I shot myself out of his reach.

Through the silver blur of Fenrir's empty strikes, I saw an even blurrier pattern of red, bursts of it bouncing about like a ball. Hesiod leapt at Fenrir's legs, his talon of light slicing at ankles as if they were trees. But hardly any damage was done; he was simply too large for us.

I stored up all of my might until I felt ready to burst, and shot out a focused concussion blast at his nearest hind leg and it struck true, yet in its dissipated glow, Fenrir hadn't even stumbled.

"Nothing works!" I yelled, rolling out of reach as his jaws snapped shut.

I followed my shout with a flurry of energy bursts that brought another swipe of his feet at me. I launched myself into the air, my light fueling my limited flight.

"We need that staff!" Hesiod yelled back, his talon raking through fur as smoke sizzled in his wake.

"Well, where is it?" I ducked a sweep of Fenrir's woolly gray tail. "Have we not completed all the virtues?" My question hung unanswered in the air as Hesiod launched himself high with bursts of red light beneath him, and he scraped his claw through Fenrir's quads to no avail. He landed clumsily, his stumbling luckily saving him from Fenrir's bite.

We were being resourceful, using every trick we could think of to dodge and strike, so it had to be the last virtue, the ninth. Perseverance. We persevered in our own power, our own flesh and might yet nothing was proving effective. We were certainly acting out the virtue as we continued hopelessly struggling in this apparently unwinnable battle. Perseverance most certainly didn't mean foolheartedly continuing what wasn't working, but it meant more to not fall prey to emotions: to fear, suffering, or pleasure, as I could not deny the thrill of combat, even one as fruitless and dangerous as this. But all those feelings were faded, it was not quite that either.

I leapt forward, angry at my thoughts being interrupted and scattered by constant shifting and dodging. I set my fists aglow, centering the light in each hand and I punched in a flurry of jabs followed by a right hook and then a left, right at the wolf's calf but once again, not even a stumble. I tried to think as I weaved in and out from Fenrir's legs, striking just to keep him honest and on guard. Perhaps the perseverance went deeper. Yes... that was it. Perseverance of the Hyperborean spirit, of the heroic blood of ancestors remembered and honored. To feed from their source of strength, to be rooted in tradition, to the history of a people so heroic they'd become myth. This light exuding from out of my marks was not the limit of such strength. I remembered bursting into an eternal fire and consuming Kronos, before any rituals or added strength were imparted to me. To tap into that, that would be perseverance; for how could one continue on through time if that which came from before was forgotten? If one forgets, then there is nothing to persevere with in the first place.

"We persevere with our blood! We persevere with our ancestors! We are because they were!" I proclaimed to Hesiod and the heavens alike.

With such an epiphany shouted out, my ancestors stormed together within me and without. Clouds of gold gathered in the heavens, blotting out the gray blotched sky. And from the glowing clouds, an ornate chest descended in a beam of light. It was carved with gilded golden wolves that spiraled into a whirlpool on the front. Each wolf had citrines for eyes that shimmered with yellow light. Fenrir howled at the chest and suddenly ceased his attack, cowering backwards as if it could kill him if he got too close. I walked over to it as it floated to the ground, the beam of golden light still shining down on it from above.

I shuffled backwards with my eyes trained on Fenrir who snarled and shivered, the now gold bathed landscape reflecting off his silver coat. Hesiod followed me and kept his eyes solely focused on Fenrir. The chest had nine cracked seals atop it, each seal a half black, half yellow circle, like the moon and sun split. I opened the chest and stared at Lævateinn. Fire and darkness swirled over its white ivory wood. I grabbed it and raised it out of the box. The staff shined with a freezing white light, pulling me into a frigid sense of despair. A black shroud suddenly enveloped me and my body was pulled into darkness, and all my life was sucked into shadow. The chaos of non-being. And I was naught.

. . .

. . .. .

. . ..

. . ..

No... No! I refused this... this nonexistence. This darkness. What had the chest thrust me into? It wasn't merely internal as I could still feel my body. I gripped the staff tighter in my hand, numb and cold. I walked blindly forward into the black expanse. While I couldn't see, I could at least hear. Uncertain whispers stroked the nothingness around me, words impossible to grasp. The whispers floated, a circle of voices holding themselves adrift, as if deliberating whether or not I should be addressed.

Rangabes

The voice rose from a whisper to a declaration of masculine strength. A heroic baritone, deep and strong—this was a voice that was worth heeding.

It is I, Aeneas. Long separated by time and blood, we share a sunlit start and the same shining task. The light of the sun stirs our blood. No matter how distant, a star's light cannot be blotted out; it only takes time for it to shine towards the right spirit—from mine to yours. Rome was a successor, and before that it was my tragic homeland of Troy. That solar soul, that spiritual blood that sings high into the heavenly realms.

"Aeneas. Great hero and father of Rome, why do you speak in this darkness?" I said.

The staff you hold sets your blood aflame with cold truth. Your spirit is meant to supplant those weak cows above, now fallen below. The human has become a herd animal. But you are not called to stand alone. No, never! You are called to be a man, to stand above—and from this height, this rising up, this ascension up the mountain, you become yourself—a self. As a self, you now can find your flock. For a herd is faceless, but a flock is known by its fleece. Where are your brethren, Rangabes? Will you succeed in founding a new people, a powerful empire matching my own holy mandate?

"I've been ascending from youth and now even from death."

And now you will see what fleece the flock of the sun wears. Light!

The blind black crystallized into white and shattered into a brilliant and pristine gold. I stood on white ground, with a blank expanse of gold above, shimmering and sparkling like metal made into sky. And there before me was a line of men so legendary, so mighty that I nearly tripped over myself. But I remembered my own strength and my connection to them, and I watched calmly as they stood in their perfect line. Beyond their wall of heroism was a multitude of dull shadows standing still and together in mass; an army of silhouettes with hunched backs and dropped heads. An army of men forgotten in the dark, an army made up of mere cattle.

"Join your brothers, this is a fight for you and your kin."

I turned around at Aeneas's voice and took in the mighty progenitor of Rome. His hair was thick but cut short, its amber color a field of golden wheat set aflame. He had a prominent nose, straight and royal, and his jawline was strong with cheeks squared and wide. A face of classical power; his blue eyes peered out at me with the cold rage of an avalanche. His armor was immaculate and silver. His legendary shield that had been crafted by the god of fire Vulcan, was enormous. Only he could carry such heavy metalwork with ease. The shield depicted a future that was now past, the promised glories of Rome. Aeneas's wide and muscular form was impressive, and he gazed at me with a patient understanding. I nodded at him and walked towards the line of heroes.

There stood Julius and right beside him was Augustus. They each had their swords raised, their dominating spirits set forward. And there, Alexander the Great, with tan skin and curly dark blonde hair, he grinned with his big olive eyes taking in the promise of battle and glory with glee and excitement. Next to him stood a straight-backed and stiff looking man with a trim curled beard that was a light brownish blonde. He had clear gray eyes like the winter sky. His face was worn but calm and he gazed ahead with a serenity possessed only by those who knew their own greatness. He turned away from the herd army and looked at me.

"I'm Hannibal Barca. There is no military mind as great as mine," he stated in a calm and even voice.

Alexander scoffed next to him. "I'd say the rest of us might argue our own case." He smiled at Hannibal who only let the corners of his lips slightly spread in response.

A man on the far side, several paces away from Hannibal, stood there with a billowing dark blood red cape. His shoulders were massive and spread wide, and his body cut inward at a steep angle that showed not the slightest bit of fat. He had brown-blond hair and a thick pointed beard. He wore a helm with a stiff horsehair plume. He had a hefty Hoplite shield painted a bloody red. A Spartan.

"Leonidas, great son of the Lion, of the line of Heracles, you don't want to welcome this new hero to join our ranks?" The man who spoke was another Roman, and I recognized that no-nonsense face. Trajan, the great expander of Rome. He spoke with mirth, yet his face remained stiff and watching the unmoving herd.

"He has much more to do yet," Leonidas grumbled, his voice heavy and rasping; he kept his eyes trained ahead the entire time, not breaking form or discipline in the slightest.

A man standing alone and off to the left with a five-pointed silver crown atop his fiery red hair turned to look at me. His eyes were a clear green and his face was aflame with a thick red beard.

He said, "My name is Brian Boru; I am a king who fought for my own and died doing so. My banner was solar, a sword bathed in the sun. We are of light. We fight for the right reasons and I am glad you and I are one." He lifted his hefty longsword and pointed at me, nodding and then turning back to face the darkness.

"This is what you must be, and what all who come from the sun must strive towards," Aeneas said.

I turned back to look at him. Two proud looking warriors now flanked him, one on each side like Varangians from my Constantinople. Like my blessed grandfather. They had that northern look, dressed in chainmail and horned helms as they were. They were certainly of Norse blood.

"Egill Skallagrímsson, warrior-poet," the shortest one said, stepping forward. His stout form was as wide as a chariot and his beard was pulled into a long knotted auburn tail. "I plunder what I see, my ship an axe to the sea. Water broken into land, my strong sword cuts words out from tearful enemies as they drown in my drag."

"I am Eric Bloodaxe," the other man said, grinning at the poet. "A King I am, and I raise this axe in hopes of quenching its scarlet thirst." He lifted a large black axe that was spiked at the top and double sided with a wicked rusty blade. I looked closer and realized it was not rust, but dried blood from who knew how many years of slaughter from successful raids.

And then a third man stepped out from behind Aeneas as if from the very golden air in this strange plane of existence—this realm of ancestral connectedness. He wore a plain bluish gray cassock with a tan chord around his large stomach. The man was mostly bald but for a stubborn sprout of gray hair atop his pale, round head. His beard draggled low and it was as gray and greasy as the hair that remained on his head. His face was fierce yet kind, the sort that demanded respect but gave affection and wisdom in return. His eyes were clear and hard like crystal and a soft sparked kindness in his irises invited me in.

"It is I, Snorri Sturluson. It's a shame Hesiod could not join you, but you are the one who holds the staff." He gestured at it, his youthful and vigorous voice surprising coming from his old and portly form. "A poet all poets owe patronage to, but could he combat the warrior spirit and wonderful songs of my Eddur? Iceland is my island, and my writings will always remain as they were written—in stone. But you have not read them, have you my eastern friend? Well, our nobility unites us! Our sovereign spirits sing with solar blood! Turn then, heed the herded hordes with the brilliance of your brothers. Destroy darkness!" He shouted with infectious glee; his arms spread as if he were a prophet.

I raised Lævateinn high as I turned. My uncovered skin shined pristine, a glowing gold mirroring the aura of the heavens. With my staff raised high, lightning cracked out from the firmament and crashed into me—an electric arm reaching down to press power into my being. That familiar ecstasy of eternity held me rigid as the blue light dissipated, leaving behind bulky, deep blue armor that covered my entire form.

I took my helmet off to see what it looked like, and it was a glorious sight to behold. Two white antlers jutted out from the forehead so large, that I felt as if I could rush right into the fray, goring through them all like a charging stag. The antlers glowed with veins of blue electricity that snaked through the surface. The helm itself was a solid blue, smooth and simple with eye slits and tiny holes for the mouth. A strange white-lit rune glowed softly and covered the entirety of the face. It held a circle in the middle; eight branching symbols carved it into eight equal sized pieces. The branches looked like pitchforks, three jutting crossbars just before their three-pronged, forked ends.

"The Helm of Awe," Snorri called out, his voice drowned with reverence. He slowly started to sing a poem.

"The Helm of Awe
I wore before the sons of men
In defense of my treasure;
Amongst all, I alone was strong,
I thought to myself,
For I found no power a match for my own."

He coughed as he let the words sink into silence. "It gives the worthwhile hero glorious might. But only one worthy of it can wear such a mark. What is your treasure?" he suddenly asked.

"My people," I answered.

"And who here is greatest?"

"I am." With no hesitation, I knew it as truth.

How could I not consider myself the greatest, no matter the company? To not consider oneself the greatest was to lose before ever beginning. It was not to lie, but to believe without false hope. A pure focus of power. It was a will that was always striving for more and rested not in pretense but in the always present ascent of the being that became greater in the now—in the always.

I looked around. Alexander the Great was smirking, no doubt he still considered himself the greatest man of all time. Augustus glared at me, clutching his sword tight and dragging it on the ground in repeated circles. Julius paid me no mind, still focused on the unmoving herd before us. Leonidas looked ready to fight it out right there to prove me false. Hannibal and Trajan like Julius, had their eyes focused ahead. Brian Boru smiled at me and shook his head. I looked back to Aeneas, who looked at me with a loving defiance, a silent support simultaneously disagreeing with what I'd spoken. Eric and Egil both chuckled.

Snorri nodded at me. "Place the helm back upon your head." He paused, waiting for me to do so.

As soon as I donned the helmet, my vision was reduced and focused through the slits.

"*Ægishjálm er ég ber milli brúna mér!*" Snorri shouted.

White light filled the inside of the helmet and shocked my sight into a bright daze, before it settled back to a glow and I could see clearly once again.

"This formula spoken has unlocked the power of the mighty rune. Your head is rimmed with a soft circle of white light, angelic and halo-like. The rune glows as the sun! You do not know it, but your eye slits are pools of blazing white light—beacons pushing back the dark."

I felt invincible in this worthy suit! My dark blue amour was colossal, a mass of crystalline mineral that jutted out like icicles of stone on each shoulder blade. The armor was covered in tendrils of blue electricity that pulsed with light in veiny paths, similar to my antlers. The energy of lightning was stored within my armor which served as a sort of engine for the power, my spirit the flint to set off the flame. A large white glowing sigil shined on the center of my breast plate. It was made up of a circle with eight straight lines shortly extending out from its center. There were tiny stars on the edge of each line, with the four corner lines hooking slightly like scythes.

"That is Þjófastafur, the stave to stop thieves. The rune is named for the degeneracy for which it stops: Thief. Fitting, for the thieves of darkness on the battlefield want to steal your glory, to make you as meaningless as they are."

With my soul dipped in a divine pool of heroism, I was aflame with lightning blood and thunder strength. I stepped towards the line and held my white staff up, its carved ivory swirling in patterns of black mist mingled with fire. The shadowy herd in the plain below at last moved, their black heads creaking up, an eerie sound of moaning wind drifting up from their soulless shadows. The moaning rose into a shriek and then a howl, and as their cries rushed through the air as a whipping wind, in the far distance a familiar form towered high, materializing from a black cloud of ash made bright by the shrieks of the silhouettes. Fenrir, giant and growling stood at the back of the shadowy forces, looming over the battlefield like a silver mountain. A roar from behind made me turn around myself.

Cerberus stood there as large as ever, yet his fur was no longer black, it glowed with a golden sheen and was pure white. His serpents were now silver and all their eyes, along with Cerberus's own, were gold. No longer a hound of death and darkness, but a hound of light. A hound of the sun. He reared back his three heads and spat out three white balls of fire that arced through the sky, loping high into the air before tumbling down from the heavens and into the shadows. Apparently not wanting to be beat, Alexander leapt into the herd, his sword a flame of silvery-white light as he cut through the howling creatures reaching at him. Cerberus's fireballs splashed into the field and explosions of flame cascaded over the shadows in rippling waves.

I shouted, my roar echoed by the rest of my brothers as we plunged into the darkness and carved our way through with weapons of brilliant light. My strange staff glowed with a pale light of foggy gray, and it wiped out the shadow warriors wherever I swung. I whirred it in my hands, spinning it in a circle as the strange light burned away my foes. They air was frigid on the field, and the strange shadows' touch was cold and painful. They screamed and cried, scraping at me with tendrils of black smoke that served as their arms. Standing as I was in the midst of them, a shallow sea of shadow, there was no avoiding their touch. Mercifully, my armor seemed to pain them as much as my staff did. They pressed against me, trying to overwhelm but they tremored back, squealing as several of them evaporated from rubbing against my runes.

The shadows around me shivered away, shaken by whatever my armor had done. I charged into them, lowering my horns like a ram. Lightning crackled through my antlers and wherever I swung my head, the shadows burned into a bright blue before exploding back into whatever nothingness they'd emerged from. Fully charging ahead, I unleashed all my energy in a reckless push forward and through, aiming my progress towards Fenrir who was striking down at someone, though I couldn't quite make out who. Balls of fire still rained down, Cerberus playing the part of artillery. My heroic brethren were sweeping through the shadow warriors with apparent ease. Both Caesars were deep in the center of the fray with their backs pressed against each other as no shadow could get through their sharp swords. Eric Bloodaxe was leaping about like a wild man, crushing the black mists as if they had skulls, uncaring if their shadows burned him with their freezing grip.

I charged once more ahead, spinning my staff and swinging my head back and forth, my eyesight blazing white and so clear that I felt as if I could see their attacks before they fell—the helm giving me a mystical foresight. I pushed through the shrouded foes with ease, but to my horror, as I spun back around to see the damage I'd done, it was as if I hadn't even made a dent. There were no holes in their ranks, and where the shadow men had been burned away, it seemed as if two had come to replace them. Julius and Augustus were no longer back to back, but separated and being overtaken fast. Alexander had vanished somewhere, lost in the darkness. The rest of the heroes were in dire straits. Hannibal had fallen, and he swung his sword trying to keep the shadows back. The great general had chosen the area of attack smartly, there were none behind him, but how could you defeat an enemy that came back twice as strong every time you dispatched one of them?

Bloodaxe no longer leapt, he limped and staggered, and with my divinized eyesight I could see his numerous wounds sizzling. Frostbitten and broken down, he was at his end, still hobbling towards the shadows, refusing to go on the defensive. Leonidas was off to the far corner of the battlefield, he'd managed to march through their ranks with his heavy hoplite shield glowing red, and his helm with its scarlet horsehair crest marked him out amongst the blackness. But his jabbing spear and blazing shield were beginning to give way to the sheer amount of shadows closing in on him. Egil was slicing with his sword in one hand and chopping away with his thick blunt axe in the other. His face was mad with joy, apparently unperturbed by the dire state of our attack. Brian Boru stood tall above the herd, swinging in every direction with his sword, but even I could see that he was hurting.

Cerberus had his heads lowered alongside Aeneas with Snorri as well. They were no doubt deliberating on what to do to end these replicating demons. I breathed slow and long, a sharp chilled air bringing me back to myself and in the present. The Helm of Awe had spread my sight and self out over the battlefield like an army of ants with antennas alert, all in a moment as if time had bowed to the majesty of my might. Now seeing there was no obvious way I could win amongst these grunts, I charged through them and headed for Fenrir. The dark wolf was being pestered by Alexander, which shouldn't have surprised me; I knew the great conqueror wouldn't be so easily taken. He'd been the first to charge in and he must have headed straight for Fenrir. As I neared, an exhausted Alexander rolled out of the way of the striking Fenrir's attack.

"Nothing harms him," he said, his breath thin and his chest heaving. He lowered to a knee and paused.

Fenrir stared down at the both of us and growled. I ignored the shadows behind me, I could only hope that my solar blood brothers would persist in keeping the darkness at bay. I stood there and waited. Fenrir had not attacked, he was back to staring at the staff I held, the same sense of fear in his eyes as before.

"This staff Lævateinn is like you, isn't it?" I shouted up at the wolf. "A darkness and light, forced together. You devoured Odin, you took Hesiod and Týr's hands—the power of the Allfather, an ancient poet, and a god of war absorbed into your essence. All those forces... light and darkness mingling together... paradox. Like you, that is what Lævateinn stands for." I held the staff out further. Fenrir stepped back, snarling. "You hid away this relic; a key to keeping the chaos of your world and the order of mine, in balance." I chuckled, holding up the staff and studying it closer, its fire twisting in helixes around the dark mists hovering throughout. "You want to bring the world fully into darkness, into your realm. But you did not think of the result of swallowing the sun, you didn't think that this light would persist. For where there is a little bit of light, there cannot be darkness. And where there is a little bit of dark, well... whatever exists around it, *exists*. You are an absence. A decay. A little bit of poison ruins any well. But what does a little bit of purity do to a pit of waste? These forces aren't meant to exist within one another. This dark mingled with light... but unlike you, I've taken my dark and transmuted it into a purer light, a light above mere existence. My purity comes from descending into the filth, and overcoming it by filling it with power. I've transcended while you remain unbalanced and unwell." I laughed, letting out a Dionysian joy as I danced in front of the scowling wolf, swinging Lævateinn like a baton.

"Do something, you madman! The shadow warriors will be the end of us all. Kill this wolf!" Alexander yelled.

I scowled at him, but a quick look back at the battlefield changed my mood. The shadow warriors had multiplied to the point of forming a completely connected black mist. There was no battling that now. I turned back to Fenrir and charged with the power of my runes and armor, leaping up and soaring high into the golden heavens. I threw and thrust my body with staff and antlers leading the way, straight at Fenrir's teeth. He snapped his jaws while whining in high pitched fear. My antlers struck his cheek and the staff shattered in half, breaking inside his mouth. He gagged as he swallowed half of it. I fell to the ground and landed with a booming thud that put my armor to the test. It held together, but my bones strained and my flesh ached. As I slowly stood to my feet, careful not to rush, I found that my body was bruised, but still intact. My antlers dangled in front of me, snapped in half and clinging their like broken twigs. I dropped what remained of Lævateinn and yanked off the ruined antlers, throwing them in a shattered heap.

Fenrir stood tall as ever, unfazed. He had his head tilted and his ears perked, but nothing happened. My bravado and his fear had apparently both proved pointless. Or so I thought. Suddenly, the great wolf of darkness howled so piercingly high that I staggered backwards and clutched at my helm. The agony and retching pain that carried Fenrir's soaring howl into the air was a wicked and awful sound. His body tremored and shook, distending and bloating, rippling as if of liquid, gas, and solid all at once, unable to settle on just one. His cries of agony became three-fold, the wind howling along with him and the sky thundering too. In a sudden burst, Fenrir's body exploded. A burst of pale green light followed his raining blood and guts. The army of shadow was gone, leaving us tired men of the sun to remain, wounded and confused. My brothers now rallied to my side, Aeneas along with Cerberus and Snorri at last entering the fray.

"Don't step closer!" Aeneas shouted, sprinting alongside Cerberus with Snorri bringing up the rear.

"We've figured out the purpose of this all. It was what we were discussing during this impossible battle that was set only to bring about this metamorphosis," Snorri said in a hurried, rasped burst of words.

The wearied warriors and heroes now all stood beside me. Nothing of Fenrir remained but some large diseased chunks of his carcass, with the rest spread out across the field in gory bits of flesh, rotten and foul.

"Before she comes, you must know what this place is," Aeneas said, his strong hand upon my shoulder. "This place is you. A manifestation of yourself. Not merely an inner battle, Fenrir was quite real...in a sense. I and all these great men are very real yet gone, as we've moved on into the great after. We also remain tethered to reality, because of blood. The blood of the Hyperborean Hero, the solar spirit that transcends mere biology and mortality. We all..." He let go of my shoulder and spread out both his arms as if to hug the lot of us. "We all are one in our purpose: to destroy any darkness that blots out our glory, both within and without. Our purpose is to ascend to the sun, its rays pathways that only we can walk. We are power. That is our purpose. Be a tyrant of your soul, Rangabes. Break your weakness into submission, tyrannize it for that is the only way to walk the path of the sun. A burning must always be within, that painful fire of fulfilment that comes only from the worthy suffering of the infinite becoming. Always pursue glory. We are all one in this path."

They bowed their heads and my heart sped up as I doubted my reality. "Is this real? A dream? A hallucination?"

Cerberus, glowing in ethereal light peered down at me and said, "It is real. All of us, me as the hound of light and Fenrir, the wolf of dark... we exist inside you in a way. And this battle is what the Lævateinn forces the wielder to wage. It drives most mad, or darkens some into absolute evil or others into lethargic light. A transforming light transmutes darkness, as you said. That is why this staff was locked away. That is why Fenrir fears it so. And perhaps others do as well."

"So, none of you are your actual selves from eternity? From myth and reality?" I asked, removing my helm and looking them all in the face.

Aeneas smiled at me and said, "These selves you are looking at, these mirrors of greatness, both light and even dark—this source of power and being is yours, and it shows your connection to both aspects. We are related in that sense, but most do not get to fight such an inner battle with such clarity and reality. Most let their unconscious mind suppress it or internalize into a weaker form. So, in spirit, we that still stand give you our strength. We watch over you from outside of time, just as we all do here inside your own eternity. Though Cerberus is a living friend among you still, his soul radiates and reflects a man as only a hound can do. You need each other, do not let his darkness win, open his eyes to this reality." He pointed at the shining Cerberus at his side. Aeneas then looked at me closer and his face flattened. "This will hurt, but we mean to give you our combined light. Remove your amour."

I quickly shed the armor and stood naked before their great power and I opened my arms wide.

"Look down where the staff has split and the shattered antlers rest," Aeneas said.

I did so, lowering my arms and kneeling. The white antlers, still pulsing with blue light, had grafted themselves into the staff and formed into an axe. It was now a double-bladed axe, pure white in its power, and the darkness that once coursed through the staff was no more, only red fire remained in its immaculate twisting helixes. I grasped the axe and heaved it high. I closed my eyes and thought of those once again that came before me, and those that would come after, and how I and they all related to the sun. My kin. My people of light. I opened my eyes and a swirling vortex of burning golden light roared above in the heavens. A pillar of white golden light shined down in a perfect beam that enveloped my raised axe, and then the light vanished in a blink and my axe of the sun remained.

Its hilt was now an orange-red with yellow swirls carved into it like a sea of flames. Whatever material it was made of, it was impossible to say. It was not heavy and it felt cool to touch. If fire could be made into a solid, this is what I imagined it would look like. The double-sided blade that had come from my broken antlers was now pure gold, each side of it sharper than even Fenrir's terrible fangs. The double blades glinted and gleamed, their bright gold hue like the sun itself, and the fiery hilt of the axe looked like a ray of sunlight extending down.

"You've made it pure," Aeneas said as he bowed his head.

All the great heroes around me shimmered into bright and golden silhouettes. They all stepped into me, their warmth and power making me whole. A peaceful power, one that felt as if it had always been and always would be, as long as I kept my gaze fixed on its truth. Smiling and now alone, I looked affectionately at my new axe.

"No longer Lævateinn, I'm calling you Solisinanis. You've transformed all to sublimity." I nodded, and turned to the gore Fenrir had left behind.

A *she* still had to come. And then what? The metamorphosis, the monster after. Regardless, I was ready. And sure enough, there in the carnage, a woman of pure glory and beauty stood. Wyrd. Her dress flowed in ripples along with her perfect hair, the olive tone subdued in the light of her yellow mane. Those blue eyes melted with understanding, warm and willing to listen and love. She stepped out of the filth and glided towards me, her dress swooshing over the ground and peeling back to reveal slender, pale feet. I breathed in her scent of day, the fresh clarity of a misty morning heavy with a cleansing dew.

"Rangabes, my child. You move with a might befitting of my son, and fitting of a story that needs to be told." She drifted up to me and placed her soft hands on my cheeks. "Aeneas is at home with me and our Lord. So many people have misunderstood the truth of me. It is why my name is now what it is. Like the Blessed Mother, I birthed a powerful man. Not Lord, but a servant of Him. I am her handmaiden now and I come to you at her charge."

"Venus?" I mumbled.

She drew back her silky hands and frowned. "I was called that once. Aphrodite before. Some said Persephone was my darkened reflection, my Chthonic Sun. You smell of Dionysus." She laughed and swirled backwards. "Do you see us in the mirror? Do you see *what* we mirror?" She leaned forward to stare at me with a sudden and shocking solemnity.

"I do," I whispered.

"All night long, all day, the doors of Hades stand open. But to retrace the path, to come up to the sweet air of heaven, that is labor indeed," she chanted.

"Virgil," I said.

"The iron race has ceased and is ceasing. The golden will arise over all the world." She smiled at me. "A holy poet who spoke as a prophet. He saw much truth in me and my son. This truth has now found you." Her eyes moistened, immersed in holy tears that softened her blue irises into spotless skies.

"I believe—help my unbelief." I reached out a finger and caught her tear.

"I will, for He wills." She took my hand. "Come, you must see what is promised."

Still holding my axe, I held her hand as we were covered in white light. It warmed me and a chorus of voices sang out, ripples of pure music stirring my spirit while Wyrd's grip tightened. The song rose up, the voices flying away as the light removed itself in a whir of gold. We now stood atop a mountain of gray stone with white snow dotting the pine tree landscape below.

"We stand on the highest point of the mainland of your promised home." Wyrd stood beside me, beckoning her graceful arm at the wide expanse below. The sky glowed red as the sun awakened for a new day.

"My promised home," I repeated, the cold wind slapping at my naked flesh. I was numb to its touch; the glory of this land was the only cover I needed.

Jagged gray mountains rose up from the earth like massive rows of fangs. Snow dotted their towering brilliance with a gleaming white. It was as if we were standing in the mouth of a giant serpent whose entire jaw had detached and fallen, its ruin the majesty of might. The landscape far over the mountain-tops was rolling, more peaks and valleys beyond, blue mingled with the red of the rising sun, setting the watery visage aflame in purple.

"We stand in the west of your promised land, it is for you to spread out towards, to strive for once the east becomes your own. But this you must know and tell your future kin: your home is not meant to cease at the end of this land. I speak now of a manifest destiny of glorious overcoming, thriving and subduing. But can what be made manifest ever cease its manifestation, if it truly be your destiny? Like the always increasing tower of glory, to top it off, to cease its ascension is to topple it down. There is no stagnation, only building or tearing down. The powerful, the mythic heroic might of the new gods, the mortals who move with eyes and body aimed at eternity, that is what this destiny requires. If for a moment you tire and accept what already is, or what someone else has already done, that is the moment the tower collapses, for it cannot be held up only by those who built it in the first place. It must continue to be upheld by every age, and this continuing is done through pursuit. Look up at the sky when out of land; the stars await your manifestation of power and glory. Always ascend."

I nodded my head, eager myself to leap off this peak and wrestle the land into submission. "When will this be mine? How will it be done?"

"It is not a when or how, but a what and a why. The what and why are both love—but what kind of love? A love that is required. A love that carries a shall, nested in its essence. For if love has the potential to change, then it is not the shall saying love, the love based in eternity. The eternal love that is built with the shall as a foundation, is a love that transcends and carries with it, everlasting greatness. That love is free, and truly the only kind of love that is free. So, you must love this homeland that will be yours, but it must be built with the shall. No matter how far you spread, no matter how much you succeed, others will come after you—teach them not to let the tower collapse, to maintain and repair, and build. Build! Even if the land is aflame with weakness and decay, this love must never falter. Only those who understand such a truth can claim that they are of your glorious stock."

"And now I will begin my taming of this land." I nodded to myself, scanning the landscape and strategizing how I might make it my own.

"There is still more that must be finished in the land of myth. Once you finish in the land of the Norse, the Celtic land must be mastered. There lies Grian Dorcha, the terrible black castle stolen from the Otherworld and erected by Sulis in her jealous fear. Another thrust back into darkness remains. Circles to be closed. Then, with the sun not at your back nor merely above you, but burning within, your deeds its glorious rays—only then must you come. The land can only be properly tamed if bathed in the light of Hyperborea. You will be ready once you have gone to Hyperborea and taken her light. She is yours and will give you many children."

"Thank you," I said, turning from the view. Wyrd held her hand up and I kissed it.

She smiled at me, only to frown as her crystal eyes squinted. "Always listen to my song, even when it sounds strange and harsh. I sing for you and your kind. I tell you this now, something foul awaits your return. This was the metamorphosis my son warned you of. Use your Solisinanis and put an end to the nightmare. You now truly know what is at stake. This land is not meant to die without your noble flock pasturing in its glory."

Wyrd stretched her hand out again and I grabbed it eagerly. And in a blaze of white heat, our light hurled forward and tore through the sky, puncturing into the gold canopy of my ancestral plane and landing in a boom before the remains of Fenrir. I gripped my axe and stood there alone, for Wyrd had vanished.

In the shadowy remains, a figure stood; a beast misshapen and foul, double my size. It stood there with a hunched back, its body gnarled and malformed. It was grotesque and twisted like a spindly, fungi-covered rotten branch of a dead tree. Its skin was brown and spotted with pale warts, purple splotches and white boils, some of which were leaking a slimy, putrid, pale puss.

The monster's lower body was covered in thick, matted fur that was missing in pink splotches down its legs. The legs were bent and ended with black hooves. Its arms were a muddy brown, thin and curled like withered plants, and two corroded iron shackles were clamped tightly around its tiny wrists. Even stranger, there were thick chains of rusted iron wrapped around its belly, pressed so deep into the flesh as to have become almost a part of its body, sunken in as it was with the skin rubbed raw.

Its strange head stared at me crooked, blinking empty black eyes like a dumb cow. It had a long, pointed beak, pale and speckled with red lesions, and it hooked far out and downward. It had no ears but oddly enough had what looked like gills with three flaps where ears should have been. To top it all off, two red horns that were tiny points of gnarled red poked out from its mottled gray scalp. It stood there labored and limp, panting hoarsely as it stared at me with emptiness.

I gripped my axe tighter all the same. "Who are you?" I said.

Its head slowly tilted and its eyes blinked at me. "Finnihil," it wheezed, its voice a harsh release of dust deadened air.

"And why are you..." I trailed off.

What was I to say, why are you...you? It was a tortured and sad beast, so accustomed to its strange and unfortunate lot that it seemed to be numb to its suffering decay.

"Have you forgotten where we are?" Finnihil said through heavy breaths, its beak hinging open so slow that the words barely formed and found their way out.

I frowned and glared angrily at the beast. Was this monstrosity a part of me? Fenrir had been as a darkness capable of tearing my soul into a sad existence of fleshly unbecoming; he was a darkness that dwelt within and that I could fall prey to... but there was a power in it at the very least. Finnihil was a tortured corpse of weakness. This did not belong in my soul.

"You are no part of me," I snapped.

"I am you when you take off your mask, beneath your mask that is beneath the lowest mask and hung and hidden in a cupboard burned in a forgotten fire. I am the hollow you that you fill with the soil of a sordid soul. I am the grave, the tomb, and the body buried deep. I am the self that refuses to relate itself to itself, looking not at the mirror but only through its broken shards of clouded glass. You cannot dress up a corpse and expect it to be a real man."

"You are a lying fiend. A stranger here in this realm of greatness." I was snarling and I didn't care. I stepped closer and raised my axe, daring Finnihil to speak another lie in its weak and unworthy wheeze.

"Like a legged fish without land, I swim through ashen light, heavy with unworth. I'm the stranger that is so strange to your built-up façade, that my strangeness is a testament to my truth. I am you, Rangabes, without the lies, the masks, or the esteem."

I stopped my predatory stride and stood straight, smiling at the pathetic creature. "No, no. I will not attack what is unworthy of acknowledgement. You are nothing but a black hole of nothingness, a void of potential where virtue, meaning, purpose and power go to die. You are the promise of comfort and weakness. But I act, become and ascend; my being perfected in the infinite light that I strive towards, for the striving towards is the only way to already possess it." I laughed, happily realizing the thought and answer as I spoke it. "You cannot stop the moment from occurring, from always occurring. I spiral up, my circles tight and equal. My equilibrium is met with a return that only doubles in reward, and then more goals and greatness forever follow as it repeats. What you are, is what all are if they do not participate in eternity and purity. You are the power that is so self-absorbed, that the self is annulled and nothing remains but a black, meaningless non-existence. You are the finite incarnate."

Finnihil scowled, a wicked and angry fire alight in its black hole eyes. "Then how is it that I am here beside you?"

"You are not inside me though. You are a false promise, the shadow to the back of my eternal pursuit. You can only become me if I stop. I will not, and am not ever going to stop. I'm not stopping. You are unbecoming."

"Do you deny me?"

"No, no. But you are a mere shadow. To pretend you are not there is to ignore the light before me by pretending there is no back. So, you will submit to my light and watch my back. Your corruption, your empty potentiality is mine to conquer. The shadow must bow to the light of clarity. I do not deny you but I do not intend to let you run free, nor be destroyed. A shadow is needed, for how else can one know they are heading towards light?"

"I do not need you," Finnihil spat back, the wheeze suddenly filled with air and life.

"What are you to me? Are you a fear of weakness, a fear of decay? My fear of the nothingness, my fear of meaninglessness? You are my fears made flesh. The fear of the finite."

"And what if all those are true?"

"Your life is mine. I see that. I accept your weakness as my own. I cannot pretend that weakness and nothingness are no temptation. You, beast of unworth, you are me. Come, I accept your wicked sclerosis and add you to my own movement upward. A shadow at my back, pushing me forward and reminding me of the outcomes of decay, neglect and unmoving."

Finnihil writhed and screamed at my acceptance speech, and with its head back, spine arched, and its crooked arms spread straight, its diseased corpse collapsed on itself and whirled into the form a black tornado that stretched up and tore through the gold firmament above. I held up Solisinanis and it burned with a powerful orange-white glow. My marks surged along with the axe, and I poured my red and blue light into the powerful weapon and held it up. A shattering crack of spiderwebbed light leapt out from Solisinanis; threads of red, white and blue coursed into the black tornado and spun it with fire, lighting it aflame.

The tornado wobbled unsteadily like a spinning top. I held my axe higher, the light still surging into the murky black. I drew inward and pulled the tornado's shadow to me as it collapsed on itself. The black mass spilled into me and I accepted its power. As I drank the bitter cup of black, the sky cleared and all on my ancestral plane fell silent, shining and perfect as it was meant to be. Then the landscape shimmered and in a burst of cold white, I jumped out of the dark and back into Jötunheimr once again. The chest popped open and I sprang free. It was the chest that had held me locked inside. And now, I was ready to finish this with my newfound axe, blazing like the sun.

Hesiod was flat on the ground; my emergence apparently had knocked him backwards. Past him, Fenrir was gone and Cerberus stood tall, watching me with a quixotic glint in his eyes. This was the real Cerberus, black as sin and with eyes red as fire. I wondered if such a change of color was possible and whether or not the spirit of the Cerberus within me might unify his with mine. We were cut from the same cloth of fiery light.

"What happened?" I said.

"You fell into the chest and it latched itself closed behind you. I couldn't make it budge and Fenrir still cowered, even with you shut away. And then a change went over him, his eyes went dark and he faded into the air. I feared that he'd followed you into that realm in some way."

I rubbed the back of my head and wondered if the Fenrir I'd defeated had not merely been a part of my psyche but the real dark wolf, feeding off of the darkness that was my Finnihil, who in turn gave him that army of infinite shadow. Questions perhaps best left unanswered.

"He's defeated now. And what of Skade?" I glanced around, looking for my armor. I spotted its red glow off to the right. "Come, let us clothe ourselves and finish this cleansing of the land."

Cerberus suddenly barked, his three heads howling in unison. His noses twitched and his snakes writhed. "I sense it... I feel it. Yes. She's gone. Perhaps she's returned to her natural form, standing high as snow peaks and strong buttressed mountains. Perhaps she has fallen into the nothingness she longed for. The light, or what is left of it bleeds back into the realm. She is no longer as she was. Your axe, your transfigured staff seems to have broken her hold... for better or worse."

"How can you tell?" I asked as I finished strapping on my armor.

"A change in the air. A sense of cleanliness that I can only just catch a whiff of, the slightest smell of unpolluted life, a freshness drifting in."

"You got all that from smell?" Hesiod asked with a grin, King Arthur's mantle adorning his shoulders once more. His chest bloomed red, and the ember lit robe covered his body. He bent down to put back on the cloudlike shoes before chuckling up at Cerberus. "Be honest, Apollo told you, didn't he?"

A strange yelp purred out from Cerberus that I guess was his way of laughing. I laughed as much at Hesiod's mirthful doubt as I did at Cerberus's strangled guffaw.

"I caught the scent of light when Apollo raided the dark gates of Hades with his sumptuous, melodramatic glow." Cerberus laughed louder which broke me and Hesiod in half as we bent over laughing along with his yelping. Cerberus managed to grab hold of himself and he waited all straight and dignified for Hesiod and I to stand up straight again, doubled over as we were. "But once his overbearing scent and light lift you free, you get a distaste for what is foul. My scent is already attuned to senses and powers you cannot begin to understand, but now that I've tasted the light..." Cerberus paused his stream of thought and grew gravely serious. I thought I might have seen a light mist in his eyes but with his height, it was hard to tell. "I want to be as Apollo shines. The light beckons me forth and I will walk in its power along your side, Rangabes."

I put my fist to my heart and bowed my head. I hoped Skade had found her nothingness. I could only hope that much of what she had said about Apollo and my quest was untrue. At the very least, my two companions here were worthy of my trust and we would see this through the end. Wherever we had to go, I knew we were worthy to walk in the light. No matter the darkness, we had each other to shine forth.

Book 4

Endless Circle

The black stone lifelessly towered there amidst the vibrant landscape of lively green. I stared at Apollo's toned and golden back. He'd returned to us right after Cerberus had declared the realm freed from the darkness. He'd taken us here in a cloud of light, as according to him, grave matters had fallen and caused much to shift. Valhalla had to wait. But it was a movement, however strange, and I was grateful for it. The land of the Celtic people, the land once again of the living. It was bizarre—I breathed with lungs and drank the fresh worldly air of earth yet I felt as though I were still tethered to the land of the dead, or at the very least, the land of fading myth.

"Apollo, why is it that I do not feel... alive?" I asked.

"You still are not in part. The netherworlds of the great myths had to be overcome by your might before you were supposed to set foot on earth. But these realms are bleeding, like Jötunheimr before, and this is not earth as you know it. It is a festered wound. It should not be. Yet duty calls and chaos reigns. You walk here only by my light."

"How much further must I march underneath your glaring sun?" I said, angry at what I knew was likely the truth.

"What underworld remains? Egyptian, Greek, Norse, what more?" Hesiod said, throwing his hands up.

"You did not pass through the Norse underworld. You merely walked in the land of a dying breed's darkening kingdom." Cerberus spoke with detachment.

Unemotional and seemingly uninterested, he simply spoke the truth.

Apollo kept walking and without looking back, said, "If you must know, Hel is all that remains, conflated sickeningly with mighty Valhalla. The Celtic Otherworld has bled into Hel and a strange tear is ripping both realms to shreds. Great Valhalla has been thrown into the darkness and surrounded by a black, boiling river of warm blood. There is where you will finish your task as a dead man, and there you will at last free yourself from the chains of the void. But we must take care of this nightmare here, in this sad seepage of Celtic glory. The Celtic people are not so far removed from their Hyperborean ancestors. Rangabes, these people are needed for your promised land, I assure you. Even in this half-whole land, walk on this ground with holy reverence as you must not profane what is sacred and pure. This battle is one in which purity will be attained, and the glory of the infinite lit aflame. Follow the fire and its spark might set you aglow with the power of resurrection."

"And what can we expect here?" I said.

"The renegade goddess Sulis played me for a fool. If I had foreseen her treachery, she would have been thrown to Fenrir as dog food too. But she acted the part; she agreed to bow to our coming reign, but then as she saw you gaining power, she resisted and this castle—and our being here—is the result."

"Why do you need us? Or why do we need you? She is one goddess, nothing I haven't bested yet. One goddess of light is not even a flicker to me," I scoffed.

"She has her armies of corruption. But worse, she has those powerful Celtic gods of light. The Hyperborean spirit might be blotted out here for eternity—yours with it—if we do not finish her and save the dying light of this land from the darkness that is the absence of good, the absence of the true one and only good, that being power." Apollo stopped walking and shouted at the great black stones of the castle, "Sulis, your sun has set as the true one has risen. Come out and face us!" His voice echoed, clattering around the stones before bleeding out into a dead silence.

"Nothing," I murmured.

"Everything is wrong about this place. Apollo, we would be wise to watch where we walk. A wrong step and I fear we might end up as Lugh." Cerberus pawed at the ground, his noses twitching nervously.

"Lugh?" Hesiod said. "What has she done to him? He's the true solar god in these parts." He looked over at me.

"The Celtic sun has been blotted red with blood. Its rays severed from the source, now Sulis sits in her inverted throne with Lugh set in the land of the dead. He, Arawn and the Morrígan are drowned in the black blood of swine. She has her Gwydion setting tricks and traps all about us. Cerberus is right, a wrong step might be enough even to end my own reign of light." Apollo tensed, his ankles flexing, his golden calves in silver sandals delicate and divine. The god of wisdom looked as if he had no answer to this disaster.

"Onward, let us ascend this castle." I strode forward to lead the way, ignoring the worried grunts and gasps behind me.

The field before us was an empty green with mounds and hills surrounding it, all leading to the giant black carapace of a fortress that protruded out on the horizon. And there in that sword-like tower, I knew that this unworthy sun queen was waiting. So, she feared me? Good. She should. I was tiring of being the gods' plaything. I wanted my people, I wanted to carry forth my own glory and live for that, for in that glory my people rested. But they could not awake until I myself awoke from this death thrall journey. And Apollo's light upholding me... the thought made me sick. I was not one to take kindly to relying on the strength of another if it had puppet strings attached—chains to an artificial becoming. I was my own jailer, and the only prisoner was my weakness which I always tyrannized into submission, making it bow at the feet of power and suffering to transfigure it into an ineffable glory. That was how I lived and died, and it was how I would continue.

I still did not trust Apollo. I wasn't entirely sure I couldn't head towards my promised land as I was now. Wyrd's words were what kept me straight. She'd told me where I needed to head, and her fate was one worth heeding. But still, who was to say Apollo wasn't just using me to defeat his enemies, and that this quest of mine was really an excuse for him to run free and unchallenged amidst the diminished mythological realms of divinity? I stormed forward, angry at my suspicion and even angrier at the lack of clarity and truth. I almost welcomed Sulis and her trickster god friend to intervene, at least that would provide some form of action, an answer in itself.

Alas, no action came and I sadly made my way alone and hurried up to the black stone of the wall. Ignoring shouts from Hesiod behind to slow down and wait, I rushed forward, preparing to launch myself over the wall and up towards the roof so I'd have a closer look and easier time ascending the tower. I stopped and leaned forward, staring at the craggy onyx stone blocking my path.

He is false and so are we.

The words cooed out from the stone. I shivered. They burned. They froze. I knew this pain. A corruption. A temptation. A desire. Who had planted it here?

He is false and so are we.
You are blind and cannot see.
Apollo wants and does not get.
This trap of his is always set.
So many lies, so many proofs.
There is deceit in finite truth.

My hand ached and I stretched it out, longing to touch the singing stones. I placing my hand against the wall and gasped as icy air filled my body. My blood slowed and the light and my surroundings vanished. More black. Again. Again. Again. Standing in the black expanse, I fell as if my feet suddenly realized there was nothing there holding them up. I tumbled down. Tattered and translucent souls pushed past my face, cobwebs of unworthy existence. It was odd that the longer I fell, the more at peace I felt. The expanse of nothing, the massage of death, and my endless descent soothed me. Falling without any sense of direction, it became more like a relaxed floating in cool nothingness. My eyes weighed heavy and threatened to fold closed, shutting off my faculties in this strange void.

And as my eyes fell dimmer and dimmer, a pale blue light hung off in the distance below... or above. I squinted at the light, and my sudden attention shot my body towards it and a blue glow enveloped me as I tumbled out of the dark void and into an entirely different land. I swallowed, realizing where I was. Hel seeped into the Celtic Otherworld with glorious Valhalla blasphemed and torn apart, right there in the center. Surrounding me was a black river of blood that bubbled and reeked of rot and burning flesh. Past the river, the light of this strange land was non-existent. Above and on all the outer sides was that same void I'd been falling through. Fortunate was I, to find a way out of it, or so I hoped. The stones had sang of Apollo's trap. But why trust them? Why trust anyone? Not here. Not now. Hesiod was the only one. Maybe Cerberus, but I knew him not well enough.

Whoever planned this, whether Gwydion or Apollo, I knew what drove me forward was my own will. The pure will aimed true, always. Surrendering to the torrent of time and letting it rush you into greatness was how to taste its delicious decay without succumbing to the dusty ashes of its banks, beached into obscurity. One couldn't forget oneself either in this surrender as then the temptation to sink into time's depthless waters and not work through and with its ceaseless surge, would end in nothingness. To let oneself go into the eternal, that was the powerless power that all great men drew deep from. The well of pure will. The well of true singlemindedness. The mind set on the blazing sun. Time's river forever surges into the sun's fire, water shining forth as rays. The sun the beginning and the end.

I rolled both my shoulders and stretched my arms. I dusted the ash from the ground off my pants. The ground was made up of gray soot that smelled similar to that sulfurous nightmare, Tartarus. Within the limits of this enclosed space, a hulking and elegantly carved wooden building like an upside-down ship stretched for what looked like a mile. No doubt this was the cursed Valhalla, or at least a portion of it. Around the building there were four circles of stone, all equidistant from each other and the center.

I walked straight towards the hall. As I neared, sounds both merry and vigorous, like a whip urging on a horse already in the lead, echoed through the hollow wood. Large interlocked doors barred my way, covered with gilded carvings of prancing white stags that shimmered with a magical, ghostly glow, alight with life. I lifted the latch and thrust my way inside. While the outside had been impressive simply by scope, the inside was twice as magnificent. Like the inside of a whale, the wood crisscrossed above like that of a monstrous spine.

And the men inside these halls—the men! Heroes abound from all ages and kind; men who'd died heroic deaths and lived heroic lives. Some were in armor as magical as mine—shimmering white here, silver there, gold elsewhere, and every shade in between. There were other men in various states of undress, some wearing nothing at all. There was rusted armor, bloody armor, some of leather, some of rags. Regardless, each man I could see had the gleam of glory exuding out from his spirit. If only I could spend time here in fellowship! The tables ran along the hall the whole mile, men filling every seat with good cheer and drink. They lifted their mugs at my arrival, their greeting rising with the merry music already resounding inside. To partake in the pleasures of the flesh again! How I missed feasting with friends. But my body remained tethered to this fate, and Wyrd's song was the only one that seemed worth dancing to. How else could I truly live again? But the sumptuous and sweet scent of succulent food made my mouth water all the same.

"Rangabes has arrived!" a familiar voice yelled. "I'd hoped you might have somehow persisted. How fares our great city?"

I gaped at the humble emperor. Even in this glorious hall, even as the last emperor of Constantinople, Constantine XI Palaeologus still remained clothed in the same plain banded armor worn over the white robes of the penitent. A holy man who had given his all to his people, fighting amongst them, praying amongst them, living amongst them, and dying with and for them. I stumbled forward. Constantine's jaw was as square and strong as ever. His crystalline eyes were pools of mercy. His brown hair of medium length framed his manly stature with regal strength.

"They breached our walls. Our unbreachable walls. I was overcome," I said with my voice cracking.

"We were holding them at bay where I stood. Truly, us mere hundreds at our stretch of the wall slaughtering thousands of their men. God was on our side. But Satan struck and the worst of misfortunes befell us. Someone—we'll never know who—left the gate open. They stormed it, pushing through the outer walls like rats through sewage." He shook his head, his fist clenched at the irresponsible fool who'd cost us so dearly. "Yet even still, we held them back at the inner walls. Great Giovanni Giustiniani Longo, the fearless man from Genoa, marched along the walls like a god, St. Michael holding him aloft. But then, Satan's luck came again and Giovanni was struck in the head by cannon fire. The man somehow survived, but in his stupor—his wound causing him fear when nothing else had—he called for aid and a singular retreat. Only for him, not the others!" He shook his head and sighed. "But his men panicked and abandoned us once they pulled him away... and our wall fell. If he had somehow stayed or his men hadn't fled their post, we might have held. I truly think it might have been prolonged. The Sultan's men were losing their lives and fervor the longer we endured." He sighed deeper and rubbed his chin. "I stood with my men, cutting the heathens down as they stormed through—but alas, I was overrun." Tears brimmed in his eyes and he breathed deeply. No doubt he'd often thought about the loss of our people and the evils that occurred afterward.

I embraced him and wept. We wept for our glorious home forever lost; our women and children manhandled, dishonored and profaned by those foul heathens raping in the name of their demonic god. The hall grew respectfully quiet as voices lowered to murmurs. The heroes and warriors in these halls knew what it was to sacrifice themselves for their people.

I grabbed Constantine by his shoulders and stared into his clear eyes. "You must know, I've been given the holy task of carrying our spirit into new lands. This light that unites us will shine again. We will carry the spirit of Rome—East and West. United. United. Yes, we won't leave either side to die alone. I promise."

He nodded at me. "Go then, Rangabes. Both of us were kept from Heaven for reasons unique to our paths. Once you cleanse this cursed realm, and these hallowed grounds return to where they belong, I will sleep. When I awake, as it is prophesied, it will be to return triumphant to my city and reconquer it. However far off that might be, however long I slumber, it will be mere moments, for I live and die for that holy place. But you, you carry not merely a place within you, but a people and—even greater—a spirit. Go forth on your noble task and free me from this place, as jolly and glorious as it is, it is not for me."

"I will, my dear emperor." I released his shoulders, crossed my arms to my chest, and bowed my head.

"And Rangabes, if you come across Giovanni somehow in your travels, I ask that you forgive him. He sacrificed much for a land that was not his. He did not need to come to our aid. His retreat was more from his own men's fear than his coherent command. He should be remembered a hero, but I fear he's been forgotten and maligned as a coward. I pray you come across his troubled soul."

"If I see him." I nodded.

Constantine gestured at the heroes behind him. "Another king wishes to speak to you," he said, returning to his seat.

And there, further down along the table, a man of powerful stature sat, his spread of food and drink more glorious than any other I could see. In front of him was a large golden goblet filled with scarlet wine, a roast duck and pheasant on a plate of silver, and an assortment of all kinds of other meat along with plums and chocolates. I licked my lips and forced myself to look away and at the man. He stood up and smiled at me. He was tall with a commanding posture and broad shoulders. His hair went down to his neck and it was a gentle golden-brown color. He wore a three-pronged crown of gold, each point encrusted with a different gem—one emerald, the other ruby, and the last a diamond. His eyes were green and intense like my own. His nose was straight and strong, and his jaw was blunt as a hammer. His face was hard and sharp, and his scythe-like cheekbones only added to the severity of his appearance. His garb was fitting for a king; a gold and green collar encrusted with more emeralds covered his thick neck. He had a violet mantle over his shoulders that draped him in waves of velvet finery. He wore a rich blue shirt that hung low over his burgundy trousers. Three golden crowns glittered on his chest, made from what looked like golden serpent scales. This was the kind of man that made people bow without saying a word. A man that mortals wanted to worship. I stared at him in awe, anxious to know who he was and what he wanted.

"I am King Arthur," he said.

The uncertainty twisting the folds of my face collapsed like a sink hole. "My friend has your mantle," I murmured.

"It was I who gave it to him. I could hear his glory from this place and I sent it forth. This bleeding effect allows for such strange connection, but it must be resolved. Many of us do not belong to this realm. The realms, they all bleed into one now. Only when there is one to stop the bleeding by drinking it as his own, only then can we all return to our rightful places. We need you here, brother. We are all worthy folk, but our spirits are hemorrhaged in this wound," he said with deliberate annunciation, sounding like someone who was used to having a person record his every word.

"What must I do to heal this wound?" I said, nodding and crossing my arms.

"At each circle of stone, there lies a challenge. This bleeding realm requires a show of prowess and victory. You must compete in the Ichor Games—like the great games Aeneas held while honoring his father's funeral. Only, the Ichor Games are an inversion. It is what happens when what belongs to the light is twisted in the dark, when degeneracy is propped up and honor is maligned. These games, these four events in each circle must be won. And then the dark lord who is the cause of this abomination will come and challenge you himself."

"Fine. But who is this lord?"

"I cannot say, for I do not know. It is something you must seek out alone."

"So be it." I nodded at the legendary king and headed out the gilded doors without a look back at the heroes behind me. They had their place and I had mine.

The closest circle of stone was not much to look at. I walked over to it eagerly, its smooth black rocks mere rounded spheres that circled out from the center in a spiral pattern of black, each boulder increasing in size as it got further away. There were four paths of stone spiraling out from the center, and at the edge of the paths was a thin line of smaller boulders making a circular rim that contained the spiral inside. I didn't see how some sort of challenge could be held in such a small space—one I could cross in perhaps twenty paces. Seeing no indicator of what I should do, I simply stepped into the circle and as soon as I did, my sight flashed gray and I stood in an entirely new place.

"The Impalement Game," a sultry, feminine voice cooed out from somewhere deep in the wooded area.

A fog drenched forest surrounded me. I took a step forward, trying to breathe through my mouth as this place stank of death and decay. Like spoiled meat in the hot sun, this was a place of rot worse even than the chthonic realms I'd left behind. I looked closer at what I'd assumed were dead, branchless trees—the haze made everything appear uncertain and mirage-like. I gasped as I realized what the trees actually were. They were stakes with writhing bodies impaled on them, their still living forms twitching like crushed cockroaches. My cleared sight seemed to unlock the silence of the surroundings, and sounds of suffering crashed over me. Groans reverberated, a haunting melody blowing about like a wind of plague and death.

I walked up to one of the stakes and looked closer at the man there. His body was swollen and bloated, his purpled skin pierced from his rectum and up through his skull. Yet his hands each held black plums. He clung to the strange fruit as it seeped a liquid just as dark and thick as his clotted blood. The man's eyes were battered but he blinked at me, his blue mouth wheezing and coughing.

He groaned, "You've heard of those who throw the javelin, you've seen those who throw it far. But here, instead of competing to see who can throw the javelin the greatest distance, one competes to see how far the javelin can throe you. Birth and death."

"I will not do what the rest of you have done, piercing myself with the hope that my selfish pain might win this challenge." I shook my head and squinted at the dying man. "No, for you and all those here do it for yourself, not for all nor for the many. There is another way, and I will find it. It is somewhere here in this forest of decay."

"You must find Miseria. You must eat her fruit." He extended his hands holding the sopping plums, but I ignored him and headed straight for the heart of this decrepit wasteland of wood.

Voices called out to me from their places of impalement. A chorus of woe and weeping, their gnashing of teeth deaf to my forward focused ears. So, I needed to find Miseria? There had to be more here than just these barely living kebabs. An Olympic Game, inverted. So, the javelin pierced the man in his own throes? How was one to win a game turned on itself? By not playing it. By forcing the hand of the gamekeeper and severing her corrupting touch. I would win by being right. But where was she? There was nothing here but fog and death. Everything the same: the bodies, the pain, none of it differed to one detached from weakness.

And then off to the left I saw something that caught my eye. Not a dull gray stake, but a golden javelin glittering and bright in the gloom of the forest. It stood alone with no javelins nearby. I ran towards it and leaned close to inspect. An unclothed and healthy-looking man was impaled perpendicular on it with the stake through his stomach. His body faced upwards and he twisted his neck to look closer at me. The man had a protruding lower lip with a thick and straight barred moustache shadowing over it. He had deep-set brown eyes so dark that they seemed black, almost appearing as though they were without iris. His hair fell all the way to the ground, dragging in the dirt like black tasseled cloth.

"I've impaled many during my days. Most deserved it. I fought to keep them out of my land," he said, his voice measured and sharp.

"Who are you?" I asked. I looked closer at his face. "You look familiar." I frowned. I reached out my arm and left it lingering in the air. I'd seen his look before. I knew I had. When there'd still been hope of resisting. A Wallachian. This man's people had aided us when they could—the last bastions of a dying and unified Christendom. "Did you visit Constantinople? Or was it your father? I am unsure of how much time has passed."

"Perhaps, but Constantinople is long gone. Time continues. I kept the hordes at bay. I kept them away while the rest of the so-called Holy and united Christian Empire left me to fend for myself, just like they left you and yours to die."

"You know me?" I said.

"You are a Roman, that much is obvious. Oh that East and West were whole, but now that is forever lost. I became the east once you fell, and we were left mostly alone. I fought the Turks, that same Sultan Mehmed II who ruined your people. I was kept his prisoner as a youth so that my father would be forced to do his bidding. Their oh-so holy slave army. A truly wicked empire that we never should have let flourish. Yet that all changed, and eventually I ruled my throne with a fist of justice."

"So, you came after me. After Constantinople had fallen." I paused, staring at the pained expression of this man. Could it be? How much time had passed since I'd died and been set on this quest of unliving myth?

"I reigned with terror, for that's the only thing those inbreds know and respect. I forced the German grifters from my land, whether through impalement or banishment. I fought valiantly with my men, leading charges and defenses alike. I've fought alone against the best of men, and have come out victorious. Valhalla should be where I dwell. But I chose this stake, my penance for a terror too strong. For I cannot lie and say I did not enjoy the pain I made others feel. Their scent of rot, their screams of agony, I thrived off it. I even impaled rats out of joy. Torture was a part of me, so now I experience the torture myself to tear away that wicked skin. For excess is always unjust when wrought for pure pleasure and nothing but."

"Your name?" I said.

"Vlad Dracul, son of the dragon. Most called me the Impaler. I saved my country and died for my excess. I shouldn't be here, but I was pulled from purification by Wyrd at our Lord's command, an extra penance that I so truly desire. For she told me of what is to come and what is promised, and that you would come too. So, I am here now in this inverted game as if it had sprung from my own mind. A forest of impaled souls with my own stake gold and gilded to mock my prideful madness." He sighed, and he grabbed the shaft of the stake and grunted as he pulled himself slightly up, adjusting his position to speak easier to me.

"You hold no fruit like the others," I said.

"I've eaten it and await its caustic effect," he said.

"How do I win this first game?"

"Throw this javelin at its own throes." Vlad vanished as he nodded, his body blown away in a sudden cloud of ash.

I clasped the golden stake, pulling it up with all my might. It broke free from the ground and split in half, its golden wood glowing in splinters as it fell apart. Letting my light course through my arms, I surged the energy into the remaining half of the shaft and threw it straight at the forest of impalement, exploding the stakes all in a burst encompassing the full spectrum of light—a solar-flared rainbow. All that remained were shards, broken and weak like spindly toothpicks, the bodies once inhabiting them gone.

A roar resounded from the heavens. Soaring mightily above, a maroon dragon with golden wings flew out from the gray. On its back a bare breasted woman with a dark cowl covering her face sat, a skirt of shadowy fog misting below her waist. Her pale skin shined with a moon-like glow as the dragon crashed downwards and landed close by me in the remains of the shattered forest.

The dragon glared at me, a sparkle of righteousness in its eye and I stared back with recognition. Vlad the dragon flew away to where it was that he truly belonged. I smiled and nodded up at him as he disappeared into the gray. I hoped he'd find peace in his penance. I turned my attention back to the strange shadow woman. Her head was covered in the black abyss of her cowl. She sauntered over to me as her breasts swayed with her hips, her skirt of smoke leaving a trail of ash behind. Her skin that wasn't doused in shadow, was pure and pale; a soft sheen of moonlight seemed to emanate from her smooth flesh.

"I am Miseria," she said, her voice a bottomless hiss of whispers, sounding like it came from my own mind, all around me, and from her.

A voiceless voice, an ever-present whisper so constant that it faded into white noise and became a backdrop of static. I shook my head to try and stay clear minded in the face of such a strange goddess.

"Did you eat my fruit?" she said.

"I found none worthy of eating."

"Good. Never fall into the trap of eating fruit from others. My suffering must not come from others, but from you. From within you. Those impaled fools ate the fruit from the suffering world, thinking the suffering their own. That is not true darkness. That is only the fruit of those masturbatory, pity worshipers."

"Is suffering in the world not a fruit we must all digest?" I said.

"That is merely life. To not eat it is to not live. The pity worshipers who impale themselves on the trees of such fruit became entranced by what they take to be the world's death throes. They pity the nothingness that they imagine to exist, pitying their lot so much that they become the nothingness they imagine."

I crossed my arms, the hissing everywhere-ness of her voice frigid and distant. "So, the fruit they offer is not yours, but merely the fruit of death?"

"In part, but those so devoted see the death and suffering around them, ignoring that same suffering that pours out like sewage from their own mouths. They spread despair and decay just by espousing their supposed love for humanity. They climb up on their own trees of rot, pretending to care for the many when in turn, they want only to secure a meaning in themselves. Their fruit is excess, it is the will to death. It is the pitying will caught up in the exuberance of feeling bad for others, and feeling good about feeling bad for others, as though their fruit was righteous. No! You did well in refusing the common fruit that we all swallow, that we all breathe like air. They think it special and seek its decay."

"So then, where is your fruit?"

Her cowl tremored and fell back to reveal the face of a young woman with wide spread soft gray eyes. She had a ghostly yet angelic complexion with a delicate nose and an even more delicate mouth flowering beneath it, the lips pale-pink petals drained of blood. Her eyebrows were wispy and light brown, and her hair was pulled back in a loose and messy bun. This was the goddess of misery? A pretty young woman? She tilted her head and smirked, her lips pouting before spreading like the thin wings of a butterfly, revealing her rounded, soft-white teeth.

I looked down and watched as her skirt drained away, its tendrils reaching out towards me before vanishing, leaving behind pristine white skin and shapely legs. She stood before me uncovered and smiling, the goddess of misery innocent and pure in her nakedness. I had no wife or family. I'd been wed only with war, but could I now succumb to my own suffering, sleep with my own misery? Miseria was my fruit to pluck and taste. Yes. Yes. This was it.

I shed my armor as I reached out and held her chin. Her eyes beckoned me forth as I pulled her into my arms. Her lips were cold and tasted of ash, like kissing a slab of marble, yet her breasts were ripe and her body soft and warm. We kneaded ourselves together, a knot tied and bound as one—flesh and spirit, divinity and mortality, eternity yanking my mind into the ecstasy of full abandonment to the current of timelessness and perfect relation. I was awash in an ocean of oneness that churned us together until we became as the other, while remaining perfectly ourselves.

As the waves finally subsided and the current slowed, I untied myself from her, sliding back into myself as I let go and drifted to my lonely shore of self. We stood up, unbound from the heap we'd become and we stared at each other with the shared knowledge of union.

She pointed her long white finger at my heart, her long nails the same off-pink color as her lips. She lightly touched my chest and it glowed black, my heart a shadow pushing my skin and rattling against my rib cage. And in a grotesque gush, it plopped out from my chest and rolled itself into my hand through a sheer will of its own. Seeing the blackness and realizing its union with myself, I surrendered to its dark and shadowy force. I lifted the heart to my mouth and bit it, its taste bitter yet sweet. I consumed the rest of my heart and let it descend back inside of me, worming through my throat and inching back into my hollow chest.

And I saw inside me what I already knew. There were black eyes within, staring down from a moonless night. The eyes possessed a somethingness that was more of a something than my somethingness—more of a something than my nothing that was myself, staring up. A nothing. A something. A someone. Me. But the nothing slept within.

I stared through this moonless night of my reflected self's reflection, the I staring not an eye looking, but a mass of meaningless marionetted flesh with a limping gaze attached to a half-broken form. Most of my strings were snapped, detached by my own doing in this continuous moment of digesting the fruit. I closed my eyes to the moonless night. Therein lied my lying eye. To get through the heavenly abyss required a passing into something, and my something still seemed as nothing. My eye could not see, because my I was not me. So, I closed my black eyes, the invisible moon setting to the purity of powerlessness. In this perfect purity, my soul burned and the wound of my empty tomb chest was cauterized shut by a boulder of burn—my heart resurrected as caustic fruit.

And Miseria stood there naked and smiling. I reached down and put my armor back on. The black cowl returned to her, shading her face from my gaze and its darkness leaked over her whole body until she was covered in black mist. And finally, she vanished and the surroundings shivered, and once again I was back standing in the circle with my armor donned. The inner spirals of the circle were now gone and only the outer wall of small boulders remained. My blood was mine. The darkness was below me. It surrendered to me as I did to purity. This was to be whole.

I breathed deep and walked out of the circle and headed towards the next. This one had but one boulder in the center with five small boulders surrounding it in a circular, unfilled border. I stepped into its bounds and my settings whisked themselves away like a quilt being torn off then thrown back on with new fabric. The fabric of my changed reality was a wide, soaked space of deep red. The sky dripped like wax, yet nothing fell. I stood in endless shallows; there was warm scarlet water all around me that mirrored the sky and covered my ankles.

I heard grunting behind me and I turned around to see two men boxing each other. Each man stood unclothed and of powerful form. The one had curly hair cut short, red and thick like wool with a beard draped over his face from just under his eyes to his chin, shaved close yet still shaggily carpeted. The other man had a long yellow-white beard and medium length hair that was fine and splayed out down to the nape of his neck.

Every time they swung their fists in attempt at fighting each other, a crack of an invisible whip sounded, and each man grimaced as his punch struck something solid, as if they both were encased in an impenetrable shield of glass.

"What is this?" I said. Neither of the men turned at my voice.

The yellow haired fighter unleashed a flurry of jabs which caused him to wince with pain just as much as his opponent, who needlessly held his arms up.

"Two men of power," a voice said from beside me. I spun to my left and there a brawny man garbed in exquisite black armor stood, with only his wide, unshaven head and ox-like neck exposed. "Hercules is the curly headed one, Beowulf the blonde."

"And you?" I said, studying the armor closer. It was covered in etched skulls; the eyes of each skull shined with red rubies serving as unblinking irises.

"Turnus." His gray-coal eyes smoldered with passion and hatred.

I shook my head. "Oh hateful one, has defeat at the hands of Aeneas and his justice not taught you anything? You cursed destiny, there was no righteous fulfilment."

"I fought against the unjust favoritism of the gods."

"Is perhaps this favoritism due justly? Was Aeneas favored because of his perfect will, willed upwards and into the eternal moment?" I knew all too well of this in my own experience. "Blame thyself, not everyone and everything else."

"Spoken pompously from a favored mortal himself. You should be dead." Turnus frowned and crossed his arms.

"I should not be, for I am not. Shoulds are mere weakness. Musts and wills are strong. I willed this through making my own must," I said.

"Then what must you do?"

A loud thud sounded from the fighters. Hercules threw down quaking strikes, his fists fruitlessly landing from above and against air. Beowulf weaved and threw his elbow. They kept fighting as those unseen whips continued to snap. I shuddered, thinking of how long they'd been going on in this dance of numb death.

"What's the use of power unused? What if one cannot use it?" I asked, turning back to Turnus with a wince. Seeing these great heroes so strong yet so stuck, pained me.

"Here fight two of the most powerful heroes of all, and yet their power is useless here. They neither hear us nor see us. They are trapped in their useless power."

I sighed. The man was tiresome. I smiled, "How must I right this wrong and fight and write my own song?" I laughed at Turnus as he clenched his fists and scowled. "I think your old master Aeneas would have appreciated such a line. Virgil certainly, that Latin poet who wrote your own demise. He wrote your wrong! It was right."

Turnus took a loud breath to calm himself. "Is it a wrong? Mine was unjust. But is it wrong what has happened here? Or have these two heroes not chosen this fate?"

My smile collapsed and I grit my teeth. "An inversion. An injustice. Let them strike each other then!" I said, my fists shaking as my helpless gaze was directed back towards the legendary fighters throwing their purposeless, painful punches.

"This is what happens when might is lied into the wrong," he said.

"They did not lie!"

"No, but the gods did," he added.

"Your victimhood will not contaminate me. The gods did not lie, for that implies that the mortal believed."

"What is it then to be mortal, if not to believe in something? Whether in a here and now, or in a forever after?"

I breathed through my mouth, the warm and wet air of this strange place making me sick. "It is the mortal's choice on whether or not he will believe. It is the mortal who drinks from the wellspring, who conquers the empyrean, invading into the infinite. The mortal does not believe in the past, the now, and the future. No, not in the infinite sense. The true mortal—the immortal mortal—believes in the always, which implies a dwelling place housed and solidified in the sun. Aeneas's rays shined forth on gods and men alike. Can you blame the sun for not providing enough light, when you hide yourself away in darkness? No. But you can come to the sun and dwell within it, but only when its rays have damaged you to the point of perfection."

"A fool's rambling, nothing more. Hercules and Beowulf are cursed because the gods hate our ilk."

"You hate the gods," I snapped.

"Then what of those two?" he screamed, veins popping angrily at his shaved temples. His wide shovel nose sniffed greedily at the air as if to inhale added fury.

"Perhaps they fight this impossible fight to make up for the weakness of the world. Maybe power unused is in itself a use. Withholding or suffering, so others might one day possess such strength," I offered.

"This is a prison. None of us wanted to dwell in this twisted circle; we were tossed here in chaos as the mythical realms continue to bleed out."

"So, their righteous deeds have become corrupted by the degeneration of the herd. But they themselves continue onward in purity," I said.

"And it fails. You see their strikes, hitting nothing but air." His eyes darted back and forth between them and I.

“Have you not thought to join them? Perhaps their victory cannot be had here until you step in.”

“It is my job to guard this sword," he pulled out an ornate silver weapon. “Hrunting, the sword that failed.”

I understood what was required here the moment he unsheathed the weapon. I spun and kicked his hand, his loosened grip allowing me to pry the sword from his grasp. I blasted Turnus before he could strike me with a burst of blue light and he flew backwards, skidding through the shallows and spraying the scarlet water high. I walked over towards the two heroes who had yet to pay me any mind. I chopped at their bodies with the sword, and as silver struck flesh, they evaporated.

I turned back and slowly walked over to Turnus, who was on his knees and staring down at his empty hands. The angry champion was too distraught to even fight. Again, he no doubt blamed the gods. I shook my head.

I said, “And now it succeeds. Their fight required their own blood. This place prevented their holy fight from finality. To be in the always, one must belong to finality, the endless end of eternal surrender. Then destiny and atonement can come. Those who do not fight, render the sacrificial fighting of others an impossibility. If one refuses to be strong, weakness will win and can have no end by any other than that pathetic individual. They fought for those who did not deserve their fight. So, they fought hopelessly, as against thin air, for those people they sought to save remained in the dark. Their rays shined outside, but the individual remained. Eyes shut, head lowered, and back turned.”

Turnus looked up to me and I held no pity for the chosen resentment and madness of this sad man. I nodded and brought the sword down into his skull, splitting it in half. The circle flashed a bright red and I was back to the bleeding realm.

I held Hrunting in my hand and smiled. Another worthy weapon beside Solisinanis. Still, I wondered what that game of the circle had been called? No matter, for now those great heroes were freed. And this sword, Hrunting... it belonged to Beowulf. I did not know how I knew, but it was as if it spoke through its silver gleam. A connection to my spiritual past. However, it had failed so I would need to redeem it; its path was far from finished. I nodded and headed for the third circle of stone.

This circle swirled outwards, stones spiraling out in an almost fluid curvature like that of the water's wake. The stones curled in odd wavelike formations and swirled into smaller circles out to the edge. There was no outer rim of this circle, but as I stepped by the farthest swirl, I was instantly plunged into icy water. I gasped as black water piled atop my body and currents dragged me under. My wind shoes were of no use submerged as I was, and my armor weighed me down, pulling me further into the merciless depths. With Hrunting still clammily clasped in my hand and Solisinanis latched to my waist, I forced both weapons above my head and bathed them each in blue and red light from my marks. Solisinanis burst in golden fire, flaming alight despite being submerged in this liquid tomb. Hrunting glowed a pale blue, its frigid flame brilliant and pure as a pearled sky. With both weapons bathed in my powerful light, they pulled me as if they were wings and I tore upwards, yanked free from the icy sea's grip. I sliced through the surface and pierced the black, launching into a gray sky like a showy dolphin.

I soared upwards; the salty sting of the water drawn out by the relentless wash of wind. All below me was a black and stormy sea, its waves peaking upwards after me like outstretched and greedy fingers, but I was free from their cold grasp. Above me there was only an endless gravestone sky. I flew in a loping arch as a beacon of light, my rays of power extending out to push away the gloom of this dreary realm. Ahead, there was a large ashen stone formation of several raised pillars, a stairway fit for a giant. It was the only land I could see in this sea of dread. I aimed my falling flight at the formation and as it neared, I pulled my weapons back and the light drained out as I landed softly on the stone stairs.

With the spray of sea-salt stinging my eyes, I stood there drenched and chilled, wondering what inverted game I'd have to win here. The waterlogged air, heavy with the scent of rotted fish, pillaged my nostrils of any hope of clarity. I turned to look at the sea and there from the water arose a bare-chested man with a blue band wrapped round his flowing brown hair. He rode a boat-shaped chariot made of pale sea-green leather and animal skins. The ship was tethered to a large stallion of white sea foam, stamping its hooves as part of the billowing surf. The chariot surged ashore and the stallion become a solid, beautiful white mare. It waited there at the bottom of the isle as the man stepped up the stone pillar stairs.

He wore dark blue trousers tapered tight to his legs, and his chest was toned and wide compared to his narrow waist. His face was covered with a salt-sprayed gray and black beard, and his oval face and clear blue eyes peered at me with a slow and condescending look, like that of a bored teacher. I glared down at him from my perch as he walked up, and I kept my hands at my side with both weapons ready for use at the slightest threat.

"Rangabes, you've come at last. That down there is Enbarr, my foamed steed." His voice was calm like the surface of a lake with the power of an endless abyss lurking below. "I am Manannán mac Lir, god of this here sea, and delightful deliverer of the dead. I see that you have come to me for a sort of surf game, or should I say served play. This is a game after all, is it not?" He smiled and winked, holding up sinewy arms wrapped with two leather bands of dark brown around the wrists. The bands were interlocked with a glowing blue pattern that curved through each like rivers of watery light.

"And what have you served me? On this surf I've come, and I have no interest in playing. I want to finish this worthless wave." I glared at his wry smile and frowned. I could play his game of wits and win. This fool!

He stood a few steps below me, stopping his ascension and resting his one leg on the pillar before him while leaning lazily forward. "A chariot race, on chariots of the sea. We will ride around my great serpent friend who for the moment sleeps. The mighty Stoor Worm, reborn from Iceland, has melted back to life!" He grinned, flashing teeth as white as his horse. He flicked his wrist and a goblet of pink pearl appeared in his hand. Six sapphires circled its front with an onyx stone in the center, larger than the rest of the gems.

"This is the goblet of truth. It is what we will race for. Though you will soon see, to get this truth you must lie, threefold." He laughed and did a jig, clicking his bare heels like a man mad with wine. He pulled a sword out from the air, its brilliant white steel gleaming bright.

“Fragarach! Lugh has lost his sword! Lugh is no light god anymore!”

I started at the mention of the god’s name. “Where is Lugh?” I shouted.

“He cannot answer, for his Answerer is my answer now! He can’t question either!” He hopped backwards from one foot to the other, leaping to pillars in various directions in a mad flurry of ferocious mirth. “Come now, come! We race first and then you might perhaps have an answer yourself—perhaps you’ll sip from this cup of truth.” He stopped his hopping and flicked the sword and goblet into the air, and they both vanished in a sudden cloud of evaporating mist.

Manannán motioned for me to follow as he walked towards his waiting white horse. He stroked its silken skin and whispered to it. He then turned to face me as I continued warily behind, stepping down the pillars in his stead.

“Alas, you have no chariot or steed, so I will ride in my ship. She’s called Scuabtuinne—she sweeps waves without wind, for the water is happy to sweep her off her feet. She has none! She scrubs the ocean well, she does.” He smiled, nodded, and then shook his head up at me as I stood there waiting at the ocean’s edge. “But you have no ship. I told you we won’t use chariots or steeds, for you didn’t think to bring one. But a ship, well, how can one get here without a ship, right? A sea requires one, if it ever might be subdued, or at least ridden as a sailor should sail.”

I stretched my arms wide and said, “My body is my ship and I will sail your wretched water with my arms as oars and legs as rudders.”

“And what of your sail? Is it your hair?” He chuckled and leapt into what had served as his chariot before, though it had since changed its shape and color—a sleek black boat that was of medium length and had no sail or oars.

“My sail is my spirit,” I said, his loud laughter tearing my speech and tattering it windless but I continued, “for my flesh, my form is better than what any lot of wood might rot upon me. You cannot see it, god of the sightless sea, your eyes lulled by the gleam of sumptuous craft. Yet when one is left with the only craft that is truly his own, then the body peaks above the watery valleys, for I follow this creed: body and soul together is perfection, and where one goes, the other follows. My mind is sharper than any sword and my fitness more durable than any ship. You might have designed yours for this, but what I have here is life, being. The valleys of this sea are not seen by my mind’s eye, the intellect sees through and over your elected wood, parry-less in the face of my own body’s thrust. My sail is spirit and my body a ship. Both are better, for both are meant for more.”

“All right then Master Boat, hop right in and let’s finish this.” He tapped his foot in his boat and tousled his hair in a flurry of impatience, pulling back at it as if it were a squirming snake escaping his grasp.

I nodded and shed my armor and shoes while keeping on my weightless trousers. I looked at both my weapons, Solisinanis and Hrunting. Each weapon begged to be grasped, the silver of the sword and the gold of the axe equally enticing. Yet I bent to hold Hrunting and turned away from my glorious axe. If Manannán only had his one sword, I would not seek unfair advantage. I strained my ears, listening for Wyrd’s call. She would know if what I did was right... or true, for truth was this game’s play. Or was it deceit? I listened harder and there in the distance, a sweep of shorn strings high off in the heavens confirmed what I'd known. This was now my sword and it needed its failure to be fixed; I felt as if its redemption was not complete and that its salvation was a sort of metagame within and above these cursed circles. Perhaps a key? Wyrd's song soared and vanished at the thought. Manannán showed no signs of having heard, he just stood there impatiently with his arms folded at his side and his feet tapping.

I set my jaw and cracked my neck, and after a few rolls of my shoulders, I plunged into the icy water, its black embrace covering me like soil in a grave. I whipped my head out of the water and floated over towards Scuabtuinne.

"The Stoor Worm!" Manannán shouted with his arms raised and head thrown back in anticipatory rapture.

A rumble shook from beneath the water as waves arose like quaking mountains, tossing me up and down as the frightful creature climbed out from its cold depths. The monster was blacker than the black sea it rose from. Like a coiled mountain it broke the water around it, shattering the black into fleeing white waves. The giant sea serpent blotted out huge swathes of sky, casting the realm in an even drearier darkness. Its individual scales were the size of ships alone, and its slimy black body dripped a venomous yellow liquid. Its yellow eyes were round and reptilian, and its snout jutted out with striped bands of that same venomous yellow on each side, split only by the black empty color of its scales in the middle. Its head was that of a dragon—less serpentine and more horse-like in the length of its snout and jaws.

It reared its head upwards and opened its mouth, letting out a yawn that sounded like the earth was breaking in two. Yellow gas poured out from the beast's mouth, poisoning the sky and turning it the same vomit-colored hue. Its teeth were bright and sharp like icy mountain peaks. It lowered its head back down to the surface of the water, strangely keeping its mouth propped open. Tendrils of toxic gas still leaked out from its maw, but the Stoor Worm settled into its position and floated there like an island, no movement other than the endless trickle of gas from its still agape mouth, and its eyes that followed my bobbing in the sea.

"I lied!" Manannán yelled over the racket of rolling waves. "We are not racing around the Stoor Worm, we are racing through it! The first one to its liver wins!" And with that, his boat sped away.

I grunted at his head start and swam forward, my already tired arms dragging like stones through the unforgiving surf. I let Hrunting drink both my blue and red light, each mark feeding the weapon with energy. I sped after the ship, trailing in its wake but unable to come close. The putrid air stuffed with the sour spoil of the Stoor Worm tore at my flesh. I lowered my sword so as to avoid the air and submerged just beneath the surface as I skimmed along like a dolphin. But still, that slippery god was carving through the water with ease, white sea foam crashing after him like an avalanche of snow. My body dragged behind like a caught fish as my sword flung me forward. I could barely see through the black water stinging my eyes.

I at least knew where I was headed. For the mouth. For the toxic worm's mouth. I flung my sword upwards, my arm latched on like a notched arrow to a bow. I shot out of the water and into beast's black maw as its pale green gas sizzled my skin. Numbness wrapped my body as I went in and landed with a plop in pulpy liquid. The stench and feel of the worm's cavernous maw was of sludge and slime. Despite the stink, a strange calm in the beast's murky mouth descended and all was quiet but for the groaning of the worm's innards. I could not see Manannán anywhere; perhaps he'd already made it through the worm's dark depths.

The Stoor Worm roared and my surroundings flipped as I was thrown against slimy walls. The worm's mouth closed shut and a dark black fell over me like the earth itself had swallowed me whole. Its throat flexed and the water surged downwards, the gas and smell of rot reeking to the point of making me weep; even with eyes shut I could not prevent the tears that streamed in vain, for there was no purifying myself in here.

The slippery wall I was stuck on slid out from underneath me as the Stoor Worm reared its body vertical and swallowed at such a force that water, noxious gas, and what little of the untainted air remaining, were all sucked downward. I fell and plunged my sword into the beast's inner wall, sliding downwards as Hrunting carved a jagged line until I stopped, clinging on as the sword held true. Hanging vertical as I was allowed for the air's toxicity to thin, the gas falling back into the stomach. I cautiously took a few slight breaths. What was I to do now? I'd followed the rules of this inverted boat race, yet Manannán was a cheating wretch. Where had he gone? Had he actually plunged into the Stoor Worm's mouth or had it been a ruse?

I sighed, my body tense and secure, and I pulled myself upwards and rested my chest on the sword's hilt to ease the burden of holding myself aloft. It was oddly peaceful now. It sounded as if the worm was holding itself upright and waiting in perfect stillness for me to dissolve in its stomach acid. There wasn't much I could do stuck here like a canker sore. I needed a song. Where was Wyrd? I heard a humming that accompanied my thought, yet it wasn't Wyrd who sang. The voice was a soft yet throaty echo from somewhere below. The humming arose pleasantly with an aroma of warm smoke like that from a cozy hearth. The humming swelled slowly up, building in volume until words burst free from the soothing rhythm.

Into the ash the rootless tree digs
Its branches gasping, its trunk already dead

Light arrives. The drought lingers in shadow.

Into the darkness the rooted light shines
Its rays quenching, its path aflame with life

The song was now a full tune, echoing somberly about the darkness. I could no longer tell where it came from for it had coursed over me like a stormy sea, spinning me under its surf and into its melody. That lovely smell of smoke made my entire body tingle, incense holy and right like that once used in Hagia Sophia. I smiled, holding myself on Hrunting as if I were lying on a soft green pasture, gazing at the sun. And as the scent ascended in swirls of smoke, my soul seemed to join in. And now the music grew louder, the voice filling out into a choir, no longer low in tone but angelic and high in its tenor. The words burst free from the dark humming cocoon, the flight of voice like light shining forth into a new lyricism.

Arrival is departure, a paradox of motion
Light loves dark, an unceasing ocean

The song exploded, rising with that last line in a sustained note. As rapturous as it came, just as powerfully it vanished, and once more a slow hum of melancholy filled the darkness. The lingering smell of burnt-out flame was all that remained. And from the whispering hum, words sputtered out like dying embers of the last of light.

Evil is great, and good is evil
Great is good, and evil is the nothing

The nothing
The nothing

Good is something, but sometimes something—
Sometimes something belongs to the nothing

Light burnt shadows
Dark swallowed sun
Absence and presence together as one

We are one

Vapor to ash, and ash back to sun
Shadows burning the light
Light swallowing shadows

No duality.

The good evil. First among the last—
From the beginning there was a first and end.
A start amidst a never started.
A something before the nothing, and then with it.
They existed together, nonexistence and being.

The Good Evil.

This is a snake that has finished swallowing.
This snake has consumed itself, not in perpetuity—
in finality.

The swallowed nothingness is our digested somethingness.
Neither end, for when it started, it was already eaten.

Eat.

At last the strange song finished its whisper without melody, a flutter of flaring moth burnt in the glow of the flame. And in the stillness, all sense faded away. Even the motion of the Stoor Worm lowering itself back to the surface was somehow silent and without feeling. And then, a soft yellow glow emerged from the back of the beast's throat, and a boat with a tattered sail came towards me. I stayed there dumbfounded, Hrunting still piercing the wall.

"I am Ashipattle," the man called out, his boat slowly inching towards me. "I killed the Stoor Worm back when nobody else could. I killed the wicked wizard too. Yet this pulling, this strange bleeding of myth has brought it back to life and me with it. Somebody is causing this. But I've been here since the cause, whenever that may have been, I do not know. And now you are here to bring about the cause's effect. Make it your own cause, I beg you. Do not follow through with an effect that is someone else's design."

As far as he was, he didn't shout but called out in a smooth and comforting manner, the kind of voice that carried itself without needing an affectation of tension and forced volume. Now that he had drifted close enough, I squinted and was able to make out his figure beneath his soft-lit lantern that hung atop a mast. The lantern's light was a fading flicker of yellow-orange like that of autumn leaves. The man was no fall and he stood in a wintery fashion. His icy demeanor was fitting of his gray robes. It appeared as though he was wearing a strange sort of silk ash. His eyes mirrored his clothing's color. He was of medium stature and lean. His oblong face sported a wide brow and a long and narrow chin.

His red hair hung straight down, curtaining the sides of his face just past his chin. Atop his head sat a plain silver crown without adornment. He was pushing his way through the water with a large broad sword serving as his paddle. The sword was as gray and piercing as his eyes, and its white diamond-studded hilt glowed as bright as the lantern above his head. His boat lurched beneath me and at last he stopped rowing, looking up at me perched there on my sword with kindness in his eyes. He offered his hand and I accepted, pulling Hrunting from the beast's meat and hopping onto the boat.

"Can you tell me where Manannán mac Lir went?" I said, standing next to Ashipattle as the boat rocked in place.

"He came in here. Yes, he came in." He sighed and looked back towards the darkness he'd emerged from.

"And where has he gone?" I said.

"To hide the truth of course."

I frowned, staring at Ashipattle's ashen face, gray as his robe and eyes, and just as dulled. As simple as the crown was, it at least shined. I stared at the crown until his face blurred into a cloud of unclarity. Truth. That was what this race was for, that goblet of truth. Manannán had claimed I'd need three lies. But what could that mean?

"Three lies to win the truth," I muttered, itching my chin through my beard.

"A riddle, no doubt," Ashipattle said. "I once defeated this worm as a mere child, my wit winning the day. Where is your wit? This is not my truth to win."

"Three untruths. I wonder. Like St. Peter's three denials. Could a lie be true if denying the truth of a lie?" I rubbed my eyes and lowered my head to concentrate.

"Whom do you love? Why do you do this? What is it that you are doing?" Ashipattle said.

"I love myself. I do this because it is better than the nothingness. I'm journeying to live again."

"Truth or falsity?" he said.

"I only love myself when I love my people. I only exist in somethingness because the love for my people drives me away from nonbeing. I'm journeying to make my people live again."

"And thus your selfish deceit and truthful lies become true untruths. For it is untrue until it is finished. And can such a task be finished?"

"Never and always," I answered, raising my head smiling. Ashipattle smiled back.

"Manannán mac Lir comes," he said, his mouth tightened straight and serious.

I looked over Ashipattle's shrouded shoulder, and there from the dark depths of the Stoor Worm's belly, the infernal black Scuabtuinne came. The ship was suspended in the dark water in a strange white glow of light that exuded from the boat's black wood. It glided out from the darkness and towards us as Manannán smirked and waved his hands about as if to a crowd during a victory lap.

"What kind of race is this?" I said, my words weighed with weariness from the inverted games of this strange realm.

I'd faced much thus far, and this by much was the shortest in stature. Where was the glory here? I hardly felt like my ancestor Aeneas. No celebration. No glory. Only tired aloneness. If these were my funeral games, I wasn't sure who was being honored. Perhaps I was being mocked by those who'd survived me, my enemies spitting on my grave.

"A race of untruth. I have my Answerer here," Manannán said, holding his gleaming white sword aloft as the boat slowed to a lazy lull, floating a few feet away. His face waxed wicked in the white light, carved shadows intensifying his evil mirth and highlighting the concaves of his narrow countenance. "Ashipattle has his Sickersnapper: a sword that bites severely, but can its bite breech a sword that retaliates with a force that is always in perfect reply? Can a response be bitten when it is the answer to the bite?" He tossed his sword from one hand to the other, chuckling as he turned his bright eyes my way. "And your sword, that Hrunting, that sword that failed! How can you expect to hold your weight against a biting sword and an answering one when all your sword is known for is failing to hold up against Grendel's mother? She was a ghastly, old beast that Beowulf had to slay with another, better weapon."

"You're a fool. This sword is no longer the one that failed. It set Hercules and Beowulf free. It killed Turnus. It has shed worthy blood." I pointed the sword at Manannán's direction. "Insult me as you will, but this inverted boat race finished the moment you went backward. You came back here to what... gloat? You fool!" I laughed and swung Hrunting through the air, its gleam silver and cold, icily waiting to shatter the shadowy sea god's might.

"Yes! Yes! A battle for truth, a battle for truth while the race to it was untruth!" He bounced from one foot to the other and laughed. "But here is the lie, you fight Ashipattle first!" He cackled and danced.

"Is it true?" I said, looking at the great Celtic king who had weary lines pressed into his face.

"I do not belong here. Free me from this untruth. In victory or defeat, I achieve an act. I must act. I must. It is the only way to break free from this monstrosity, this place that should not be. It is a lie. I will be freed in the fight. If you win, your heroic victory will send my spirit into the land it belongs. I will try to win. I act in truth. I must, to be true. I pray you do as well, friend." His tone was solemn and he held out Sickersnapper in all of its awesome ashen aesthetic; its gray blade dull and smoky, and its hilt glowing with white-infused diamonds.

I nodded and tapped Hrunting's silver against his metallic ash sword, and we stepped back as far as we could on his small boat. We stood with knees bent and swords raised, ready to fight to the death. Manannán laughed with glee, his clapping obnoxious in the silent, slow groaning mouth of the Stoor Worm. The only light came from the lantern above us, our swords' magical gleams, and the white field of glowing mist that leaked out from Scuabtuinne.

And so, we danced. My blade caressed his, the steel sparking as we spun. I punched with my free arm, striking his stomach, yet he merely grunted and parried my following slice at his throat. He leapt backward to the edge of the boat and dissipated into a cloud of ash, truly worthy of his name and cloak. He vanished as smoke into the air and reappeared in a puff above me. I threw up my sword to ward off the blow but he managed to clip my shoulder, drawing only a slight trickle of blood. He vanished again in a haze of smoky-gray ash and I spun around, looking in all directions for him, my sword waving desperately about. Not wanting to remain trapped and exposed, I covered my arms in light, aiming them down. I shot out bursts of light into the water and propelled myself into the air. As I flew up towards the worm's walls, Ashipattle reappeared in the air beside me and I twisted with my sword and cut into his side. My legs landed high on the beast's walls, and with my arms still glowing, I planted my feet and shot myself back like a cannonball at the boat. Ashipattle reappeared grimacing and slow as I plummeted down onto the boat. I landed rolling, slicing at his other side. I then rolled away into a crouch, ready to spring up with another attack. Blood poured from both his wounds, each side gushing geysers of red, yet he refused to give in.

I watched his sluggish arms and labored movement, and I shimmied to the left of his desperate attack. He thrust right past me and staggered as I rolled and dragged my blade along the boat, yanking it up and plunging it into his stomach. His wounds painted his gray cloak black. He held his stomach but refused to cry out. I pulled the sword free and he clenched his jaws in agony, but held his voice. He impossibly remained standing, truly worthy of the crown on his head. Yet he was beaten, and he stumbled to the edge and toppled into the water. I leaned over the boat's edge, yet there was nothing left but a cloud of dark red. And as I stared after him, the cloud of blood suddenly was sucked downwards, disappearing into the black of the water. A terrible and sudden screech scorched the air. The awful sound was high-pitched and stabbed my eardrums, pushing through my palms even as I tried to cover my ears. Everything started to shake and the Stoor Worm opened its mouth and flung its head upwards.

The water surged beneath me as I clung to the boat. The worm spat me out and I flew out in a spout of water through the air. The black ocean rushed towards me as my boat plunged down through the sky. It mercifully held together as it crashed into the sea and I lay there clutching the sides like a child to its mother's bosom. The Stoor Worm towered above me, waving its head in erratic circles. If mountains could move, they'd still fall short compared to the might of this beast. How had Ashipattle bested such a foe?

Mercifully, its shrill screaming had relented and now it moaned in a haunting, almost peaceful manner. Its strange groaning was not fitting of its manic gyrations, but more belonging to a wise old whale of some forgotten deep. In the shadow of the Stoor Worm, Manannán mac Lir stood on his boat with his pearl goblet held out as if in toast, and his stolen Fragarach lifted in the other hand. His boat coasted towards me and I stood up and ground my teeth at his insolence.

"So Hrunting succeeded against an apparently not so severe bite. But it will not succeed against the perfect answer. Do you even have a question?" Manannán laughed loud with his arms extended, inviting attack as his boat came closer.

I was not going to put up with this jester any longer. I bounded to the nose of my ship and leapt off of my right foot and into the stormy air. Hrunting guided my leap as I plunged the sword into the laughing god's chest, the force of my blow sending me into a crouched landing that pushed Manannán onto his back with my arm buried in his flesh. He gurgled and I yanked my sword out of his chest and sliced at his neck, his head rolling away like discarded fruit. Scuabtuinne rocked back and forth, trying to throw me off before it suddenly stopped like a tamed horse, and its wood groaned, mourning its master's defeat.

I bent down and picked up the pink goblet along with Fragarach. I crouched over Manannán's headless body and pulled free a yellow cloak I'd failed to notice before. As I held it up it vanished, yet I still felt its cloth in my fingers. It seemed my fingers covered by the cloak had vanished too. And I realized now how it was that he'd disappeared in our race. A cloak of invisibility.

Féth Fíada

The wind whispered the words, and the invisible cloak fled my fingers and turned into a pale mist that curled into the sea. I looked down and wasn't surprised to see the body gone. The faithful mist had taken its master home to his sea, even though he could no longer see, or it see him. And alone on his ship, I looked at the sword and goblet, and then back up at the Stoor Worm. The great beast, its head like a dragon, stared down at me. It no longer moaned or moved but was watching, as if waiting for my permission. I looked at the goblet, then looked back up at the worm. I nodded, and held it up in toast to the mighty serpent. It bowed its head to me, purring like a cat. Its black body glowed a deep violet color that shined brighter and brighter as the purple glow lightened to a reddish-blue. And then, the Stoor Worm burst into a blast of pure light. The bright light spread out white effulgent wings in a hundred directions, before coming back together into a single orb that hung there in the sky like a descended star—a pure white ball of energy.

The light lowered down to me and hung over the water, its size twice that of Scuabtuinne. The goblet of truth was still clasped in my hand and lifted up in perpetual toast. The orb of light lifted above the goblet and poured itself into it. Like sand through an hour glass, the light trickled in, never filling the cup despite its size, as bits of light flecks fell into the chalice in a perfect funneled form. As the last of the light leaked into the goblet and the orb disappeared, I lowered it and peered inside. A glowing liquid like white lava filled the goblet. Not wasting another moment, I pressed the goblet of truth to my untrue lips, and swallowed the light whole.

Book 5

Over the Moon

"Just like that... The dark took him." I shook my head, scraping my new talon along the black wall as I sighed at feeling so useless.

"Hesiod, the dark didn't take him. Whatever trap he rushed headlong into, only he could have willed the where. He is where he needs to be. Perhaps the wall was only for him and it called out to his ears alone." Apollo spoke frankly as if all had gone according to plan.

I stepped away from the wall and looked at the god of wisdom with doubt. I remembered when he'd first come to me in the hopeless hell of Hades. He'd reminded me of who I'd been and what I was called to do. He'd come to me in that darkness with the light of the present, and the promised light of the future. He showed me his wisdom. He showed me my own light too. Yet the strangeness of the journey through Jötunheimr, the inconsistencies in his reasoning, and other gods' words of warning had me suspicious. And he'd never quite told me the why behind it all. Why would a god of the bleeding, mythological past be so invested in exalting a modern Christian soldier? Why would he expect all the other solar gods to relent while he alone continued to stand? I had the feeling something sinister was brewing, but for the moment, we were all at the reticent god's whim. There was nowhere else to turn.

Apollo frowned at me. "Why do you look at me as if I am some stranger? How many times have we sung together? How many times have my muses guided your own light of understanding? Hesiod, we are working towards something more. Rangabes will surely succeed."

Apollo walked closer to me. His smooth, flawless face was radiant in its natural glow of beauty. He placed his hand upon my shoulder and I forced a tight smile and nodded.

"The both of you need to focus. We have more than enough to deal with at the moment." Cerberus stood behind us, looking up at that ominous tower, a middle finger of darkness to the Celtic sun. "Why have we met no resistance? I came expecting war." His thoughts were clear and measured. Not even a bark accompanied his strange method of speech through thought.

"Sulis will show herself soon enough. If she bested Lugh, Arawn and the Morrígan, then we must be prepared. I think she wants us to come to her tower unimpeded," Apollo said, itching his cheek and looking up with a hesitant glance flashing across his normally imperceptible face.

"Sulis hides in her heights, too risen in the night to shine down amongst the stars. Not even the moon can catch her glance, how much less for us lesser suns. She's forgotten me." The voice crashed down upon us, its startling heat pushing us all into a defensive frenzy.

Sitting atop the black wall and off to our left was a man clothed in a loose purple robe draped over golden flesh, covering little more than a small sliver of torso and his groin, stopping at mid-thigh. His hair hung to his feet, its yellow rivaling the strained, hanging sunlight of tree-canopied rays. He kicked his feet at the air and smiled down at us.

"Now you come? Now? Belenus, you shining sun god, you hid your light from me!" Apollo shouted, shaking his fist but standing still, at least for the moment. "Sulis had the will to at least resist, and Lugh the honor to join, but what of you? How many Celtic suns are worthy to be sons of the true solar soul, the true movement of the one sun?"

"Easy for you to say. You have us all bow to your Roman pawn and for what? We give him our draining light, and dissipate as you rub your hands in the greedy shadows of your strange sun. Why is it that Ra is no more? Why is it that Helios and Hyperion are gone from the mythic existence? Do you mean for us all to join as one, to have an avatar carry our dimmed light into a brighter future? No... no. All you mean for is to have our lights burnished in the furnace of your pawn. Methinks you plan to let that worthy light burn him to ash as you drink from our fountain. This whole quest, this Rangabes, all of it a lie!" Belenus sprang to his feet and glared down at Apollo.

Apollo's face went blank and he lowered his arms and stood subdued. I watched with arms crossed, my allegiance as unsure as it'd ever been. Had Apollo not given me the secret of his bright wisdom? Had he not instructed me on the myth and power in lands unseen? Had he not led me to aid Rangabes, to become brothers with a truly worthy soul? There was no way to turn my back on his blessings, to turn my back on my own people's light-born past. If Apollo was the Hyperborean god, the founder of the people of light, how could I distrust his noble soul? Could he be so maniacal to orchestrate such a darkening of light; had he lingered too long?

If the realms of myth were so weakened, perhaps it wasn't so maniacal of Apollo. Maybe nothing else could awaken a sleeping sun so blotted out in its own eclipse of memory. Whatever it was that Rangabes possessed, Apollo saw in him a soul worthy of being sent forward with his blessing. The light Rangabes carried, could it be taken from him? My own accusations joined with Belenus's were not enough. For if Apollo truly wanted to possess these dying gods and their solar spirits, why would he not do so himself? Still, I had to ask.

"Why send Rangabes? Could you not take these dimmed flames yourself?" I said. Belenus laughed but Apollo merely glanced at me, his face still blank and pulled back from it all.

"I've explained it before, Hesiod. Of such little faith you are, you who authored the faith of so many for so long. The irony of your unbelief is mad."

"Stop it already and speak plain," Cerberus said with a sharp bark. Belenus tilted his head, meaning the thought had surely been meant for us all, and it had been one that had sounded loud and clear like a cannon shot.

"I've told you already that Rangabes is a beacon of my light into the new world of the mythless masses. A hero forged with a bronze spirit, and a hero meant to bring about a new age through walking in the power of that glorious old. To drink from the sun of the great pantheon of powerful peoples, all who were ignited in some way by that original Hyperborean man and soul, that is what I wanted for him. Is he my vessel? No. He is one who walks as his own because he carries his people. You all doubt and doubt my goodwill, but here I stand and say I am bowing my own might in the face of a mortal." Apollo shook his head, then turned to directly address me. "Why have I not taken this task myself? That is your question. I have in part. But I do not need these other suns," he said, his arm gestured up offhandedly at Belenus. "Could I recreate the Hyperborean man, just as he was in the beginning? No. Their blood is sacred, as Pindar sang. Can a sun create separate rays, or are those rays mere extensions of itself, the same substance undivided but united in that first emanating cause? Those rays are the Hyperboreans, and I can no more create them than a man can separate himself into two different persons."

"Why don't you finish that line of thought then?" Belenus looked down at Apollo and leaned forward with gritted teeth. His golden skin had taken on a frightening pallid yellow as if he were a tanned corpse.

"We come from the same source," Apollo said.

"And what is that source? Mere light?" Cerberus questioned knowingly.

"Power. Divinity. We Hyperboreans are no less gods than you lot," I said, looking at these mythic beings with equality—no... superiority. I was the sun's ray, just as these few were too, though perhaps not Cerberus—that old hound of darkness and death. "You are not the sun Apollo, and neither are you Belenus. This noble people, my noble people, were born in light pure. That essence energized us into existence. Our actions belong to the light." I shook my head as I looked around at the myths I'd once written so devoutly about. "A Hyperborean is not made, he simply is. And to be Hyperborean is to walk in this being, this gift of godhood. My footsteps follow eternity and are pressed with the infinite. To be of the sun, one has to shine forth from it in the first place. But regarding those rays that come discolored through shadowy distortion... well, perhaps those rays no longer can feed at the root of power. Your skin Apollo is thin and pale, and your black boned structure is beginning to protrude. You would take all the light in the world if it meant your flourishing, but your refusal against the eternal being of Hyperborea has poisoned you, and a poisoned well is tainted beyond repair. Your stained soul prevents you from taking light in its pure power. The purity of powerlessness is foreign to you, impossible even. But as Rangabes bowed to his being and willed the one good, you hoped his cleansing power might cover your own shadows in a forgiving light of worth. He is your vessel, yes? Is this because you want to empty his purity dry in hopes of cleansing yourself from this stain—this fear of the shadow that has already covered your soul? You are no Hyperborean. You remain. Rangabes becomes by being."

"Are you done? Is this your next work, Hesiod? Jealous of Homer? Must you write an epic now?" Apollo paced to the wall, stopping just short of it and turning back again to walk towards me. "These insults hurled by all. All of you. Cerberus, you doubt me when it is I who awoke you. Hesiod, you question me when it is I who gave you an answer in the first place. It was I who gave you life and light again. And Belenus, you suddenly appear only to accuse and cause strife amongst my own? Has everyone gone mad?"

"We only want a simple answer," Cerberus said. I nodded in agreement, standing tall despite Apollo's aggressive striding back and forth like a cornered tiger.

"Why have you put Rangabes on a quest you yourself should be able to embark on?" I said. "Could it be that the god of light has been darkened?"

Apollo stopped stalking and stared at me, his golden eyes aflame. "My soul is a flame that does not flicker, but burns continuous. I am not capable of suffering shadows. You claim I have some stain, but that is a lie, Hesiod, and be thankful I don't burn you to ash at such blasphemy. Your Hyperborean kinship and my love for you, whether or not you're willing to remember and still see, is enough for me to hold back my wrath. Honor. I have honor." He looked at me as the flames in his eyes dimmed to a softer glow, and he squinted and looked above my head at some unseen thought. "I woke you up to guide Rangabes to the land of promise, the land made for the children of the sun," he said as he turned to Cerberus. "Even you question. Can you not see that I care?"

Cerberus sat erect as high as the wall, and perhaps thicker. His three heads glared proudly back at Apollo, apparently not interested in apologizing for any perceived affront. "You care about our kind's end. You care about our power fading," he said.

"Of course. Of course I do. And you did not, that is why you slept. There was nothing to uphold, nothing to guard. But you were wrong. The solar spirit lives on, that heroic will that belongs in bronze yet ascends towards a new form. I saw Rangabes die defending his beloved Constantinople. He leapt off the ramparts and held his own against hordes of hungry invaders. Alone and cutting down so many that truly I could not ignore such heroism. I saw him die, his worthy emperor and city along with him. Was this city an heir to Hyperborea? Or was its people? Perhaps, perhaps not. But in Rangabes... as his soul ascended, the sunbeam of Hyperborea connected him right to that eternal source. I saw it. I watched."

"And did you prevent that ascension? Did you cast his soul into the dark pits of Tartarus?" I yelled, my fists clenched. I remembered my brother's nothingness, the pain he endured—the pain we both endured while Apollo gallanted free, concocting his strange schemes.

"You know what Erebus told you. He called Rangabes a failure and you believed his words. I said no such thing. Rangabes was cast into Tartarus, but not by me... no, and I'm sick you'd think such a thing. All of you," he said, tiredly heaving his arms around at the three of us in a weary and ragged gesture. "His heroism those last days in his impossible war was a burst of light, true. But from the beginning, his pure and perfect will towards the utmost glory of the infinite was united to his Hyperborean ancestors in such a way that no mortal has ever been able to accomplish. This balance, this glorified and transcendent focus anchored to eternity and the historical, had all us dying gods watching him from his younger days and onward. Light and dark, far and small, it didn't matter who or where, all the gods watched his march towards the end with worry and intrigue. Most saw our end in him, and those wily Fates screamed it the loudest, though they relented to the rest of us with quaking terror that even they could not see what he truly meant. Wyrd took a liking to him, which is no surprise. But her guiles belong to someone else, and I merely hope to survive her higher whims." Apollo sighed as he leaned back against the wall. The black stone didn't swallow him whole like it had with Rangabes, and so my suspicion remained. Yet, I kept quiet as did the rest of us as Apollo continued. "His life was watched with fear and trembling by the full pantheon of all gods. I trusted in his promise but it could not be ignored that his appearance and destiny was to bring about a final change to our order—an order that had already fallen to some decay. I did not cast him into Tartarus... maybe that was Wyrd testing him for her unknown plans. She never was quite as you wrote. You and your people pictured her wrong: she was always on the other's side. But I accuse without proof and am not entirely sure who it was that dragged him there. Perhaps if you'd been awake Cerberus, you might have stopped it, but there is no telling who—if not Wyrd. Was it

Zeus? He's been absent and silent for too long. Some other god I've never heard of, perhaps? My mad brother Dionysus? Doubtful. He was always on the side of glory for the most part."

"You spin and spin, be careful you do not get caught in what you've spun. You sir, are a dark sun." Belenus clapped his hands and laughed at his rhyme. I shook my head at the strange god's jokes. I was in no mood to laugh, but Apollo's speech certainly had the feel of crafty weaving. What was true and what was trap?

Apollo stared off at nothing, uninterested in offering a retort. Finally, he spoke, "The dark forces that are at work, the bleeding of the mythic realms as they swirl down the drain—it is hard to know who decided to act. Was it willed by his own spirit? He no doubt felt guilty at failing his city, however impossible the odds, perhaps his will weakened at the end. I think his will was wilted with guilt and a sense of failure, and that this weakening allowed for some god to act and interfere with his soul's release to that eternal light. That interference set off this whole thing. Once he was cast into Tartarus, then I decided to act. These harried plans, this confusion and rush was the result of my own indecision and unforeseen anticipation of what might go wrong. Much has, as you can see from Rangabes not being here and three Celtic solar gods being reduced to swine. But fate has played to a weird tune. Blame her, not me. I do not see what is beyond the setting sun, but I intend for the sun to rise again, whether I am a mere ray, the sun itself, or a distant speck of light—it does not matter. I do not want Hyperborea to die." Apollo breathed deeply, sighing at the release of such spirit, yet he seemed stronger for it in my eyes. I felt better, but would be a fool to blindly look into the sun and accept its light as harmless. There were questions still unanswered, but for now, it would do.

"Thank you." I walked over to the slumped god of wisdom while he leaned against the wall with the weary weight of confession on his shoulders.

Cerberus leaned down his three heads and nuzzled against Apollo's head affectionately, a dark purple tongue lolling out to lick his cheek. Apollo laughed in response, wiping his sopped skin and standing straight, away from the wall. Belenus sat there on the wall, leaning so far forward and with such a wicked glare that I was surprised he hadn't leapt off and attacked Apollo, the way he stooped like a hungry vulture.

Apollo stepped towards him, squinting up with suspicion. "You come now out of darkness, a supposed god of the sun yet you sow discord and accuse, action belonging to one who works with shadows. I'm a fool for not realizing sooner. Gwydion, why don't you show us your true form and take us to your pathetic master?"

"I have no master!" Belenus shouted.

His form rippled, breaking apart and bubbling like a sudden landslide as his golden flesh fell off to reveal a small, peevish looking fellow beneath. He was bald with beady red eyes, and thin orange moustaches hanging to his chin. He wore only a loin cloth that was torn and dirty. He was so skinny that he looked like a skeleton haphazardly wrapped in a thin layer of pale, dirt-splotched skin. Like a monkey he sat there hunched and unclothed, a grotesque little god unworthy of the form he'd disguised himself as before.

"The god of trickery and deceit lives only for himself. Where are Lugh, Arawn and the Morrígan?"

Apollo said through clenched teeth. His bow was already aimed and at the ready, its gleam of sunlight a fearsome sight that had appeared in a subdued flash I'd somehow missed.

"They've become the pigs they always were. An exterior fitting for an interior so swinish," Gwydion said.

"Take us to Sulis," I said, my talon raised and my robe aflame with a deep-orange glow.

"Suliiiiiis!" he whined, a high-pitched shriek pouring out of his mouth like that of a bratty child.

The tower above lit up black, and a streak of white light thundered from its peak, soaring down towards us like a missile, yet it landed quietly atop the wall, right next to Gwydion. The light dispersed, revealing Sulis standing there above us with her dark violet dress billowing out around her. Her forlorn locks of red hair were coiled like several fiery serpents, gathered together and contained with a silver crown topped with dagger-like amethyst diadems the same deep purple as her robe. With her face of distinguished porcelain, delicate and angular, royal and haughty, she stared down at us in such a way that revealed she was used to getting whatever she wanted. The way her kissable chin was tilted back and her green eyes stared down her straight, narrow nose: I couldn't deny her beauty.

"We're reaching the end now, aren't we Apollo? The end of your games that is," her voice drew in all the surrounding sounds, forcing an unnatural silence the way her speech swallowed the air. If not for the flapping of the wind and her still billowing dress, her voice would be the only sound in a silence she commanded. "Rangabes and his chthonic convergence is finally coming to that fine point of solar deceit. Will you take him to your ruined home? Your curse on this wall did the trick and served its purpose." She smiled and Gwydion leapt up to his feet and hopped back and forth like a jester.

"The wall was his will. Accuse me as you might, you cannot turn my own kin against me. Cerberus and Hesiod saw through Gwydion's deceit." Apollo spoke as if he were convincing himself of the veracity of his lies. Again, my doubt bubbled back into my mind.

With such an admission, whether or not he'd realized it, I knew that when the time came, I'd be prepared to cut him down.

I glanced over at Cerberus and he met my eyes with his right head and whispered in my mind, "Apollo is not sure where his own plots are leading. Let it be so, we mustn't bow to his words, no matter how eloquent or wise sounding. Be on guard." I clenched my jaw shut and held my taloned hand close to my side, ready to wield it at Sulis and Apollo alike.

Sulis smiled a wicked grin. "Rangabes thrown into a twisted Hel that is not even its pale, Norse shadow. No, instead he is in some strange Otherworld amalgamation, a wound of myth with Valhalla blasphemously tossed in. You wanted him there Apollo, to win that goblet of truth. You wanted him there because you yourself are not capable of besting such twisted sporting games, an inverted Olympics of blood and dark. Who is the games master? Were you not the founder of your precious Olympics in Ancient Hellas?" She laughed and Gwydion joined in. Apollo scowled in silence. "Well, he won that goblet, but he did one thing you didn't think possible. He drank it—drank it all. The Stoor Worm's sacrifice is your death sentence."

Apollo's light seemed to dim; the golden god paled into a pallid corpse of himself. For the first time since I'd seen him and known him, he looked utterly lost and shockingly—afraid.

"Does he know?" Apollo whispered.

Sulis slowly smiled, a crooked and haughty grin maiming the delicateness of her face with masculine harshness. She pointed a long finger up and off to the horizon. I turned to look and fell to my knees. There in the sky loomed two giant beings, their bodies suspended high in the heavens and larger than the disk of the sun. Yet they appeared firmly fixed and standing despite being perched on the nothingness of the heavens.

The one giant was a misty silhouette of shadow. A darkness taking on the form of primordial power—the form of a giant rolling up the heavens as if it were a map. The other giant was composed purely of light, a hot white heat that was stronger than the sun and pushed back just as powerfully as the other giant's darkness did. Beside the giant shadow being there were three other shadows shaped like swine. Like black pig-shaped clouds, they bowed at his feet and snarled at the being of light.

"We can only watch and witness now. Rangabes fights darkness. Whoever wins, decides our fates," Apollo murmured.

***

The great nothing. Colorless color. Opaque and translucent. Above and below. White light: walls, skies, and oceans of white light. White light. But the white was not white. It was clear and bright. A nothingness where light shined. Was this what black looked like when exposed? I looked down at my calloused hands, mottled in grime and blood from this strange journey I'd been set on.

Nothingness had blanketed me more than enough. Yet this nothingness, this was not a quilt I was willing to roll under—to rest in. No matter how warm. No matter how pure.

A quilt. I held up my arms and stared at my scars, my glorious, sacred scars. The bite: two perfect blue dots. The wolf's head: a branded silhouette, burning red. A quilt. This whiteless white, a quilt. I remembered. The words came back to me as if Kronos whispered them alive again.

Escape Tartarus and you will be rewarded by founding a powerful people, fulfilling Apollo's mandate. If you look below, one patch of this quilted black is not like the others. The answer is in the past but present.

Had I not already escaped Tartarus? Yet, had I not done so without finding that patch unlike the others? The past but present. Not the relived memory of my Constantinople's sad fall. Past but present. Quilted black. I stood in quilted white now. Now. The present. The past was a black quilt. The present was a white one. What had the goblet's truth, its light of pure sacrifice, done? Quilt. The word was there, and I couldn't unroll it and awaken. No, not yet.

That goblet. It had answered the riddle, solved it for me when I hadn't known it had gone unanswered. So, a part of me remained in Tartarus—or more accurately in death. As long as I was chained to death, it was an abyss that could not be climbed out of unless the Lord himself raised me up. What was this quilt? The quilt perhaps was an extension of, if not itself, Tartarus. That dark chaos, that dark concealing mist, blinding the light from seeing its own glory. Blinding the living from seeing the sins and power of the dead... that unseen mythic heroic world where light was rewarded, where power was celebrated, where the now could remember the glory of the righteous tyrant and the loving, traditional past.

Did I need to look below? I looked down at my feet to make sure there wasn't some trick beneath me, but I stood on solid.... solid white light. Not there. When did I look below? When? The past and present. How could I look below them both? I itched my brow and smiled as I remembered. When rowing through the Duat, Hesiod had spoken wisely. But with Sobek's interruption and constant conflict, I'd never considered his words in light of this riddle. I'd assumed Tartarus was gone forever. I'd forgotten Kronos's cryptic murmurings.

Hesiod had spoken of a moment, a perfect moment not beyond past or present, but in it and joined perfectly. If I pictured those moments as forming a circle, could this quilt, this answer, lie at the bottom of the circle of the past and present? The moment. The repetition. The eternal being and becoming in harmony, the finite to infinite, remaining pure. My joined will, the speartip as I'd called it to Hesiod. Oh, how I missed my brother who'd been away from me for too long. His words, wisdom, and love would do me well now.

It was Wyrd's string I plucked—that redeemed mother of Aeneas, a true god-mother of mine in the literal and spiritual sense. I nodded. I'd made the abyss my own. Embraced it by becoming it, yet retaining my all. Reenacting the repetition of power in the every moment of the eternal now. I remembered that. Hesiod had said to look inward and guide my soul like a ship towards the heroic past and my own heroic future. The past, present and the future. I was going somewhere. I was nearing my answer. I could see it, feel it. But there was more to peel back, this riddle a stubborn, impenetrable orange that had me considering swallowing the skin out of a starvation of wits and will.

I chuckled, and narrowed my eyes at the white below me. The speartip. The being and becoming that pierces the shroud... no, no. The quilt! Pierces the quilt of time! The speartip pierces the quilt and catches the flying fish, that single fish, that uncatchable fish! Yes! Eternity in the piercing! And to pierce through such a quilt, to catch a fish, one has to look into the river, one has to aim below. The below... not under, but within. The within. Will directed within, reflected without and back again in a circle of eternal heroism. Pure will. Purity of powerlessness. The great surrender, the great embracing of the all.

One patch of this quilted black is not like the others. The answer is in the past but present.

This one patch—the only patch in the quilt of time. The patch of pure will. The patch over the elusive fish. I'd speared it. I was spearing it. I would spear it. Yes. Yes! My answer. This white quilt of light. That black quilt of dark. Together, folded into one, they formed my patch. I could not grasp it without the goblet thrusting me here. But now, now nothing could stop me. Nothing!

"Do you hear that!" I shouted, my voice a surging siren of ecstatic triumph and vigor. I shivered, my body wavering with excitement. "I cannot be stopped. For I act. I am. And I will!"

My words burned, shouts singed with song. Musical notes imbued them as they crescendoed into the white light, and I laughed as a sudden pleasure shook me. And then pleasure exploded into an ecstasy that ripped through me, searing into pain. It burned my insides then chilled them with ice, only to melt and freeze a hundred times over, all in a moment. The rapture at last released its terrible hold on me and I dropped to my knees, gasping for relief.

"You didn't think I was finished, did you? Our race had only just begun!" Manannán mac Lir said.

I looked to my left, to face the god. In a flash of white light, cold steel embraced my flesh and I shivered at its sudden touch. My trusty armor had summoned itself to me somehow, perhaps Wyrd's doing. Perhaps of the magical steel's own will. Perhaps it was my own. Regardless, I was covered once again and both my faithful weapons were latched to my side. I flexed my cloud-shoed feet and breathed deeply as the tremors of painful ecstasy dwindled. I was the speartip—the point tearing through. Even in this place of perfect light, darkness had bled through too.

"I feast on swine that dies and lives, again and again, just for me! That same cauldron that bubbles their flesh so sweetly, cooked my rotting skin back to this lovely hue. Ruddy cheeks such as these cannot be bought!" He slapped his two cheeks and grinned wide. His hair was long and shining; the man looked even healthier and more powerful than he had in his own sea.

"I drank of the goblet, Manannán. The worm was all too willing to give its life to truth. It took me here. Yet how is it that you've followed?" I said.

He shook his head, his grin spreading wider, and I clenched my fists as he loudly laughed, drawing it out like entrails shat from a pig. My mind was darkening next to such a swinish stain of a man in these hallowed heavens. Perhaps it was the talk of swine that was hogging my mind's pure focus. I clenched my fists harder.

He said, “I followed? My foolish, tiny little friend. I followed? The audacity! That goblet is mine and remains as such. Remember our little game? Lie three times to receive the goblet of truth. The paradox of life in the land of the dead! You lied three times and spoke truth in the same breath. Typically, the three lies break the goblet and render it useless, but your accidental blunder did something else. It... it cracked it and remade it at once. In a moment.”

“I spoke the true untruth. A paradox is required to make sense of it all. Regardless, Ashipattle was there. He led with the questions that I’m sure you no doubt force fed him during his accursed imprisonment in a beast he’d already slain.”

“Very astute. But I’d assumed you’d stick with just untruth and the goblet would be yours in useless shards as I decapitated your ugly mug from your even uglier body. But no. The goblet made into a paradoxical moment, of being made and undone. For one such as me who is always cooked right back anew, your...” he paused, put both his hands beneath his chin and pressed up in pretend decapitation as he made a strange clucking sound as if my sword had been a cock. “Your decapitation freed my life blood right into that cup. Right into those filled in cracks, that unbroken breaking. You fool. You fool! The worm’s sacrifice was for naught. Whatever you stumbled into doing made me even greater. For now, I am in you. You drank me along with the worm. And even the tiniest bit of dark is enough to dampen any light. An absence, eh?”

“An absence... An absence,” I said, shaking my head. The reborn god wanted to talk. Was this the further prodding into that quilt unlike the others? Was the end finally at hand? I had to find out. "I know, I know, darkness is an absence of light. Evil an absence of good."

He coughed, and raised his finger, wagging it like a cobra's tail. "Evil is the presence of absence."

"Semantics. You speak meaningless paradoxes, fool."

"Evil is irrationality. Evil is necessary, because it never is. I do not twist my tongue here in confusion. I speak those true untruths you're so fond of! Evil is never necessary, because it is always good. How can an absence of good, be always good? How can this void filled with nothing, the present absence, be something when it is nothing? Because nothing exists, as long as something remains some, and not whole. Therefore, all the something is touched by nothing," he said.

I frowned and crossed my arms, thinking once more of that enlightening conversation with Hesiod on the nature of purity. We'd figured it out then that to be pure was to be untouched by the nothing. But here was this fool claiming the something implied the nothing's touch. But he was speaking in the theoretical, the nonexistent mind frame. Not from the eternal, and not even merely the finite. He was speaking in terms of decay. The rot of shallow being. The stench of low becoming. He spoke as if nothing was not better than something, but it simply was all—was the everything. Nothing corrupted all. I squinted at the smiling god's hungry face.

I shook my head and said, "You speak of not merely the irrational, but the irrelational—the man without relation. My words are my own. I made that one fit into this talk. Can you not see though that my word could not exist without language and all its parts? You speak in the grandiose terms of the great nothing. Then what are you doing here fighting with me? Why? Any why you hurl out from your nothingness is tainted by unreason, untruth, and darkness. The decay you espouse has rotted any truth you purport into falsity. Nothing matters, when nothingness is the end." I nodded, but my heart clenched in my chest so as not to drop too far into that pit of nothingness. How could I not fear eternal darkness? How could anyone live as if that wasn't there? What mattered was why one answered the dark.

His face drooped, then tensed back up like a turtle into its shell, hard with the determination to survive with his strange worldview intact. "Evil as the presence of absence. Evil as the nothing. What do you call good? The something. Existence. I propose another definition: the good can only be something that cannot decay and fall fully into my nothingness. So good is the perfect existence in the eternal, infinite being. But then you must ask yourself, is not everything and everyone evil, for all are not fully eternal—they all rot. But there my friend, where the dark and light shine together in relation—I know you like that word—there where they impossibly, paradoxically shine, there blooms Good Evil. A flower with petals of solar rays and a stem pushing out from the eternal night. Ashipattle for all his good, agrees with my evil. It was in his song."

I frowned, for he was not wrong about Ashipattle. If only I could have asked that ashen king what he had meant, what he himself had believed. What had Manannán forced him to do? I knew Ashipattle was a hero and a good man. Whatever happened, I knew he belonged to and in the light.

I crossed my arms and scowled. "I am untouched by your Good Evil for I will one thing, and that is the eternal.

You will death, I will life. May this be a fitting battle then. I've been fighting death this whole time."

"Let's see how pure you are after this, you little angel. Look, here is Lugh!" Manannán gestured wildly to his left.

A shadow arose from the depths of the perfect white light we stood on. A man emerged from the dark with black tattoos that shifted like smoke all over his pale skin stood there with teeth bared. His eyes were swirling pools of black mist that leaked out of the corners, trailing behind him in putrid trails of fiery ash. He held out his arms which extended into fine points: shadowed swords of black mist serving as his hands.

"Lugh has no Answerer anymore!" Manannán laughed, flourishing the grand Fragrarach in his hand. "But he has his friends! The Morrígan, the crow who tried to circle the light. You are a carrion, my dear!"

Another black silhouette emerged, this time from the light above us. A woman with her pale breasts exposed and dark black hair spread out like wings, hovered above Manannán. Her bottom half was wrapped in smoky gray robes that hung low on her slim waist. Her mouth was an evil pout with lips black and smooth. Her eyes sported the same leaking black mist that Lugh saw through.

"This cannot be the fourth circle! What has become of that accursed soil?" I shouted. "I was not finished!"

"The Ichor Games, inverted and foul; you really think there were four? What were those circles but spirals of time that when neared, draw one to a faraway nothingness. Do they not appear as the graves they were designed to be? The fourth is me. Again and again. The fourth continues onward. You will not redeem these lands and peoples! That sword you redeemed is a lie! It still failed and you cannot take it away," Manannán said.

"But I can make it better." I held up Hrunting in my left hand and hoisted up the returned Solisinanis in my right.

"But wait, my eager angel. You are a bear cub stumbling into a wasps' nest. There is another shadow come to aid my war against the light, against what once was but never truly is. Here is Arawn, a green knight turned into violet night!"

And from the far horizon, a dark purple shadow burned into being. The clacking of hollow horse hoofs boomed as if the steed were made of thunder and the sky it raced across was of glass. The horse shrieked all the way through its weeping gallop. It was a hulking beast of black with muscle rippling in sheens of shadow. Its eyes carried a piercing red glow, fiery pits alight with rage. I leaned to my right and left, stretching as I readied myself for the challenge of battle.

Astride this horse was a deep violet knight who wore armor of such a dark purplish hue that it appeared infused with an even darker black. It shimmered and crackled with swirls of a lighter violet shade. His horse thundered to a lightning crash of a stop beside Manannán. I watched him with sadness as he sat there accursed atop his shadowed steed. It was a kind mercy that his black mask covered those hideous leaking eyeballs of black mist the others had. But his black helmet was an even wickeder sight. Like a skull with its mouth burnt away, the bizarre ribbing of the helmet made him look like a corpse brought back to life. There were no holes for the eyes either, just two empty sockets. I looked closer and shuddered as I realized it was no helmet. That was Arawn's tortured skull. The skull moaned like a man gagging on his severed tongue.

My armor intensified its red glow in the face of such darkness while surrounded by such perfect light. I could feel that power burning inside me, a volcano about to erupt. My armor did not smoke with decrepit, twisted black mist like the dark ones surrounding me—instead it glowed like the sun, blood-red rays extending out from me. I'd become a bloom of beaconed light. My arms glowed their distinct hues and I held up my glorious weapons bursting with power. Our talk had been made cheap by the nothingness that gripped these foes so ferociously.

"Come, you fallen god! You pollute the light with your presence. Even as you say all is naught, I will show you that you are naught!"

I leapt into action, light bubbling in my chest and exploding in a fountain as I bounded into the air. I swung my axe and sword down, heading right for Arawn's skull. The horse reared back on its hind legs, kicking its hooves at me. Like a cannon ball to the chest, its hooves cracked my armor right in the center, but the landed blow couldn't prevent my own swinging weapons from tearing through the beast's flesh. Solisinanis cleaved a chunk of dark meat from the horse's underbelly while Hrunting dug a straight, fine slice that spilled the horse's guts out. The horse bayed and wailed. It reared back, flailing off its feet and onto the ground. Arawn flipped off his horse unharmed, but his steed had been rendered useless like a broken stud.

My chest armor's cracks glowed an orange hue like lava pushing through the surface. Staggered as I was, I barely had time to throw up my weapons to parry Manannán's strike. I threw my arms up, holding my weapons crossed together to stop his blow. I pushed my parry back at him and he swayed away. Lugh and the Morrígan attacked in unison as I rushed to dodge. She cackled and cawed like a crow as she flew back and forth, zipping around while hurling orbs of black shadow down at me. My axe and sword were able to swallow these strange orbs, their light burning away the dark. But with my attention focused upward, I was vulnerable to the rest.

Lugh leapt to the left of me, swinging his arms as I turned my shoulder and tried to ward off his blow. Unable to move fast enough, his misty sword-arms sliced into my triceps and I screamed, swinging my axe wildly at him as he stepped easily out of my reach. My arm was cut deep, blood cascaded down it like liquid rust. He snarled and set on me again and I parried his blows with Hrunting, while keeping Solisinanis raised and blocking those annoying bursts of black energy from the Morrígan.

Realizing that I'd have to take one of them down before Arawn and Manannán attacked too, I rolled backwards and aimed both my weapons at the Morrígan. Beams of red and blue light burst forth from my arms and amplified out through my weapons, shooting up in a concussive blast of bright force. The light struck her straight on and consumed her, leaving nothing behind as she vanished.

I rolled out of the way of Arawn's steel fist, blocking Manannán's stab with my axe and Lugh's overhead slash with my sword. I jumped backwards and retreated to survey the three remaining foes. They cautiously stalked forward, and I breathed as deep a breath as I could. Could they block my focused light? I poured it once again into my weapons and shot it out towards Lugh.

He threw up his sword-arms which held for a moment, then crumbled into ash as my light burnt him away into nothingness—or hopefully somethingness. I prayed these former gods of light might still be redeemed.

Manannán growled and leapt forward but was too slow to prevent me shooting another burst at Arawn. My light bounced off of his dark armor, useless. Arawn charged forward and I ducked and spun backwards, barely blocking both blows. This was going to be a tough one to finish. I sighed, tired and alone, and held my weapons up, readying myself for another attack.

***

Two lights like falling stars burned down from the battle between dark and light in the heavens. Two of the shadowed swine had disappeared. Could these falling streaks of light be Lugh and Arawn, or perhaps the Morrígan? The meteors neared, and I started as I realized they were headed straight for me. Using my talon, I scrambled up the wall and out of the way. Sulis scowled at me and Gwydion laughed.

"What's wrong poet, never seen a battle like this?" Gwydion said.

"Silence fool. Their fall is not a good sign," Sulis said, watching the approaching lights with worry creasing her pretty face.

I turned back and stared as the streaks of light crashed into the ground before us, and the air splintered with a loud crack like ice splitting a tree. The fiery lights tore through the earth and struck the wall with a thud as they skidded to a halt. As the dust settled, I allowed myself to breathe again and stared at the two bodies lying there. One had blue tattoos covering his fit physique which was covered only in a loin cloth. The other was a beautiful naked woman with raven hair. They lay there unscathed, as if merely asleep.

Apollo bent over them and gently held up the man's head. "Lugh?" he whispered.

Apollo breathed into his face, his breath a puff of golden mist that entered into Lugh's slightly open mouth. He repeated the same process with the Morrígan. They stirred, but before either could open their eyes, two spikes of black burst from Sulis's outstretched hands. The first pierced the Morrígan right through her chest, pinning her to the soil. Apollo pulled out his lyre and held it out to stop the second from striking Lugh. The Morrígan screamed as the spike spread its dark poison, highlighting her veins black against her pale skin. With one last cry, she burst into a cloud of crows and flew off into the sky.

Apollo removed the spike like a splinter from his immaculate instrument and stared at Sulis. Before he could act, Cerberus and I attacked her. I shot a burst of red light from my chest while swiping down at Sulis with my claw. She was consumed in light, and the flesh that remained was torn to ribbons by my talon. Cerberus's snakes struck the trickster god, stunning him. Cerberus lowered his gaping maw down and with a wretched crunch, ripped off the god's head, spitting it out like a pit from a plum.

"Why did you wait?" Lugh said through strained words as he slowly sat up, leaning against the wall.

"We watched the battle," I said, pointing up at the sky, where the darkness still battled the light.

"We didn't know if we needed her to save you. She refused to cooperate until it was finished." Apollo sighed, and sat beside Lugh. "I didn't know what to expect. I didn't know if my breath would be enough. In my shock, I forgot like a fool that Sulis waited."

I was stunned at how haggard and tired Apollo looked. The doubts and accusations I'd hurled at him, this impossible task he'd started upon, truly none of us had any real answer to it all.

"I'm sorry about the Morrígan," I said, sitting on the wall with my feet dangling down.

"She flies free now. No longer tethered to the darkness of the fading pantheon we belong to. Her omens are her own." Lugh rubbed his temples. "She belongs to the air now. She is animal, her godhood broken for good."

"I am sorry," Cerberus said. I bowed my head.

"Perhaps she's better off that way. Better to be remembered as something, than to be forgotten as nothing. The raven remains," Lugh said.

"I suppose," Apollo added.

We stopped speaking and stared back into the heavens. The light and dark were still even, still striking and retreating in an endless dance.

"Rangabes fights pure. He will prevail. He must," Lugh said, looking at the sky and unable to hide the tear that had fallen free. He sighed and set his gaze strongly upward, and I turned to look up at the sky too.

***

Arawn and his fists had added plenty of blue-black bruises to my blood splattered arms, purpling the flowing red of my wounds. Spots of my skin had been torn off, and lakes of blood filled in the valleys of my arms. My armor was soaked in scarlet and its light was diffused into a dim red where blood filled in its cracks. My eyes were permanently fixed in a squint, dried blood and sweat stinging my vision into a swirled sight.

Arawn stood there tireless, his blank skull unscathed. Manannán wore a mien of mirth, even with his bloodied face. My landed blows seemed only to enflame his sick joy with a sadistic jaunt. My beams of light had proven ineffective against Arawn's unbreakable armor; it still looked as whole and polished as ever. Its violet shades of infinity sparked purely, mocking the grime I myself was covered in. Manannán seemed to have his answer in Fragarach to my light—Lugh's old sword absorbed it all. My blade could cut his skin, but I'd not yet managed to strike cleanly, not with Arawn keeping my attention divided. There had to be a better way.

It was odd, this temporary respite. I was panting, hunched over and drenched in pain. Arawn and Manannán both stood there waiting, as if longing for more of a challenge. Manannán smiled with ever-twitching lips that spread and warped each second. Arawn and his mask of death was faceless, but his body stood rigid and tall, apparently waiting for his master to move first. So we stood, the silence distilled with decay as I drained myself of life by staying on my feet, dying standing up. My ragged breaths were loud enough to roughly rub the quiet with hopelessness.

"Rangabes, you must see this is folly. The other two perished because they were not part of the Otherworld like us; even with their dark metamorphosis it was not enough. But we... we cannot die because we reign over death," Manannán said, his voice zapping his grin into a suddenly straight, grave look of concern.

"You are wounded and I've killed you before, Manannán. I cannot fear what always is, never was, and always will be." My voice gathered strength and invigorated me, a surprising bubble of energy burst in my soul, my words awakening it.

"Is death and dying an always to you?" He laughed. I think Arawn grunted in an attempt to laugh, but his mouthless skull remained as dead as ever.

I said, "Living, I live! That is my always. That is why I cannot fear. But what I cannot comprehend is your sudden interest in speaking with me as if I'm not covered in blood and on my last breaths. Why?"

"Because you drank from the cup. The Stoor Worm's sacrifice is no simple sip. That burning light you drank, even with my poison—it still burns. And neither we nor you will end without unnecessary suffering," Manannán said.

"And what is that suffering? Whose suffering is it?"

Manannán's face paled and he looked uncertain. Whatever secret he hid, he had hinted at something. Something that Arawn seemed struggling to spit out. Manannán and I both stared at the hulking beast, as he started grunting and sputtering, words muffled by his mouthless skull. His body shook and he raised his armored arms to his faceless face, and punched as hard as he could. He struck his face with booming blows as chips of black skull flaked down, and inky black liquid spilled out from beneath the bone. Arawn's strangled voice shouted free, gurgling out with the black geyser of blood. He bent over screaming as it continued its terrible torrent. Manannán watched without moving, his face even paler and his grin evaporated, condensing back into an unsteady balance beam, tilting back and forth with weighty fear.

"We are in the fourth circle," Arawn choked.

"What is this!" I shouted at Manannán.

"The black of the surrenderless surrender to the silhouetted shadow god of the finite. The god that is all in his ever-present nothingness. He does not exist. And so Arawn vomits the untruth in an attempt to speak truth. Your own cup has overflown," Manannán said, his voice flat and quiet as he watched unmoving.

Arawn's spilling ink slowed to a trickle, and he stood to his feet with the lower half of his skull gone. He wiped his arm through the soiled space where has mouth should have been. What remained of his skull was cracked and crumbling, but at least the foul liquid had at last gone dry.

"The fourth circle was the cup you drank," he rasped, his voice like dust-gnawed bones. "This fight is not true."

"Stop!" Manannán shouted, "Do not awaken him." He stretched out his sword arm, pointing its blade at Arawn who stood unfazed.

"This light and dark in the heavens is only true to the beholder's eye. Where is yours? Where was mine?" Arawn said with his words whispering out strained and ghostly.

"What is the meaning? What is my task?" I said, stumbling towards the broken knight.

"Your task? Your task!" Manannán cried. His hands wavered but his sword remained pointed at Arawn.

"We fought an impossible fight. You slew two, but you cannot slay us. Manannán will resurrect and I cannot be harmed by another. This game is not a fight. This circle requires a final point."

"Was my drinking not that?" I said.

"No, that only brought you here. And now you must aim. Pull back the bow of your intellect and fire inward—a target of the soul," he said.

"That's it!" Manannán screeched.

He leapt at Arawn like a shrieking monkey and swung his sword. Arawn's sockets watched me peacefully as Fragarach crashed his skull into pieces. His body dissolved into black goo until there was nothing left but Manannán and I... and the still waiting white light. I nodded to myself. Aim inward. A final point. It was what I had to do.

I fell upon old Hrunting and let its blade pierce into my heart. Manannán's desperate screams were burned away in the heat of my pain. My heart's beating thudded into nothing, and the light of my eyes exploded in a waterfall of color before washing to gray. The white was no more and I was released, leaving the failed god behind in that expanse he didn't belong in. A beating drum shook my gray blindness. The thumping of a heart pierced by a redeemed sword—the turning of the earth's wheel, its grind the sudden words that rushed into my dying mind.

The Moon calls.
Pursuit of the sun requires its reflection.
I am Sin—
the quilt you sleep in is me.
I watch your restless rest.
I, the ancient god of the Moon.
Lunar light darkens the Solar.
This quilted black is blotted by the sun.
You must look below the sun to see the moon.
But to see the sun, you need to stand above me.
The Moon calls.

The words filled my dimmed sight as I became the blind gray.

***

The sky spilled over into black. Rangabes in his fearsome form of light had vanished. The remaining figure of black thundered, and in his thunder he spread his arms as if desperate in his strange victory and he too became nothing, his black encompassing the heavens. My dear brother had lost, it seemed. But there was something falling from the dark, a slow descending light, laboring down weakly. I sprinted ahead and into the field.

The light spiraled down, thudding loudly as it crashed against the beaten down grass. Cerberus's loud steps boomed behind me, but he kept a distance. I looked back and the great hound bowed his heads and waited. Apollo and Lugh remained by the wall. I stared at the fallen man with confusion. This soul was a stranger to me. He lay there unclothed. His hair had fallen beneath him, cushioning his head. An angelic face that belonged to a prince, a man who could make a woman blush just through the flex of his full lips and spreading of pristine cheekbones. Yet this beautiful man was dying, his skin sallow like sackcloth and his head fallen back, too weak to lift up and acknowledge me.

"Apollo!" I shouted needlessly, as Apollo had already come to my side. I sputtered, gesturing at the fallen man, "Breathe over him like Lugh, save him!"

Apollo held out his hand and a golden lyre flashed from the air and glowed like a ray of the sun. He stepped in front of me and stood over the fallen man, and he began to play. The air seemed to dance along to the harmony of his pristine playing, the plucking pure like gentle streams rolling over pebbled creek beds. Nature bowed to the perfection of this song of light. Apollo opened his mouth and sang: the nightingale's chirp, the rush of the pouring rain, and the mingled tree leaves swaying together in gentle ease—that was what this god's voice brought, and still more. His humming was an instrument better than even his immaculate lyre. Yet the man stayed still in dying form. And then, Apollo's hum was built into words.

Arawn once waited for the dead to come
Arawn once sated with red and rum

The light combed its long fingers in collection
The light of life breaking glass dew of reflection

The mourning of morning is for one who is night
This morning is forever, the one sparked sight

A ship moored to land, broken and still
You joined light and life yet fell for the kill

Arawn sees time that leapt away
Arawn can climb the ladder of day

Awaken, you king of deathly green!
Awaken, you king for eternity is mean!

Apollo abruptly stopped his playing and the wind, the trees, and the harmony of nature snapped into silence, guillotined into submission to the solar god's will. I looked over Apollo's sleek and strong shoulder and at this fallen man, this Arawn. He still laid there but now his chest lifted slightly, up and down, the beat of his heart murmuring life into his lungs. As if nature sought to sing him back to being, its breeze flowed over him and the smells of green Ireland lifted lively into the air, pushing into our bleeding realm with pure reality. A wave of wind carrying soft glowing four-leaf clovers washed over his body. The swirls of green clovers came down three times from the heavens, resting themselves like a pyre over Arawn's body. The green light of the leaves hummed there, piled up in a loose pyramid. All fell silent again as we watched and waited.

A green gloved hand abruptly burst through the top of the pyramid, and a body emerged, garbed in green glowing armor that looked like glass bathed in a seafoam fire. The clovers whisked themselves away with the wind as he stood up. Green runes of glowing emeralds covered his armor. Yet the brightest emeralds were Arawn's brilliant eyes, somehow greener than before. And on his head now sat a crown of gold, studded with seven emeralds on seven points.

Arawn breathed deep and spoke to us all, "Sulis turned me into swine and in that muck, I forgot who I was and am. Manannán tried to play the part of being king of the dead, but he forgot that he himself was already dead. He can still come back, but nobody will care. He is weak and I doubt we will ever hear from him again. I left my kingdom of death to my herds of swine and my red-eared dogs. Nobody came to me anymore. Not until you, Apollo." Arawn bowed his head, and then looked up and stared at Lugh. "And Lugh! You awakened the light, reminded me of my rooted power and path. This is the only way forward. All else will crumble into the dust of nothing. The sun shines and it will not set on those who follow its path. It sets only on those who forget to look and go up. To ascend. You brought me from the depths."

Cerberus hummed, looking at us all with his three heads in each direction. "I know of those cold dark grounds—I guarded them for so very long. But it was false. The sun set and did not rise again only because I slept. But I awoke to what I was and am called to bring." Cerberus took a step closer and lowered his center head, his other two with their tongues lolling out joyfully. Arawn hugged the massive hound's cranium and itched behind his ears.

"It is true that those who know darkness are better than those hidden only in light. For we know the folly of that black way and have overcome it. We don't long for what was weak. Those who do not know it, do not grow quite as strong through resistance. It is like a child who never had to make a choice of its own. It is like steel forged without fire. That is a weakness in and of itself. We are brighter for it," Arawn said, kissing the top of Cerberus's head and stepping back.

"And what of this black sky?" I asked.

"Manannán is trapped in his own despair, dispersed in the dark he so coveted. The path of the moon is one that misleads. It reflects truth and tries to claim it as its own. The moon's light is meek myth," Arawn said, turning to me.

"So now we make the heavens whole and flood them with light," Lugh said as he walked towards us. His lines of blue tattoos glowed brighter as he neared.

"But Rangabes, where has he gone?" I asked.

Arawn rubbed at his face and said, "When I beat the darkness out of my soul and ripped off its parasitic mask, I spoke as true as I could to guide him free. He has left that quilted darkness and has traveled through. Where, I do not know, but I do know he has to do what he is about to do. The four circles are finished and Valhalla and its confused inhabitants have returned to where they belong."

"So it is left for us to clear this sky. In the ocean of light that follows this flood, we must hope that Rangabes surfaces anew," Apollo said, his golden eyes blazing and cast upwards.

"Pour out your light, pour it out together!" Lugh yelled.

I focused the glory of my light in my chest and shot it out in a flow of orange-red fire into the heavens. I screamed with power, pure pleasure and joy coursing through my veins and gathering explosively into my heart. I laughed and drank deep from my soul, the power welling up with eternal flame. Lugh's tattoos cast him in a blue glow as he thrust his chest forward, and a polar white light burned through the atmosphere to join my stream in the heavens. Cerberus reared back his three heads and belched blood red fire into the sky. The flames shot out in three separate streams and then burst together, forming into a thin line before billowing out to embrace the already blue-orange sky. Arawn's armor lit up green, his runes crackling with energy as his emerald light flooded the heavens.

Apollo hovered into the air and spread his arms, pouring out golden light from his entire being. His light tore through the sky and exploded into the wash of blue, green, orange and red. The heavens burst open in waves of pure gold; electrified rainbows carved through the sky and swam back and forth like eels. Gasping, I cut off my light as the others ceased as well. The sky tremored and rippled, settling into an expanse of gold.

Apollo gently floated back to the ground like a petal of a flower and sighed as he landed. "It all rests in Rangabes's hands now. He has reached a realm none of us could dream of. Now, we wait."

And with that, he sat there on the ground with legs crossed, staring up at the clear gold sky—yet his eyes were clouded with a lingering dark.

***

The air was absent, yet I breathed in a stale something, that at the very least, was fitting of the darkness hanging above me. Whatever I breathed, it was not my lungs keeping me alive. The frigid freeze of this empty space bit my skin with frost, yet it didn't manage to pierce through to my blood and bones. My cracked armor still remained, but my dear Hrunting had finished its race and was gone. Solisinanis was still latched to my waist. My arms were heavy and covered in a landscape of carved, canyon flesh. Something was keeping me afloat in this dark land. I stood on rocky gray ground and I felt almost weightless... this land was surely not of earth. Could it be that I stood on the moon?

"Turn around." If a planet could speak, it would sound like this voice. Deep and low, the rumble of an earthquake carried further by the rush of an avalanche.

I turned to where I'd heard the voice and stared in awe at the glory before me. I collapsed to my knees as I saw the top half of a giant sphere that was bright and blue, swirled with white and green. The earth hung there like ripe fruit from Eden, dangling above. I wept, knowing it was beyond my reach. I grabbed clumps of ashy dust and threw them away in disgust. Despite all the horror I'd seen, despite all the impossibilities I'd faced, this was the most terrible. For even as a Christian, the mythical still belonged to earth, even if in some strange realm. This, the moon—this was not meant for me. It was wicked. Wrong. My home was a far-reaching blue light—a beacon of birth, power, and humanity. Now I stood in the land of darkness, the land of stolen, not borrowed light.

"Do you know how I am I?" the voice said.

I shook my head at the strange cadence. "I do not care how you are you, I care only what you do," I said, still on my knees and staring in awe at my beautiful home, with the moon ash sifting through my fingers.

"Do you know when I was I?"

"I care not for when either, but instead a why." I sighed, the airless atmosphere a nothing to my emptied chest. More riddles. Always riddles. I breathed a deeper, emptier breath.

"Open your eyes then," the voice said.

Open my eyes! I frowned and closed my eyes in protest. Closing my eyes did not bring that familiar black, but instead my shut eyelids were somehow ineffective. The landscape was still the moon and I still saw as if nothing had changed and my eyes were open. I shook my head and opened my eyes and saw the same. My stomach heaved and my heart dropped as I recalled the fleshless feel of Tartarus. I looked down in relief to see that my body was indeed still there. Solisinanis was tucked at my waist and faithful Hrunting was still gone like I'd noticed before.

The old sword had gone full circle, and its redemption had closed off those wicked circles. I patted my axe and ran my hands through my thick hair. I breathed a deep sigh, a breathless breath in this impossible air, and closed my eyes again. Through my shut eyelids I saw a strange being that stood before me. I opened my eyes again in shock and the being disappeared. I walked forward, stretching out my arms where the figure had stood but touched nothing. I stepped back and closed my eyes once more, and now the same being stood there towering before me, mere inches away.

The stranger blinked at me, his eyes two large walnuts hanging deep under full, heavy-lidded eyelids. He had thick black eyebrows that arched above like silhouetted domes of a cathedral. His beard was thick and pulled together; the hairs looked to be impossibly made of gemstone. His beard's color was a bright and vibrant purple-blue that could only belong to the lapis lazuli. Even stranger, he had four pale feathered wings extending out—two from his back and two angled below his waist. The wings glowed a sickly gray, a strange mimicking of the moon's own diffused light. His legs were as wide as oxen, and his muscles were comfortably covered in a rippling robe that caressed his tan skin as if not there. He had six large breasts stuffed beneath the robe... what kind of god was this? He... or it, reared over me like a beast; I barely stood up to his knee.

"So, you are Sin, god of the moon?" I said, longing to spit at the feet of such a being.

"I am Sin, an ancient god hailing from Mesopotamian myth. While the rest of the gods linger in weakness as the world forgets their might, I gather strength here always, all the world's ills fueling my delight. I need no mention by name. A mere glance from the herd at the night sky and I've won over those weak-willed ones who see only material, rot and death. Fools fuel my cold flame."

"And yet you've brought my fire here. Do you wish to burn?" I said, staring up at his bearded face, which showed no emotion. I opened my eyes once more, and again he vanished. I blinked and he flashed before me. I closed my eyes again and placed my hand at my waist, holding Solisinanis's hilt.

"Open your eyes," he said.

I frowned, but this time took him at his word, unsheathing my irises to cut his image into this fleshless landscape. And now there he was, standing as the same being, the same exact features, only now he stood at eye level with me at my height. I quickly shut my eyes again, relieved to see the darkness of flesh shielding me from false light once more.

"And which of these images is true?" I said.

"Can you trust an image that is a mere reflection, a dimming of light too pure to see?"

"And what would you have me see?"

"Come. It is why I have brought you here." He curled his fingers at me and turned, his wings flexing and swaying in his gait.

He walked as if he were still twenty feet tall, but I followed all the same. What else was there left for me to do? Was I to slay this god, as his deity stood against my very blood and purpose? Or was his invitation and my listening necessary to move forward? Now was not the time to rush—where was the purity of powerlessness in that? Time was my whip, and as its wielder, I stood behind it by not letting it force me into fear. Its sting was my own to feel.

"Where are we going? There is only nothingness," I said.

Sin stopped and spun around with a toothy grin. The way his dark, hungry eyes gobbled me up made me want to split his face with Solisinanis.

"My ziggurat and throne. Look behind you."

I turned around and sure enough, on the hill we had first set off from, a massive temple now stood. It was made of gray sandstone—moonstone perhaps—as it reminded me of desert architecture. Only the desert here was gray, and so was the temple. A sick and pale glow exuded out from the stones. Shaped like a rectangular pyramid, the ziggurat had sloped walls in front of it that flattened out into a wide plane of surface. A stairway of shiny silver material went right through the middle of the walls and two gray stairways crossed the silver one horizontally, descending out like spread arms. And before those stairs another wall split through the silver stairway, turning it into a t-shape at the intersection. The silver staircase at the top plane of the ziggurat had a silver archway over it, a sort of gate that shined with an even brighter and smoother sheen.

On top of the ziggurat, right in the center of the plane, another arch stood with its own set of silver steps leading up to it. The arch was larger than the first and made of the same silver material, yet atop this arch was a large orb like a miniature moon that shined with the gross pale glow of weak moonlight. Under the top arch was a throne made up of two slabs of brutal black stone, rugged and blocky. It stood there in its brutality and grotesqueness as if to challenge those in front of it to say one negative word, so that the one sitting there might have excuse to execute its attendees.

"This is my house, the house of the little light, the great dark," Sin said.

"Yet it was not there when we left it. Why have me walk in the wrong direction?" I said.

"Why this direction is no more wrong than right. It led us to the end, did it not?"

"Not the end, but merely an end." I did not like the god's fluidity and avoidance of the firm and foundational. The untruth of him was palpable. His breasts were proof enough of that.

"Come. We will speak in finality once I am seated upon my throne." He smiled and jumped high, his wings flexing and riding the airless air, flapping until he fluttered down into his chair.

I leapt after him with surprising ease, bounding as if I too had wings. With two loping jumps I leapt over the strange stairs that shimmered as if of silver liquid, staring down at them as I soared over. I landed in a crouch right in front of Sin, my fist scraping the dusty stone. Sin sat there waiting on his throne, watching me with an odd smirk. His disgusting breasts rested on his lap and I had to look away to reorient myself. What was this god?

"It is well and good you leapt over my stairs. Wise to follow my flight. You see, those stairs look almost like they are of water, some strange silver stream solidified yet not, no? When water flows so smoothly, it is as if it is frozen. Think of this regarding time."

I stood up and bent over to dust my midnight pants off. Of course, it was unneeded as they somehow remained pristine, their charmed exterior as pure as ever. Unfortunately, my armor was still dented and damaged, and blood still slickened my skin, though it had started to dry on me like rust over a faucet.

"What does that even mean? And why have useless steps?" I said.

"But were they not used to describe time?"

"Riddles, riddles. I'll riddle you with my light, you dark jester. You could use being skewered and made cheese of." I shook my head and stared into his soulless eyes. "As if it is frozen... it either is or isn't. As ifs only abstract. A distraction. You dance your notional jig in an ocean of air, your boat nothing but a solid rock sinking with the weight of reality as you sing that nothingness keeps you afloat."

"Rhetorical flourish, very fine indeed. Good fun from one who claims to be of the sun. Can you face my night? No matter, for the matter at hand is liquid, which in a strange way is a moving matter, or at least it appears as such. To be moving is to be not still, not of matter, perhaps? Regardless, my riddling has its purpose, purposeless as I may be." He chuckled, his wings cushioning his body as he leaned back with his right arm stroking his knee and his left firmly fisted under his chin. "Time as liquid that appears frozen because it flows so smoothly. What might that imply? Eternity. Forever flowing, yet frozen in a moment."

"I agree," I said, shaking my head, surprised that the lunar god spoke so wisely on the issue. Perhaps his as ifs were not so empty. I'd come to a similar conclusion before. "Then what is this time, right now? Are you willing to admit the eternal moment, or will you circle back and hide through your already riddled wings? I see through your holey logic."

"You joke and insult, but you are not wrong to doubt. No, this is no eternity, this is the great nothing. What is this house called but the one of little light and great dark? When the dark is so great, it consumes the little light."

"You are wrong. Light pierces any dark, no matter how small."

"But the dark remains."

"Not where the light shines."

“This here is the great nothing because whatever light shines here, becomes dark. It is filtered through shadow, and the scratch of my cold fingers leaves an itch that can only be cured by drinking deep from my well. And now that you are here and you itch as you do—will you drink my cup? It is one that will pollute, and in this corruption, you will be made powerful.”

“What relies on broken light is merely a shadow of real power. You merchant, you broker! I don’t need your wares, even if the whole earth gladly ogles and desires them. You twist the light! You claim what isn’t yours and say it is your own.” I unlatched my axe, holding it up with my teeth bared like a tiger. “Without the sun’s light you are a useless hunk of dark rock. Without the eternal light you are merely a hunk of meat. You husk! You insect!”

Sin sat there and smiled, clapping his two hands together as if I were a jester entertaining him in court. “Go ahead. Cleave your axe into me! It’s the only way!” He lowered his head, grinning like a child about to open a gift, and he spread his arms wide and his four wings too.

I stopped myself from cutting the fiend’s head from his shoulders and tried to think. He spoke of his light being a corrupting source. Did I feel his itch? I surely wasn’t immune, considering I walked his lands. But no, I did not. For he had not touched me with wit, will or force. I had remained myself, despite the danger of coming so close to such a corrupt source. But what would chopping him down do? It would pollute me with his weakness, his inversion. He’d brought me here to bring about this. Why else would he be so willing?

“You will not carry my solar soul into the shadow of the sun.”

"But if you let me live, think of all the souls I might still claim."

"And if I cut you down, you will claim my own and more. I am no fool. To burn you with the light of my axe would only reflect your dark in a broken, distorted form. Your shadow lingers in the light, and I will not let you linger in mine. I am my own man and I am finished here. This quilted black has been burned through. And above you, I stand for the sun."

"Burn with the rest of your kind!" Sin screeched, his head lurching forward while he remained seated.

Then I felt heat arising in me, burning away that ever-present cold that the moon had brought to my bones. My armor broke away, flaking off into ash as my body was covered in a golden-white flame. My pants of healing fabric at last met their match, and the flame burned them away. The fire lifted me, and I could see nothing but the all-consuming golden light. The fire scalded my soul, yet soothed my being. Solisinanis was still in my hand and it drank my golden flame with eternal thirst—it felt as though it was a part of me, its heat my heat, its light my own. And in a burst of sunlight, my soul a solar ray, I shot back to earth and into a land of white snow and ice. The cold could no longer touch me and I stood as I was born and as I would die, my body my home, unblemished by unnatural decoration.

***

"You saw the sky. There was the sign. He goes to Hyperborea at last," Apollo said with a nod, his gold eyes squinted in an intense and seemingly angry focus.

A glorious golden orb had torn through our already golden sky and made it brighter. The streak of light had vanished at the horizon, but its path of firey gold light still hung in the sky like a rainbow. I knew at once that it was my dear brother Rangabes. How I hoped Apollo would remain true. I watched him closer than ever now. Cerberus watched and sniffed, all three of his black noses twitching in Apollo's direction. Lugh was unreadable. Of course, he hadn't heard Apollo's strange explanation of everything. The same went for Arawn. The two of them still seemed a bit out of it.

"And how can you be sure? How can we know it is Rangabes, and that he is headed there?" I asked. Of course, I knew it was him, but I wanted to goad Apollo into sharing more of his plans.

"It is he and you know it." He shook his head at me and his jaw tightened and jutted. "Hesiod, what is it that you think I plan to do? Do you really question my wisdom when that is what I am lord over?"

"I think you plan something that the rest of us do not know." I crossed my arms, my red talon rubbing against my robe.

"You told me I was to watch over Rangabes and be his steed to carry him forward, yet I've barely had the chance to be near him," Cerberus said, his snakes hissing and his voice whispering into our minds while he neither barked nor made any sound other than his serpents and their writhing about.

"They make interesting points," Arawn said, leaning against the wall, off by himself.

Lugh stood beside Apollo. "We go to Hyperborea. I've been stepping with you from the beginning, I see the end is near. Once he completes this cycle, he can at last be born anew. And then his promised land and new people can be birthed."

Apollo slowly nodded. "Yes. It is as I have said. He is to be the one to carry Hyperborea forward and not let its true light die in darkness. Hesiod, I do not understand why you continue to doubt this. And Cerberus, your true journey with Rangabes will begin once he is born anew. He needs your guidance in those savage lands that wait to be tamed."

I said, "And yet that question lingers that you did not answer before. Why have Rangabes go through all these trials, that you yourself refused to complete? And why did you fear his drinking of the cup? I saw your face. Your doubt. That cup is what allowed him to ascend."

"You feared the cup of truth and the Stoor Worm's sacrifice?" Arawn said, pushing himself off the wall and walking over to Apollo.

"Only because it was unplanned, unforeseen," Apollo said, his mouth a pale, tight line. "It might have made him... unclean. We do not know its effects on him."

"Unclean. You blaspheme a pure sacrifice that not even Manannán mac Lir could ruin. That cup was salvation. You make me wonder what, or better yet who, he needs saving from." Blue veins tensed against the pale and arched throat of Arawn. His temples throbbed and his eyes burned a bright green—a forest consumed in emerald flame.

"Arawn, please my brother, do not step where you do not know the truth," Lugh said, standing between Apollo and him. "I brought you and the Morrígan into the fold, because I knew you desired light. But do not forget the dark you emerged from. Fates have spoken; allies and enemies have been made on all sides." Lugh stared stony faced at Arawn who looked even more ready to burst. "We knew he had to drink the cup to move to the fourth circle. We spoke with the Fates. We spoke to Wyrd, though she remained uncouth. Neither mentioned the Stoor Worm sacrificing itself. That brought the strange battle into the heavens. The circle was supposed to be in the twisted realm that glorious Valhalla had been so profanely thrust into. He didn't just complete the circle, he pierced right through."

Arawn shook his fist. "You dare to explain to me the meaning of the sacrifice? I tore the darkness that had stained my soul and colored my skin, right from my corrupted flesh. It was so I could speak the truth, even as swine! To drink the cup alone, without sacrifice, would have sent him into impossibility—a task that dissolves into an infinite minimizing. Forever trapped there. Is that what you two wanted for him? I do not understand. The sacrifice of the worm allowed him to finish the games by rising not merely above them, but by bursting through them like a comet shot forth not from the stars, but the planet—the finite returned to its infinity."

"I did not know of this Arawn. How did you? I saw only the fourth circle as another inversion. But he bested the other three. There had to have been a way to finish it," Lugh said.

"Maybe, and thankfully we'll never have to find out. Manannán removed my mouth for a reason. I was the true king of the dead, he a mere pretender. Whatever he planned, whatever he knew, how could I not know as well? I know of legends and murmurs, whispers of dead souls and monsters you could never imagine. I know much and he feared my knowledge, rightly so. I did not anticipate it either." Arawn breathed deeply and relaxed his body, loping back to rest on the wall as if he hadn't moved aggressively forward in the first place.

I was not satisfied but I would wait. I looked up at Cerberus and met his eyes. The great hound looked graven, frozen with a dread that drooped his ears and slumped his snakes.

Cerberus whispered only to me, "He feared the cup because it brought Rangabes into the infinite, into the truth. Apollo will no longer be facing a mortal, a mere vessel he can empty. I do not know if Lugh is aware. Be ready for anything in Hyperborea." Cerberus's thoughts proved my own fears and suspicions true. I nodded with my eyes.

"We go to Hyperborea. I've waited for Rangabes to find the path there for so long, and now it is at last his own. It had to be his own. Let me now open the door to the kingdom that has for so long remained closed. We will watch and wait, and hope that Rangabes is made pure in the light," Apollo said.

He walked several steps away from us all and lifted up his hands. Gold fell from the shining heavens, waterfalling down in a sparkling shower of light that formed into two streams, leaving the sky a clear blue. The light we'd used to cleanse the sky with drained into this fall and collected itself in growing orbs that hovered above both of Apollo's raised hands. The one above his left hand was icy-blue, and the one above his right was fiery red. The waterfall was a torrent of golden effulgence that was being swallowed whole by the ballooning orbs of light.

The sky at last was cleared, drained back to its natural blue. Apollo raised his hands even higher, a straight angle above his head as if he were the pillar of a temple. He spread his arms like wings, the orbs following his hands' motion, and in a sudden burst he clapped his hands together and the orbs exploded. Their explosion of light funneled directly before Apollo in a swirling vortex, and there where the light dispersed, a door of ruby appeared. Its handle was made of blue sapphire in the shape of a scowling demon—horned and clawed, its tongue sticking out like a scythe.

"Through the door, the ruins of Hyperborea hide. They lie unseen, unknowable, but Rangabes's burning will reignite their ashes. We must watch. Come now," Apollo said, stepping to the door and grasping the gargoyle's tongue.

Before he could turn it, Arawn said, "I will stay here. Hyperborea might guide me but it is not truly my home. The Celtic grass calls me and I long for deep forests. I want to push out of this in-between world and return to the true. My time as king of the dead here fell as I arose in this new emerald armor. I am happy to carry the pure breath of crisp dewed air—to float in salty sea. I will defend my home here. In nature I rest. I become it. I think that is what all of us are meant to be."

His eyes flashed green and before anyone could say another word, he rode the invisible wind like a stallion, galloping through the air with speed so swift he vanished over the horizon in mere seconds. The breeze lingered, but he was gone. Maybe it was the way all his kind had been meant to go, back into nature, into earth. I winced as Apollo flung open the door, his tightened face annoyed at the god's refusal to pay privy to his plan. Beyond the door was an expanse of white that bled into our fresh green with greedy ferocity. Apollo stepped through without glancing back. I lowered my head and plunged in after him. The white light was cold; beyond it, it was colder.

Book 6

Farther North

This white expanse was one of desolation. Snow, ice, and nothing but. Yet I remained untouched by the cold. I looked down at my naked body and flexed my now healed arms. I'd been washed and made new in the flames above. An eternal fire burned in my soul and this cold could not touch my pure blaze. I stretched my body and pressed my feet into the snow. It melted under my soles and I grinned. I no longer needed my old armor. The flame had been too powerful for its enchanted steel. But my soul had been burnished. I was too powerful for any flame to burn me to ash. I was that flame now. Yet despite my own renewal, everything around me was still dead.

Why had I arrived here? Was this supposed to mean something? This was not the sun. Was it Hyperborea, or at least where it once stood—in the land of the north where the sun never set?

"You came here like an arrow of flame, have you struck true?" Someone called out behind me.

I turned around without fear, the power of my pyro plummet still pumping my heart, my mind infused with infinity. A man of average stature stood in a cloak of soft purple that had the look of a snowy landscape reflecting a cloudy sunset. His hood was drawn over his eyes and he had a youthful smile and smooth white skin like the untouched snow surrounding us—though his flesh held a slight yellow warmth.

"Who might you be? And is this all that is here?" I said.

"They called me Abaris the Hyperborean. I fled this once noble land because it was plagued with death. A plague not merely physical, but a sickness of spirit. When the sun sets on the land always drenched in daylight, it is no natural phenomena, but a will of weakness." His voice warmed the arctic air like a slow stream of gentle flame, bathing the cold in a calm burn. He walked towards me now, his gait unhurried and his hood still drawn. His smile tightened into a thin ridge as he remembered his home—our home. "When a people forget what it is that they are, were, and should be, they cease to live as more. They collapse into the sameness of beastly, lowly living. Instinct is well and good, but instinct severed from glory is best left to the mongrels. The plague clouded our judgement, and nature's freeze yanked away the sun, plunging us into half a year of darkness. People died. I had to go."

"So, you left your people and home to die, so that you might live? Is that not what mongrels do when they leave for strange bedfellows?"

"You came as an arrow yet you fly like a penguin. Even with your renewed flesh, your mind cannot comprehend. My arrow was given to me by Apollo. He sent me forth and I healed nations who would have me. I did mighty deeds."

"But not here."

"How else would the world know of Hyperborean greatness, when its very pillars cracked beneath the terrible weight of its ancestors? As long as a people remain, the land is not lost. When desolation came and the Hyperboreans fled, wept, or were indifferent, I healed as many as I could. But my gifts were not meant to thaw a stone soul. They took on their now glacial surroundings and, when frozen in despair, the best way to burn is to prepare the way for the next. So, I did with Apollo's blessing. But it seems as though his blessing is more of a curse."

"And am I next?" I said, thrusting my face over his completely shorn mountain of a chin. He stood just slightly shorter than myself.

He smiled and lowered his hood. A face like golden ice stared at me. His forehead was wide and his face long. His nose was as sharp as a glacial peak yet it sloped in such a way as to appear small against the powerful expanse of his appearance. His eyes were even icier—so light a blue that not even a clear bright sky could replicate their brilliance. His hair was golden and wavy, messily pushed to one side and of medium length. So, this was what an original Hyperborean looked like. Not pale white like northerners, nor brown like easterners. He was white-gold with sun-filled skin despite this frigid land. But the light in both our eyes were unmistakably of the same kind. The sun shone differently according to the land one lived in, but it was still the same sun, as long as the people were of the sort that looked up.

Still smiling, he said, "You are next. For not only do I heal, but I see. I am the seer of this land and I see that your ears listen to your hand. Be sure to be pure." His eyes melted into a contemplative gloss as he latched his glare onto and into my eyes. "You will bring us a new people and a new Hyperborea. To do this, you will need to cross treacherous seas and savage lands. You will have to kill monsters and armies of men. Your friends will die, as will you, but your people will live on. Beware the gods, Rangabes! Beware even those you believe. I see three priests coming, not in the future but now. They will talk with you here and will never cease speaking as long as you exist."

"You prophet, I merely want to fulfil my task so that like an arrow struck dead center, I may be retrieved not as a trophy but as a divine weapon to be used again and again. My deeds will allow for greater ones to be done in my name. Sharpen me and point me away! I long to strike the savage land in the heart," I said as I searched the empty landscape in vain.

"Then speak with these priests but do not fall victim to their honeyed words. The priests are the sons of the god of the North Wind, Boreas." Abaris placed his hand on my shoulder and leaned close. "The priests are called the Hyperboreades. They lorded over Hyperborea and the more they drained our people of light, the more this once perfect land frosted into nothingness. These wicked priests were not in submission to any king, they sucked this land dry of any power or good. Do not let priests be kings! Ever! Do not let the weak-willed rule! For if you do, your new land will suffer this same fate. Wyrd's warble cannot set either path clearly, it truly is your fate to love, cultivate, and garden. Lord over it! But these priests remain, haunting the land they froze. Their father has long since passed into a forgotten gale, howling with a wind that carries only cold. They come now, look." Abaris pointed over my shoulder and I turned.

Three figures ghosted out of the cold air. With their robes white as snow, only their pitched eyes stood out clearly, like fractal Tartaruses amongst the blank of the tundra. Their robes billowed with tendrils of snaking smoke that wafted about like a putrid breeze from a dying corpse on a summer day. Their stench carried a heat, a deathly plague fitting of a summer spent in a sickly Venice. They weren't translucent like ghosts, but they weren't quite whole either. They floated in a gaseous manner and from the way their faces tightened and creased, I couldn't help but imagine that this was what a dead body forced to live on would look like. This... deformation. They all held pale blue lanterns, one in each of their left hands, swinging and creaking like rusted hinges. Cold light flickered from the lanterns, the flame weak and impure. The priests held them out as if to keep away some unseen force.

The three of them drifted close to Abaris and I, floating before us like dead bodies in a polluted lake. They spoke with one voice and their mouths opened up like crypts, black as their eyes and with no teeth to be seen. If wind had fingers and it scratched them into bloody stumps against a locked door, that still wouldn't capture the shrill whip of these screeching priests' wails.

"Who are you to think yourself worthy of carrying the light of Hyperborea? Do you think your spirit can hold such fire without burning to ash? Do you?" They hissed, their wilting whispers rotting in the air.

"I've outshined the moon, its darkness unable to reflect myself back in blindness," I said.

"But we possess the sun. You will be burned alive!"

Abaris stepped forward and pointed his finger at the ghostly priests. "Demons! Filth! Hyperboreades unworthy of carrying such a name! The sun set on you long ago, and you heralded its demise. This tundra, this deathscape is your doing. Rangabes is more Hyperborean than you three!" Abaris said, spitting into the snow.

"Look," they said as the three of them split apart like an opening door, arms held open and beckoning the impossible vision that shimmered into being.

Green trees soared up from the icy ground and the lifeless hanging sun suddenly lit up to an orange-white, burning with extra warmth. Buildings of gold grew right up amongst the trees, the massive oaks dwarfed by the golden columns and white roofs that covered large swaths of land, the massive forest forming a perfect garden. A city now stood before us with shining domes glimmering there like stars hanging in dark green heavens. But this perfect city was without a sound. No birds chirped. No music played. No children sang.

Abaris shook his head and started to sing,

"*Never the Muse is absent*
from their ways: lyres clash and flutes cry
and everywhere maiden choruses whirling.
Neither disease nor bitter old age is mixed
in their sacred blood; far from labor and battle they live."

Abaris sighed and looked at me. "Pindar said it best. Yet what is this but a husk? Hyperborea was a land of love and life. This is a vision of despair and death. The priests have not the power to bring back the tropics here in this vision. We stand on what was once warm water and beach, teeming with blazing life."

"Why show me this, you deceitful spirits? You who reigned so pathetically over this perfection. How could Apollo appoint such fiends?" I said.

As if heeding my call, the air in front of me sizzled and cracked in two as a ruby door burst in red flame. Out came Apollo followed by Hesiod, Cerberus and Lugh. So Lugh had lived, something I was glad to see—but even more, Hesiod my brother had returned. The two of us leapt into each other's arms.

"I'd worried you'd been lost; it's been so long my friend! How I missed your companionship and our longwinded talks, brother," I said, laughing while hugging him.

"I thought the same. The wall took you in and I feared I'd never see you again," Hesiod said, still embracing me.

Cerberus, the loving pup, leaned his big heads down and nuzzled the two of us. I laughed and scratched behind his ears while Hesiod pet his snouts.

"And what of your armor? You are without clothes." Hesiod stepped back and shook his head while looking at me and chuckling. "Your axe?"

I surprised myself as I acted on instinct, holding out my hand and letting a gold flame flicker in the center of my open palm. The flame burst and unfurled, and out of its grown blaze Solisinanis emerged from the vanishing fire. Hesiod stared at me with wide eyes. I held the warm hilt and said nothing. The thought of Apollo pulling his weapons from the air in bursts of similar light made me wonder: why stay listening to him in submission? I looked over at Apollo who watched me blankly.

Cerberus said to only Hesiod and I, "Beware Apollo. We do not trust him here at the end of this road. You are too much of an anomaly to him now."

My face tightened but I knew he spoke the truth. I stepped away from the two of them and glanced at Apollo and Lugh who both nodded. With a wave of my hand, Solisinanis disappeared in a flash of light. It was truly a part of me now.

“Apollo, our god and king,” the Hyperboreades said, wisping over to him and bowing their heads.

“You come at last. Yet you let your home die. What is it that you want here, Apollo?” Abaris said, his body relaxed but his voice tense and forcefully slow. “No road can lead here and no ship can reach these once pearled shores, yet you open your strange door of magic, chasing after the worthy path of sunlight that Rangabes burned into the heavens. Why? I’ve ridden your arrow around this globe for so long now, searching for a cure, and yet you ceased to return. I always return, hoping that somehow everything will be set right here once again. Was it you who told your priests to set things so wrong?” The disdain colored Abaris’s voice black; he had no sense of reverence for the god of his people, the god who had so starkly left them to freeze. Yet he still stood in a confident and easy posture—neither stiff nor slumped, but leaning royally as if they air held him up at his command.

“Your tongue was put in place by me, and so it might still be severed. Watch your speech or your eyes might follow.” Apollo glared at Abaris and turned to acknowledge his priests. “Arise, and tell me what you see in Rangabes.”

“Unworthy. Unworthy. Unworthy.”

“This vision? Hyperborea is no more,” Lugh said to the priests. Apollo tensed at the interruption, his mouth flickering into an almost frown.

“It is so, to see if he is worthy,” they said, turning to point their lanterns at me.

“What is it you would have me do?” I said, wanting to get away from everyone but Cerberus and Hesiod.

"Now is the time to be his steed," Apollo said to Cerberus with a look up and a nod. "Rangabes, ride with Cerberus into the forest. Seek my temple that has been resurrected for your glory to be gained. There, you will find the final essence you need to truly begin."

"And what of I?" Hesiod said, his talon balled into a fist of sharp shards. "I am not being separated from him again."

Lugh looked at him with disgust. "You walk amongst gods and breathe again, not on your own accord, poet. You may have sung once of Apollo, but now you whine like a toothless pup. Have you forgotten why you live?"

"I'll show you teeth," Hesiod said with his chest glowing red and his talon unfurled.

"Go with him then," Apollo said in a solemn voice as if he were pronouncing funeral rites.

"Be careful Hesiod," Cerberus whispered.

"We go," I said firmly.

Cerberus lowered his three heads and I climbed aboard. Hesiod stayed there staring down Lugh and Apollo like a madman before three of Cerberus's serpents extended down and pulled him up by the waist to sit right behind myself. I was done with the scheming solar gods and those three priests. Abaris could do whatever it was that he'd come to do. Apollo's mysterious, old servant couldn't yet be trusted.

I held tufts of Cerberus's black fur and leaned forward, and the great hound of Hades leapt ahead. His bounding sent us speeding straight through the trees. The forest and its golden buildings towered so high it felt as though we were shrinking. We rushed under the canopy of green and gold, and I expected at least some semblance of life, yet the emptiness of the air that lacked fragrance or sound exposed this glorious vision for the deceit it was.

Cerberus slowed to a walk as the trees bunched together and the undergrowth, thick and blooming with white flowers, reached up to his knees. There were many smaller trees scattered about, dwarfed next to the endlessly towering trunks belonging to the oaks of the forest.

"Why don't you let us go on foot from here on out," I said, patting and scratching right between Cerberus's shoulder blades.

He might have been a mythical, deadly beast, but he was still a dog, and I might have imagined it, but his serpents were wagging about like tails while I pet him. He stopped his trot and lowered his body to the ground, and Hesiod and I both leapt off. Even lowered as we were, it was still quite the drop, and I almost fell as my foot got caught on a vine. Hesiod bumped into me but managed to stay upright as he shot me a wry grin. I pulled my foot free and shrugged.

"This forest, this dead lie, is throwing all my senses into the dust. Nothing. I smell nothing. I hear nothing. But there is something. I feel it. Something. Be ready, we are at our journey's end," Cerberus said, his heads looking in all directions.

"Which dome do we head to? Which building? They all appear similar, all garish in their gigantic uniformity. I doubt Hyperborea was this simple, this plain." Hesiod walked to a flower and eyed it with suspicion. He then kicked at the trunk of a tree, checking to see if it was truly there. "It's real, whatever that means here."

"Those priests were warped and decrepit like ghouls, evil intention manifested by their physical existence. They ruled this once perfect land. Why? And why would Apollo create them, and let such monsters plague the city to death?" I said, massaging my forehead. I was so close to leaving behind death that only now was I beginning to realize how alive I felt.

To taste of sweet life again! How I longed for roasted lamb and a glass of wine beside a warm fire. How I longed for my bed. But the time for rest had long since gone to sleep. I was awake now. Cerberus abruptly turned his heads and tilted them at me, raising his ears, watching me as if I were a stranger. His lips pulled back and he growled. He shook his heads back in forth as if in battle with himself, and his snakes stood still, all of them pointed at me.

"Cerberus?" Hesiod said, inching closer to me as he eyed the suddenly rabid hound.

I ran to Cerberus and stroked the black fur on his chest. "I'm here, it's me," I said with my head pressed against him.

"Get away!" Cerberus screamed in my mind, tearing into my soul with an impossible anguish that I screamed aloud with.

"Rangabes!" Hesiod yelled as he grabbed my shoulder and pulled me away.

Three of Cerberus's mighty serpents snapped down at me, just missing my head. I stared at him in a stupor. There was only beastly wrath burning in his red eyes. Flames blew out from his nostrils and he roared as he bounded forward. I propelled myself out of the way with a side burst from my arms.

Hesiod leapt into the air and aimed straight for the serpents. Cerberus's head stretched and snapped at Hesiod's flying form, but his twisting, red glowing body was too fast and high to reach. I watched in horror as he dove down onto Cerberus's back and raked his talon through the biting serpents. He ducked his head as he carved his way through, but his talon couldn't cut deep enough to sever. Bursts of black blood showered him and he threw his arms up to ward off the snakes' deadly bites.

But he was one and they were seven, and that seven swelled to ten as Cerberus turned his heads as far back as he could, biting from behind. Still I sat there helpless. What was I to do? Could I harm him after all this? Why had he turned? I'd thought he was destined to become a hound of light, if he hadn't been already. He was as much a part of me as Solisinanis was now.

I winced as Hesiod stumbled, and two snakes wrapped around both his ankles, hoisting him upside down. The other serpents struck in a flurry of bites at his body. I clenched my fists and let my marks glow, but before I could send off a burst, Hesiod's chest scorched red and shot out a burning, scarlet stream of light that flung him free and sent him hurtling at a tree. He thudded into it and tumbled to the ground, but the flowers mercifully padded his fall.

Cerberus turned his attention back to me and charged as he belched out a wall of flame. I crossed my arms and shielded myself in blue-red energy as the fire passed over me. Cerberus leapt with his claws swinging down, tearing through my field of light like it was paper. I fell to the ground, rolling out of the way of his giant paws.

Running away from his burning fire, I yelled, "You are a hound of light! Whatever this is, it is a lie, a nightmare! Do not fall asleep to who you truly are!"

Hesiod sprang to my side and said, "Listen to him! I once called you a glutton, an eater of raw flesh and an offspring of darkness. I wrote this down, but I was wrong!" He unleashed an aura of red from his chest, covering us in a blood-like light of protection.

Cerberus breathed his flames at our shield while scratching it with his claws and striking down with his serpents. I added my light to Hesiod's own, and our shield held as we poured out our strength. Cerberus backed away and eyed us, the evil in his eyes weakening as he shook his heads in frustration.

Hesiod called out to him from behind our light, "Cerberus, your parents Typhon and Echidna, two of the most powerful beings to grace this earth, they are your past but not the everything that is your present. From where did you come, hound of darkness? No... not darkness, for Hercules carried you into the light. Your blood has been redeemed. This curse cast over you, from this land and/or from Apollo's blackened hand, it is only for those who sleep. Apollo may have awoken you at the gate, but his lingering song has become a lullaby. You chose to stay awake then. You can choose to awaken now."

Cerberus shook his heads harder and he roared, yet his voice was silent in our minds.

I lowered my arms, letting the shield lessen in size and brightness as only Hesiod kept it aglow. I said, "You were pulled into the light, Cerberus. Will you stay or go back to the dark, closing your eyes to the power of pursued glory? It is either/or. The dark is only your shadow."

"Purify me," Cerberus groaned, his voice bouncing off the walls of our minds with a ferocity that staggered us both.

Hesiod and I combined our light again, this time forming a white orb of increasing light that hovered out in front of us. Cerberus howled, his bark an anguished roar and his voice a screaming cry within our minds. We pushed the ball of light straight at him and it rolled through the air growing until it completely swallowed him in its path. He howled from its midst and the light burst open, cracking like an egg. Cerberus stepped out as the orb was absorbed into his fur. He no longer was colored black, but now stood with a shining white coat of fur, just as I had seen him in the ancestral plane. Yet now he stood even more glorious than he had then. His serpents were gold and their eyes a bright white. He slowly walked to us, looking at us with a peaceful gratitude that words could never capture.

Peering at us both with his now golden eyes, he said, "I am now what I was meant to be. I do not guard death. I do not sleep as though dead either. I step into this light pure, powerless to stop its touch, but willing to embrace it fully. I walk awake now."

"Was it Apollo?" Hesiod mumbled.

Cerberus shook his heads. "A curse brought about by his priests—this land hollow and dead, it awoke a darkness in me that could only be consumed by an even higher awakening of light. I believe this is why he first came to me in Hades, to unlock the light of his homeland. We must end Apollo. This land and this people—your people, are not his."

"Cerberus," I said, running up to him and hugging his chest, his fur warm against my breast. He nuzzled against me and licked my head. I stepped back and looked up at him. "I saw you as a hound of light. I knew it was true." I smiled and nodded my head.

"But now what? Do we still search for Apollo's temple?" Hesiod said. "Was your cleansing the key to unlocking the temple's location? A sacrifice of darkness at the altar of light?"

I sighed. "Why has Apollo chosen me to carry the light of Hyperborea if he wants to end me? Does he truly? Is he the one who devised this quest or is he supplanting Wyrd who herself answers a higher call? Apollo cannot think he will be able to use me to do his bidding, not after all this. Either he's lost it, is being controlled by some other, or truly wants me to make it through this all. Perhaps none of that." I rubbed my chin and shook my head. "The priests. I think the answer lies with the priests." I pulled back my hair and cracked my neck, looking up at Cerberus and admiring his ascended form. The glory of his light manifested in physical truth. To think how close he was to ending in darkness. To think how close we all were. I breathed deeply and turned to Hesiod. "The temple first. Let us get out of this miscreation as soon as possible. This place is not supposed to be."

Hesiod walked ahead and said, "If this is the land beyond the North Wind, then let us continue north. We might as well keep moving forward. The temple likely lies ahead."

And so we continued north, the billowing white flowers still blooming coldly around us, and the trees staying distant and austere. The golden buildings even higher up remained hollow and vacant as they stood silent. But what would the temple be like? It would be different. It would stand out. Yet our walking was leading us nowhere. There were no markers and everything looked the same. Up close, the majesty of this place proved imagined and in jest. From afar, it certainly had been glorious, but now that we were in its midst? It was like a scarecrow lacking even its straw.

Our walking in silence was heavy, unsure. The shadow of Cerberus's almost death loomed, even overcome with his present brilliance. Our lack of clarity and the uncanniness of our surroundings only made it all the worse. An air of corruption seeped from the beauty of the empty illusion, the trees and flowers had long since lost their charm. This northern path we walked was not leading us anywhere. A temple hidden in this nothingness was fitting of those twisted priests. Another test, the last one to put a cap on the nonsense I'd been through. I walked ahead, letting my surroundings blur and my thoughts bloom. I'd suffered the ritual pain of my Hyperborean scars, infused with blessed light and power. I'd earned Ra's guiding light and my heart was judged worthy. I'd proved myself in possessing the nine virtues of the Norse. I'd gone through the four circles and earned my truth. I'd torn through the quilt by overcoming the darkness of time, and finding myself in it as a speartip. And I'd left behind the lying light of the moon, supplanting it as the sun.

What was I to do to unlock this hidden temple? What? What? Perhaps not what. What if its discovery required a negation, like the rest of this place? Our walking was not it. To cease, then? To wait? More inversion to cut through the lies. Fire and fire. Dark on dark. The nothing. Perhaps... I laughed and stopped walking, shouting at my two startled friends to stop as a sudden idea shattered my stupidity. I laughed louder, ripping the suddenly startled silence into submission and sending Hesiod into a start so sudden that he jumped around to face me. Cerberus's now pale-pink ears and noses twitched at me.

"We keep moving as if we could overtake the sun. Can you walk to the sun? Can you catch it?" I said.

"What are you talking about?" Cerberus said with his three pairs of golden eyes squinted tight at me.

"You can't catch the sun," Hesiod said, pulling at his beard with his brow tight, curtaining his dark eyes in folds of shadow. "It shines on who it will regardless. But it seems as if its rays touch a chosen few in such a way that no man can force on his own. The sun's kiss and caress that can only be known if manifested. Abaris had Apollo's arrow yet not even he dared fly to the sun. We cannot look at it without blindness. Yet here we are looking for Hyperborean light, the sun's holy power, as if we might see it with ease." He shook his head at his foolishness in rushing forward. "So desperate was I for movement that I couldn't see. I see, Rangabes. We can't catch this light, this sun here, no. Not in a land that is dark and reflected. The only way to win the sun's affection is to stay in its light and let it shine where it wills. We should wait," Hesiod said, his eyes unlatching from whatever vision he'd imagined before him and focusing back on the two of us.

I nodded at Hesiod in agreement. "And what is the one trial, the one aspect I have hitherto avoided and failed to prove? The ability to wait and do nothing. Further, the ability to trust in the divine will. So, let us sit here and wait. This temple will come, I am sure of it."

"Then we wait. May your faith not be as blind as those who look at the sun," Cerberus said as he crossed over his two front paws and laid down to rest his heads on them.

***

"What is this Apollo? How is this going to end? When is it going to end? Why are you doing this?" I said, my voice shaking with a desperate and anxious rage.

Apollo stood there staring into the forest, and his priests glared at me, holding their lanterns high and in my direction.

"Lugh, follow Rangabes and make sure he is on the right path," Apollo said, pointing at the woods. Lugh ran forward, his legs crackling with blue light as the forest swallowed his charging form in darkness. "Abaris, only two of your questions are worthy of answering. The what and why are what matter here."

"You send Lugh and not me because you fear what I might reveal. Or is he as dark as you? What of my questions?" I said.

"I want Rangabes to be worthy. That is why. What I'm doing is putting him on that path. You know this."

"You want him to be worthy yet you yourself aren't," I growled. Apollo stood there unbothered while his priests hissed.

He held up his hand to silence them. "Your power and ability to survive, to leave behind the plagued Hyperborea, came from me. You still live because of my blessing. Now you question it?"

"Your Hyperboreades oversaw the destruction here, yet you keep them in your service. I once came back here after learning from the most powerful sages and physicians in the world. I came back to heal my people. Yet when I returned, nothing remained. As if it were mere myth and I myself were a lie." I clenched my fists and fought the urge to strike at Apollo. I snarled at his ghostly priests.

"You keep repeating that blasphemous accusation. The plague came from sclerosis. When society remains stuck, it is better to start anew. The Hyperboreades were righteous rulers from the beginning, the plague was not their doing. You accuse without proof. They did not set the sun on the Hyperborea, the people did it themselves. Yet their pure spirit and blood can be renewed and cleansed from such filth. Rangabes is that renewal. I've waited a long time and have seen my fellow pantheon collapse under the weight of this modern world. All this unbelief is forcing many of my brethren to return to nature, their identities diffused into the green."

I scoffed, "Oh god of wisdom, where is your wisdom in reigning so sickly over a pure people? 'Know thyself' is what was marked on your temple at Delphi, but did you know thyself when calling yourself wise? How can you claim to be a god of light? I see why you did what you did. Sclerosis, what nonsense. I lived there, you didn't. You were off fornicating with some Greek pretty boys and playing your lute to enthrall them. Sclerotic is what you are. You only know how to please yourself. That is your great, so-called wisdom. You set your priests on us because you feared our murmurs. You feared our strength. We were becoming gods! Gods! As powerful as you, and with our power we saw through your degeneracy. And so, you plagued us out of weakness and envy. And the people wept and forgot what they were, and what they could become."

Apollo turned to face me. His eyes were burning red as flames leapt out and cast his golden body in crimson shadows. "You are an accuser who sucks at the teet of power, remaining merely mortal without the nectar of the infinite. You accuse. I should have known you'd come here. The Fates didn't see your face. Wyrd must think it some joke to send you my way. How did you know?"

"Are you the god of idiocy? I saw the flame tear through the sky. With Olympus empty, I've spent much time meditating on its frosty peaks. Centuries. I knew this would come. You made a mistake by making a god out of me."

Apollo's bow flashed into his hand and his priests screeched as they flew at me with their lanterns swinging. They carried the light of plague, but they would not carry me into their eternal graves. A golden arrow burned from out of the air and into my hand, and I flung myself forward, the arrow carrying me away as my body dragged behind like the sail of a boat. The priests swung and screeched, their cold flame chilling my bones as their three lanterns just barely brushed my cloak, but I flew free from their evil reach and sped towards the forest. My vision blurred and my body whipped as I glanced back. Apollo had already let loose a volley of his deadly accurate arrows.

"Ascend," I whispered to my arrow, and it flew up in a direct and vertical line as Apollo's shots struck at empty air.

I soared into the heavens, the icy clouds cloaking me in the true frost of this land. The heat below was as artificial as that hallucination of a city. Hyperborea had been beautiful—perfect—walled in with impenetrable gold and paved with gardens flowing amongst swaying trees. The sea had licked our shores and was a most becoming brother of our homeland. This monstrosity the priests had concocted was simplistic with no originality; it was a uniform chaos that was mere pretend.

I hoisted myself up onto my arrow, straddling it between my thighs, and hovering high. The clouds spread out before me like an ocean of snow. I skirted above them, my feet dragging lines through the clouds' cold, wet touch. I had to find Rangabes down there. Lugh would lead him to Apollo's trap, whatever and wherever it might be. Apollo wanted a new people for himself, which meant he would have to create a darkened and submissive will from the start. How he planned to do such a thing in Rangabes was beyond me. But I refused to let this madman pollute my peoples' legacy any longer. This was a fight for the right to bear the sun in one's veins. I only hoped Rangabes didn't bleed out to darkness.

***

I peered down at my prey from my perch on the high, green shrouded branch. The three of them hadn't gone all that far into the forest before I'd been able to track them down, but they appeared to be close to solving this riddle the way they were all sitting there waiting. So, I would wait as well, for the time being.

I smiled. Apollo was wise, and for the plan to come this far, to be so close to its fulfillment... it was maddening to sit and wait. I wanted to act. How could I, the Celtic god of the sun, not desire Rangabes's power to be swallowed by my own? Apollo and I as the gods of a new Hyperborea while the rest of the deities faded into the background—yes! Rangabes was a vessel that neither of us could be, but neither could he be us in his mortality. The strange chord of fate that had brought him about, and that perfect will of his set into the eternal—a man such as he, at such a moment in time or outside of it, could neither be ignored nor misused. Apollo knew of Wyrd's infatuation; he recognized that Rangabes was a sort of new Aeneas to her and that she, a so-called higher god, had spelled so many of our ends. She served a god that tired of our free reign. No matter, she was the only one I knew of that had returned to that ancient council. I was just as much a god as any other!

I tried not to remember those distant days of submission and focused inward, nodding. Apollo, the creator of Hyperborea had seen that his ancient lineage was being resurrected in a new way. Of course, he came to me soon after. Was there any better way to seize control of this strange play of fate than to claim Rangabes as our own? All of it, this whole path merely a proving ground to glory, brought on by himself and continued by Wyrd's harp, with Apollo's quiet lyre strumming softly in the ether. I missed my Celtic kin, but with Arawn and the Morrígan gone, it only gave me and Apollo more control of our new nation. So close! And what brilliance, misleading all the gods!

I chuckled, clinging to the tree with a childish glee. How I wanted to shout out our successes! It was something I never grew tired of reflecting on. Even with my forced darkening at the hands of Sulis, this reflecting on our brilliance had kept me as me through it all, even during and after our worst missteps. We'd given those other gods the promise of their power and eternal nature being carried into the finite, continuing in glory while they faded fully into light, and it was not pure deceit. It had been truth. Nobody wanted to submit again to that ancient way. There wasn't much else one could do. We'd all fallen too far, and had risen as our own. But of course, there were those who questioned why Apollo and I did not offer ourselves up as well. Odin was killed for such resistance. Zeus vanished, resigned to his own withdraw to nature. He'd lived long in fear of the son god who'd been prophesied to take Olympus from him. So fearful was he that he forgot to fight. But Sulis fought and nearly won—I still felt the black pain of that darkness. I shivered, focusing down at the unlikely trio.

They sat there in a circle, unmoving and silent. Wise of them, as this forest was unnatural and ancient, possessing a dark silence that if stirred too saucily, would boil over into a corruption I wouldn't be able to comprehend or deter. Once again, Rangabes had proved resourceful and worthy of the light he continued to drink. And Cerberus, now white and pure. So, he had wrestled his darkness into submission? Apollo's song had fallen on deaf ears then. No matter, it had been a desperate play; we'd hoped Cerberus might somehow serve us. The Fates had suggested it and we'd been foolish to listen. We'd given Rangabes another ally against us. But if it had succeeded, they'd both be in our thrall now. I suppose it had been a risk worth taking. Much like using the ancient poet as a proxy into tricking Rangabes into trusting us. It had worked at points, but our path had been too jagged and we'd cut that tie to us as well. We had our successes, but there were many failures too. Still, we were so close to the end. It was easily within our grasp. And Cerberus and his darkness were required if the temple was to be found. Apollo's own creation, hidden in its own shadow that not even the sun god could banish. The Fates had said Cerberus was needed to break this binding. I sighed, thinking on how little we knew and how much was out of our hands.

I had to at least respect the hero's guile thus far. Rangabes had overcome much that we ourselves had failed to see. And this final riddle was by no means too difficult for him to solve. It was simple: Apollo's temple couldn't be reached just like the sun. A ray of light touched the individual based on the sun's own accord. And was there ever such an individual as Rangabes? Smart of him to not force the inevitable. Patience—the temple would be coming and my time to act was nearing. So much could go wrong here, with just the smallest of steps away from the current of time we were attempting to dam. If only Wyrd would sing for our tune once, instead of her jealous and all-knowing god! And Abaris... he would be coming soon if he escaped Apollo's grasp. That was something we'd both foolishly overlooked: that of the old Hyperborean returning. How were we to know that he still walked the earth, not going the same way of the gods much greater than he, untrue immortal as he was?

I looked closer at the trio, sitting so solemn and grave. All of their heads were hung low as if in prayer. I couldn't tell if their eyes were closed but that hardly mattered. Senses were useless here—yet I felt a sudden stir in my soul as solar rays sung out from an icy tomb below the false soil. I could feel it, and I fought to cling to my branch so as not to hurl myself down to that hidden light. It sang so purely that no sound was needed. Light! It was coming. My breast swelled and my heart soared upwards, a surge of desire mixed with urgent terror at such power.

The limb I was perched on shuddered as the trees screamed—a shrill cry, as if the whole dead race were accusing us of blasphemy. Perhaps they were, or perhaps they feared the coming light. I looked down one last time and incredibly, the three of them remained with heads bowed, unbothered by the chaotic screeching around them. My tattoos glowed blue and I leapt off my branch just as it misted away into nonbeing. I hovered with my hands burning blue, holding them down to keep me aloft in the air. And then at last as the trees faded into putrid vapor and the buildings collapsed into ash, swirling away in billows of black smoke, life sounded out once more in this icy wasteland. The howls of wolves rode the cleansed air with frigid soul, an ache of forgotten power and an ache for a new future. Gray wolves appeared all around—not as apparitions, but as if they'd already been there waiting, in all their magnificent reality.

Rangabes and his companions stood up at the sacred sounds from the worthy wolves. They looked all around at them, but thankfully did not look above. I floated higher to avoid their glance just in case, wrapping myself in the arctic chill of curling clouds.

Graceful auburn deer arose from the snow and pranced among the wolves, their bounds in tune with the soaring heights of the howls. And then an orchestral backdrop of cicadas hummed, their chirping rising and falling in a symphonic wave of sound. They swirled out of nowhere and into the heavens, just below my hovering form. Their shining, slick bodies blackened my view as they swirled and twirled together in apparent choreography. I could still catch plenty of glimpses below, and what a sight it was becoming!

The impossible was coming true! No temple had yet arisen, but now, sleek gray dolphins leapt to and fro, swimming through the snow as if it were an ocean. Thousands of serpents shivered out from the ground, all of different lengths and shining colors, forming a reptilian rainbow that shimmered, their vibrant scales flashing below like millions of tiny lights. The song grew colorful now, those haunting howls taking on the tune of sublimity, transcending my senses to the point of causing me tears, the only expression proper to such beauty. I wept. Now ravens and crows rolled in like black thunder, their caws neither harsh nor discordant, merely somber as if to remind us all what had been lost. They rolled in the waves of the sky with the cicadas, in harmony and now almost completely blocking my view. I would wait above. My fated time to act was almost at hand and my fingers itched to scratch at and hold this destiny. I continued weeping. This was our legacy.

***

The sky no longer swirled only in black, it lightened as glorious swans arrived. The black waves of ravens and cicadas parted in deference to their pure white. The swans' garbles rolled amongst the sweeping canopy of music and only added to the uncluttered, infinite expanse of nature's solar song.

None of us spoke, but my eyes did for me as they teared. Hesiod's face was a light of childlike joy. Hope and love were the only things capable of creasing that face into such a grin as tears ran rivers of youth through the old crevices of his tired mien. Cerberus's ears were twisting in all directions as he stared at the glory surrounding him, his snakes hissing along and lulling back and forth. Even his impressive size was dwarfed by the swirls of eternity singing around us. My eyes streamed and I knew not what to do but weep with joyful gratitude that I lived, and that these animals lived, and that life was beautiful, even in death.

Hyperborea was not finished, not as long as these creatures continued their song. The snakes slithered around my feet in an affectionate manner, and the gaily dancing deer and still singing wolves lived together and acted in a harmony that drove me to my knees. I prayed to the Lord and thanked him for his mercy and love in creating such a world filled with such abundant life as this, no matter where. Why had Apollo buried this away? Was it not his? Perhaps the temple was truly the Lord's.

A triumphant and eternal roar drove my head into the dust as griffins soared over us. They were magnificent, golden winged lions with manes made of fiery feathers that were fitting for their eagle heads. The seven of them swam through the filled sky and sang a song of triumph, a trumpeting bellow of pure light. By their hind legs they carried large Doric pillars of red-painted marble. Was this the temple?

The animals had destroyed the lie of the vision and unleashed the powerful and primal truth of return and recurrence. They belonged to the same soil that drank deep and gnawed hard on our spent and hollowed bones. The griffins flew, singing songs of flame, their feathers and manes so gold and bright that the orchestic dancing song of the other creatures was swallowed in their glory, a slight shuffled hum to their triumphant roars.

The griffins circled their flight into a tighter and tighter spiral, funneling down and dropping the pillars in a circle around us, the seven of them spread equidistant. As the pillars landed and stood firm, the animals bellowed together and in a great sweep of color and life, they pooled as one, soaring into a giant wave like a teeming tsunami of rainbow. They burst free and together into the heavens, vanishing to leave behind silence and nothing but the seven red pillars, and the returned desolation of the tundra. We stood there unmoving, not wanting to break the silence and bring an end to the sanctity of the space and moment.

Your friends must leave.

The thoughts swept through me, heavy with dust and age. I saw nobody, and Cerberus and Hesiod showed no signs of hearing.

They must leave or the light will not come.

"Hesiod, Cerberus... you must step outside the circle. The light will not come otherwise," I said, my stare inward and searching, trying to uncover the voice.

"I will not abandon you," Hesiod said.

"We will not," Cerberus added.

"You must," I snapped. I took a long breath and said softly, "Someone is speaking to me. The spirit of this temple, perhaps. All I know is that for me to finish this, it must be done alone."

"Then why did we come? Was there no threat outside Cerberus's own shadow? Are we to stand idly by as you face peril?" Hesiod said, storming over to me, his face cut with dark lines of concern.

Cerberus stood quietly in the same place. He nodded his middle head. "Hesiod, we need to let him do this. We cannot aid him here. No matter what, we must leave this circle. Even if he suffers, even if he were to perish, to intervene would be to forever close the path of righteous tyranny Rangabes is on. He must be a tyrant over himself and what is his to possess. A tyrant stands first alone, and second, on the foundational pillars of power from his worthy ancestors." He stopped and looked at Hesiod, then turned his focus to me. "We go. We cannot walk on a one-man path. Each has his own. Ascend the mountain and take this light, Rangabes. We are nearing the end." He turned away and walked past the pillars and sat: a guard dog once more turned observer.

Hesiod slowly walked away, his face ashen and his shoulders stooped and sharp. Each of them watched from outside the circle like statues, cold in their sudden distance that might as well have been infinite. And then, the red pillars glowed orange with flame, and a wall of red light encircled the pillars and burned Cerberus and Hesiod from my view. The decision was made.

"Are you pleased?" I shouted to the heavens.

"Pleasure is a state of being, so your question for one that belongs to the light is meaningless. Pleasure is my being, no matter the cause or effect. Pleasure is always for one already pleased."

I lowered my gaze at the voice and before me sat a sphinx. Its head was that of a beautiful female with blue eyes, pale ivory-toned skin and braided, chestnut-brown hair. Her chest was covered in bright blue feathers, with spotted, red and white sharp wings that waved upwards onto her back. Her body and legs were that of a golden lioness. Was this all that guarded the light? I'd bested far more fearsome foes than this. Yet, there was a sudden stuffiness in the air and I labored to breathe as if there wasn't enough of it to be swallowed.

"A sphinx? So, you speak in riddles like the rest, but what is it that you guard? Where is this final light?" I said, stepping forward and focusing on the beautiful face and not the beastly body.

She blinked and cocked her head like a bird. "Do you know pleasure?" Her voice wheezed out in an ancient sigh like that of a forbidden book pulled off a dark corner shelf, sending off a plume of dust.

Annoyed at her aloofness, I said with a frown, "I've torn myself asunder to reach you here. I stand here naked and weary," she looked down at me and smiled. My frown deepened and I crossed my arms as I continued, "I've faced treachery, and the purported purveyor of my journey is not even for me, and might cast me into darkness once he's had his fill of my power. Unworthiness everywhere! Pain in every step! I was torn apart by crazed women. Reborn again and again. Darkness at my back and light in my eyes. What have you done?" I flung my arms angrily about. "Have you suffered? Who have you bested? Are you even the best creature here? Those griffins were more impressive than you. A sphinx! A twisted female *it*, thinking that all is pleasure. Harlot!" I walked closer to her, waving my hands with disgust. "When will the riddles end? Buried truth is a grave of deceit. I am no grave digger, but I will empty all the tombs and catacombs where the hollow bones lie, and resuscitate the rotted flesh that speaks silent."

"I loathe the loquacious. Rhetorical posturing is weaker than purposeful riddles, for yours stands tall while remaining short, and mine props up the purpose to the actual height of discernment and true knowledge. If you must spin your words in silk, do so with purpose. Perhaps a well-placed pun might earn you this light." The sphinx sat there unmoved, my approaching steps not even resulting in the slightest physical response. She simply sat and watched, like a bird staring at dying prey. The image caused me to pause and consider caution.

"I know no pleasure. I pursue power for its own sake," I said quietly, reining in my rage and relaxing the rigidity I'd assumed with my previous verbal assault.

"And what is this pursuit? Better yet, what is pleasure?"

"Whatever feels good. What kind of question is this? Am I a child?"

"A child knows pleasure in the warmth of the womb. A man knows pleasure not. Pleasure is to be taken from all and everything. Power is pleasure. Pain is too. With a will heightened to joy and always bathed in light, all experience is transcended into pleasure. It is to be not finite in finitude, but finite in infinitude. If all is washed in forever, then even death is pleasure."

I shook my head and then smiled as I thought of a pun. She wanted silk words, did she? "You must be in jest; chin up you fool for your words are drool—my heart burns and my stomach clenches at such empty speech. If all is pleasure, then nothing is." I nodded and stroked my chin.

"But in the dark, do you not have the light of your eyes? You can look inward. All is only pleasure if one loves being. To curse existence and to flail against your flesh, is to deny purpose and the eternal light of joy. Pain is only pleasure if the cause is necessary."

"What is the point of this? I am here for the sacred light of Hyperborea."

"If you cannot find pleasure, you cannot find Hyperborea. This was a land of joy and celebration. A people of light and affirmation. What can you affirm when you deny what is good?"

"And if I say it would be my pleasure to kill you right here, then what? Would the light come to me then?"

The sphinx laughed, her voice musical and free. The dust of her voice lifted off with her mirth. She smiled like a sultry woman while her wings stretched and her curtained tail raised. "It is a start. Kill me, or I you. Make sure you enjoy this death."

She growled and flew at me like a hornet, and I dove to the ground and rolled beneath her hurtling sting. I tore Solisinanis from out of the air and spun to the left as she flew and swiped at me, her talons clashing against my steel, showering us in white sparks. Retreating, we eyed each other like two boxers sizing the other up as we paced. Her wings fluttered and she pawed at the ground, her face poised and ecstatic—the combination of calm and exuberance, a fearful elixir that sparked her eyes with fervor but smoothed her face with a flat boredom.

I held my arms out, clutching the axe in my right and flexing, opening myself up to the light sizzling in my marks... but no light came. My axe suddenly appeared dull, its gold ornamental and its fiery hilt merely opulent and useless. As if the mythic power had ceased pumping in my veins, my heart beat faster, acknowledging my sudden and ever-present mortality that I'd hitherto forgotten. My confidence crumbled and my breath came ragged. I held out my hands and stared at my flesh in its weakness. This was not like my fight with the false god Sobek-Ra—this was an unchosen weakness.

"What have you done?" I said, my voice shaking at the sudden loss of power.

"What have you?" she said, prowling and slinking along the ground.

"My power... I earned this!" I yelled, holding up my axe and gnashing my teeth. "I don't need your light to best you. You can darken it, but you cannot darken me."

"I cannot darken, I only shine my light where it necessitates a shining forth. Best me with your own light, and you will have your ancestors'. To gain their might and spirit, you must be worthy first."

"Have I not been? All this was earned from my worth. The stains of darkness trying to corrupt my light have been burned into another form of shadow, a dark light. I possess it on my own. I shine in shadows and light; no darkness can consume me. Yet now my light is snuffed out? What have you done?"

"Before we trade blows once again, is this pleasurable?" she asked, her words spinning and venomous like a spider about to devour its mate. She chuckled, sounding of all things like a flirtatious woman. I shook my head at such madness.

I chewed my lip and breathed deep, swallowing the weight of my remembered mortality and letting it first hold me down, then yank me back up as I stared inward at the infinite calling me back to the surface. I nodded my head as I began to understand the strange sphinx's purpose. "My will is pure, focused on ascension. I see what this focus means. Willing one thing—this pure heart of mine loves its purpose." I looked at her smiling face and grinned back at her. Pleasure! Pleasure! I chuckled, before continuing. "When all this is willed purely as one, that is how I reach the infinite. In this reaching out, pain, loss, and gain all become an ocean of glorious pleasure. That is living as a mortal drinking from the mirror pool of immortality." I laughed and shook my head at yet another riddle solved in the heat of battle. "Perhaps this loss of light is to see the infinite source shining deeper. Joy at striving! Joy at becoming! And most of all, joy at being. I am pleased sphinx, for I am myself."

She smiled wider and bowed her head, dipping her plumed chest and extending her front paw. "You see what you always and already saw. Let us finish this."

She swooped up into the air and arced in a steep loop upwards. She paused at the peak of her flight and cannoned straight down at me. I held my axe with both hands and spread my feet. It was inevitable. I side stepped and chopped up at her head. Her outstretched talons scraped down on my left arm, carving deep claw marks from my shoulder to my biceps. But Solisinanis sang, and it struck her neck like an axe to the trunk of a tree and her head tumbled down, a smiling fruit rolling free as the timber of her body collapsed skidding, leaving her head behind.

Yet no blood sprang free and her spirit stayed within. I walked over to the smiling head and was unsurprised to see her blinking up at me. I bent down and picked her up, her head warm and hair soft as silk. She smelled of the desert oasis, fresh and hidden, strange and distant. She smiled as I held her aloft, and she blinked her deep blue eyes, their heavy lashes curling like tiny fingers and canopied under thick brows that held the elegance of a British queen.

"Sphinx, what is it now that must be done? I need this light." I spoke slow and quiet, holding her warm flesh in both palms of my hands. Her lips were drenched scarlet like cherries as she smiled wider.

"Hold me aloft and give room for my body to grow. You have freed me from my monstrous prison." Her voice was a river of honeyed life, smooth, sweet, and rich.

I did as she commanded, holding out her head by the temples and up high enough to give room for a body to form. Light emitted from the base of her detached neck and then extended, white and pure, into a blazing silhouette of feminine form. As the light brightened, a body emerged with pristine white skin that sloped like Olympus—perfect peaks for breasts and a valley of smooth snow sliding down her sleek form. She stood there unclothed, unashamed, and smiling, her body grown to perfection like the choicest of flowers in a royal garden.

"I cannot simply call you sphinx now," I whispered, lowering my hands to her cheeks and letting my fingers linger before pulling back.

She laughed and pushed her brown hair over her shoulders with her slender fingers, and stared into my eyes, her blue the water to my evergreen. "My name belongs to the future. You will soon meet a man that will shape your own future people and land. I take my name from him. Not for his love, but for the honor of his discovery. My light demands it. My name is Columbia. And yours is Samuel."

I laughed. "A beautiful name, but I do not know how I feel about you being named after another man. And I know not anyone named Samuel." I shook my head.

She stepped close to me and peered up into my eyes, her upturned nose begging to be kissed. "A name demanded by the future. He is a great man, but he is not the father of those to come. He is not you. You are neither Greek nor Roman. You are Hyperborean and your name bathed in my light, in our light, in the highest light, is Samuel."

"If I am now Samuel, have I then at last received this vaunted light? Am I ready to face Apollo and leave for my promised land?" I said.

She leaned so close now her breath salted like seawater, tickling my tongue and nostrils, her scent and taste washing over me in aromatic waves. "Adam needed a helper. He was given Eve." She ran her fingers over my ribs. Tracing their outline, she said, "I came from your rib. From you, the man. My bones are caverns filled with marrow light, and the bones that bloomed out first were yours. That is Hyperborea. I do not have this light of my own, it was yours first. Will you enjoin me to it? Will I become as your flesh, aglow with your blood?" She stared up at me with fear, biting her lower lip and folding it in half with pearled teeth. Her eyes were wide and innocent.

I stepped backwards and her face froze in horror. How I longed to rest in that warmth of hers—how sorry I was to cause this perfect being to suffer cold. But she misunderstood my movement, and as I dropped the axe to the ground and stepped back towards her, her eyes burned with passion. Her face was singed with pleasure, and she stepped closer to me, the both of us as natural as Adam and Eve. I took her hand, its warmth like butter melting into my palm, and placed it back onto my ribs. I pulled her to my body, and her head rested against my breast. We moved as one, and became bone of bone, flesh of flesh—the way of paradise. This was the light of Hyperborea, and Apollo was unworthy. I released myself in waves of her, and she in the sea of me, and we rode inward with pleasure at every toss and turn.

***

On Apollo's arrow, I shined like a pillar of light; a gold wake stretched from my ascending flight down to the sea of cold clouds below. I couldn't cease my climb yet, for Apollo wouldn't let me go so easily. His ghastly priests were probably already scouring the forest. The air snapped at me with icy teeth, yet my aura of light fueled by Apollo's arrow warmed my soul with a perfect peace. The atmosphere thinned as I climbed and the frosted scent of arctic air was sharp against my nostrils.

As my arrow arose in its fiery pillar, the urge to ascend forever was overwhelming. My will resisted having to leave the light and stop my flight—the glory was too much! With great effort, I held my breath and clenched my chest, and the light crumbled off of me like dust, and my flight ceased and sharpened to a hovering standstill.

I shook as the sudden reality of my mortality overwhelmed my being, and as I shivered and clung to the arrow, seated on it like a child hanging off its chair, a tear drew itself out like blood and trickled down my cheek, collapsing off my chin down towards the clouds, lost in the haze of the heavens. I hadn't flown so in tune with that immortal light since I'd fled Hyperborea in desperate search of my peoples' salvation. Now the only thing salvific was Rangabes's beating heart, and Apollo wanted to suck it dry to a shriveled standstill. My immortality was a mortal curse. Not true. I didn't quite understand it myself, but it was a trick of being so near to Apollo's light with this arrow. But my immortality felt like an always dying, without release. I sighed. A release was coming at last. I was here to protect these waters. I'd spoken with Wyrd. I'd listened to St. Michael; he told me that this was decreed. I swallowed, accepting the fate of death that would undoubtedly come. But not yet. Not yet.

The frigid peace of this empty arctic sky was of a hollow kind. As if this part of the world had given up, and in its lying down, in its last sigh of rest, an uneasy and somber peace would forever remain in the pure air that was once breathed by so many here. The blanket of white clouds was billowing so thick below me that it looked like an ocean overflowed with cottony snow, softening the darkness of the desolation beneath it all. My family and friends, my people and civilization, gone in an instant. Those that escaped spread their blood thin through the other peoples, and in my search for salvation, I did not heed the call to sire one of my own. Cursed with this mortal immortality, I longed for a moment of worth. It was coming now, and this silence, this shivering peace had to be thawed and melted into a lava this land hadn't seen in many millennia. It was my destiny to burn. For I'd lived as a flicker, and it was past time that I used my remaining flame to make a difference.

I breathed heavy and aimed my arrow down, slowly descending as I searched for Lugh. If the priests came after me, their combined might would be too much along with the Celtic sun god. But if I faced him alone, with Michael's sword alight in my spirit, I could cut through his darkened sun. He and Apollo both were Chthonic now. They belonged in the darkness, in the underworld of unliving. They lived not, they merely drained the world of glory like lunar leeches. What had happened to the sun? The good solar gods had bowed to Rangabes and offered him what remained of their diminished might. They had not fallen for Apollo's plans like he undoubtedly thought they had. They'd done it out of goodwill and honor.

I lowered myself down further, the lazily curled clouds begging to be disturbed. I watched for any sign of movement, but if there was any, it surely was beneath. For Lugh to spy he'd have to ascend, but how high, I couldn't guess. I saw nothing, but then music of indescribable glory tore through the clouds below. I felt myself fall into infinite peace, while the finite me lowered steeper to get closer to such glorious song.

The clouds still sheeted below, shielding me from what a glorious sight those musicians must be. If the earth could sing, this would be her song. Better yet, if the sun sang, this would be his song serenading the worth of his earth. I stopped myself just above the clouds, their thinning swirl tantalizing me with what might lie below. But it was not for me. It was for Rangabes. I had failed that once immaculate temple, its seven pillars holding up an impossible rotunda that towered like the dome of the heavens. Whatever it was now, I deserved not to see it aflame once more. I was here to see off Lugh, and that was it. I let my toes dip into the cool bath of fog, letting the chill rise through my body and freeze out the immortal music carrying me where I didn't belong and to what I wasn't worthy of—not until I killed Lugh. And even that wouldn't be enough to excuse my lingering existence of inaction. My heart thudded faster at the thought of Lugh. It beat and rattled at my bones as if screaming for a release from the cage of my breast. Its terror at failing in the heat of this song was a welcome stirring, it pulled me further from the glories below.

The song was mercifully ending, and as its throes of life went through my dead ears, I sighed with the last note as it breathed itself into the empty sky. And there below me, his head emerging from the white clouds like Dionysus from Zeus's thigh—Lugh floated upwards with his hands aglow in blue light and pressed downwards. He lofted himself higher and the clouds' cool grasp released him as its tendrilled grip dissipated. No doubt he hid above the clouds now that the song had cleared. He couldn't act until the light was possessed by Rangabes. So, the snake had come to slither in the shadows.

I silently drifted my arrow backwards and up, away from where he'd emerged several feet in front and below. He hadn't turned to look behind him yet, and he appeared lost in the afterglow of the glories he'd witnessed, no doubt wondering if his course was the right one. The light of Hyperborea chose her own, and her silence for both Lugh and Apollo was telling enough. I aimed the arrow's golden point just below Lugh's scarlet topknot and filled myself with the blaze of the light's energy. I shot forward straight and true.

Lugh turned his head at my burning form and threw up his hands in a clap of blue thunder. We exploded together in torn blue-golden light, and were both throttled backwards. I clung to my arrow and hoisted myself back on, and Lugh's whole body glowed blue as he hovered there with supernova, white-pitted eyes. No words were needed, and we whipped at each other like wasps in the air. He blocked my arrow's point as I flew, and I dodged his sweeping bursts of blue thunder. My arrow alone wouldn't be enough, it was time to show him why I'd been known as the supreme magician in my day, and not just for healing!

My cloak billowed out behind me, shimmering purple as my eyes and fingertips crackled with pink-purple lightning. I shot out my violet light in veins of violent, forking bolts, and my arrow burst forward for another gold-streaked attack. Lugh soared upwards in a flash of blue, and dove back down at my hurtling arrow. I shot lightning up at him but he absorbed my attacks with blue orbed light in his hands as he tore down at me. I dropped off my arrow and with both hands, yanked its point upwards by the tail just as Lugh crashed into me. The tip of my arrow pierced right through his throat, but the collision jarred my grip loose and I fell. As I dropped like a cut anchor at sea, I smiled up at the death that glazed the face of Lugh as he and Apollo's arrow tumbled right after me. The cold swallowing of the clouds was a welcome respite as I fell to my death.

***

The pillars collapsed as we finished our embrace. I stood now as Samuel and she as Columbia, and we reflected each other in our eyes. The red barrier of fire flamed out with the pillars' destruction, and Cerberus and Hesiod came surging forward, their anxiety announced in each of their harried steps.

"Who... What happened?" Hesiod called out.

"This woman?" Cerberus said, his thoughts only for Hesiod and I.

"She is Columbia and she is my light—the light of our future people and the light of our past. The forever light of the shining now!" I cried out, leaning in again to kiss her upturned nose, so delicate and short.

"Rangabes? Is this true? Was this what you fought for in the flame of this now fallen temple?" Cerberus said, again, only to Hesiod and I.

"Speak to all of us friend, do not leave her out. And I am no longer Rangabes, but Samuel. As Simon became Peter, so I must become this new rock. God heard my cries in the deep, in the desolation of Tartarus. He heard. We will not be forgotten. A rebirth is needed for myself, just as a rebirth is needed for Hyperborea."

"My apologies," Cerberus said, bowing his heads.

"Noble hound, do not apologize. We need your fearless fury," Columbia said.

"Rangabes?" Hesiod said, his voice creaking with hurt and confusion. "Your name? This woman? All in an instant?" He stood in front of me now with a grim look of defeat sagging his body.

I took his taloned hand, cold to the touch, and his other into my own, and looked into his olive eyes. "I am still me, but I must be someone new. Rangabes stands as a relic of a fallen empire, a city that failed. Samuel is for a new people, a land that will live on. You are still my brother Hesiod. But this renewal is needed, for to remain as Rangabes is to stay chained to the yoke of Apollo and an empire that no longer is. And we both know that Apollo's yoke is one best forgotten."

Hesiod nodded and pressed his forehead against mine. There seemed to be a finality in the gesture—a farewell. Before I could examine the sense of foreboding further, a blurred body fell from the sky and landed with a sudden, cracking thud, followed by another body slamming down right behind it. Lugh was crushed, his head split like a rotten melon with Apollo's arrow pierced through his neck. Abaris laid next to him with his violet robe pooled around him like a moonlit pond. He looked untouched and undisturbed by his plummet. He lay there on his back with his head tilted and his eyes closed as if he were in a deep slumber.

Columbia leaned over his body, and kissed his forehead. His eyes fluttered open and he smiled up at her.

"You have found him worthy?" he murmured, his eyes barely open.

"Yes. And you are worthy as well. Sleep, Abaris. For you, the last Hyperborean, served our people and light well. Your love will live on. Embrace the mortality you once lost. Embrace the true home of the infinite." She reached down to hold his hands.

"I leave behind my cloak, madame. Take it and make it yours. Stained red with my blood, purified with white and snowy light, and branded with the blue of the seas I flew over all those years. The purple is gone. Columbia, great light of Hyperborea, carry it forward. May this one act make me worthy of joining St. Michael's army."

"You are worthy, great sage and healer. Abaris, rest now, true Hyperborean man." She kissed him again and lightly pressed the center of his forehead.

He looked up with a sudden burst of life and love flaming within his deep eyes, like an infant greeting the first light of its mother's face. His body sank into the purple folds of his cloak and he vanished into them. The cloak gathered around itself like a serpent, shimmering with colors flowing through it in a rainbow-like vortex until it stretched itself out, then shrunk, then reached up towards Columbia as if alive. Its color settled into red, white, and blue, and it snaked onto Columbia's outstretched arm and spread over her like vines over a temple.

The cloak became a robe-like dress, like one an ancient Greek goddess might wear. Columbia's perfect, sloped shoulders remained bared as thin straps of striped red spread out into a white top, with the bottom of the dress blue. A new goddess for a new people. I took her hand and pulled her close, running my fingers through her rich, brown-cinnamon hair as I reveled in the perfect beauty of her being.

"Apollo and his priests are all that remain. This is the path he wanted me on, but he will not be my final destination." I kissed Columbia and turned to the horizon.

Apollo rode forward in his chariot, its bronze gleaming with gold, its four white-winged horses casually trotting forward through the snow, lightly carrying him behind. The three Hyperboreades sat behind him, their lanterns held up as if it were night.

The four of us stood tall and still, ready for a final end to our Chthonic journey. Apollo's dark sun was set to never rise again—I would make sure of it. The chariot approached, the horses' slow gallop scraping through the icy snow; it was an oddly peaceful approach, like that of a distant and passing storm—the foreboding remained.

"Congratulations, Rangabes," Apollo said, his voice tight and his face strained as he descended from his chariot. His forced joy wasn't fooling anyone, not even himself. His priests drifted after him, floating behind.

"I am Samuel," I responded.

Apollo squinted, and seemed to just then notice Columbia standing next to me. "You chose him? You chose him over me? I am your lord," he said. "But the deposit has been made. Time is met, and Rangabes is ripe. I am your god."

"I guarded my people and land. And your people, your Hyperboreades, destroyed us. You are not the sun, Apollo. The sun is already in the sky." She pointed up at the pallid, winter orb, still brilliant even in this arctic desolation. "The sun is my light, not you. We existed apart from you, and when we were together, there was a thriving. But your greed is why your kind has fallen from its heights. Olympus belongs to the Other now. It was always the Lord's and so were you. Hyperborea is His sun."

"Rangabes, is this how you choose your end? I've brought life to you and Hesiod, guided your path. And now this so-called light, she speaks blasphemy," he said, almost pleading as he held his arms out at me.

"We've heard many different stories. But Apollo, your light is of the dark. You sought to guide us into your own shadow. You knew that was the only way to survive," I said.

"You are all that remains," Cerberus said.

"I awoke you for a reason. Why would I take on treason after waking you to the light? All of you... how can you not see that I helped guide you? And now Lugh lies dead. Is this what you wanted?"

"Wyrd showed me the promised land. In her true light, I saw you for what you were, a mere reflection, dimmed and untrue—of the moon." I stepped forward, and stared into his yellowing face, the gold paling at my accusation. His priests waited, their faces dead and ghostly, their lanterns propped up and unmoving.

Hesiod pointed a long talon at Apollo and said, "He is not your avatar and there is no taking his light. You deceive!"

Columbia nodded and said, "I've given him my own light now, and he has the last of the solar gods' blazing power smoldering his soul. It would consume you, Apollo. You who are drawn by fear. You who try to supersede the Fates and steal Wyrd's strange-stringed eternal lyre from her. Only she can play it in her designated station. You saw Rangabes's destiny of power, and you feared it and sought to make it your own."

"Empty accusations," he said.

I laughed. "Empty words. You could only take my power if I submitted to yours. But why would I do that? I stand on the towering foundation of my forefathers. The same foundation you and your priests sought to tear down," I said.

"Hesiod, have you forgotten our long time spent in the dark? Have you forgotten the second chance I've given you?" Apollo said, turning to the poet.

"It was not yours to will or give. I am my own man." Hesiod spat on the ground, the hiss of his phlegm sizzled in the frost and silence, the snow welcoming it with haste.

With even greater haste and in a terrible, lightning quick motion, Apollo's bow flashed into his arms, already strung. He pulled back the bow so fast that by the time I even yelled, the arrow tore through the quiet and shattered Hesiod's fiery robe, piercing right through to his heart. He collapsed, his face drained and blank, not even sure he was dead; he had no time to register the sudden killing blow.

I growled, and my axe appeared in my hand as I sprang like a tiger at Apollo. The three Hyperboreades soared in front of him, thrusting their lanterns at my biting attack. My axe sparked against their ghostly blue lights, showering me in burning flecks of silver. They surrounded me and I roared in fury as Apollo remained out of reach. I vaguely was aware of his golden arrows flying out at the rest of my company, but I couldn't see if they hit their mark, as the priests required my full attention. They swung their lanterns down at me like maces and moved with such speed that as I swung my axe, I could only catch air, not even managing to clash with their lanterns. As my rage cooled and converted to clarity, I realized they were merely keeping me busy. Their speed and strength surely could have overpowered me. Perhaps Apollo needed me alive after all. With this in mind, I sprang backwards and rolled over while blocking their lanterns, stepping back towards Columbia and Cerberus.

I focused my power and sought to send my marks aglow, but was stunned to find them still empty. What had Columbia done to me? I shuddered, realizing I was alone here with my mortality. Could Apollo have been true all along? What kind of man was I doubting the Lord for a fallen god? And Columbia. There was a purpose, but these useless thoughts coursing through my mind only hastened my retreat. Thankfully, Cerberus and Columbia appeared untouched.

Columbia had climbed onto Cerberus's back, and his snakes whipped about, biting and swallowing arrows like anacondas, apparently unaffected. Cerberus's three heads were spitting out jets of white flame that shielded them well.

"Columbia!" I shouted over the tearing of the arrows and roaring of flame. "My power is diffused!" I blocked the priests swinging lights as they followed my retreat. I ducked and dodged, fully aware that they still sought to distract me. The fools!

"No! Samuel, remember your new name." She called down upon me with grace and confidence, as if we weren't under attack. "True immortality requires mortality! Only one can possess perfection of both. The promised land, and the light you carry, is your soul. Abram to Abraham! Those marks are vacated, because you've become who you are and who you were meant to be."

"Couldn't it have waited?" I joked, gritting my teeth and spinning out of the priestly gnats' endless prattling.

I tensed, and yelled out with anger. Hesiod, my brother, the man who'd awoken me and given me purpose once more; the man who loved me through this whole nightmare! Now he lay there dead and torn away by the whim of a selfish god.

"I'll show you blasphemy!" I screamed at Apollo over the heads of the Hyperboreades. Apollo was still flinging his arrows, his face aglow with red fire, hatred fueling his attack. "Cerberus, the priests!"

The great white hound turned his heads and shot out a wondrous, blooming flower of fire as I dove through the Hyperboreades' attack, their lanterns banging against my arms and burning my bare skin. I sprinted at Apollo who spun to face me. The fool still held off attacking me; his pause would be his death. He pulled back his bow at last and let loose a shot as I threw Solisinanis as hard as I could at his chest. I twisted at the tearing arrow and jumped, but it clipped my shoulder, sending my leaping flight crashing to the ground. Searing pain burned my bones, and I held the wound while screaming and writhing on the ground.

But my desire to see Apollo dead was greater than any pain could bring, so I forced myself up, biting my lip and drawing blood, the pain burned so deep. Holding my shoulder, I lumbered towards Apollo. He was sputtering, holding his chest, where Solisinanis remained lodged, right in the center, tearing through his armor like a rudder through water. His face was twisted with wretched rage and disbelief. The anger was weak, and his face sagged under the sudden weight of mortality.

"What would you have done had I joined myself to your cause? Speak free and true, do not let your last words be of the dark and belong to the shadow of deceit," I said through clenched teeth, still holding my wound and shakily standing over his fallen body.

"Cracked you open like an egg and drank your yolk fully. We needed you alive: another Prometheus to torture. My priests and I had the means, but your friends were too much. Cerberus... we thought we had to bring him to prevent one fate from happening, and to make another occur. But Wyrd played her chord once more. And now I leave through a one-way door, shut forever."

The gleam of his golden skin faded, and his eyes lost their glow. I yanked my axe free and limped towards

Cerberus and Columbia, the both of them standing close-by and watching me with worry.

"Where are the Hyperboreades?" I said.

"I don't know if it was my fire or Apollo's death, but they vanished as my flames extinguished," Cerberus replied.

"Samuel?" Columbia said.

I didn't respond. I stumbled over to Hesiod's fallen body, and fell to my knees, weeping for my brother. His face was cold, yet peaceful like a man who'd died in his sleep. Apollo was weak for striking out like that! Not even a chance for him to defend himself. What was left now? So many had died to get me here.

Arise.

The voice of an angel. I stayed on my knees.

He is in eternity now. A place meant for him long ago. Do not forget he had been dead long before you awakened.

"Was I not dead too? Why should I continue alive?" I mumbled, still staring at Hesiod's colorless face.

Rangabes is dead, Samuel is alive. This journey of yours was your own. Look at me and see that you are meant to bring about a new people in a new land. God's country. Will you be the forebearer, or do you want to die as Rangabes after all, and remain as such?

I stood to my feet and turned to face the voice. St. Michael stood there in all his glory, the gallant archangel mighty and strong. His golden hair and white-lit sword gleamed. He held out his white blade in front of me. Cerberus and Columbia bowed their heads.

"Great Michael, where do I go now? What must I do?" I slowly moved closer to him, his figure pristine yet welcoming, the kindness glowing in his eyes was one that transcended the finite chains of mortal love.

He took his sword and tapped my wounded shoulder. The blade cooled and warmed—a crux of infinite power focused into the now—and my wound was gone as the blazing sword was released. He tapped my other shoulder as well and placed his sword into its diamond jeweled scabbard.

"You will found a powerful people, Samuel. With Columbia as your bride and Cerberus your dog, you must travel forth with a crew of worthy men. The oceans are treacherous and many perils await you on your long voyage. And once you make it ashore, you will find that your promised land is a savage one with many beasts to be tamed, and many noble peoples to be battled. Are you up to the task?"

"Of course," I said, my fist to my chest.

"As am I," Cerberus said with Columbia nodding.

"But know that you leave behind the land of the other, the land of myth and bleeding magic, to go to the land of mortality, the land of men. Monsters still roam, many greater than those you've already faced, but now you will have to best them alone. You will be weaker in one way, but infinitely stronger for it. Samuel, you have already felt your glowing power diffused, but know that your power is stronger for this exact reason. You will see in due time. Your great axe Solisinanis will remain, but no more can it carry such magic and light. It is still as trusty as ever, but requires an even defter hand now that she is humbled with reality. Your marks will remain as reminders of what you've gained here; but your armor, wherever it may have burned off to, will be traded for mere cloth. You did well in your skin. Like in Eden—fitting for paradise. And so I ask, are you willing to give up all this, to continue forward?"

I nodded and said, "Without question." I crossed myself and gave silent thanks to the Lord. The grace and glory!

Michael held out his hand and a wave of white light flooded over me. I glanced down at myself to see that I was now wearing a simple olive-green tunic with brown trousers and black boots. This would serve me just fine. I'd been a soldier in Constantinople, and at times dressed humbler than this. It felt freeing to wear clothes that fit so simply, though I'd gotten used to the freedom of uncovered flesh. But the mortal world required what it did; I was not in paradise yet.

"And Cerberus... a three-headed, giant beast with serpents writhing about cannot step simply into the land of men and mortality, even transformed as a holy hound of light. You will keep your wit, thought-speech, and your loyal strength will remain; but are you, too, willing to undergo a transformation to the form of a humble canine? You will still be a Molossus dog but no longer gargantuan, merely a bit larger than the average hound. Of course, you can only have one head, and I am afraid no serpents."

"I am the hound of Hades no more. I left that behind when I slept, and now that I've awoken and traveled home, I too am ready for a rebirth—a reawakening. This current form is blessed, but if it keeps me away from Rang... Samuel, then I refuse it. He is my light and I welcome it," Cerberus said. He lay down and bowed his three heads. His seven serpents wilted like dead flowers.

Michael held out his hands and white light bathed Cerberus until I could see nothing. Then as the light diffused, a powerful Molossus dog stood up. white and pristine, his face smiling and tongue lolling. In his black eyes, I could see Cerberus remained himself, but now we had both taken on mortality to face the new.

"And now you go to Portugal. A man named Vespucci is about to set off on his fourth and final voyage. Christopher Columbus might have spotted your promised land, but Vespucci will take you ashore," Michael said. He turned to Columbia. "I know you saw that time which was a future, but now has passed. Columbus sailed and saw that land, and your name comes from the great explorer. Wear it well and honor his path. Yours and his are names that will echo into eternity."

"Time... how long have I been under? How long have I been dead?" I asked.

"Rangabes was dead for more than 50 years. You come back carrying your peoples' worth. Be worthy of them all, Samuel. Much depends on your journey," he said.

"And how do we return to the land of the living?" Columbia asked. "To the land of man and mortality, I mean."

"Listen to Wyrd's song," he said with a smile. "Close your eyes and listen. You will awake where you need to be."

Cerberus trotted over to sit next to me and Columbia moved close to rest her head on my shoulder. Together, we all closed our eyes and listened to the sudden, strange pluck of an invisible harp string.

Made in the USA
Middletown, DE
23 December 2019

81894091R00220